Also by Douglas Unger
*Published by Ballantine Books:*

**LEAVING THE LAND**

# EL YANQUI

## Douglas Unger

BALLANTINE BOOKS • NEW YORK

*For Steve,*
*and in memory of*
*Álvaro and Alejandro Colombo*

Library of Congress Catalog Card Number: 86-45159

ISBN 0-345-34940-7

This edition published by arrangement with Harper & Row, Publishers, Inc.

Manufactured in the United States of America

First Ballantine Books Edition: June 1988

Cover photo © Peter Frey/The Image Bank

"A novel of the other life,
translated to this one . . ."

Luis Vélez de Guevara

The author wishes to express his gratitude to the John Simon Guggenheim Memorial Foundation, the Corporation of Yaddo, and the Arts Americas Program of the United States Information Agency, for their generous support while writing this novel. Special thanks also to my wife, Amy, and my daughter, Erin, for their immeasurable contributions.

# Changes

The chill in the breeze was a relief from the stewpot of summer. It climbed in slow gusts out of the port of Buenos Aires, up over the broad, columned avenue called the Paseo Colón that had lines of musty shops and smoky bars and that ran just down the hill from the Plaza de Mayo, surrounded by government offices. The little wind stirred the smog that was as thick as a thunderhead around the obelisk, an imitation of the Washington Monument in the far distance. It ruffled the colorful plumage on the tall hats of the honor guard decked out like hussars in front of the Casa Rosada, the pink presidential palace that, along with the Air Force building, still showed minor damage from the bombing raids the Argentine Air Force had carried out when *presidente* Perón had been driven from power. Maybe the little rough craters in the flat stone facings, the tiny nicks and scattered shrapnel patterns in the pink plaster filigrees of this house of the presidency had been left there as a reminder of what had happened many years ago. Some Argentines said that it wouldn't be until Perón took power again that the damage would be repaired.

It was my favorite walk in the afternoons to start at the

1

Plaza de Mayo then to head down the steep hill and clip along under the antique covered archways of the Paseo for block after block, looking through the big smoky windows of the bars at the uniformed public employees, the soldiers, the sailors, and especially at their women, some of these port bars the only places that seemed alive during the siesta hours. Tango music could be heard through the transoms of antique doorways; recordings of quickly beating accordions and sad violins, scratchy tenors singing out their nostalgia for their lost years and homes and lovers in a thick port dialect I was just beginning to understand. I worked my way along this avenue that ran close to the mud-colored River Plate until I could slowly climb back up into the heights of that part of the city called El Barrio Norte, where the people called *la gente bien*, the well-to-do class, lived, where my new family lived behind their iron-grilled windows, their French balconies overlooking quaint streets lined with silver *plátano* trees. In this neighborhood, on almost every street corner stood a cop in the blue uniform of the federal police—a blue soldier with a machine gun around his neck as if a matter of routine. At night, black Ford Falcons roared through the streets at full speed without sirens. None of this bothered me at first—they seemed like my police, protecting my new neighborhood, my new home.

I was amazed at how far I had come, the distance I had covered. After the confusing, stiflingly hot summer months full of struggle with the language, tongue-tied and always translating in my head at a frustrating pace that lagged way behind any thoughts, this day had arrived when the weather changed. There was a feeling of autumn in the chilly breeze coming up from the port, and I noticed a transformation in myself that had happened all at once. After nearly five months of wrestling with words I was suddenly thinking and even dreaming in Spanish with a Buenos Aires accent. On seeing my reflection in the glass of shop windows, I realized that I also looked like an Argentine now, and a rich one at that, sharply dressed in my new blue blazer with a crest on the pocket, my tailored gray slacks and blue silk tie, my hair all plastered down with gel and combed straight back in the more conservative Argentine style. My wallet was stuffed fat with pesos. My new family were real upper-crusters, and made me as rich as they were. I had a hot little Peugeot to drive, and a complete new wardrobe of Italian-style suits, English tweeds, French shirts and these wonderful handmade loafers with soles so wafer thin that I could feel the crosshatched ribs of the tile sidewalks as if my new shoes were as alive as the skin of my feet.

The city of Buenos Aires was in my blood. I walked all over its streets after school, climbing up the hill from the old archways and from that stretch known as El Bajo, past the expensive Plaza Hotel with its flags of many nations, then past the hotel and through the parklike Plaza San Martín with its weird-looking trees called *palos borrachos*, drunk stick trees, with pendulous hard green fruits that made them look like their branches had been strung all over with hand grenades. I usually didn't mix with the crowd in the Plaza San Martín—mainly tourists on vacation, soldiers and sailors on leave, people in from the provinces to see the famous sights of the city, senior citizens relaxing together on the benches, taking in the new crisp air in the shadows of the huge monument to San Martín, The Liberator, on a horse with its front hooves kicking high, the rose marble pedestal under him thick with friezes depicting the perilous crossing of the Andes, the battles in which the heroes of the first revolution were shown gallantly raising their flags and dying under Spanish cannon. In the victorious face of The Liberator on horseback there was very little that looked like the other San Martín I was learning about in school, the much more common face of the older man who had found it so dangerous for himself in Buenos Aires after winning the war for independence that he was forced to flee his beloved new country for France, the whole continent behind him suddenly carved up into factional violence. It was the sad face of an old man dressed in a dark coat and string tie like Lincoln's, the face printed on most of the bills in Argentina's currency, a portrait taken from his period in exile, with a dark, perturbed expression focused on the space in which absurdly increasing denominations were printed—the old general even looked a little embarrassed to appear in blue and mauve inks under the figure 100,000 pesos, banknotes which after many monetary reforms became about as common as yanqui hundred dollar bills. But his younger, victorious self was preserved in bronze in the beautiful Plaza San Martín, on horseback, with his army, surrounded by a little park with its pretty drunk stick trees. The young San Martín rode there high above it all, overlooking the tourists picnicking on the grass and benches on the heights above the lawn that gently sloped to the clock tower in front of the Retiro railroad station that was a miniature copy of London's Big Ben, his face looking proud of his city, his country, his future.

I always walked past this statue a little awed by its majesty. Usually it was at about the same hour, just as the city was waking up from its big lunch and siesta. I took a left down the avenue Santa Fe into the wealthy district, walking fast, the *porteño* walk as it was called, a pace that everyone in Buenos Aires seemed to use. I watched the avenue Santa Fe lazily coming to life after the siesta, the expensive shops and five-star restaurant windows still tightly shuttered, the dark and pretty young housemaids just beginning to push their mistresses' babies toward the parks. I stood at the head of the grand Parisian-style boulevard that glittered with so many elegant windows, and I felt lucky.

A few months before, back in the States, I had first felt this sense of luck, the kind that comes to stay. I was on my way back from getting stoned in a favorite copse of trees behind the Port Washington High School when I happened on a line of kids behind the gym. They were waiting to take exams to qualify for scholarships to go abroad with a program called International Student Exchange, or I.S.E., and the particular kid who told me this was condescending enough to yours truly in my hippie rags that I decided to stand on line and blow smoke into his face until we were called in to sit down. I went in with the others and sat down, too, since I had discovered that taking the exam could get me a pass to skip social studies, my only afternoon class aside from study halls. I sat down beside the kid who had told me what was going on so I could shift around, groan, scrape my desk and that kind of thing just to bug him. That was boring after the first few minutes, so I read the questions over on the exam, mainly about capitals of the world and its leaders, current events and all that, like a huge quiz on last year's "Week in Review" section of *The New York Times*, and I filled in boxes on the computerized answer sheet quickly, so I could get my pass and go back up to the woods to get stoned all afternoon.

Ten finalists for the I.S.E. program were selected from the exam. Nobody could have been more surprised that one of them was me. I took trains into New York City for interviews with a panel of judges, ducking out to the men's rooms to keep my hash high nice and levelized, all the other kids wearing sports jackets, suits, ties, smart dresses, and preppy hairstyles, me there with them in a pair of clean jeans, my longish hair falling down over my ears. For about two weeks there was a steady fog of waiting rooms full of competitive I.S.E. finalists and I didn't care. Who was going to send a freak like me with grades long ago slipped into effortless blanket B's abroad, man? What was I doing in this waiting room full of wimps and little miss diplomats?

There was a nervous talk with a psychiatrist in which I almost blew the whole joke by confessing I took any drugs my brothers turned me on to anytime. Instead, I went into the time the old lady started to drink a can of ant poison to prove to the old man how miserable her existence was, feeling like his dowdy wife and chief cook and bottle washer to all us kids. A clicking timer rang and I got out of the psychiatrist's office as fast as I could.

Two days later, news arrived that I was the one student selected from a group of more than three hundred in my region who had applied. My assigned country was Argentina, all expenses paid, and I would be living with an Argentine family named Benevento in Buenos Aires, my date of departure in just four weeks. The principal made an announcement over the high school's P.A. system, saying how proud the school was that one of its students had won the I.S.E. competition, and my teachers kept looking at me like they found this news impossible to believe. Following that there were batteries of vaccinations, photos for passports, trips to the Argentine consulate for a visa, a set of fingerprints and forms to fill out for the FBI to make sure I had never been convicted of a felony. I was told to wait around afterward. I sat in a little caged-off room for about an hour feeling like a criminal until a Nassau County police officer came in and handed me a pamphlet that explained the dangers of carrying illegal substances overseas.

It was a busy time. Suddenly the old man and the old lady were working together, "to get you off to a new start," as she put it, driving me to stores along the Miracle Mile where I picked out clothes—purple jeans and red sneakers, a cool olive drab jacket with hearts on the sleeves, green T-shirts, tie-dyed jockey shorts, my folks just handing me the money. Then almost my whole big family, Donny, Tommy, Kevin, Willy, Carol, and the folks, everyone except for my brother Harry, piled into the station wagon and drove me to JFK airport, all of them laughing, happy, proud. That's the way I remember the scene years later, though at the time I couldn't wait to get away from them. No matter what my new life would be, it was at least away.

I knew from the briefing kit sent to me by I.S.E. that the new family I was being sent to was rich and that they had three sons. The school I would attend was a large Catholic prep school administered by a brotherhood of priests founded in France and sent as missionaries to Argentina a century before. An Argentine consular staffer had translated from the brochure of Colegio San Andrés that it was "prodigious and exclusive." I had no idea what that might mean, and on the plane, still half believing it couldn't possibly be me, I tried to imagine what my new school and my new country would be like. Who had taught us anything about Argentina in my high school? From the few picture books Mrs. Begeneau, our librarian, found for me, I imagined a place something in between Mexico and England, halfway around the world by plane. I asked one of the nice stewardesses for any extra meal trays and managed to keep eating for most of the sixteen hours and seven thousand miles. A drunk Uruguayan in the seat next to me tried to feel me up as soon as the lights went off. I changed seats, engaging the sympathy of a stewardess, who served me a fourth extra tray, this time the shrimp from first class, with two little bottles of complimentary wine. Luck was with me, I knew that much, though what I was on my way to I couldn't have dreamed.

Now five months later, the city of Buenos Aires, like its language, had suddenly fallen into place in my mind, its directions, its limits, the way the names of its streets changed at certain dividing lines of its avenues. I was standing in the doorway of a shop called Chaco Sport. The door still had an iron cage drawn across it and the lights were off behind the colorful window display of wire mannequins wearing Chaco brand sweaters and French cut Chaco shirts that were long-sleeved now for the change of season. An imported camel's hair overcoat stood on its own at the center of it all like a Christmas tree with brightly colored socks and ties and scarves piled under it. I admired the coat for a few minutes. Then I went to the door and made a fist. I pounded on the cage a few times thinking somebody had to be in there, some clerk was just too lazy to get up from his lunch in back, *hijo de puta*. I had things I needed to buy, a lot of studying to do, then getting dressed and ready for a big dinner, man, or *che*, as they said it in this tango city. I had never been able to sleep the siesta—it still made me impatient that a whole population could button itself down, eat a huge piece of meat, then close its eyes two hours a day as if Don Cristóbal Colón's globe itself had stopped turning. I gave up knocking and looked at the overcoat again. I thought of how I might bring the matter of this overcoat up to Papá and maybe talk him out of eighty or ninety thousand pesos. Then I stepped back a little on the sidewalk just as the three o'clock sun cast the shadow of a building behind me onto the shop window, and there I was— it was my reflection, but it was nobody I recognized. Even my name was different. *Diego* was standing there, that's what they called me, because it was one of the Spanish equivalents of my real first name. At school I was mainly called *El Yanqui*, a nickname started by my buddy Hernández-Marelli, but otherwise I was called Diego, the name my new family used. And this Diego was a high-class-look-

ing kid, his face clean and straight-looking, discrete nests
of acne pinpricks in the hollows of his cheeks, his dark blue
Colegio San Andrés tie fastened in the symmetrical triangle
of a Windsor knot at the pale, starched blue collar of his
impeccably ironed shirt. The gold buttons of the wool blazer
flashed in the darkened window, the sky blue shield of the
Colegio San Andrés coat of arms lay over his heart. It
showed the smiling sun that symbolized Argentina on one
diagonal slice, and a bright red droplet and a cross in the
shape of an *X* that represented the martyrdom of St. Andrew
on the other. A long black scroll trailed off the shield like
an unfurling flag with the school's motto in Latin written
on it, some kind of Roman mumbo jumbo that meant *Reason and Theology in Double Truth*, as nearly as my new
Papá could translate it for me.

My new family had insisted on these changes. No long-
haired yanqui kid getting off the plane with Jefferson Airplane, The Doors, Paul Butterfield and Led Zeppelin albums
clutched in his arms was going to embarrass them in society. No way were they going to let me be tossed wearing
sneakers and patched blue jeans into the social atmosphere
of club dates, debutante balls where penguin suits were required, the elite schooling with the French brothers or anywhere else for that matter, not if I was going to live as one
of them. And I soon found that I wanted to live like them,
no question; I hadn't even looked at the pictures of my
North American family in three months. Compared to my
new life in Buenos Aires, the one I had left back home
seemed impoverished, though we weren't poor by any
means, with graying memories of my five brothers and one
sister, most of them working after-school jobs, the old man
and the old lady battling it out to make ends meet on non-
union wages. No question that the transformation had been
almost total, starting with the first day I set foot in the
spacious, high-ceilinged flat that belonged to the Beneventos, which took up the whole second floor of an apartment
building and had a small flat inside it just for the maids. It
had original Miró lithographs and Rodin sketches on the
walls, tapestries from Florence centuries old, Persian car-
pets and rich Spanish furnishings of tooled leather and dark

wood. Even the air that blew through its ornate French design took on a quality of wealth.

My new Mamá went through most of my clothes on the first day, all the colored T-shirts, my leather pouch with the bells and fringe, my faded and new purple jeans, my Rajah sandals, my red Converse hightops that had cool holes I'd cut out of the toes for ventilation. She disapproved even of my jockey shorts, wrinkling her nose at them and having one of the maids show me pairs of boxer trunks with fancy designs that all of her own sons wore. Mamá tossed most of my clothes into the shabby plastic suitcase I had brought them in and I just stood by watching, fumbling for the words to stop her, but all my protests were ignored. She handed my suitcase to the maid with a limp gesture in its direction, using a tone of voice as if giving orders to her janitor. We waited for the barber, who had agreed to make a house call under these special circumstances. As my long hair was falling in bunches to the floor, I regretted most the loss of the tattered band uniform coat I had just bought for two dollars at a Salvation Army store and that was just then the rage back home.

But there was nothing I could do. I was like a gibbering child again. I had studied basic Spanish for three years in school but somehow, with everything coming at me at once, it was a struggle to remember enough of the language to ask for a spoon at the table. I felt caged in by a rattling of voices unreached by my comprehension. Starting with that first day, my personality began caving in if from nothing more than the fatigue, loneliness and humiliation of being reduced to tongue-tied gibberish and frantic hand gestures while at the same time trying to translate strings of words out of a Spanish-English pocket dictionary that seemed useful only for Mexico. Everyone in my new family except Mamá could speak some English, but my new Papá forbade them, explaining to me on the first day, in the only words in English he ever spoke to me, "From now on, we speak Spanish. Only Spanish for you. That's the fastest way you can learn." Then he told his sons that even when they were explaining words and phrases to me they should make themselves clear in their own language. It was like a game to the

boys, Martín, Alejo and little Miguelito gesturing at me
with meanings I couldn't get and all of them talking at once
in a chattering barrage. It was a lot of fun for them, like
that evening, at the late supper called the *cena*, when I tried
a few practiced phrases from my dictionary, trying to make
my first conversation, and somehow I mixed up the word
for lawyer, *abogado*, with the word *albóndiga*, and ended
up asking my new Papá, "What kind of a meatball are you,
Papá?"

From that day on, it was the Benevento family who taught
me my speech, as well as my rules of dress and etiquette,
my tastes and my leisures, as if our contract together from
the beginning was that in their Buenos Aires, as a member
of their family, I was expected to sound and dress and act
as one of them. But I had a fantastic huge room with dark
carved woodwork and a marble balcony that looked out over
treelined Arenales Street that was like a pointillist painting
of an elegant scene in Paris. Silver services were everywhere and with more than enough maids to keep them
shined, cooks to cook for me, plenty of money to spend on
myself. Every Saturday morning, thousands upon thousands
of pesos were handed to me in wads of colorful bills, my
new Mamá doling them out in thick rolls on the dining room
table to each of her sons, and I began to get used to the
idea that I was rich like them. As I stood on the balcony of
my new room in those first weeks under the hot summer
sun of the afternoons when I wasn't able to sleep the siesta,
Arenales Street shuttered and quiet except for the occasional
taxi ricketing over the cobblestones, little else stirring, not
even a breeze at midday to move the leaves on the overhanging *plátano* trees, I kept thinking to myself that living
like this was a *joda*, as my Argentine brothers would call
it, a real boss time. I stood there for a while, breathing in
the boiling airs of the street, then I went back to the desk
in my room where the language books were open that my
new Papá had bought for me, all of them in Spanish. I tried
to cram my brain with another list of verbs and phrases,
repeating them over and over to myself in a low voice while
the rest of the family was napping. And sometimes, too,
when I was tired, foggy, and nothing made sense on the

page anymore, I thought of the voice of the old man long ago at the International Departures Lounge at JFK. "Some of us get a chance and some of us don't," he had said, then a strong embrace from him, a firm shake from a hand with the fingernails stained a chemical orangish yellow from his smoking and his trade as a darkroom technician, followed by hugs and kisses from the old lady, from my sister Carol and from all my brothers except for Harry. Five months later, caught by my well-groomed reflection in the shop-window glass, I no longer even felt like the same person.

The metal cage on the door of Chaco Sport slid back with a clattering. A balding, sleepy-eyed man in rumpled clothes regarded me with a bored expression. In his cheap rope-soled slippers his appearance was out of place in the bright, pine-paneled store with its polished racks for Polo, Jockey, Lacoste, Lee and Levi—an English flavor attempted by lithographs of fox hunting and a display of English saddles and bridles mounted on the walls. The store was tastefully in order save for the man in his shoes called *alpargatas*, who was slowly on his way into the back of the shop to finish his coffee. "You look around until my salesman gets here," he said. "He eats his lunch all the way over in Barrio Constitución."

"I just need a sweater," I said. "The one for Colegio San Andrés."

"Just a little moment and I'll get the ladder," the man said, but he didn't stop on his way to his coffee. He left me to look around the shop for things to buy with all my money—a really cool belt made out of white crude leather, for example, and a set of silver cufflinks that were tiny replicas of Incan idols with chips of emeralds set into their mouths like offerings. The man came back in noiselessly, coffee cup in hand, and said, "Good school, San Andrés, no? I know a *coronel* in the Air Force whose son goes there."

"Who's that?" I asked.

"Dipaoli. Of the Air Force."

"Ah, *sí* . . . Dipaoli. Geraldo. A tall, skinny kid."

"That's the one. The skinny one. You know him?"

"We play *fútbol* together, in the same year. Everybody calls him El Judeo because of his nose."

The man's bored but friendly expression darkened, his eyes narrowed as he looked quickly around the store as if somebody else might be listening. He regarded me differently then, as if reminded that this was no Argentine he was talking to, no matter the smooth Buenos Aires accent. He stepped back a little, raising his shoulders in just enough of a movement to show his new indifference. He cast a blasé glance down the rows of boxes above the clothing racks, files and ranks of boxes that reached to the high ceiling, and said, "I don't think I have any more of the ones for San Andrés."

He went behind the counter to his cash register, where he set his cup down and opened an afternoon paper to the soccer page. "Maybe my salesman knows where they are," he said. He leaned out over the counter, his coffee raised too casually, too *qué sé yo* as the saying went, like how was he supposed to know? He buried himself in his paper for a moment, then glanced up at me trying to read the labels on the rows of boxes and said in an unfriendly tone, "Are you a yanqui or what?"

"How did you guess my country?" I asked.

The man frowned tautly behind the rim of his cup. He looked in the direction of the doorway carefully, as if to make sure there was no one else in the store. He took a long sip, rolled the coffee in his mouth, swallowed. "Only a yanqui would be *boludo* enough to talk about a colonel's son that way," he said, using the word in Spanish that meant something like *swollen-balled idiot*, and that was applied in roughly the same way as "asshole" was in New York slang. "You've got to have *ojo* in this county," he said, pressing a forefinger against the lower lid of his right eye and pulling the skin back until the blood-red crescent showed under the white. "You've got to 'keep an eye out' and watch what you say."

For the first time since I had lived in Buenos Aires, I felt pass between us what was to become a common fear in Argentina—the fear of everyone else. But I didn't understand it then, so I casually shook it off. "It's just a joke,"

I said. "Geraldo doesn't mind, *che*," I said, laughing a little nervously. "It's just his nickname from *fútbol*."

"What should I care?" the man said. "I don't own the country."

A moment passed in which the man seemed to think I was going to leave. Then when he saw that I was going to wait for his salesman, he said, "*Che*, I just remembered. The San Andrés sweaters are over there. You're tall enough that you can probably reach the box. That's it, third row up, over there. Just take the box down. If it doesn't fit you, I don't think we have any other sizes. There we go," he said as I was putting it on, "a real playboy." I wasn't sure if he said this because of the reputation of my San Andrés classmates or because of the way the white sweater with maroon trim and the school crest actually looked, like I'd just stepped off a yacht on my way to Oxford. He kept on jiving me, "*Che!* How pretty it looks! No kidding! Stand over here closer to the mirror. That's it. That's right. The girls are going to go crazy over you, don't you think? Do you look like a playboy or what?"

I walked home down the glamorous avenue Santa Fe, watching the city come back to life, the beautiful upper-crust women in their new autumn clothes out shopping in the expensive boutiques, and the maids out on their errands, the dark-haired *negras* in the short-skirted uniforms that were popular that year, a coy acknowledgement in the way they returned my greedy appraisals of their legs. I turned the corner onto narrow Junín Street and then once more to Arenales, my street, and the huge stone archway that marked the entrance to my building.

I heard music from our second floor flat as I leapt up the circling marble stairway, light and breezy, Vivaldi or Bach or somebody like that, unusual at this time of day, meaning that Papá was home at an hour when he would usually have gone back to work. I used my keys and pushed open the ornately carved door, and my new youngest brother, Miguelito, called out a greeting from down the hallway, "*Hola, Diego!*" As if at his cue, other voices joined in, Mamá's from the library, "*Hola, Diego,*" with an obligatory sing-

song. Then Alejo from the reading desk in his corner bedroom, the sensitive son with the pecan-shaped brown eyes
who always seemed to be carrying an open book in one
hand while he used the other to munch on heels of bread
that he carried in his pockets. "How are you doing, Diego?
What do you say?" Then Martín Segundo, the eldest, who
was sitting alone and brooding in the little dining nook that
seemed to be the main province of the boys, poring over
the afternoon editions of the newspapers. Martín didn't look
up as I passed but grunted at me a quick and restrained,
*"Hola,"* still absorbed in his paper.

The maid, Isabelita, appeared before I could reach my
big bedroom. First using a felt baton to clean off any dust
from the streets, she took the blue blazer off my shoulders
and hung it up. The sensation of these dark hands running
over me was still the strangest thing, these hands that were
so often at my service, and the voice behind them, old
enough to be my grandmother's, addressing me always for-
mally. "How are you, *sir*, after your walk? Was it cold
outside? You ought to be wearing an overcoat, *sir*," she
said. "Winter's going to fall on us soon." She chattered
away at me, straightening my shirt and tie. It was somehow
part of the formality expected of me, not unlike the formal
patterns of a new language, to comply with being served,
to learn how to be served.

*"Gracias, Isabelita,"* I said.

"Papá wishes to see you, *sir*," she said. She took my
jacket and package. Then little Miguelito was suddenly
there, having covered the long hallway on the run. An open
schoolbook flopped in one hand, his index finger sand-
wiched between the pages to mark his place. In his other
hand he carried an airmail envelope of flimsy blue paper
with stars and stripes in one corner.

"This came for you today, Dieguito," Miguelito said. He
was pleased to be the one to pass me the letter. I looked at
the return address—A.P.O. San Francisco—and near it,
there was a long brown smear across the paper just beside
the G.I. postage metering, a brown smeared thumbprint
across the postmarked date. Why had it taken two months
to arrive? I was anxious to tear the envelope open. "You

want to see my homework?'' Miguelito asked. ''What shit they're making us swallow today at school? It's a real hassle, *che*,'' he said.

I looked at Miguelito's book. It was a children's edition of Dante's *Divine Comedy*, specially edited and printed for the sixth-grade level at the school, like a kind of Junior Classics Illustrated comic book edition. Miguelito's index finger rested on a colorful depiction of Dante himself cowering before a line of tormented figures shrouded in a fiery dust cloud. They were chasing after a figure that carried a banner that bore no symbols, their faces twisted into ugly metamorphic expressions as if they were human beings on their way to changing into griffins. They were rushing around for eternity, chasing after that blank, tattered flag. ''This is just after Dante has crossed through the gates into hell. These are the souls that are being punished for wasting their lives, for cowardice and for vanity,'' Miguelito said. I looked at the caption under the grotesque illustration that said, *To themselves alone were they true.* ''I have to memorize this passage for tomorrow, what a hassle,'' Miguelito said. ''You want to help me?''

''Recite it for me later, kiddo,'' I said, not adding that I hadn't read Dante myself, and that I thought it strange to be using this kind of thing in the sixth grade. I scrubbed a hand through Miguelito's dark hair that was standing straight up on his head, and the little gangster seemed satisfied. He followed me down the hallway to my bedroom, past the long rows of well-dusted books with copper lithographs hanging over them, a series of depictions of the Argentine Indian wars, *la guerra al malón*, showing soldiers with rifles facing off hordes of charging Indians armed with lances and *bolas*, battle scenes that hung like aging family portraits over the hallway bookcase that also held all manner of china and sterling knickknacks, including a collection of gaucho knives in tooled silver cases.

''Papá is waiting for you, señor,'' Isabelita said. ''He told me to send you in, sir, as soon as you returned. Should I wait tea for you, sir?''

''That's all right, Isabel. If I want something, I'll ring for it later.''

"Later is too late, I beg your pardon, sir. The señora is entertaining for tea and I have to serve them in the living room. So I have to get you boys out of my hair first, do you understand? I'll leave a tray of something out for you. Now don't keep your Papá waiting, sir, he has something for you."

I wanted more than anything to sit down and read my brother Harry's letter. But it was a big day for me, an important day for my new family, and it was unusual for Papá to be waiting for me at this hour, a surprise that he should have remained at home until teatime. The times Papá was at home, he usually set himself up in his large front room study with its exposed mahogany beams, its French windows opening out onto a balcony from which it was possible to reach out and touch the uppermost leaves of the trees below. Papá set himself up behind the thick wood slab of his desk with its handchiseled edges. He leaned back in his leather chair and surveyed his neat ranks of paperwork or his open leatherbound books, his French telephone, his bottle of Cinzano with its accompanying siphon of soda from which he continually served himself. Sometimes, he rang a little silver bell on his desk and Gisela, the day maid, or Isabelita, the live-in maid, would cut fresh limes into little wedges and carry them in to Papá on a wooden tray. Papá maintained a kind of formal distance from his family in this sanctuary, as he put it, *para descansar del yugo*, to rest like an ox out of its yoke.

Later, at the dinner hour, Papá ate in a merry, relaxed way with Mamá and his boys, enjoying his wine even as Mamá kept her eyes focused mainly on Miguelito, waiting to catch his violations of her code of table manners, which he would do to make the rest of us laugh—like quickly licking the serving fork, eating his salad with his spoon or picking up a chicken leg with his fingers, all with the fast mischievous reflexes of an artful dodger until Mamá finally caught him and sent him away from the table. Papá would then tell Isabelita to serve Miguelito dinner in his bedroom, after which Papá would rise and go off to his study for his customary evening audience with his older sons, me included.

We milled around in front of Papá's desk as he talked to us, or we sat before him and answered his questions as if we were litigants facing his highbacked judge's chair. We were required to recite for Papá our activities of the day and our plans for tomorrow, to which he usually gave his approval. Or if he disapproved, he lectured us about his reasons with the rhetoric of a Roman senator—why none of his sons should be too friendly with our classmate Hernández-Marelli, for example, who was a wild kid and might get us into trouble. Or why we should make sure to buy mezzanine seats for the *fútbol* games at the River Plate stadium and not go to the game if the tickets with seats were sold out because the bleachers were dangerous, the fans so crowded together shoulder-to-shoulder that they sometimes fell in *avalanchas*, as they were called. An *avalancha* had happened recently at River Plate stadium when a riot broke out between fans of opposing teams. Seventy-two people had been killed, some of them in a tumbling of hundreds over the high cliff of the packed upper deck; others, when the crowd had panicked, were crushed trying to get out of the stadium.

Generally, Papá approved of our plans, relaxed his tone with us and asked Alejo to put on a certain record as he poured a vermouth and soda for each of us. We sat together and listened to Vivaldi or Bach, or to Tommaso Albinoni, his favorite, or, despite the faces Alejo and Martín made at such old-fogy stuff, old tango records. He tried to explain some of the difficult words in dialect for me—tangos like *Her Eyes Closed on Me, My Beloved Buenos Aires, Goodbye Boys* or *I Missed Her by a Nose* and that kind of thing, the melodies always swift in beat, frenetic accordions merging with the violins in passionate resonance, or lone singers with guitars ramming out the melodies as their voices broke into nostalgic tears at their saddest memories of love and youth and how their lives had changed.

Martín could hardly contain his relief when Papá would switch back to his baroque music and take down one of his books to read to us. While we listened to this music, Papá recited passages from his history books or popular novels or the newspapers. Alejo's favorite was Albinoni's Third

Trumpet Concerto and Papá often read to us accompanied
by that record, the melody like a frilly series of white clouds
passing in the first strong light after a storm, a brassy sound
of bright expectations, of high spirits like the charms of
Italy. Opened on Papá's desk might be a leatherbound book
with the pages so yellowed they looked ready to crumble.
He was very proud of a first edition of an obscure work by
Machiavelli he had bought in Florence, a treatise about a
popular revolution in an Italian valley, and he read the words
out loud to us in Italian, then gave us summaries of what
they meant, phrases coming from him like, "*In a revolution
supported by villagers, the village itself must be treated as
an enemy camp.* Don't you see? This is one of the first
guerrilla actions in history, and the way they dealt with it
in Machiavelli's time was to make war on the whole population." Once, Papá read to us *The Daughter of Jorio* in
Spanish, a play by D'Annunzio about a young girl pursued
to death by a town jealous of her beauty. He was also particularly interested in the Civil War in North America and
sometimes read to us chapters of a translation of *Lee's Lieutenants*. He tried a novel by Alejo's latest favorite Argentine
author, Roberto Arlt, called *Siete locos* (Seven Madmen)
but the language was difficult for me to understand, and
much of it too profane for Papá's tastes. I tried to read it
myself later, and it was a very sad and hard book. "Just as
it was impossible to change lead into gold, it was impossible to transform the soul of man," is what I most got out
of it. When Miguelito was with us, Papá went on reading
aloud for him from his editions of Raymond Chandler de-
tective novels, among the most popular books ever published in Argentina, like *La ventana peligrosa* or *El sueño
mortal*. For me, these novels would always remain "The
Dangerous Window" and "The Deadly Sleep," even after
reading them again in the original, with Papá's sardonic yet
exciting tough guy voice forever Marlowe. These hours with
his sons were what Papá Benevento called his "dream
time"—smoking, reading, listening to his stereo. I was the
only smoker among his sons, and Papá didn't disapprove.
He was a habitual chain-smoker of American L&M's. He
smoked *como un demonio*, like a demon, as he put it, and

he seemed glad enough for reinforcements in the family against Mamá's persistent campaign to make him quit. "I like to smoke," he often said as he offered me a cigarette. "I smoke because I like to dream. It's beautiful just to sit here, smoking and dreaming and listening."

I reluctantly folded Harry's letter and put it in my back pocket, then I knocked on Papá's study door and let myself in. I stood quietly for a moment in front of Papá's desk; his concentration was still off with his music or out mixing with the sounds of the street. Then he suddenly reached out and pushed a red and white pack of L&M's toward me. I shook a cigarette out of the pack and reached for Papá's desk lighter that was an imitation Spanish globe, the continents drawn colorfully on it according to man's rough conception of them in the seventeenth century—monsters of Neptune reveling in the oceans, the flame clicking awake and rising from the North Pole. I sat facing Papá at his desk, behind him his wall of swords, pistols and rifles, antiques he had collected mainly for historical interest and had displayed behind him as a kind of miniature war museum. We both smoked a moment, the muted noises of the teatime traffic drifting in through the windows from Junín Street, a rapid hubbub of tires pattering over the cobblestones, distant car horns dying off toward the avenue Santa Fe. Albinoni's bright trumpets peaked, increased in speed, caught up to themselves in their cyclical melody. Papá waited until the concerto faded away. The scratching of the stereo needle between cuts of the album filled the room for a moment. "I love baroque music," he said. "There's a spirit in the sound you can't find anywhere else, don't you agree? But I like all other kinds of music, too, even that shit you and Martín Segundo listen to—you know, *los Beatles, los Erolling Estones*, all kinds of music. But the tangos and the big bands, mostly, next to Vivaldi and Albinoni, they're the best. Mamá and I fell in love to the music of tangos, and to the North American bands like Eduke Ellington, Esatchmo, Efather Hines, and the rest of them," he said. There was a blast of shrill oboes as a new concerto began, at which Papa turned in his chair to face me more directly and change the subject. "When I was a student at Colegio

San Andrés, they used to say that once you'd been to the bachelor's dinner with El Rector, you as good as had your degree in your pocket.''

''Does that mean I get to quit reciting lessons for Professor Herrera?'' I asked. The history teacher at San Andrés had for two months made me recite half a page a day from our textbook at the beginning of almost every class. He did this supposedly to help me learn Spanish, but there was a perverse satisfaction in the way he liked to listen to a yanqui stumbling through the facts of his country's beginnings, out loud, the professor correcting my pronunciation at the end of every phrase. When I no longer made mistakes, it felt like an unjust punishment for being yanqui.

''Herrera's been good for you,'' Papá said. ''He's got you speaking Spanish like an Argentine.''

''He busts my balls all the same,'' I said.

''Students your age should have their balls busted,'' Papá said and laughed. ''You've got to learn to make yourself strong in this world, strong enough and smart enough to take it in your hands.''

''Surely,'' I said.

''I'll talk to Professor Herrera if he pushes too hard on you again,'' Papá said. ''But a little pushing is all right, my son.''

''Thank you, Papá.''

''It really has helped you,'' he said. ''Look how good you've done, *che*. The way you've learned the language, and your excellent grades, and now this. An invitation to dinner with El Rector is an honor for you and your family. And he's invited you even before Martín Segundo, as if you were the eldest son of this family. By the way, if Martín seems a little rabid with you, Diego, let it pass. I know he's been acting like a *boludo* ever since you came to live with us. Mamá and I are grateful you've let that pass so far, like a real brother, and we're not happy either about his grades, all his girl troubles, everything. Just between us, I think it's good for Martín, your being here. It teaches him he can't always be at the center of his world. And it hasn't been that easy for him to bring you into it, you understand, to share the car with you, and to get invitations for you to his parties, and to try to line up his girlfriends to dance with you . . ."

"Really? Which girlfriends?"

"How should I know?" Papá laughed. "In any case, I didn't intend to talk to you this evening about Martín. I want to talk about being a Benevento tonight, about behaving like a Benevento. Do you understand me?"

"It's clear, Papá," I said.

"A dinner with El Rector, well, it's not some parish priest you're talking to. It's a Monseñor, a man with some influence in this world. Some of your less fortunate classmates, the ones with families of position but no money, scholarship students like the Crespi boy or El Gordo Rojo and plenty of other boys will probably get their starts in life with the help of the Monseñor. It's a military government now, as you know, and the church has always worked hand in hand with the generals. El Rector is in a position to help with admission to the universities or straight off with government jobs for the students he likes. Personally, I don't care for this particular Monseñor very much, and maybe you don't either, but I still want you to do your best to make the right impression, as you've done until now and as we're all very proud of you for doing. Is it clear what I'm asking of you?"

"I'll comport myself like a Benevento," I said.

"That's very good, my boy," Papá said. "And something else, my son, you need to know. When El Rector has had too much to drink, as he is known to do at dinner, when he starts to talk too much and comment about the government, about who his friends are in it and who are his enemies, or when he asks too much about my business, you know what I'm saying, my son, when you see El Rector get sloppy at dinner, take my advice and make an excuse. Tell El Rector that your Papá Benevento wants you home early for a family reunion. Laugh with El Rector, talk with him, say anything you please of a casual nature. But when El Rector talks too much himself, especially about politics, and when he asks you political questions, you know what I'm saying, that's the time to make your excuse. Give him a respectful kiss on his ring and say goodnight, is that clear?"

"Yes, sir."

"Have you ever heard of a group called The Catholic Lions?"

"What did you say?"

"The Catholic Lions, my son, is a religious and military club El Rector belongs to, very right wing, not the kind of organization I would see myself or any of my sons get involved with, a very dangerous and radical gang. So if El Rector talks about any of his activities with The Catholic Lions, or if he even mentions them, that's a sure signal he's saying things he doesn't mean and that you should make your excuse, is that clear?"

"Yes, sir, it's clear," I said.

"Very good then. Everything's clear now," Papá said. "I have a little present for you." He swiveled around in his chair so he could rustle among some papers in a cabinet behind him. When he turned back to face me he had the white, maroon and sky blue colors of a Colegio San Andrés sweater in his hands. "This was mine once," he said. "I wore it to my own bachelor's dinner with El Rector of San Andrés, a much more refined man than the present Monseñor. It was a different world back then, or maybe in those days we demanded more of our priests. At my own dinner, El Rector helped me to decide that I could do more for my family by becoming a lawyer than by going off into the *pampas* to help run the family ranch, which my younger brother Frederico had already decided to do. Anyway, it doesn't fit Martín Segundo, the boy takes more after his mother. Alejo's off in space somewhere and doesn't care a shit about his clothes. And Miguelito probably won't even make it through primary school if he keeps going like he is. So I'm lucky there's another son here who can wear this," he said, and by this time he had risen out of his chair and was holding out the sweater as if to size it on me.

"Really, Papá, I shouldn't take this. I just bought one like it today, and maybe one of the other boys . . ."

"That's enough, my son. I've already talked it over with Mamá. Martín can exchange the one you bought today for one his own size. So take it now. I insist. It's a gift from the family," he said.

Papá watched proudly as I stretched my arms up, cupping my fingers to catch the cuffs of my shirt so the sleeves wouldn't bunch up, then pulled the sweater down over my ears. Papá was suddenly on his feet as nimbly as a dancer, his sharp black shoes clicking over the polished squares of the wood floor to his stereo, where he quickly moved the needle back to the opening trumpets of his Albinoni record. Then the two of us sat down on the small sofa in Papá's study and shared a few moments of smoking, dreaming and listening. Papá looked at his watch and said he had work to do, for me to run along now, even on a Friday afternoon Papá was working, working, always working, he hoped he would never stop, that was clear, how else was it possible to keep building his family?

Later, alone in my big bedroom after my gifts of things Benevento, and after Isabelita had laid out a freshly ironed pale blue shirt, blue tie and gray flannel trousers, the Colegio San Andrés uniform, chattering at me all the while about what an event this was, I was a real bachelor and a real gentleman now, she'd make sure the whole neighborhood would know it and could she please have my dirty pants for the wash, I suddenly remembered Harry's letter. I stopped midway through dressing, socks down, tie draped over my open collar like a tailor's tape. I struggled with the glue on the flimsy envelope until I finally used my thumb and ended up tearing the fragile pages inside:

Dear James:

I remember that last time we were kicking over the sidewalk after I'd played guitar at The Winds, that little baskethouse on West 3rd Street. A woman coming towards us told you, "Keep him talking." Did she say that? Did you hear her?

Interesting times since I've been over here in the sense that I never did and still don't have the slightest idea of what goes down. And I still hear that woman's voice in my head, "Give up," mostly, and "It's too late," and stuff like that. So that makes me think it's

too late for me, I ain't going to make it. When I think
that way everything in this crazy scene turns into a
big fucking joke. Like ha, ha. Turn the music up full
blast, man, let's get it over with.

This is how it seems from my point of view. The
relationship is particularly sick—other people in how
they relate to me as a human being, how I relate to
them, and how we're all relating to the war. Everybody's copped an I don't give a fuck attitude, even
the officers, which seems to me particularly dangerous
over here. So I just chucked my allen wrenches and
volunteered to be a doorgunner. I mean, if I'm going
to stand there getting mortared on, I might as well get
someplace where I can shoot back. The boredom alone
and busting ass bagging sand half the time is enough
to kill you off. Just write the old man for me and tell
him that as far as I'm concerned, he's got nothing to
be ashamed of. While most of the crackers are pissing
in their beds, I'm up there flying around.

Most of us are here by chance. That's what it
comes down to. But that leaves me wondering just
how the hell I got to where I am in the first place.
Now she's at it again. "You've said too much already." That makes me laugh, man, like somebody
in my head is making the definitive statement of what
actually exists, a silent majority. All this random killing going down and nobody bothers about the reasons, you just go on. There are a few college boys,
the officers, and some others with a year or two of
school back in the World. Some of those guys talk
about the peace movement and free love, the revolution that's going down back home and all that shit.
That seems so silly over here. I mean, the college kids
are the silliest of all. I'm glad I never went to college.
Remember when the old man used to tell us about
college? How he came in from work with a few beers
in him and sat in the TV room with you, Donny,
Tommy, Kevin, Willy—all the sons, man, his sons.
He was all pumped up and telling us kids that we had
to go to college, we had to be the ones to close the

gap. There's some college kids over here who talk like
that, closing the gap between workers and intellectuals. It's nice, enthusiastic talk, but it still sounds
silly. Most of the others, the guys who've had a year
or two out making a living, or some who've hung out
a while, I mean, the majority of us just aren't like
that. So you write and tell the old man that in the
Nam the difference between the college kids and the
rest of us is this way—the college boys will tell you
your life's a joke and won't be laughing. The others,
I mean people further into life, harder on the dream,
they'll be calling your life a joke and laughing their
asses off. I guess that's just the way the divisions feel
to me.

You must be thinking I'm laying some kind of a
bummer on you. Most of the time it's not bad over
here. I sit in the hootch a lot, maybe looking at magazines, watching my guitar that's starting to twist up
at the neck because of all the humidity, gone all out
of tune here in the boonies. It's as hot all the time as
the hottest summer day back home. Some of the guys
go off to the river to swim it and go get laid in the
village. But I just stick around. I don't want to know
about any dumbshit crackers talking about hunting
coons all night. I just try to sleep, killing time until
morning. Then I climb up into the door of the helicopter and shoot the M-60. Like yesterday, the wind
was cool up there and we cruised up and down the
river on some kind of a recon thing, me firing off into
the trees for hours just trying to flush something out.
Reynolds—he's the W.O.—he tuned in the earphones
to rock radio AFN Saigon and I heard the old Airplane cut, *I'm going to saddle up my horse Lightning
and get out of here*. It was cool and blue up there, a
beautiful green jungle below. Then every once in a
while I'd just jink the gun over and watch the bullets
hitting the water, like when we were kids skipping
rocks at the bay only better, skipping hundreds of
rocks all at once and everybody having a good cool
day up there just doing his job. Maybe we hit some-

thing. Probably couldn't see it from up there even if we did. Sometimes I think in the middle of Vietnam you can find as much peace as anyplace else in the world.

I think I'll go find a buddy of mine, a spade named York. Maybe we'll go find a beer. It's too hot to sleep tonight.

If I were you, I'd start worrying about the draft. Stay right there in South America as long as you can, then go right on to college. None of this year-off bullshit and getting suckered into the Army. You were always the brains of the family, everybody knows that. I think about you a lot. I think about Donny and Tommy, and little Willy, too (Kevin can go fuck himself for being such a creep sometimes, but I also think about him). I think about the old man and the old lady, too, but I don't like to think about them. I should shut up now but I'm not going to. I just want to say we're all proud of you. Make the most of it and get into college. College is the right place for you. No offense, because I know you're not a joker. You're my kid brother and I think about you the most. Say hello to las chicas for me. Have you gotten my other letter with the good luck charm? Sometime send me a pretty postcard and let me know you're O.K.

Love,

Harry

Martín Segundo broke into my bedroom wearing his boxer shorts and his argyle socks, a fresh shirt unbuttoned over his suntanned chest, his shirttail snapping behind him like a flag in his quickness. "Sorry, Diego," he said in English with a nasal affectation taught at the Academia Londres, where he took classes. He was headed for my spare closet, into which some of his abundant wardrobe had spilled over. He threw the door open and stopped a moment in front of the long mirror that swung past him. He flexed and posed, admiring his suntanned build made from years of rugby, tennis and swimming. Martín puckered his lips and made a quick little kissing sound at his own reflection. "What a handsome boy, no? What a macho! What an hombre!" he said as he modeled for himself, testing the various hues of gray slacks to match the pastel yellow of his crisp new shirt. "All the girls are going to let you feel them up," he said into the mirror, and with a rake of his fingers, he pushed his hair back and started out again with his choice of slacks.

"*Che*, Martín," I said. "I'm sorry about tonight. El Rector should have invited us both."

"It's not important, *che*. I'm going out with El Gordo Rojo and José tonight with some really slutty girls we're supposed to meet at the movies. *Rosemary's Baby*. Polanski's a genius. We're going to move in and try to cop a feel while they're screaming," Martín said as he continued to dress, stepping into his pants and cinching them home, giving his flat muscular stomach two little pats after he buttoned his shirt. He stopped moving and said, "That's a great sweater Papá gave you. It doesn't fit me. It's too tight in the chest and shoulders and too long in the sleeves." He looked at me with something new in his eyes, something unspoken. "*Ciao*, Diego," Martín said and suddenly turned in a rush to get down the hall. "I've got to pick up El Gordo and then get a taxi. We're ten minutes late already!"

"What time is it?"

Martín was already slamming down the hallway to his room, where he banged through his closet for just the right tie. His urgency reminded me that I was also short on time.

"Isabelita!"

"I'm just finishing pressing your jacket, sir," Isabelita called out. "You'll have it in a little moment!"

I pieced together the torn pages of Harry's letter, blue scraps scattered over the red poncho that was my bedspread. I thought of how when I had first told the Beneventos that I had a brother in Vietnam, they had accepted the news as if I had told them that he was dying of an incurable disease. They showed concern for me by trying to avoid the issue directly. Part of this was Mamá's sense of propriety, that talk about war in civilized company should be restrained. Yet each of the Beneventos would inquire in his

own way about news from Harry, particularly Papá. Papá
would circle articles in the Buenos Aires papers and leave
them out for me on his way to his office before anyone else
in the family had stirred out of bed, the Spanish headlines
standing out in the frames of his black ink, *Westmoreland
Anuncia Nueva Ofensiva*, for example, or *VC Decimado En
Khe Sahn* or *Bombas Caen Nuevamente Sobre Hanoi* and
so on. Martín and Alejo talked openly at the breakfast table
about yanqui injustice in the war, what a piece of shit it all
was and that kind of thing to express sympathy for my
brother Harry. The few times Papá had been there to overhear them, he interrupted his sons and stated his own view,
"Any nation that aspires to power in this world has to pay
its price. The war in Vietnam is the price that the United
States is paying for its empire."

I didn't tell my new family that Harry had gone off to
pay the price for empire with hair down to the middle of
his back and both bootheels filled with acid tabs. He had
been the first of my brothers to turn on, tune in and get
political, the wanderer of the family, barefoot in summer,
wearing boots with bells in winter, and wherever he went
he packed his old Gibson Hummingbird guitar in its beat-
up case. He was proud of the fact that he had played that
guitar for a peace rally in the city only an hour before Bobby
Kennedy gave a speech. But Harry had lost the protection
of high school by graduating, then he had started a full-time
shift at a nearby rivet factory, a job that lasted only a few
weeks before he received a request from the draft board to
report for his physical. Harry went to psychiatrists recom-
mended by the International Society of Friends who wrote
extensive files that he was mentally unfit. He went to another doctor who helped him drop a capsule of serum al-
bumin into his urine sample. Later, he claimed back
problems, trying to curve his spine in a certain prescribed
way under X-ray machines. Harry stalled them, mixed up
his paperwork, made it through eight long months treating
staying out of the Army like a full-time job, but nothing
worked. He finally passed all of the Army exams and received his final, threatening notice to report for induction.

Harry quickly packed up a duffel bag and his guitar and disappeared into the city.

Living underground for Harry was made a lot easier by his brothers. We took the Long Island Railroad into the city and brought him cash, and Tom or I sometimes threw Harry's dirty laundry in to wash with our own, then delivered it to him. Nobody let the old man or our mother know where Harry was because the old man at that time was sitting at the dinner table saying things like, "That lazy asshole Harry's nothing but a bum and a traitor. He's going to end up in jail, and that's just where he belongs. And the rest of you are going to wind up just like him if you don't cut that ugly hair off and straighten up and fly right."

It was usually me who got on the train and met Harry at one of the coffeehouses or bars he called baskethouses, where he was playing his guitar and passing a basket for spare change. I was the closest to Harry, and since I was older and got the best grades at that time, I was less watched by the old man and the old lady. I met Harry at places like The Feenjon and Café Bizarro, or at the coffeehouse called The Four Winds, where he later landed a steadier gig. As long as the weather held, it seemed, Harry was doing all right. There was a festive street-fair atmosphere everywhere in Greenwich Village in those days, the peace and free-love guerrilla army out in force—sparechanging, doing drugs and taking in the sunshine. People were handing out flowers and peace movement buttons in the streets with as much sincere feeling as anyone who had ever sold war bonds.

But the season changed, and Harry and I started walking more uneasily along the icy sidewalk in front of The Four Winds. An unfamiliar face would come up to us out of a street scene of gaudy and starving gypsies, like one of the stragglers from a carnival that had moved on for the winter. Whoever it was, the dude would likely bum a cigarette. We would agree with him that it was cold out, and yeah, man, what a hassle to get a job without showing any I.D. and say, hey, the place to score smoke is the coffee shop around the corner, the kitchen slave named Tony, and you can get great meals over at the Mission if you don't mind the Bible talk, and at the guru's it's brown rice, meditation and yoga and you get to breathe in all that incense and get high. . . .

This one particular night, we got out of the cold and went back to The Four Winds for another of Harry's sets. Harry played a good version of Jerry Jeff Walker's "Round and Round," and other songs by Dylan, Dave Van Ronk and Neil Young. He had three dollars and forty cents in his basket at the end of it, which wasn't enough to pay the price of a flophouse room, but Harry lucked out that night and picked up a girl. She was like all my teenage fantasies of girls, blonde and with full hips and breasts, the kind of girl who made sex look easy. There were no secrets to it as I watched her lift a leg up onto Harry's lap. They sat at a dark corner table, making out. Then Harry made signals to me that it was time for me to catch the next train back to Port Washington. I left The Four Winds wishing I could be my brother Harry. In my mind, this girl was taking off her beaded leather skirt and peeling off her leotard. I imagined myself instead of Harry naked with this girl who lit candles and brought out good drugs and had a tub-in-kitchen pad over on St. Marks Place.

As I was heading into the West Fourth Street subway, two freaks crossed the street and approached me. One of them was a dude named Frank, with frizzy hair under a sports cap the color of engine grease, somebody Harry and I had met on the street and smoked a number with that night. Frank was with a young black dude who wore his bandanna like a pirate and had a gold loop in one ear, his fuzzy black face poking through a rip in a filthy blanket he held around his shoulders like a poncho. "Hey, man, dig it," the dude named Frank said. "Want to check out a party over on Avenue C?"

Dirty striped mattresses covered the floor of the dark apartment wall to wall. Between them, colorful lumps of splattered wax marked where candles had once burned, and how long it had been since the electricity was shut off. A black ball of opiated hash glowed at the end of a coiling green glass pipe. A pretty girl was passing the pipe, her hair hanging in beaded strings dyed purple, and she kept giving me this eerie smile in the candlelight every time I took a hit, as if she knew what happened next. I was slowed by the drugs, and sleepy, huddling against a wall and waiting for the party to start. A thought passed through my mind that something was wrong here, and dangerous, but I told myself it was only paranoia from the smoke. I leaned back and closed my eyes for a minute. The girl suddenly vanished, or maybe I fell asleep. The next thing I knew, this guy Frank was moving his body against mine, flattening me against the wall. I cried out and pushed him away. Then he slammed his forearm up against my throat and I knew what was happening, the party they had talked about was me. The pirate ripped off his dirty red bandanna and stuffed it so far down my throat I thought I'd swallowed it. I kicked at them, gagging, I was choking to death, flailing my arms all around, then Frank hit me in the face once, twice, then lower down and that was all, doubling me over was enough for him. Everything inside me panicked and moved and tried to escape my body in a long, shrill choked-back screaming that was bursting in my lungs as I felt the two of them flipping me over and pulling down my jeans. . . .

Walking stiffly up out of the subway into deserted Penn Station, blood was running down the back of my legs an soaking into my jeans. I was cut up and beaten up, ripped open inside like a sausage bursts in a hot pan. What I was most afraid of was that somebody might see and somehow know, as if the bagladies and winos trying to get warm in the Long Island Railroad waiting room could have given a shit. Still, I backed myself up against a pillar as I waited for the train. For days afterward, I stuffed Kleenex into my jockey shorts and faked a bad case of the flu with the old lady so she would let me stay home from school. I lay alone in bed wanting to die, hurting all over with a pain that stifled and weighed over my body like a tropical day with the sun beating down. In time, this feeling became lost in an attitude of strong and fixed alienation, in my efforts to damage my brain as much as possible through drugs, most education lost before I ever stepped into classrooms. At parties, I joked around and drank beer with the girls and rolled them joints until they couldn't speak, then I walked

them home without touching them. At home, the TV and
radio were on all the time as if to turn everything else off.
It was easy to get lost in our house as long as I didn't make
noise enough to wake the old man and the old lady late at
night, getting up the stairs past their room.

Then a day came when I stepped into line at school and
took the test for I.S.E. and lied my way through all the
interviews and a miracle happened. I was taken out of that
life. Luck was with me, and with a lesson, something like
*the truth gets you punished when your lies can set you free*.
One of Papá's old tangos said it, too, and at first in my new
country I listened to this record, writing down the words
and trying my best to understand them, a tango about a love
that's closed its eyes and died, *everything is lies, in lies is
where I've put you, and now my heart is all alone. . . .*

Five months later, I didn't feel anything like the kid I had
once been and didn't want to feel anything like him. The
soft wool of Papá's Colegio San Andrés sweater felt warm
over my clean, ironed shirt, the smell of mothballs from
the old sweater covered over by a generous splash of Papá's
lemon cologne from Harrods. I was his son now, full grown
and honored, with a new family and even a new name. My
new country had given me everything and more. It wasn't
a country so different from myself; it also believed its own
lies, calling itself *la Argentina, the land of silver*, when
nobody had ever found any there. As far as I was concerned, I was going to live in Argentina forever, if I could.

Harry came back home from living underground before
I took the I.S.E. test. He was starving, weighing about a
hundred and thirty pounds by then. His money had run out,
he had gone to Chicago, and while singing at a club, his
first real job as a pro musician, he had been busted for draft
evasion, and also charged with *contributing to the delinquency of a minor* because there was a young girl living at
the crash pad he had been arrested in. It cost the old man
two thousand dollars in legal and other fees to get Harry
released from Cook County jail, and the judge had made
Harry sign an agreement to report for induction into the
U.S. Army. The old man took Harry's troubles as something more than one of his normal foulups, it was a lesson

for the rest of his sons. As for my brothers, we were all disappointed in Harry, at how weak and quiet he'd grown, at how he wasn't even considering crossing the border into Canada while he still had the chance. I still felt somewhat this way even when I received Harry's letter all the way in Argentina—why the hell was Harry always getting himself into trouble? What business did he have to go off and volunteer for something? But I also felt sorry for him, in my head still hearing the old man those last days at the dinner table, talking at Harry in all sincerity and saying, "Listen, Harry, the Army's not all that bad. You might even learn to like it in the Army." And how when Harry didn't answer him, the old man turned to the rest of us and kept saying, "It's not that bad. It's not. It might even be good for Harry. The Army's just the kind of thing that might straighten him out."

On my way to dinner with El Rector of Colegio San Andrés, past Mamá's dutiful kiss on the cheek and Papá's quick handshake and "Good luck, my son," at the doorway to his study, a prayer had started to repeat itself in my brain like an endless Buddhist chant that Harry wouldn't pay the price, that my brother Harry would somehow make it home.

# 2

## Under the Crust

On my way to El Rector's dinner, the poplar-like *plátano* trees along Junín Street were just beginning to shed their leaves, handfuls of them drifting to the tiled walks to await tomorrow morning's washing down. Above them, French doors were shutting on the balconies, windows were swinging open in the kitchens to let out cooking smells. The musical sounds of dishware filled the air as tables were set, dinner was served, lights bloomed in the windows of the buildings high above like the stars coming out at night. In the streets around me, deep into the heart of the Barrio Norte, the keepers of the tiny grocery shops and corner kiosks were selling their final packs of cigarettes, large bottles of Coke, wine, quarter-kilos of coffee and other last-minute items to clusters of maids. These maids were the live-in kind, many of them heavy in the hips, most of them dark from *indio* blood, stockings rolled down to their plastic pumps or rope-soled shoes. They chattered away with news of their employers—which young playboy in the neighborhood had just deflowered a debutante, or what youngster under their charge had been justly or unjustly held back in school. It was the same way Isabelita had talked that day of

Vera Rojo going nearly full-time to a weight-watching clinic of the Jack La Lanne franchise on the avenue Callao and how it was working, or about which señora was spending too much time with a student from the university, think what a scandal that could cause. They gossiped about their employers' lives as if they were sharing their own secrets, also as a way to compare notes on the general situation, which they called just that, *la situación*—the crazy economy, the repression under the military, a world that was out of control.

I walked down Junín, smelling Papá's crisp lemon shaving cologne. It was pleasant to listen to the music of the streets, the sounds of autumn trees in the weak breezes, the occasional car or taxi slowly passing. I lit a black tobacco Particulares. Its heavy smoke had the strong smell of organic fertilizer spread over a garden. I nodded to one of the *serenos*, a doorman in an apartment lobby and one of the neighborhood watch, supposed to protect the streets from intruders. A small *colectivo* bus of the yellow 69 line rattled past. The sturdy voices of the maids called goodnight to each other as they climbed up steps and vanished around street corners with their net bags swinging at their sides.

As I approached the school, I felt a sense of anxiety about the evening ahead—it was a big event for me, and for my family, and I wanted to make the right impression. I passed a blue-uniformed federal policeman at the corner, his machine gun hanging around his neck, both his hands on it, one on the cocking lever and one on the steel butt. Why did they all seem to hold their greaseguns as if ready at any signal to point them outward and pull the triggers like mad carpenters caulking seams? I thought of the street joke in Buenos Aires, *no se toca botón*, or don't put your finger on the button, and how the policemen were called *botones* or "buttons." It was a joke passed from soul to soul on the crowded *colectivo* buses, or wisecracked by some of the bolder and more established comedians on national television. The button on the corner looked at me quickly, with eyes like empty bullet holes, just a quick inspection, then he watched me peripherally, one hand resting on the barrel of his machine gun, his back pressed against a building as

he faced outward at the street as if to achieve his widest
field of vision. I had crossed this street corner many times.
Why didn't I recognize this policemen? Why was it never
the same button when I passed this corner?

Ahead of me stood the low, three-story building that was
Colegio San Andrés. The Colegio enclosed an entire city
block, with a garden and two courtyards inside its walls.
One courtyard was for school ceremonies and the other
served as a kind of hazardous, tile-paved gym, against one
wall of which stood the ancient cement stalls of the school
latrine, which was more like a large open trough. The dor-
mers of the priests and brothers were dark at this hour. The
teaching clergy must have been gathered by then for their
dinner in the main dining hall. I started to cross the street
in front of the tiny grocery shop where an old man named
Rocas sold his soft drinks and candy bars at superinflated
prices to the blue-blazered students of the Colegio. Sensing
a figure in the doorway, I stopped and looked, then a fast
moving *colectivo* bus of the copper-colored 39 line nearly
ran me down. I jumped back up onto the sidewalk, and as
I did, a stooped-over man limped out of the doorway to
Rocas' shop and said, "*Hola*, Yanqui!" loud enough to be
heard down the block. Then the little man moved fast in a
cockeyed gait across the sidewalk and was suddenly at my
side.

El Negrito was a short, stocky man, his shoulders
slouched into a kind of hunching that reduced his stature
even more. His dark tangled hair was an oily mess on a
head that was balding in ragged patches. The sight of El
Negrito gave me *asco*, a strong revulsion, everything about
him down to his grimy clothes with their heavy odors of
sweat and garlic. He was a manservant to El Rector, and a
general school administrative aide of sorts who wasn't a
priest but who dressed in gray like our priests. He was married to one of the cleaning ladies of the dining hall and
residences, and Colegio San Andrés let them both stay in a
special servants' quarters that looked over the courtyard
where we played our *fútbol* games. El Negrito was friendly
with the students. He even sometimes joined our courtyard
*fútbol* games as a goalie, though it was a liability to have

him on the team. There was no out-of-bounds in this court-yard game. The ball bounced off three high stone walls and stayed in play like a kind of squash version of soccer, and on the side where there should have been a fourth wall, the open latrines were guarded partway up by thin-meshed wire so rusty that a strong kick sent the ball right through it. Sometimes the ball landed in the running yellow trough or, worse, in the deep porcelain pits with their footgrips on either side for traction while squatting, in which case the player who had kicked the ball in there had to take it out from the corner himself, bounce it around to dry it off, then try to put the ball back into play out of the little concrete corner of the latrine with all the players of both teams coming at him at once. El Negrito sometimes took cigarette breaks with us in the latrine and talked to the students about *fútbol*, trying to get out there and kick the ball, too, balancing clownlike on his lame leg and clumsily swinging his good one at the ball.

El Negrito often made deals "to fix things up" for certain students if they had logged one too many demerits for savage acts—blowing condoms up into huge balloons in chemistry class by using explosive hydrogen gas, or setting the old wooden desks on fire at the back of the history room by means of steady applications of butane lighters as Professor Herrera lectured on about the conquest of *la banda oriental*, the wars of the eastern part of the continent that led to the vice-regency of Argentina, later overthrown in a war inspired by the French Revolution and becoming a republic under *presidente* Bernardino Rivadavia. Or he might be droning on about the half-century of British domination when Argentina was ruled by its first dictator, Don Juan Manuel de Rosas and his Red army, followed by the civil war in which the Blue army won and reformed the democracy on the model of the U.S. Constitution, reciting in a monotone to his room full of pupils from a yellowing sheaf of pages that had years ago been engraved in his head, oblivious of the torches kindled in his classroom until dark smoke billowed up from a flaming antique desk and the students began to fall into the aisles with laughter. Herrera would shout, "*Che!* This can't be! This can't be! What kind of savages have your families raised!" then mark down every student in the back row for three demerits. Ten demerits meant getting tossed out of school for a while. El Negrito often intervened for these students, talking to El Rector about giving them another two demerits' worth of chance before suspension.

It was strange that El Negrito would talk to me on the street. The only time he had really had a conversation with me was one day during my first week at school, when I was floundering along in Spanish and, nose-to-nose, El Negrito had fingered the collar of my shirt and said in terrible English, "I geef you thees moneee, you *amigos* in *Norteamér-ica* send me thees shirt?" Then he had limped off before I could figure out what he wanted from me and could tell him my nice shirt was Argentine.

Along with his repulsive appearance, I didn't like El Negrito, and less so because of the stories of my friend, Hernández-Marelli. He claimed El Negrito was a shameless crook, pocketing millions of pesos in kickbacks from funeral directors and from the shopkeepers who furnished the church's flowers and other supplies. Then there were other thousands of pesos, or *mangos*, as we called them, that El Negrito took in bribes for his influence in getting the doors of Colegio San Andrés opened for certain unqualified children of *la gente bien*, kids who didn't test high enough to get into school, or for seeing that a student managed to pass a certain grade at the Colegio when everyone knew he should have flunked. And here the little repulsive man was grinning up at me under a corner streetlight that made his snaggleteeth look as if they'd been filed into points. "*Che*, Yanqui," El Negrito said. "El Rector is looking forward to having dinner with you. He's had this new cook fixing a genuine *locro* for three days. Then lettuce and tomato salad, a fresh catch of squid à la romana, fried potatoes, flan for dessert and I don't know what else. Have you seen the priests' new cook yet, *che*?"

Hernández-Marelli had said something about this a few days ago, about the previous cook, Ana María, having a *pan francés*, a loaf of French bread, in her "oven," which we students suspected might have come from one of our

French priests. Because of this, El Rector had sent Ana María back up North to cook in a convent at one of the *indio* missions. "Her first slipup in all these years, the poor little thing," Hernández-Marelli said. "You can see the bad mood the priests are in from someone else's cooking."

"She's a real crazy one," El Negrito said as if he were one of us gassing about girls in the courtyard. "She's really love-crazy," he said. "I'm not kidding you. All a guy like you has to do is to ask her to the movies once."

"Come on, Negrito, don't bust my balls," I said. "This is a serious thing tonight."

"With El Rector? Dinner? Don't be a *boludo*. You just watch him. He'll drink a bottle of wine with his soup, another bottle with the main course, and before dessert even hits the table, he'll be off and snoring in his bed. He won't even remember what you talked about tomorrow." As he was speaking, I looked at him more closely, seeing something ancient in him. The spider's web of brown grainy leather that was his face turned more serious, a light passing over it from the barely illuminated doorway of Rocas' shop making El Negrito look dried and mummylike, an old, old man. "*Che*, I'm serious," he said. "Don't be afraid of El Rector. The honor of this kind of thing is that you're the one who's been picked for it, *che*, not what the general says when he hangs the ribbon around your neck. You can believe me, no lie, I was with the old Monseñor before this one, the one who was thrown into the house of crazies because he spoke out against Perón."

I had heard a story about the priests at San Andrés being arrested during the first Peronist regime, but El Negrito mentioning it now made me uncomfortable. It was against the present military government's unwritten laws to talk openly about Perón or even use his name. Perón had been written out of the official history books, a period of Argentina's heritage left mainly blank or at most filled in by graphic fever charts and short explanations of social and economic decline. Yet at parties, on the streets, in the courtyard of San Andrés, it was clear that everyone knew what had happened—official silence was itself confirmation of the exiled dictator's overwhelming presence. Even the youngest of schoolchildren in the working class neighborhoods were still taught the Peronist marching songs, sometimes with different words. For example, a song about the most popular professional *fútbol* team in the country, Boca Juniors, was sung by fifty or sixty thousands of fans every Sunday afternoon to the tune of the Peronist Youth's anthem, *We, the youth of the Peronistas* . . .

"Look, let's not bullshit each other," El Negrito said. "You don't bullshit me and I won't bullshit you."

"All right," I said. "Agreed."

"You've been in this city long enough, you can speak enough Spanish to defend yourself in the streets. But maybe you need somebody like me to show you a few things, is this clear?"

"So let's get together sometime for a Coke or something," I said. "Is that what you want? What are you talking about?"

"I'm talking about anything you want. Anything. No bullshit," he said.

"I don't understand," I said.

"Maybe someday, in return, you will do something for me," El Negrito said. I relaxed a little at this; I felt like I was on ground I knew. He was hinting at some kind of scheme, involving money, probably, a bribe or something, I thought. "Very well, Negrito," I said. "Tell me your size and I'll have a friend in *la USA* send you some shirts."

"I'm not talking about shirts," he said. "I'm talking about getting free. I get free of El Rector, take out my savings in dollars, and you help me, my wife and my nephew move to North America. What do you think?"

Was this for real? If so, how could I possibly help? He had a grin on his face as if he had just told a joke at my expense, and I thought maybe not, he was just testing me. "*Che*, maybe your wife and the kid," I said after a moment. "But they'd never let a guy like you into the United States. Customs would take one look at you and mark you down as contraband."

El Negrito shouted with laughter at this, swaying back and forth, laughing until he was out of breath. I used this as an excuse to turn and walk away with a cool little brotherly wave of my hand, like I'll see you around, man, but he started to cross the street after me. "I'll see you in a few minutes!" he called out, still laughing. "I'm serving tonight. I'll run down to the cellar for wine and uncork the bottles like a fancy waiter, just you watch me, *flaco*!" he said, and I felt put off to be called *flaco*, skinny, even to be addressed with this kind of familiarity by a man who was, after all, only a crooked servant.

"Good. In a little while," I said and turned away from him with an odd disquiet, as if somehow the evening ahead had just taken on a logic all its own. As I crossed through the archway, past the statue of the Virgin with its arrangement of purple neon halos giving off a faint humming sound, I thought I could hear something behind me, the quick thrust of El Negrito's lame leg with its huge orthopaedic shoe that he lifted, pushed forward, then dragged up to meet his other leg with a noise as if the shoe were filled with cement, the sound echoing across the street behind me, following.

The main courtyard of Colegio San Andrés opened up ahead under deep blue evening shadows. I walked along over the hundred-year-old tiles in the passageway under the arches that divided the courtyard from the tiny central plaza where we students were marshaled into assembly for national holidays and made to sing the anthem of Argentina, *libertad, libertad, libertad* . . . this chorus sung out through the changing voices of two hundred boys while we waited for El Judio's father, lieutenant colonel of the Air Force Leopoldo Dipaoli, to give us one of his volunteer civics lectures, like *The Morality of Being an Argentine Citizen*, which was in complete agreement with El Rector's admonitions to abstain from masturbation and sex before marriage. Colonel Dipaoli's speeches to us in his resonant commanding officer's voice made El Judio melt into the crowd and try to hide. "Argentina was once the fifth potential in the world, and it is up to you, to your generation of patriotic Argentines, with all the moral dignity and courage of General San Martín, to lift up our nation to those standards again"—real pep talk stuff from the armed forces. When he got carried away, Colonel Dipaoli's black riding boots invariably strayed off the walk and messed up the little flowerbeds that encircled the flagpole at the plaza's heart by which he always spoke. These flowers were Father Naboa's gardening project. All afternoon after a school assembly, Father Naboa could be seen weeding through his red geraniums crushed by the colonel's boots.

As I crossed into the courtyard, the flagpole's lanyard was ringing eerily against the hollow metal in the deserted plaza. Across the courtyard, under the arches of the passageway to the classrooms, I thought I saw the figures of two priests walking together slowly, dark moving cones of shadows in their long gray skirts. One of them was bent low enough and had his hands behind his back in a characteristic way that could only be Father Naboa's. Father Naboa taught philosophy and religion and seemed always in a daze. He was mostly deaf, and anything went in his class as he droned on about St. Thomas Aquinas, St. Augustine and Aristotle in that order, *man is a rational animal* and so on, *the existence of God can be proven by an argument from absence. Everything else would be impossible if He did not exist.* Meanwhile, students in the back of his classroom were smoking cigarettes cupped in their hands under their desks. Spitballs flew across the room. At the head of the room, sitting in front of his antique Spanish desk, his legs crossed under his gray skirts, Father Naboa simply talked on to himself with little side stories about his life in the priesthood and the closeness he had achieved to God by living a philosophy that excluded everything after the fourteenth century.

One day he told a story of the disciples of St. Augustine. They had gathered at the deathbed of the saint, and immediately after his spirit had left his body the monks dropped the remains in a cauldron of boiling oil in order to render the bones as holy relics of the Augustinians. "It was said in the oooorder," Father Naboa paused between phrases and sang out his words, "whoever possessed the booones," he pushed up his glasses and pinched the end of his sharp nose a few times, "recognized as hoooly by the Pope of Rooome," he pulled out his handkerchief, looked into it, coughed, "would be endowwwed with powers of wiiisdommmm . . ." and by that time, Hernández-Marelli had begun a kind of *samba* chanting from in back of us all, *hiervan los reliquios muchachos . . . hiervan los reliquios muchachos . . . hiervan los reliquios muchachos . . .* and everyone broke out laughing, all of us shocked Hernández-Marelli had gone that far and had even started to dance his little song out around an imaginary boiling kettle, and we all joined in with him chanting, *boil those relics down, boys . . . boil those relics down, boys . . . boil those relics down, boys . . .* until Father Naboa finally looked up at us, his mouth set sharply as he gathered his books and papers with quiet dignity. He shuffled out of the classroom slowly, the song following him, then he ordered El Negrito to mark every one of us down for six demerits. Since ten demerits meant suspension, Colegio San Andrés was suddenly in danger of losing eighty percent of its senior class.

The priest walking next to Father Naboa was Father Artaud. Father Artaud was a teaching father performing the duties of a parish priest in the San Andrés chapel. He was the one who took confession, married, baptized, said masses every day, and masses every Friday for the school, a priest with red orange hair always flying in a mess. He was often gone from the Colegio, off around the rich neighborhoods of Buenos Aires with his little traveling kit. From Hernández-Marelli's vantage point on cigarette breaks in the latrine, he could see Father Artaud visiting those well-to-do women, abandoned in all but appearances by their husbands off at their clubs, or on business, or with their mistresses. Marelli described Father Artaud descending on women like a playboy in priest's clothing, picking his flowers one by one, then dumping them off by faking atonement. Marelli went into the coarsest details, *"Che,* my older brother says that Father Artaud is the only man to throw a fuck with El Gordo Rojo's Mamá in more than ten years. It was a true work of charity. You can see it, right? That skinny little freckled stick poking out from his skirts and him jumping up onto this mountain of fat, *che,* it's a miracle he ever got it in. And she's the only one whose heart was ever broken, that's why she cries at his masses all the time." Just at that moment, El Gordo Rojo suddenly appeared out of nowhere and jumped onto Hernández-Marelli's back, crushing him instantly flat onto the courtyard. El Gordo just covered him like that, one forearm like a whole ham mashing Hernández-Marelli's face into the tiles while Marelli was screaming. Then Brother Daniel shouldered through the crowd to break up the fight and to stop Marelli's nosebleed with his handkerchief.

I didn't believe Marelli's stories about Father Artaud. It was like my brother Alejo had said, Marelli was a bullshit artist mainly because he was the kind of playboy who had stopped opening any books and would turn twenty-five before he graduated, if he would even then. No senior dinner with El Rector for Marelli. It was a wonder he hadn't been expelled years ago. Marelli had problems, that was clear. His family was just then falling apart. His father was a judge, and Papá had told me he had become an alcoholic, wavering around up there drunk on the bench. Once a high court judge whose decisions hadn't gone along with changes in the laws dictated by the military regime, he had been demoted by the generals to a court that handled small claims. Marelli wasn't to be believed, he was bullshitting all the time to hide his problems. But mainly it was the tone of voice Father Artaud used when he was saying mass— clear and simple, like the voice of a friend talking—that made me feel the gossip about him couldn't be true.

El Rector's private dormitory, kitchen and dining area were at the top of a rank of stone stairs at the end of the arched-in corridor. Going up the stairway, I stopped a moment and gave my jacket sleeves a tug to straighten them. My newest winter wool jacket was a little stiff. I gathered myself at the Monseñor's door, which was tall and dark, ornately carved with a raised fresco of an open Bible with Greek lettering on its pages that I couldn't make out, something from the Book of John, I think it was, *Judge not according to appearances but righteous judgments*, under which there was a stern-looking sculpture of a lion's head with a brass ring door knocker in its teeth. I started to knock on the door but it suddenly opened as though on its own. A dark thin figure of a woman jumped back into the shadows when she saw me. Then she quickly recovered herself and stepped forward into the light, her eyes looking down at the floor, her face dark and her body keeping to one side of the little entryway in case I needed to pass.

"I'm here at the invitation of the Monseñor?"

"Ah! Of course! Pardon me, sir!" She motioned for me to step inside, the sound of her few words made deep in her throat and with a slow lilt to her accent that I saw as much as heard by the movements of her pretty mouth. There was a shyness that seemed built into her sharp features, as if a few divine strokes of a machete had carved them out of dark wood. She wasn't stooped or fat as a pear like most of the servants the priests brought in to work for them from the San Andrés missions in the North, like Ana María, the old cook, or like El Negrito, or like the shriveled little janitor who hosed down the courtyards every morning. She was small but shapely, and something about her made me think of the striking miniature figures the Indians once made out of red clay. I passed her awkwardly, nodding and smiling, but it was as if she had sensed some indiscretion had taken place that the two of us had shared as I looked her over, because she passed me too quickly, hurrying out into the archway. "Please pardon me. You'll find the Monseñor in the living room," she said as she rushed past me without shutting the door behind her, on her way to help serve the rest of the brotherhood in the main dining hall. I listened to the fading patter of her rope-soled shoes taking the steps two at a time, her white apron strings trailing behind her like the tail on a kite.

"Cornelia! Who's here!" El Rector shouted from inside the small apartment. I entered the tiny living area that was barely removed from the little corner where the table was already set, two thick white votary candles glowing in their tall glass jars. El Rector was sitting on a couch surrounded on two sides by high walls of yellowing books. Behind him was a small balcony with leaded glass French doors closed to the noises of the street. El Rector rose off his couch when he saw me, a glass of clear thick liquid in hand. He was a squarely built man, still muscular at his age, his hair a steel gray flattop crewcut uncommon in his country, an aggressiveness to his movements that reminded me of American football players. "It's our North American already," El

Rector said. "I should have remembered that you yanquis like to get everywhere on time."

"It's an honor to be here, Father." I kissed a fat gold ring on a hand that seemed as big as a baseball glove. "The Benevento family asked me to give you their affections."

"Come in and sit down, my son. Take that silly jacket off and make yourself at home. You're in your own house. Let me pour you a drink now and you sit down and tell me about yourself. This is our little time to get to know one another, you and your Monseñor, after your long fitting at San Andrés. Well, not so long in your case. Most bachelors have been with us, well, more than ten years. But it's a fitting nonetheless, and we're going to launch you off from our port like God's shipbuilders." El Rector set a glass in front of me and unscrewed the cap on a bottle, pouring out something clear and thick. "Now don't tell me when. I always say that glasses were made like glasses because they were made to be filled. This is a traditional drink I learned to like very much when I was running missions in the North. How do you like it so far in our Argentina?"

My mouth was filled with a strong burning swallow of a liquor called *aguardiente*, or firewater, that had turned into a kind of hot steam in my nose and ears. I took in a breath that felt like I was in a sauna and considered El Rector's question. How many people had asked me this same question so far? Which of the various smiling, rehearsed answers should I give him?

"I feel almost Argentine myself," I said. "It's the best thing that's ever happened in my life."

"And the school? How do you find it? How do you find it compared to North American schools?"

"It isn't anything like the school I went to in the United States, Monseñor. I didn't go to a private school before."

"It's an easy school, everybody knows that," El Rector said with a dismissive wave of his huge hand. "And believe me, it's a chore for the teaching fathers to water down their favorite books into the kind of farina that spoiled brats are used to swallowing. But the point is that they are all very capable brats, don't you think? They all have possibilities. Colegio San Andrés does its best to prepare its students for their possibilities. We let a few pass by in the wildness of their youths because we can be sure that if they avoid idiotic political activities, they'll buckle down and study their asses off at the university. Or else their fathers will take them into the family business and kick their asses flat. Or the military academies will do the same. And the wildest boys often marry rich, in which case we make them lay assistants. Some of the best families in the nation send their children here, so Colegio San Andrés doesn't have to be as tough scholastically as many other schools and still keeps its reputation as being one of the finest and most exclusive Catholic schools in Buenos Aires. We are in the business of *education* as much as *instruction*, is that clear?''

"Yes, it's clear," I said. "*Instruction* is what you're taught from books. *Education* is how you learn to live your life."

"Very good, very good, my son," El Rector said. "We at Colegio San Andrés know the difference. The teachers know it, the parents know it, but more importantly, the students know it as well. My understanding of public instruction abroad is that the public schools in North America claim they're teaching more than they really are. You think that's true?"

"I don't know, Monseñor, enough to say."

"Look at it this way. There's a difference between most yanquis I've met and most Argentines. Most yanquis seem to me like big overconfident cowboys who walk into the dining room and start to move the furniture around. If there's a chair missing at the table, he's the first to go find one, or if he admires the dinnerware, he picks up the plates and holds them up to read the labels. An Argentine will wait for his host to move the chairs. He'll stand back and smoke his nice little cigarette and admire the dishes without picking them up, like that's too much effort for him. All the Argentine really cares about is that when the plate is finally served, there will be more than enough beef on it for him. Give him that much and he's happy." El Rector reached for the bottle of *aguardiente* as he spoke, his large meaty hands jabbing out with a boxer's quickness. "But don't think I don't like yanquis. The English are much worse. The English come into the dining room with a drawn saber and an open steamer trunk and are a bunch of pirates. Same thing with the Germans, only they do it with surgical instruments," he said, laughing at his own joke. El Rector was redfaced, smiling in a friendly way as he filled my glass again. I was nodding at him as he spoke, unsure of what to say. "To the *bachillerato* degree!" El Rector said and raised his glass in a toast. My eyes filled with tears from the fumes of the vaporous rumlike liquor as we downed our glasses together. "Tell me, my son, have you ever been to Disneyland? I've always wanted to visit Disneyland."

Disneyland was something many kids at school had asked me about, so I knew what to say, just how to make the phrases in practiced Spanish, describing the Matterhorn ride, the "It's a Small World After All" exhibit, giant Pluto and Mickey Mouse leading the parades, the audioanimatronic statue of Abraham Lincoln giving the Gettysburg Address, things like that, and for a moment, El Rector listened to my descriptions and imagined the merry scene at Anaheim. The swinging door to the kitchen suddenly opened with a bang against its stopper. Cornelia moved in, gracefully holding a tureen of soup high above her waist. I was thinking she must have come in some back way; I had been waiting all this time to watch her come back in from down the hall. Her hands were covered by potholder mittens, her expression involved with her work, vapors rising into her face from the soup, her forehead damp with perspiration.

"Cornelia!" El Rector said with some urgency. "How can we have our soup without the wine opened first?"

"I'll open the bottle, Monseñor," she said as she set down the heavy silver boat.

"Where's El Negrito? He's supposed to serve as steward for us tonight."

"Maybe one of the other Fathers detained him," she said. She spun quickly back through the swinging door into the kitchen and came out again with a bottle of red wine. She set the bottle on the table as if she wasn't used to handling one, picking with her nails at the foil on the neck. She glanced over quickly at me just as I was about to reach over and hand her the corkscrew and I stopped. Mamá had

warned me about things like this, that it might show up the
servants to help them.

"That's not the right wine," El Rector said. "Here. Let
me open it," he said impatiently, moving in beside her
tightly enough that she took a careful step backward as if
she didn't want to get too close to his skirts. El Rector
opened the bottle with a dry squeaking of the cork and said,
"This isn't the right one. This is just a decent wine from
Mendoza. Better bottles are on the way."

"This is fine, Monseñor," I said. "Please don't trouble
for me."

"I'm troubling for me," he said. "A man my age starts
to think about his wines."

El Rector sat down at the head of the small table and
poured himself a glass of wine, then he reached out across
the table for my glass. I was still standing back out of the
way, making room for Cornelia as she ladled a thick soup
into two china bowls that bore the Colegio San Andrés coat
of arms. I watched over her shoulder, catching a smell about
both her and the soup that was like a spice rack with all the
bottles open. Under her blue pinstriped maid's uniform, I
could see the unbroken brown plain of her muscular back,
her breasts like two small and perfectly shaped mangoes
lifting and falling with each movement of her arms. I was
overwhelmed. If I had ever believed in angels, I could say
I had seen one, angels being unique entities, no two of them
looking alike or with the same abilities, and here was proof
at least of one, darkly pretty, too shy to acknowledge the
way I was watching her as she stepped gracefully back from
the table and turned to go out of the room. El Rector motioned impatiently for me to sit down in a chair that faced
away from the kitchen. "Let's get down to our real business
tonight," El Rector said, "the grand and marvelous business of eating."

*Locro* is one of those traditional peasant dishes that was
once a luxury meal for the poorer classes, a luxury relative
to the deprivations they must have suffered. This *locro* had
taken Cornelia three days to prepare, as El Rector informed
me. It was a hot *locro*, a regional kind known mainly in
the North. "For this *locro*, you start with a pig's head,"

said El Rector. "You boil the head for at least a day with
all kinds of spices. It all boils down until there's nothing
left but the clean bone." El Rector described the rest of the
soup, the other kinds of meat, beef in this case, then
chopped corn on the cob, okra, tomatoes, all kinds of things.
"Every cook I've ever had makes it differently," El Rector
said while spooning through his soup, a kind of reddish-
brown gruel with bits of meat and vegetables in it. I picked
up my spoon. As the *locro* hit my tongue it had a quick
sweet taste, then suddenly it was as if a blowtorch lit up in
my mouth and throat and all the way down.

"The *locro* of the North is my favorite," El Rector said.
"Most people think it's too spicy."

I made signs for water, anything, and found my glass of
wine. I held the glass out as El Rector poured, then again,
and once more. I sagged back in my chair, sweat running
out of every pore in my body, and only then could I take a
breath.

"This is a real northern *locro*," El Rector said. "I think
my new cook is going to work out, don't you agree? Of
course, the *locros* from Buenos Aires province are much
milder. Hot food, hot climate. Have you noticed that? The
closer to the equator one gets, the hotter the food?"

El Rector sat back with an amused expression and
watched me trying to eat. I must have turned by then to a
color something in between red and indigo. I finally took
off my jacket, perching it sloppily on the back of my chair.
El Rector was chewing as he spoke, his white clerical collar
bobbing up and down. "Always with the soup course," he
said, "I begin the same way. What are your plans? Then
with salad, we discuss your means of achieving them. With
the main course, your spiritual goals. Then with dessert, it's
what we can do for each other to achieve these goals, your
earthly and spiritual ones, for the school, your family and
you." El Rector reached out across the table and rang a
little brass bell. "What are your plans, my son?"

"I don't know, Monseñor. If I can get into a university,"
I started, but Cornelia came through the doors from the
kitchen, her body swinging a little to one side, and I stopped
talking. She leaned over the table to start clearing plates

and looked at me quickly as if to make sure I had finished with her *locro*. I wished I'd cleaned my bowl and said softly, "This was very good soup," but that only called an embarrassing attention to what I'd left in it.

"I have a few things to show you," El Rector said. He rose from the table and moved heavily over to a leather-covered chest that stood in one corner of his living area. El Rector removed a few books from the chest and opened the lid. "These are *indio* crafts from our charities in the North," he said. Something dark and snakelike trailed out of his hands and made a clicking noise as he held it up. "Rosaries, crucifixes, sacred hearts, little statuary of the Virgin, those are the religious articles. Then these lovely net bags made from homespun hemp, and these beautiful vases and pottery. Our *indios* are really good at the craft of pottery, don't you think?" El Rector set some of these items on the table. The statue of the Virgin was an oblong shape with a gentle oval of a face pressed into the dark clay, her simple pious expression made with a few childish cuneiform lines, the imprint of the fingers that had shaped the rough ellipse of her halo still visible. A mammoth rosary with beads as big as golfballs and a cross the size of a shoe dangled over the table's edge. "The San Andrés order has been trying to encourage cottage industries in the North. Argentina doesn't have many *indios*, I mean compared to backward countries like Bolivia or Peru. We're more like a European nation, but what few *indios* we have are generally poor and reluctant to settle on any worthwhile farmland. They work in the sugar, or maybe they travel to the cities and try to find jobs. Then a lot of them go back again and don't know what to do. The only schoolbook translated into most of their languages is the Gospel according to St. Luke, which the Jesuits left behind. So our new strategy is to try to encourage these crafts. These things come from the *Tobas* tribe, in the province of El Chaco. What do you think?"

"They're very nice," I said. "Marvelous."

"Yanqui business know-how is a wonderful thing, don't you agree?"

"That's clear," I said.

"But you yanquis don't know anything about us, do you?

We can name off dozens of your state capitals while most
of you yanquis don't even know the capital of Argentina."

"Yes, that's true, Monseñor," I said.

"So if nothing else, whatever your plans, you can make
it your business to tell people about our Argentina, is that
clear?"

"Of course I will," I said. "I'm grateful to Argentina."

"Take these few trinkets with you as souvenirs of our San
Andrés missions in the North. Show them around." He sat
back at the table and looked at me pensively. "We can take
direct mail orders and even offer you commissions," he
said.

"Thank you, Monseñor," I said.

"Buenos Aires isn't the whole country," he said.

The dinner continued. Cornelia served salad in a whirl
of my attentions. This time, I bent toward my plate with a
relish all too obvious, hoping she would notice, but she kept
looking away, at the dishes or at her serving, and El Rector
interrupted her by saying, "Where in blazes is El Negrito?"

Cornelia understood this to mean that she should go into
the kitchen and look for another bottle of wine, which she
had trouble opening. El Rector was peeved as he watched
her, unsettled as if at some sudden turn in his thoughts.
"Protestants," he said. "North America has too many of
them. And too many other heretical sects—Seventh Day Ad-
ventists, Jehovah's Witnesses and those Mormons. Those
Mormons are all over the place, attacking the beliefs of our
*indios* in the North in our Catholic Church. Now they're
even trying to get approval to construct a huge temple in
Buenos Aires. Can't they see we have enough trouble without the Mormons sticking their oars in? When you get back
to North America, you be sure and tell people that the Mormons are making clowns of themselves down here," El
Rector said, his eyes taking on a fierce and wild cast as if
little lamps had been turned on inside them.

"Yes, Monseñor," I said.

"Tell your government not to send so many Jews on their
embassy staffs, either. It's not so bad now with your *presidente* Nixon in office. But have you ever noticed that your

Democratic party sends more Jews down to us than your Republicans? Have you noticed that?''

"I've never been to my embassy, Monseñor," I said.

"We don't like Jews here. And we've got more of them in this country for our population than any other country in the world except Israel and yours, so we've had a good chance to take a look at them. They're not patriots, they're not gentlemen, they're a bunch of little *moishes* out for themselves. But I'm not telling you anything new. You've seen plenty of them in your own country. Everywhere they're the same. *And therefore the Jews persecuted Jesus and sought to slay him.* Do you know how many of them were gathered at the walls when our Señor was condemned?''

"What was that?" I asked.

"How many Jews? How many Jews?"

"I don't know, Monseñor. I guess I've never thought about it."

"Hasn't Father Naboa covered this in religion class? It was always a question on the exam when I taught the course. Just for you, I'll repeat the answer. The church has it on best historical authority that there were no less than two thousand five hundred Jews in the crowd who chose to save the life of a thief and a murderer over the life of our Señor. Think about that every time you meet a Jew, as we all do in this world, God knows. We don't like Jews here. We only tolerate them as long as we have to. It's like this,'' El Rector said, and he interlocked his fingers in front of me like the church and steeple game that children play. "The people of a nation should fit homogeneously together with a common passion and common beliefs. Like this. Like two hands in an attitude of prayer. But look at my thumbs. My thumbs don't fit with the others. They're like the Jews, and the Protestants, or worse, those new Catholic heretical sects, the village priests in Brazil who are teaching a heretical mixture of Marxism and religion, and believe me, we've seen a few of them in Argentina lately, too. But the Jews are the real problem. Yet because of all their dirty money, and their influence, and their support from abroad, it's almost impossible to pick anything up without them. Look how much my hands need my thumbs," he said, and El

Rector reached out suddenly, thumblessly trying to pick up his wineglass in demonstration. "So we remain tolerant. Our government is cooperative. Our generals believe in human rights, even for the Jews, and our society is in danger of going down the sewer. One of these days, Our Catholic Lions are going to send the Jews packing back to their beloved Israel and the rest of them straight to hell where they belong," El Rector said. He caught his breath, letting his hands drop back to the table. "And what else can we do? What can we do about the Jews?"

"Please forgive me, Monseñor, but I don't think I can stay any longer. There's a reunion of the Benevento family, relatives from out of town. Papá Benevento wants me to get home early enough to meet them."

"Have you ever seen that singer in your country? What's his name? Esammy Edavis Junior?"

"Is there a clock around here, Monseñor?"

"He's a Negro and a Jew," El Rector said. "Can you imagine such a thing? It shows you how decadent popular tastes have become."

"But he's a great singer! A really great singer! There's a song called 'Mister Bojangles' that he made famous all over the world!" I started to say more then caught myself. El Rector wasn't listening in any case. My mouth was dry. The lettuce had turned to wood shavings on my plate and I was thinking there must be some way out of this situation when El Rector reached out his left hand suddenly, the large fingers open as if he were ready to pick up and crush a tiny crowd of Jews, Protestants and Marxist priests gathered on his table. His wineglass toppled, a dark red stain running over the tablecloth and cascading over the edge onto his skirts.

"Cornelia!" the Monseñor shouted. He jumped up like a shot and slapped at his gray skirts with a napkin. Cornelia rushed in with an air of emergency. I stood up and tipped El Rector's glass back upright. I watched Cornelia trying to use a dish towel on El Rector's lap as he jumped back in a rage and shouted, "Where's El Negrito! I want him now! Now! You go right now and get him!"

Cornelia stepped back, unsure of what to do. She looked

in my direction as if she expected I could help her, and I wanted to help, but what was possible under these circumstances?

The door to El Rector's apartment opened slowly, with a groan of its hinges. "Good evening, Monseñor!" El Negrito called out merrily, and I heard him steadily moving down the hallway, his heavy shoe dragging, and the sound of bottles clinking together in his arms. As he entered the living area, he puffed too heavily, a show of being out of breath. "I've just come all the way from the cellar with something special that took some time hunting around. And before that, Father Artaud needed to talk to me about a matter of some wedding flowers this coming Thursday."

El Negrito set the wine bottles down with a flourish. El Rector was attending to patting himself dry with a napkin embroidered with flowers the color of Lent. El Negrito finally steered him back to his chair and sat him down. "There we are, Monseñor, the main course is on its way. Everything's under control," El Negrito said and looked at me from behind El Rector with an overplayed smile of gracious servitude. A fog was rising in my brain from the wine and spices, and I was feeling a vague, passing nausea I was trying to get a grip on before the fried squid. "One of the most prestigious schools in Buenos Aires. One of the most elegant chapels this side of the ocean, for its size, anyway. And look what the poor Monseñor is lumbered with," El Negrito said. El Rector seemed to be staring off somewhere thousands of kilometers from the table. "The Monseñor would no doubt have gotten rid of me long before now except that I've always provided him such impeccable laundry service."

A bottle of wine opened with a cheerful pop, a nice clear fruity white wine from San Luis province. El Negrito found fresh glasses and poured with the air of a professional waiter. "He's been with the order for thirty years," El Rector said. "The brothers found him naked in the jungle and dressed him in street clothes."

"The Monseñor is making up stories, it's clear," El Negrito said.

"Nowhere else on the continent could servants get away

with what they get away with in Argentina. It's the under-population problem. Only twenty-five million and all this good land to feed them. Nobody wants to work as a result. We have a discipline problem in this country. That's why we need the military. Nobody wants to work, isn't that clear, Negrito?"

"Of course, Monseñor," said El Negrito. "Everybody's lazy in this country, especially the servants. I know servants who haven't lifted a finger in years."

Cornelia pushed the door open with her knees, barely able to hold up her heavy tray, her elbows bent out and straining because of its size. There were piles of crisply fried squid like exotic mounds of onion rings heaped on the tray, *calamaretes* à la romana on a bed of lemon wedges, and there were side dishes of pasta in a white sauce to go with them. I watched Cornelia building a mound of *cala-maretes* on my plate.

"Please allow me to congratulate you on your cook, Monseñor," I said but El Rector simply dismissed this comment with a nod at Cornelia that she had served him enough. She cleared out of the room fast into the kitchen, followed by El Negrito.

"Now tell me, my son," said El Rector, "what are your spiritual goals?"

"My spiritual goals aren't clear yet, Monseñor," I said.

"Do you go to mass?"

"On Fridays with the school, and on Sundays with my Benevento brothers."

"Not with the Beneventos?"

"What was that?"

"Papá and Mamá Benevento?"

"No, Monseñor, we never go with them."

"Are you living well with the Beneventos?"

"Of course, Monseñor."

"Did Papá Benevento ever tell you about his activities with the Conservative party?"

"What did you say?"

"He was a big wheel once, pamphlets and speeches, I don't know what else. During the time of the Justo regime, he was put in jail for stuffing ballot boxes."

"I don't believe that, Monseñor, pardon me for saying it.
I've never met a more honorable man in my life."

"All the big bankers and lawyers are Conservatives, or
old Radicals, which is even worse. Yak, yak, yak in Congress when we have one, nothing more, just talk, talk, talk
and nothing ever gets done. The currency goes straight to
hell because they keep printing money to keep the unions
off their backs. The trains don't run on time. Under the
military government, the trains run, the unions can't strike,
and there's a chance for order and discipline in this country.
The military keeps the Peronists from coming to power. As
long as we have our generals, Perón can't come back. It's
going to be hell in this country if the Peronists take power
again. Whenever they control things, it's a case of robbing
from the rich to give to the corrupt union bosses. And you
can see how it already is, bombs going off everywhere in
the city because of the Peronist left wing that's no better
than communists. It's the duty of any patriotic Argentine to
fight the forces of Peronism in this nation, just as your country is fighting the communists in Vietnam."

"I have a brother in Vietnam," I said.

"Yes? In Vietnam? You must be proud of him."

"That's clear," I said.

"And how do you feel about the war in Vietnam?"

"My brother went off to Vietnam the same week I went
to Argentina," I said after a moment, as if this somehow
explained something. "I wish he were here with me."

"We'll get El Negrito to let you into the chapel later to
light a candle," El Rector said. "I hope you know our
military regime is very strongly in support of your war in
Vietnam."

"Clearly," I said. For a moment, there was little else but
the sound of our eating, the first of the flavorful *calamaretes*
going down easily with the wine. Eating seemed the best
way to avoid conversation, and the food at least was worth
staying for, so I had seconds and thirds, and full glasses of
wine with each helping. El Rector seemed as if he were
drawing the dinner to an early close, eating quickly and
with concentration now that he had assessed his student's
personal and spiritual goals. As for the means of attaining

these goals, El Rector talked a little about "including Argentina in your plans" again, things like telling people back home about its leather goods and crafts, the best beef in the world, Argentina's former status as the fifth potential power in the world that it hoped again to regain. "And you can help our Colegio San Andrés by thinking of us when you're a success in life. Our charities count very heavily on alumni contributions," El Rector said.

El Negrito came in from the kitchen to clear the plates and filled a silence with his congenial chatter. "Squid tasty, Monseñor? I'll just take this out of your way now. Should I serve the coffee or are you going directly on to bed?"

"No coffee for me," said El Rector. "And no dessert. I don't believe in eating between meals," he said and laughed at his own joke. "This has been one of the extremely pleasant bachelor dinners," he said then and rose out of his chair, extending his hand out limply across the table. "Please don't rush yourself on my behalf. I know you have another engagement at the Beneventos', but I hope you'll still enjoy a nice dessert. Let's just say goodnight here then so I can go off to my little bed. I'm up with the birds," he said, and I took El Rector's hand awkwardly in both of mine, a silly gesture, as if the Monseñor were a woman, and I ended up kissing the hand instead of the ring. "You'll find a letter recommending your character to future employers in the office on Monday. Ask El Negrito to remind me in case I've forgotten," he said.

After El Negrito saw the Monseñor out down a hallway past the kitchen, his bedroom somewhere in that direction, I sat back at ease for the first time that night. I could let myself weave around in my chair, for example. I could loosen my tie and take a long cool drink from a wineglass even though I was already drunk enough that anything alcoholic seemed to make my teeth shiver. My plan was that I would leave after that, but a strong smell of coffee was coming from the kitchen. El Negrito came back in brightly, his teeth bared in a grin, a bounce in his cockeyed movements. "See what I told you, Yanqui?" he said. "El Rector never makes it to dessert."

"Don't bust my balls, Negrito," I said.

"We've got a nice little flan for you now. No bachelor can leave the table without his nice little dessert."

Cornelia came in from the kitchen and served the flan, a perfect upside down ring of custard with burned sugar giving it a crust and brought in on a cut glass platter. She seemed more at ease, too, as she set the platter down. She smiled at me for the first time that night, a relief filling the room since the Monseñor had left it intense enough that there was almost a party atmosphere. El Negrito sat down to join me in dessert, and Cornelia brought cups out and served us strong Brazilian coffee. I watched all of this in a daze, feeling as if the wine had somehow packed my skull with hot steaming washcloths, and my attention followed the olive curves of her arms through the steam, the taut lines of her high throat under her falling curtain of dark hair. At some point while watching her, I had to shift in my seat, lower my hands under the edge of the tablecloth and loosen my pants. How old was she? Nineteen or twenty maybe?

"You like her?" El Negrito asked. "You just tell me if you like her," he said.

I liked her, no question. I watched El Negrito's small fat hands as they reached out for the pretty glass flan platter to serve himself some more. With a mischievous glance across the table, he passed the platter to me, and I set it down somewhere past my right elbow. What was El Negrito thinking about? With this girl? This girl was a saint, no question, nobody had ever touched her. I felt suddenly queasy then, swallowed, and started to get up from the table, fumbling into the sleeves of my jacket.

"We get her to have a whiskey with us and you won't regret it," El Negrito said. "Why give a woman flowers when she drinks rum?"

"*Che*, what kind of a ball busting is this?"

I heard water running in the kitchen, and the sounds of plates and silverware being washed. She was humming. I could just make out the sound—a high sad melody like the music of wooden flutes. Did the song have words? What would it sound like if she were singing them?

"I tell you what to do, Yanqui. When Cornelia sees you to the door, you go ask her to the movies. There's a great little Western playing on Lavalle Street, and she likes Westerns. Eclint Eastwood in *Puñado de Dólares*. She hasn't seen it yet and is afraid to go out alone in the big city."

"You're not bullshitting me?"

"I'm serious, *flaco*. You haven't had much luck with Argentine girls, everybody says so. They don't like you yanquis very much because the social position is so unsure. You always get stuck with the ugly girls at the dances, isn't that right? It's even the same for the lower-class girls Hernández-Marelli and your brother Martín try to dig up for you. Always the fat ones or the ones with braces, isn't that so?"

"I'm working on a girlfriend," I said.

"But *che*, nothing like this one. No girl you know has anything like what this girl's got, isn't that right?"

El Negrito was right. Even to dance once with this girl might make the whole indignity of this dinner with the Monseñor seem worthwhile. Then I realized my thinking was too slow, it was crazy, a young man of my class didn't cross lines like that, El Negrito was just putting me on again, another joke at El Yanqui's expense. "You're a lousy bullshitter, Negro, and a total *boludo*," I said. "I'm going home."

As I stood up to leave, the lace edge of El Rector's tablecloth caught a button on one of my jacket sleeves and the cut glass flan platter went flying and landed with a crash. El Negrito jumped like a wildman around the room, slapping the table, the walls, taking his breaths in quick little shrieking laughs like an attack of hiccups. There was burned sugar syrup splashed over some books on the lower rows of El Rector's bookcase. Some of the yellow custard sat like a mashed cowpie on the Monseñor's imitation Persian rug. Glass was scattered everywhere, on the rug and hardwood floor. Cornelia rushed in, her eyes wide, her hands still wrapped in a dishtowel, and said, "What's happened in here?" as if she'd just heard a gunshot.

"He . . . knock over . . . flan plate . . ." El Negrito was still gulping in drafts of air from his laughing.

She looked at the thick sticky trails of brown syrup running slowly off the bookcase onto the floor; it was clear from her expression that she knew what it would mean to clean it up. Something settled on her features, a determination as if looking at an overgrown field to be slashed, burned and plowed. Shards of glass sparkled on the floor under the table and all over the carpet, scattered around like a broken string of beads.

"I'll go get the bucket and the sponge," she said.

"No, don't bother," said El Negrito. "It's your bedtime. I'll clean it up myself later," he said. Little pieces of glass were stuck to his shoes, and he brushed them off as if they were so much beach sand. I couldn't believe the mess. I couldn't believe anyone could have been such an asshole as to make it. I was speechless looking at it, then El Negrito limped over and whispered in my ear, "I'll get her all set up for you. Give me a minute alone with her in the kitchen."

"Go back to your whore mother," I said. "You've got me so fouled up because of this I could kill you."

"Me? Was I the *boludo* who did this?"

"Quit hassling me, *che!*" I shouted.

"All right then," El Negrito said loud enough for Cornelia to hear him. "I'll leave you two lovers alone. Remember what I told you about the movies," he said with a grin that made me want to punch his mouth. Then he wheeled around on his good leg and started for the door just like that, not turning around to say a word to Cornelia or anything, not even saying goodnight. He worked his way quickly down the hallway and went out, leaving the door standing open. A sudden inrush of air filled the room with its sharpness, rustling the yellowed tatters of book covers, the faded parish bazaar posters on the walls, stirring a mess of the Monseñor's papers on a little writing desk.

"I'll go get the bucket and the sponge," Cornelia said as if to herself, as if there were no one else in the room.

"No, señorita," I said. "It's my fault. I did it."

She looked at me without comprehension.

"The one who did it should clean it up," I said.

"Ah! No, señor! That wouldn't be proper!" she said. Then she turned at once and went into the kitchen.

"Where I come from I should clean it up!" I shouted after her. I heard her banging around in the cupboards, the sound of water running into a pail, and I followed her as far as the swinging door to the kitchen and pushed it open. She was leaning over the pail, wringing out the sponge with strong movements of her delicate arms. "I'd feel a lot better about this if you'd let me help you," I said.

"I'll get the broom for you, sir, and you can sweep." Then she smiled at me in a friendly way and said, "But don't you tell anyone, sir, or I might get into trouble."

I pushed the broom over El Rector's polished floor, swept up around the bookcase where the syrup had struck in a gooey brown splatter shaped like a butterfly. Sugary fragments of glass were sticking to the broom, so I ended up feeling over drunkenly with the palms of my hands El Rector's dusty carpet and in under the dining table, gathering bits of glass on my sticky palms and then carefully picking them off into the dustpan. Cornelia was behind me, on her knees and scrubbing the floor where most of the syrup had splashed, then she moved her sponge up to the wall to try to blot out a stain. I watched the lithe movements of her arms and body as she scrubbed intently on a small square of wall. She seemed aware of me, I thought I could feel that, but in a frightened way, as if marking my exact position with a kind of radar and ready to jump if I made the wrong moves. Nothing was said, though I was trying to find the courage to ask her where she was from, how long she had been in Buenos Aires, to compare notes with her like a pair of outsiders.

I dusted away at the bookcase after I had cleaned up the glass, whipping my rag past all the dusty books, mostly sets of great books editions of various kinds, the full Voltaire, for example, the history of philosophy according to somebody named Patricio Hopkins, the complete plays of Calderón, Lope de Vega taking up half the shelf; I caught spots of burned sugar here and there and tried unsuccessfully to wipe them away. Cornelia's fearfulness seemed steadily more relaxed with the sharing of our work. I wanted to tell her how pretty she was. I wanted to ask her out. I wanted to reach over right there and just kiss her without words. I was about to do this but instead I leaned into the bookcase, feeling sick and breaking into a sweat.

There are moments in a man's life when he makes such a mess of himself that he agrees in spirit to everything he despises. Nothing can help him, he's so dissolute inside that he doesn't know anymore what to believe. Sometimes, the reaction to this isn't to doubt himself; he hangs onto himself. He fights for his own worst side to the exclusion of all others; he's rebellious and does terrible things. He's too cool to believe in God or goodness anymore and suddenly, nothing he does makes any difference. This girl wouldn't have known anything about that. She was from a world so different that she wouldn't want anything to do with me. Anyway, I'd just get her into trouble and she'd end up shipped back to her village or let out into the streets to wait for another job, wasn't that the case?

I pushed off from the bookcase dizzily and did my best to light a cigarette like Alain Delon in *Adiós Mi Amigo*, which was just then drawing crowds in its rerun on Lavalle Street—that cigarette the cool actor lights just after he discovers he's locked himself in the very vault he's trying to rob. At the same time, I felt the power in my closeness to the girl, especially in these circumstances—how often did I ever have a chance like this? I leaned casually with one arm against the bookcase, crushed out my smoke, then in a single movement reached out my other arm and placed it over her shoulders. She didn't see this coming. She stopped scrubbing, all her muscles tense at once. Her sponge stuck there on the wall, a stream of foaming ammonia water running down her wrist. "The Monseñor," she said in a quiet, frightened voice.

I was already lifting her up from her kneeling position on the floor, gripping her arms and turning her to face me. She caught her breath as if she couldn't escape—she must have known this would happen from the moment she had entered the room with me, as if she had already let me compromise her. Even if she shouted for El Rector or El Negrito or the police, the story would have the same ending for her, she would be sent away somewhere, maybe to another parish, maybe back to her village, maybe just kicked out into the streets. And I thought she wanted me to kiss her as I put both arms around her and drew her in, and as

I walked my fingers across the warm ridges of her ribs until
they reached the secret they wanted, my fingers sliding in
under the buttons of her dress. She started to struggle in my
arms, moving side to side, but I was strong, and there was
nothing she could do but say, "No!" but not loudly enough
for anyone else to hear, "No! *Por favor!*"

I pushed her against the wall and pressed against her, a
lump as hard as a baseball moving against her stomach as
I pulled her face toward mine and leaned down for a kiss.
Her lips went slack, lifeless. Her teeth clenched, her body
gone rigid and pulling away. My hand was feeling under
her dress, my lips pressed against her lips, but they felt like
the back of a cold hand, with only the strong sweet taste of
her mouth and the heavy odors of her hours of working to
let me know she was still alive; it didn't even feel as if she
were still breathing. My hand kept moving, exploring, and
she began to struggle in my arms. She let out a terrible
weak cry of mortification as my hand passed, just once,
over the dark moist wool between her legs. I let her go then
and stepped back, wilted back, my whole being repulsed
suddenly at what I knew I was doing and what a mistake I
had made, a terrible, terrible mistake. The room was filled
with the smell of ammonia from the pail. Her fists were
clenched and one of them was squeezing the life out of her
sponge, her only movement to kneel back down by the
bucket and drop it in. She stood for a moment pressed
against the wall as if she were nailed there, her hair falling
in a mess across her face, the front of her dress ripped open.

"*Perdóneme, por favor, perdóneme usted,*" I pleaded
with her. "Forgive me, please forgive me, please. I've made
a terrible mistake," I said but it was too late, nothing could
save this situation. One of her hands was pressed flat against
the wall. She was inching along the wall, ready to break
and run for the kitchen. Stupidly, I reached out for her hand,
wanting to say *please don't think badly of me*. The hand
flew off the wall like a startled bird and she took a small
leap in the direction of the kitchen.

There was a quick *shush shush shush* sound of El Rector's
slippers in the hallway before he stepped into the room.
There was a sleepy befuddled look to him that made me

think he hadn't seen what had happened. But just as he entered, he saw Cornelia quickly bunch together her dress and push through the swinging door, and me there with a broom and dustpan spilled at my feet. He seemed to wake up at that instant with a shock. He turned from the door to me and saw his books and the mess on his floor, taking this in as if I'd committed sacrilege. "What have you done here?" he asked me in a voice that made me feel as if every object in the room had just tripled in weight. "Cornelia!" he called out. "Come in here, please," he said and made the *por favor* into a command.

"Monseñor, let me explain, please," I said. "The señorita comported herself in every way like a modest young lady."

Cornelia came through the door, slowly, slipping through it as if she might somehow remain unseen the quieter she came in, one hand clamping together her dress with the buttons torn off. She was humiliated, and she was about to cry. El Rector made her stand that way a moment before he said, "I'm disappointed in you, my daughter." Then he added in a tone of voice like a executioner's, "You may go to your room now, Cornelia."

"She didn't do anything, Monseñor," I said. "It was my indiscretion and totally my fault, a terrible, terrible error I've made here tonight," I said, but it was clear from Cornelia's expression that I was making things worse. Without looking back or once raising her eyes, she slowly moved in a small circle around El Rector and disappeared down the main hall and out the open door, then she was running along the archway to her room.

"You're a guest in my house," El Rector said, "and a guest at this school. What you've done here doesn't sit well," he said, using the phrase *no queda bien*, a formal admonishment for indiscretions. "You should be ashamed of yourself," he said.

"Yes, Monseñor, I am," I said. "But the señorita did nothing wrong, you've got to understand that. It was me. I broke everything, and everything's my fault. I'm the one responsible here," I said, but it seemed the Monseñor was no longer listening. He pulled a book out from the bottom row of his shelf and turned through a few pages that were already sticking together. "I'll be responsible for any damages here," I said.

"In all my years inviting you bachelors to dinner, nothing like this has ever happened," El Rector said, the book frozen there in space, raised up like he was ready to hurl it at me. "You may go home now. Tell the Beneventos that you are not to present yourself back here until I have decided that you can continue as a guest of our school."

Something waited to be said, and I was the one who had to say it. The Monseñor stood squared off at me as if ready for anything but I was a coward, the breath had gone out of my lungs and had filled my throat with poison gas, so I said nothing. My Colegio San Andrés jacket was slung over a chair where I had taken it off to begin sweeping and I found it, then had trouble with the short step up into the hallway and out, knocking into a wall near the door that was still opened onto the unlit archway. I blindly felt my way in the night to the stairs. Then crossing the courtyard, something broke inside and I was suddenly like a wildman, flailing my arms all over the place to rip off my jacket, and I was shouting in the courtyard, "This school is a piece of shit! You hear me, you *boludo*! A piece of shit! *Chúpame el culo, boludo!*" I screamed. "You can suck my ass, you asshole!"

By that time I was tearing up my jacket, holding one part of it down with my foot and pulling back on a sleeve until it ripped in two, then doing a crazy kind of dance tearing up the pieces. Somewhere in the night above the courtyard, the door to the Monseñor's apartment slammed hard, a loud echoing boom.

It was a cold damp night, the courtyard tiles looking wet in places as if it had just rained, an autumn mist coming in off the river under the gray clouds of a starless sky. I found my way out into the street and I was lost and reeling around. Then on impulse, I began tearing at my neck and arms, ripping off my Colegio San Andrés sweater, and I found myself on my knees in the gutter at the corner trying to stuff the sweater down the sewer grate, one sleeve twisting up around a steel bar of the grating. I bloodied my knuckles untangling it until it dropped free and I heard the sweater

fall like a stone into the sewer. Nausea hit me like a plunge
into a boiling tank of vinegar, so I stayed right there a long
time, on my hands and knees in the filthy trickling stream
in the gutter at a corner of what I recognized as Junín Street
by the new layer of asphalt. I was sick, drowning and dying
in it, knocked over by the waves, and I kept hearing a voice
in my head talking in English, it was strange to hear the
words, then I realized it was my voice talking out loud to
me in my own language, saying how sorry I was, it was all
my fault and I was sorry, sorry, sorry, all I had fucking
wanted to do was to ask her out to the movies.

Getting up and trying to walk was a problem. From there
on, I staggered up to Arenales Street and into the garage
where my family kept its cars and I gave all the loose money
in my pockets to Ramón, the nice night attendant, to take
the keys off their peg and bring out the family's Peugeot
504 and help me in behind the wheel. Driving was unreal,
as though I wasn't attached physically to the machine, my
mind just taking in the fast pictures through Buenos Aires.
The car whipped out onto the avenue Santa Fe with its elegant store windows, and I opened up the little French engine to everything it had, dodging traffic through a red light
at the corner of the avenue Callao. The windows were down
and I was leaning my head and shoulders out of the car
going eighty or ninety klicks per hour across the intersection past a button with a machine gun around his neck. The
wind was hitting me in the face as I raced off the avenue
and through the deserted streets of Barrio La Recoleta, past
the doormen and the glittering lights of the Hotel Alvear
that was like a palace, then on down the hill and along a
broad, wide dimly lit boulevard that ran through the parks
of Palermo. I was hitting a hundred and sixty klicks in the
dark empty lane bordered by overhanging trees. There was
a suicidal turn in a mad Grand Prix in which I had to pass
all the other cars on the street, then for the hell of it going
that fast I hit the brakes and let the car swing around in a
crazy long slide and slam up over the curb onto the sidewalk.

Sometime later, I crawled out onto the grass near the
statue of Bartolomé Mitre that was up on a little hill over-

looking a large rectangular fountain, the park and the broad boulevard. Further down, the College of Law building stood like a black Parthenon against the slate gray of the clouds. I climbed up over a French romantic statue of a knight defending liberty and onto the base of the huge horse and general overhead. I wasn't able to stand up between the horse's legs, so I sat down there and listened to the long arc of my pissing like a music splattering away on the white marble backs of a crowd of statues. Then I jumped off the pedestal and hit the grass hard and lay there sprawled in the shadow of General Bartolomé Mitre, the famous humanist general and president of the nation, a gentleman lawmaker who had taken up arms to fight for Buenos Aires against another general named Urquiza after the civil war between the Blues and the Reds that had finally kicked the butchering dictator Don Juan Manuel de Rosas out of the country more than a hundred years before. It was *presidente* Mitre who worked to restore the Argentine confederation after the chaos of the war and the butchery of Urquiza. When Urquiza's Blues had won the battle of Caseros, which decided the fate of the city, five thousand ragtag soldiers of the Red army were hung by their necks from the trees in Palermo.

From up there on the hill, General Mitre looked out with a sternly wise expression on a park full of trees. Behind him stood the tall, elegant apartment buildings of La Recoleta and Palermo, some of the windows still lit up, the general looking big enough to reach out his arm and touch the glittering ranks of buildings on the skyline. And then it was like I was up there with him, as if I could fly over the city like the general. We were sailing over the barrios and looking down on all the rooftops, and we could reach out and peel the roofs off all the houses like so many crusts off pies. Over there, off across the walled cemetery of La Recoleta where only the rich and the powerful were buried, the head priest of historic Recoleta church finished his midnight leak and flopped back into bed, a Monseñor so thick-jowled and heavy with beefsteaks that he looked like a dolphin breaking water. Down the way, across the tracks, in the distance towards the outskirts and the poorer districts, a maid named Fáfula was giving birth to a child with her husband, Toribio,

proudly attending her, while her employer in the Barrio
Norte who was the real father was climbing into bed with
somebody new. In the same big house a teenaged girl who
was a priceless beauty raised to be a beauty of great price
was putting on her Pond's and wrapping her hair in rollers,
listening to *los Beatles* singing "Ob-La-Di, Ob-La-Da,"
and she fell asleep that way, her hairbrush in her hands, an
expression on her face as if dreaming of all the romance
that was coming. Off in the city's center near the Plaza de
Mayo, the recently made full colonel Leopoldo Dipaoli in
civilian clothes was looking for his table in a smoky fish-
house called *Il Pulpo*, where he was charged by his commanding generals with the duty of a secret meeting with the
leaders of the CGT, the largest Peronist labor union, to
negotiate a new deal on base wages to avoid a general strike.
The CGT was demanding an equivalent in however many
thousands of Argentine pesos to eighty-five U.S. dollars a
month; Colonel Dipaoli was authorized to offer them each
a bribe of twenty thousand dollars apiece and tickets to
Miami if they settled for seventy-three. Nearby, somewhere
down on the boulevard called El Bajo, not far from the new
color television studio the generals had provided him, Hec-
tor Pérez, a kind of combination Walter Cronkite and Johnny
Carson of Argentina except that he was a notorious liar,
was waking up in his bed with a shout from a nightmare in
which he dreamed he was telling the truth. Out in the posh
suburb of San Isidro, a fat rich drunkard of the landowning
class named O'Reilly-Ramírez, who owned eight huge
ranches in the province and six houses in Buenos Aires,
was thinking about plans for the elaborate chapel and mau-
soleum he was planning to build for himself in a eucalyptus
grove, and of the fifty thousand yanqui dollars he kept in
cash in a safe-deposit box, as if these two preparations alone
would assure his place in heaven. Meanwhile his daughter
was in the front seat of his black Mercedes making love to
the young chauffeur who was the son of an *indio* caneworker
from Tucumán, unzipping his pants without taking off her
gloves. On an estate next door, in El Tigre, a gangster called
Tío Churro, a price fixer and broker who often bragged that
he had put his soul into the Argentine corned beef industry,

was lying under a blanket that bore a family crest of his
commission. He was trying to sleep all curled up like a big
beef pie but times were hard, and he lay awake wondering
why nobody eats canned beef for breakfast anymore. At the
presidential retreat in San Isidro with its barracks full of
guards where the *presidente* de facto by military coup lived,
commuting every day to his less secure Casa Rosada palace,
the lights were on in an upstairs office. *El presidente general*
was sitting alone catching up on affairs of state, his moustache waxed and wrapped in paper at its ends. He turned
on his tape recorder and began speaking orders into the
microphone that the factories and steel mills of the nation
would stay open by military force, a dictator dictating his
dictation, while outside his office, the Army buses were
filling with soldiers in camouflage fatigues changing guard
for the midnight shift, their numbers increasing by the hour.
In the halls of the Casa Rosada downtown, a reception for
naval officers was going on, organized by Admiral Massera
for the visiting captain and crew of the U.S. cruiser *Sac-
ramento*. All the admirals-to-be from both countries practiced their public postures in the ranks of mirrors in a
lavatory for VIP *caballeros* that once gave it the nickname
"hall of gestures." In the ballroom outside, the bartender
was a dark-skinned corporal on permanent staff dressed like
an exotic prince for the occasion in what looked to him like
a silly band uniform with gold braid and a pink ribbon in
his hat, but he was watching the men's room and daydream-
ing of his son one day looking at himself in the same glasses.
Over in Barrio Constitución, one of the first cell meetings
of the left-wing guerrillas called Los Montoneros broke up
in disorder when its leader, known only as "Carlos," drew
a pistol to make his point about the meaning of fear in a
heated discussion about whether or not to accept mounting
civilian casualties in the plans for Montonero bombings.
Before "Carlos" had finished his speech, his gun went off
and he shot his girlfriend in the ankle. Up on the avenue
Corrientes nearby, tango and popular music was coming out
of the open restaurants, and the movie theater showing *Ro-
meo y Julieta* was letting lines of teenaged couples into their
second late show in the best balcony in town, with its plush

red seats that all but folded back into couches. Behind them, big blue buses like big blue whales were spilling out hundreds of buttons dressed in blue. Gray armored cars were ferrying soldiers around in jungle camouflage, and gangs of uniformed police armed with tear gas and machine guns were ranging up the streets checking national identity cards and detaining for questioning any university students they found. On glamorous Florida Street, the tourist shopping center, the DiTella Theater had just dropped the curtain on its final showing of an ensemble production about the end of the world called "The Hour Of All" and there was a riot breaking out among the actors who had just been informed they were no longer getting paid. In the lobby, six plainclothes policemen were directing a two-man crew loading up the chalkboards that once hung in the theater restrooms as an outlet for public expression and that were now the military government's excuse to shut the theater down on charges of public corruption. The actor who complained the loudest was arrested by the police and led off to a gray armored car and driven into the industrial suburbs over the wide concrete shitcanal called El Riachuelo to a psychiatric hospital where he was committed on charges of homosexuality and spent three months followed around by a mad professor arrested years before during *la noche de los bastones largos*, the night of the long canes, when the armed forces had occupied the university and arrested most of the faculty. Once a full professor at the College of Philosophy and Letters, after so many years in the house of crazies he was by now convinced that he had truly lost his mind in search of the gerund of an obscure Greek verb, strings of conjugations written in ink on the skin of his knees. At the College of Medicine, further into the city and near the main hospital, a visiting biochemist from Heidelberg was having trouble with a large gang of blue-uniformed buttons as he was trying to leave the parking lot because he had forgotten his parking pass. When he explained to them that he was working on hydrogen pumps, or *bombas*, the police sergeant thought he said *hydrogen bombs* and ordered the doctor a motorcycle escort back to his luxury hotel. Meanwhile, down in the Barrio La Boca, neighborhood of tangos, the thirty-fifth reunion of retired congressmen from the corrupt regime of General Agustín P. Justo was gathered at a gay little club called Alicia Duncan's, where the twelve of them that were left had all broken into tears as the singer was belting out the lyrics, *I sat down with my friend, we lit up and remembered, and we were lost in clouds of smoke.* The Friday night of Buenos Aires was rising all around me like a boiling kettle with the lid off. A young maid not dressed for the weather was carrying a sleeping child from one building to another across a street that led onto a broad boulevard in front of the statue of Mitre, ducking quickly under awnings and into doorways, and a taxi driver stopped with a sound of tires and shouted out the window, "*Che!* Little baby! Why don't you go to the devil and your pretty maid with me!" then honked his horn and squealed his tires through the traffic light. Further down, toward the end of the Palermo parks, the residence of the ambassador of the United States stood behind its high stone and iron walls like a castle on the Rhine. Henry Cabot Lodge's younger brother, John, who didn't yet speak very good Spanish for his newest political plum, was trying to rouse a marine guard from his post to take the family's albino collie out for its nightly walk around the grounds. The ambassador, sitting under a framed and signed lifesize photo of his friend, Dick Nixon, was tapping frantically on all the buttons of his phone and making no connections. Not far off, under the statue of Mitre, a yanqui student who felt as if he had just committed rape lay sprawled out on the grass under the general's serious features and the strong legs of his big bronze horse and looking up at them, all around the general's pedestal, winged spirits of the French Revolution seemed to be flying overhead as he was trying to figure out very slowly just how it was he was going to get back up on his feet. . . .

I finally decided not to get back on my feet. I rolled down the long embankment of wet grass in a fog of my breath, the grass so damp and cold I ended up sliding down the hill, picking up speed like a sled set free until I smashed up against a low stone bench at the foot of the slope. Across an empty boulevard, a shallow fountain with long, low cement walls was smoking like a cauldron in the cold autumn air. There was a car parked over there, sitting sideways to traffic, driven up there and abandoned with the lights on and the door standing open. The keys were in the ignition and red dashlights were on from the engine that had been left to stall, and it was easy to start up again, to pound my foot into the gas pedal until the gaskets were ready to blow. Then instead of putting the car into reverse, I must have slipped and the lever found its own way into second gear, and with one foot all the way on the gas like that I pulled the other off the clutch. The car hurtled ten feet like a horse leaping straight into the cheap cement wall of the fountain, the car's front end crumpling like aluminum foil in an explosion of headlight glass. I threw my arms up before I hit the windshield, banged my head, bounced back, then sat there stuporously waiting for the police, water rushing through the wrecked fountain wall, stupidly sitting there drunk with grief, with disbelief, with shame.

# 3

## Real Bullets

The children of Villa Hendaya had one tree in the church-yard and a mile's length of railroad tracks with a bed of gravel sharp as glass for a playground. The skinny brown bodies were surely small for their ages; dressed in baggy pants and T-shirts despite the cold, they scattered over the twin sets of tracks. Two teams of boys broke loose from set positions when the one who acted as referee blasted a shrill whistle through his fingers. Dozens of dusty brown feet had gone bare so long the skin of them looked like dusty brown cowhide, and others were in ragged sneakers with their toes busting through them. They all danced over the splintered black railroad ties, running hell-bent in tight knots of team-mates with shouts and jeers and laughter as they kicked a large tin can over the ties in their game called *el fútbol caminito*, soccer on the little highway. In bounds was between both sets of tracks; the gravel bed was out of bounds. The boy who acted as referee chased the rattling, half-squashed can as it bounced down the barren weedy embankment. The railbed was like two long narrow soccer fields, side by side but a part of the same game. Goals were at either end, about eighty meters apart, unmanned and unmarked save for a deep, dirty line scratched with stones across the dark wood. It was a contact sport; everybody shoved and knocked into each other to make room, or the one who had the tin can *fútbol* would hang back and give it an expert kick that sailed it across the short gravel division between the pairs of rusty steel rails into another knot of boys who would carry it a few feet further toward the goal, fighting ahead, knocking each other over and down the long embankment or into the sharp stones.

Four times a day, depending on the schedules set by a military board of transportation that managed all the railways, the San Martín line's express freights ripped through the slum village that was little more than a long narrow collection of shacks made out of salvaged bricks, packing crates and tin. There were some houses with cement walls and more permanent tile roofs further from the raised embankment of the railbeds, closer to the high brick stacks of a rendering and tanning plant that overlooked the little flat stretch of low ground the slum was built upon. The shacks were scattered over a marginal fringe of very wet floodplain, between a spit of swampy fields that looked like the New Jersey flats and the beginnings of paved streets and low cement block houses that marked the outskirts of a federal housing project called Villa Evita that had grown up around the tanning plant during the first regime of Perón.

In the distance, the train sounded its horn and the ground began gently to quake. The San Martín express picked up speed after crossing through Palermo and the outskirts of the city, then it ripped through the poorer districts at fifty miles an hour loaded with freight from the port bound for Mendoza and the Andes. Or coming from the other direction, a train would be arriving back again from the provinces with its cattle cars filled, its hopper cars spilling over with wheat, sunflower seeds, oats, its freight cars full of bundled raw fleeces or boxes of grapes, plums, peaches and cases of finished wines. The patchwork shacks made of unpainted bricks and scrapwood, the scrappy tin roofs, the makeshift tables and castaway chairs in the little muddy backyards started shaking like the world was coming to an end.

Up on the tracks, the boys of the *villa miseria*, the misery village, as these slums were known, would stop their game of *fútbol caminito* and shout, "The train! The train! Look, *che*!" From everywhere among the shacks closest to the high railbeds other kids would appear and run up the embankment. Knots of dark little girls watched from their tiny yards. Kids pushed and shoved at each other to get up close to the tracks, shouting and jeering, and then nothing but the train could be heard as maybe a dozen boys from the *fútbol* game stood fast up there balanced on the rails and ties, facing off the train like a gang of little bullfighters. They scattered at the last possible second like so many monkeys down the steep embankment, laughing and shouting, one of them so quick that he held out his hand and yelled at all the others that he had touched the engine before he jumped. There was an argument. Two boys went down in a fistfight that turned into wrestling. In the middle of this, somebody tossed a new can up between the rails and started off on the run, kicking the can ahead of him toward the goal with a gang of boys chasing after him calling out, "Give it here, *che*! Give it here! Over here!"

Brown dust rained down and hung in the air long after the train had passed with a long, sustained screaming and a wind that ripped a few rags of laundry off the lines. I crushed out the butt of my Particulares in the mud behind the tiny San Andrés church in Villa Hendaya. I leaned against a low, half-finished wall of rough cement blocks, hands slapping at my sweater and jeans as the dust whirled around us and began to settle after the San Martín express had passed. Hernández-Marelli was sprawled out against the wall in a half-sleep, one eye barely open as El Gordo Rojo beside him slowly troweled a little wet cement under the stretched white string that ran down the unfinished wall of blocks, Marelli keeping watch in case El Gordo tried to drip mortar on his head. My brother Alejo was with us, too, a last-minute surprise. I was sorry that he had gotten himself into trouble but glad to have him with me, making me not the only one in the Benevento family who was being punished. Alejo was squatting a few feet away under cover of a pile of cement blocks, unwrapping a candy bar of white chocolate. He took a wad of chewing gum out of his mouth and parked it like a big gray slug on the cement block nearest his hand and then popped the chocolate into his mouth and chewed a long time. Alejo was about five feet ten in sneakers and still growing; nothing could fill him up.

All of us *compañeros* were resting. When Father Vargas left the construction site to run neighborhood meetings and organize the blocks and to give the old and sick communion and things like that, we *compañeros* would immediately begin one of our frequent rest periods. How else were we going to stretch the work out long enough to make up for all the *amonestaciones*, enough demerits to keep us all slaving for San Andrés charities every day for weeks on end until we had wiped our slates clean? Our punishment was to help work on a small school building—really one big room with a tin roof for a San Andrés grade school in the misery village—the going rate one day's labor for each demerit at Father Vargas' discretion until our totals were back to zero and we would be permitted to attend classes again at Colegio San Andrés. Alejo had been in our little chain gang only since the day before, when Professor Pérez-Pérez, our little goat-bearded, gay music teacher with fingernails filed into points, had added eight demerits to Alejo's account. Alejo had gone to the front of the room to recite a lesson on Mozart and had broken up the class by saying, "As you have taught us, professor, Mozart made very, very pretty music, and you have also shown us how much he liked to suck the flute."

So here was Alejo, unwrapping his second candy bar, sharing with me the mischief of our lounging away this cold but sunny afternoon. Maybe Alejo was there on purpose. Mamá had been very angry with me for the trouble I had caused. It was she who had to make a personal appeal to El Rector to get me back into school. She praised the Monseñor for his leniency in letting the matter go to the school's board of priests, and especially Father Artaud, who had suggested to the board that I be given two suspensions' worth of demerits and be allowed to work them off on the charity project like the other delinquent students. As Mamá was talking at the table, Alejo rudely interrupted her in my defense. "I don't think it's right to use a work of charity as a punishment," he said. "It's a shitty fascist system, that's clear. Did they even give Diego the chance to tell his side of the story?"

Two days later, Alejo was a prisoner with us, out on the rockpile with our little gang.

Hernández-Marelli's slipup had happened during our quarterly exams. Marelli had been caught for the first time in his fifteen years of cheating for *macheteando*, cribbing the answers to math and chemistry questions on tiny scraps of paper masked ingeniously but not quite enough by his jacket cuffs, the inside of his lapels, columns of formulae written in lilliputian hand on gumwrappers he had pasted to the soles of his shoes. El Gordo Rojo was in deeper trouble. El Gordo was going to be a slave forever, maybe even longer than me. He had drunk down six liters of water on a latrine break about a half-hour before the time was up on our philosophy exam. We watched him suffering until he couldn't take it much longer, then on his signal, near the bell, many of the students in the class lined up and started piling their bluebooks on Father Naboa's desk. Last of all, El Gordo, bloated like a hot-air balloon and so heavy he sloshed with each slow, tortured step, took his own bluebook up among the last students to finish the exam. With a crowd of *compañeros* gathered around him and bunched up watching from the doorway, El Gordo added his test to Father Naboa's pile, then stood a little over and behind the seated deaf priest and stuck his fingers down his throat. It was like the Iguazú Falls pouring all over the pile of finished bluebooks, all over the desk, all over Father Naboa. El Gordo couldn't stop—the water ran dry and then it was like a sewer vomiting. Our conspiracy all along was to ruin Father Naboa's vague but exacting exam on Aristotle (we had to memorize book two, chapter seven of the *Etica Nicomachea* and explain it). Any of us who wanted to cut out on the exam handed our essays in last at El Gordo's signal, at the top of the pile, written in fountain pens with washable ink. El Gordo was going to be doing works of charity a long time.

So was José Ugarte, and Manuel Llamas-Pérez, and El Flaco Peluffo, the whole slack crew of them for more minor

offenses. Then there was me. According to Hernández-
Marelli's graphic version of events, El Yanqui was a prisoner
with the rest of them because he *echó un polvo*, threw a
little dust with El Rector's new cook, telling the tale as if
the girl and I had been discovered naked in the act in El
Rector's living room. "What a barbarous mess! What a hassle! El Yanqui pulled his stick out and tried to hide but El
Rector tracked the poor *boludo* down by the little droplets
of white milk El Yanqui left as a trail, *che*! If only El Rector
had waited another two minutes, just two minutes more, El
Yanqui would have been in paradise and have made a clean
getaway!"

El Yanqui did nothing to give his *compañeros* any other
impression. Days after I had been suspended from Colegio
San Andrés, there was still a lot of speculation about the
case, fueled by the fact that Martín Segundo and Alejo
weren't telling anybody the reason. It was El Negrito who
related a version of events to Hernández-Marelli, and after
that I was transformed into a kind of hero, an outrageous
adventurer, scaler of new mountains, all of this, of course,
based on rumors and lies. The priests were already getting
used to yet another new cook sent in from a mission in
Tucumán, in the North. And the way most people wanted
to see my situation was something like Papá's explanation
of my behavior over the telephone to El Rector, that it was
understandable for a boy not used to drinking wine in his
home country, and a hot-blooded teenager as most boys
were at his age, indeed it was logical that he was bound to
fall prey to a certain kind of girl. Added to that, he didn't
yet understand Argentine culture, and everyone knew that
North American girls were much looser, so it was clear how
he had made such a mistake. After Papá had set up the
appointment for Mamá to see the Monseñor to negotiate a
way to get me back into school, he told me that it was the
drunken driving that most upset the family. "You're going
to kill yourself if you let yourself lose control like that,"
he said. "I don't care about the car, cars can be repaired.
It's you, my son, who must learn to be strong, and smart,
and clearheaded enough to get what you want in this world.
For example, if you are going to call a Monseñor a *boludo*,

you should be smart enough to do it in the right company,"
Papá said. "There's a right way and a wrong way to do
things in this world, that's all I'm saying."

I told Papá I was out of my head, that was clear. I was
sorry and it would never happen again, and I insisted that I
should pay for the repair of the front grill, fender and headlights of the family's newest Peugeot out of my weekly allowance. "The money's not important," Papá said with
irritation. "There's plenty of money to fix anything, that's
not what I'm trying to tell you. Haven't you been listening?
Isn't it clear to you? Isn't it clear what I'm saying?"

"It's clear, Papá. I'm sorry," I said. "I'm sorriest about
the sweater. I don't know what happened to it. I'd give
anything to get it back. I must have taken it off somewhere
and lost it," I lied. "You must be disappointed in me."

"So I am," Papá said after a moment. "But it's worth
ten sweaters to me, ten cars, ten nights spent hassling with
the police if you only learn something from this experience.
You may go now, Diego. And remember what I've told
you," he said.

What was clear to me in what Papá had said was that I
was guilty, and I should behave accordingly with everyone.
I thought it might even be better to change schools, to transfer to the public school down the block, but the I.S.E. organization would have to put together all the paperwork and
that kind of thing, so it would mean getting them involved.
As I left Papá in his study, I felt like a wayward soldier who
has just lost his stripes. This is the way I felt when I stood
before the Monseñor, too, ready to accept my punishment.
El Rector seemed calm enough, scrutinizing the student before him as if I were merely some lower form of life, one
of those doomed since creation by its own stupidity.

"Nothing that Cornelia did that night was her fault, Monseñor, I want you to know that," I said before El Rector
could give me my sentence. "It wasn't her fault by any
means, is that clear?"

"A young man of your position shouldn't trouble so much
about the destiny of a servant," the Monseñor said.

"What did you do to her? Where is she now?"

"You can assure yourself that the brotherhood of San

Andrés has seen to it that she won't go hungry," El Rector said with impatience. "Are you trying to tell me what to do with my staff?"

"No, Monseñor. I just want to make myself perfectly clear," I said, "and I want to know what happened to her, that's all."

"Let me make myself clear then," El Rector said. "Since you are a foreign guest at this school, a visitor in my country representing a distinguished program, we are going to offer you the leniency any honored guest deserves. Your punishment is twenty demerits against you, a double suspension from classes. You may return to the community of this school after you've worked off the demerits with Father Vargas and the other boys under suspension. Father Vargas' truck leaves at six-thirty every morning from in front of the chapel. Make sure you're on it. And that is absolutely all the time I have for you," El Rector said, ringing a silver bell on his desk. This brought in Choto, the school's little dried-up, bearded secretary who wore secondhand suits, and who was carrying a clipboard with papers on it for the Monseñor to sign. Through the open door behind Choto, there was a waiting room full of other petitioners. I nodded my head once at El Rector, turned stiffly, and followed little Choto out of the office.

For days after Hernández-Marelli had told his version of events, the boys at Colegio San Andrés passed the open window of the school's kitchen and called in to the new young cook, "*Che!* Lovecrazy! Do you want to have dinner with me?" Then they ran scattering in laughter for their classrooms before María Consuela, El Negrito's wife and veteran cleaning lady of the San Andrés dining hall, hurled spoons, forks, metal pans and blunt knives at the boys as she rushed out into the courtyard to catch them.

"*Che, compañeros!*" said El Gordo Rojo, looking up from his mealy trowel. Everyone jumped to his feet but Hernández-Marelli. Manuel and El Flaco Peluffo were up and at their shovels, El Gordo was in place, and Alejo hopped up onto the pile of cement blocks and pushed one off to me. I waddled with the heavy block until I reached El Gordo, who picked it out of my hands as if it were a mere loaf of bread. El Gordo set the heavy block on the layer of mortar he had laid, which spread out under its rough weight like drooling frosting. Marelli should have been there doing trowel work, slapping on the mortar ahead of our little assembly line, but Marelli had his timing exactly worked out. Just as Father Vargas turned the corner of the little square pillbox of the San Andrés church and came into view, Marelli rose to his feet in a relaxed, laidback movement, seized his trowel and began to use the handle to tap lightly on the block El Gordo had laid, squinting one eye down the length of the string as if he were the foreman here, the one who made sure all the blocks stayed in line. Father Vargas was walking fast, already unclipping his large yellow measuring tape from his belt, his gray work shirt covered with the gray-white dust of cement, an expression on his face of a perpetual good cheer found in those priests who feel genuinely that whatever they can do is for the good.

Father Vargas stretched his tape out with the absorption and playfulness of a boy building his first soap box racer. He measured the line of bricks and sighted down the string with a determination in his face like the whole world could be built in a week. He walked over to check the wheelbarrow filled with mortar, which after our chain gang's little rest period had already hardened to the gooey consistency of corned beef hash. Father Vargas reached down for a trowel stuck in the wet ground near the wheelbarrow and filled it with pasty cement, tiny spots of concrete splattering onto his face and drying there through the afternoon like little gray moles on the end of his nose, on his forehead and on the misty lenses of his black frame glasses. "Very good, my boys," he said, urging us on, his accent with the slow, lilting pronunciation of Entre Rios province, some r's in his words sounding shushed, like sh's. His reaction even to Hernández-Marelli was oblivious. "That's it, Roberto. Set the blocks firmly. You're doing a good job of spreading the mortar." Marelli barely gripped his trowel with three manicured fingers, spending minutes running the blade over the same little wet square of cement with an expression on his face of rebellious indolence. Marelli was tall and fine-

boned, but his playboy slouching made him seem much
shorter. He stepped back, lazily reached into his pocket and
took his time putting on his cool pair of pilot's sunglasses,
then he dawdled finding and lighting his nice little cigarette.
He curled his lips into a kind of sneer as he smoked in a
self-conscious imitation of Jean-Paul Belmondo, who was
one of his heroes.

The rest of us worked up a good sweat hustling along
with our cement blocks. El Gordo used the shovel one-
handed as if it were no more than a big tablespoon to mix
fresh mortar in the wheelbarrow, polite and humble around
Father Vargas. "You think we should add more sand, Father?" he asked. Alejo chewed away on his gum, climbing
to the top of the pile of blocks and knocking a few of them
down, then he hopped to the ground and handed one to me
without missing a beat. The square rising walls of the new
schoolroom were a testimony to the number of inexpert
hands that had gone piecemeal into them, mortar everywhere running down the blocks, some of them even out of
line, Father Vargas having built little wire and mortar
frameworks here and there to compensate for the mistakes
as the building rose. But between the delinquents during
school hours and the weekend and evening work parties
from the misery village, Father Vargas was sure the blocks
would soon rise up over his head and the tin roof would sit
in a silvery glory over it all like the certainty of heaven.

El Gordo kept up a polite conversation, chattering at Father Vargas as if to stay on his good side, *chupando el culo*,
in our words, El Gordo sucking ass, the rest of us hating
him for it. "Do you plan to make this your home parish,
Father?" he asked.

"I want to keep those kids up there from getting smashed
by the train," Father Vargas said. "They've got to have
someplace to go that's not a mudbath. But God hasn't en-
dowed me with craftsmanlike hands nor the patience for
grade school. I suppose when the school is finished, I'll say
a Wednesday mass here and leave the rest up to the teachers," he said. "And of course, we'll start building somewhere else. How many layers is this now?"

"Twelve," I said. "Or we're nearly finished with the twelfth, Father."

"Very well, my boys, we might take a little rest now."

"Why are so many people living out here like this?" I asked.

"Out here and a lot of places like it," Father Vargas said. "Most of them are women, poor women who have been, well, you can imagine what's happened to them. They're abandoned with their children. What men there are here seem too lazy to work, and there's a lot of drinking, too many mouths to feed and not enough jobs, who can say? A lot of the men come in from the provinces looking for work and find nothing in Buenos Aires, so they collect out here in the slums. Nobody else would settle on this land because of the flooding. The brotherhood discussed for a long time the idea of even building a church and school out here, that it might be better to take bulldozers in and level the whole area."

"Right over there is where Evita Perón's bulldozers were forced to stop," said Hernández-Marelli, pointing in the direction of the little neighborhood of bunkerlike block-houses in the distance behind the tanning and tallow plant.

"Roberto!" Father Vargas said sharply to him. "Change places with Alejo."

"What did you say, Father?"

"You take the blocks off the pile and let Alejo lay them."

"But why, Father, if I'm doing such a good job here?"

"Roberto! Change places with Alejo or I'll give you two more demerits and today doesn't count!"

Later, Father Vargas went off on another errand and we stopped for another little rest. Hernández-Marelli and I shared a cigarette, both of us watching the game of *fútbol caminito* up on the railroad tracks. We stood a little ways down from El Gordo and Alejo, who were splitting an orange. "*Che*, Yanqui," Marelli said. "Why don't you come with me to a student party this evening? I want you to meet some really cool people, these really cool playboys from the university."

"I don't know, *che*," I said. "I'm in trouble with my family."

"To hell with the Beneventos, *che*, they're so stuck-up it's a joke all over Buenos Aires. What do you care what the family thinks?"

"What do you mean my family is stuck-up?" I said. "*Che*, Alejo, this son of a whore here says our family is stuck-up!"

"It's clear that Marelli is a son of a whore bullshitter," Alejo said. "Everybody knows it. And if he keeps on talking, I'm going to use my fists to make his face look like shit."

"*Che*, I'm non-violent," Marelli said. "And Yanqui, this is a really cool gang, it's a boss time with them, wall-painting parties and things like that. They're trying to do something about this shitty government."

"You're a lousy bullshitter, Marelli," Alejo said. "You don't give a fuck about politics!"

"That's just the point, you idiot. These playboys run with girls from the university. They feel them up all over in the library. When these girls hit their second year at university, they really let loose. It's like they go crazy for anybody with half a stick, I swear it, *che*, otherwise I wouldn't be out there risking jail. There's a lot happening now, Yanqui, haven't you been reading the papers? My older brother spent the state of siege of '66 all wrapped up in the arms of a university girl in her little student apartment. And it's a boss time running around with these girls at night, like a carnival, *che*, and I swear you get to throw a little dust for every wall you paint."

"Quit bullshitting me, Marelli, that's all I need," I said.

"That *boludo* would get interested in politics just to get laid," Alejo said. "The funny thing is that the only way Marelli ever throws any dust is in his fist."

"Go back to your whore mother," Marelli said.

"Listen to me, Marelli," I said, "Alejo's mother is my mother, is that clear? You apologize to Alejo right now or I'll break your ass."

"*Che*, the kid is busting my balls," Marelli said. I stepped up to him, my fists clenched, watching him back up against the wall of blocks. "All right, all right! I'm sorry, Alejo! Your whore mother is not a whore mother!"

he shouted. I was about to kick him, but he looked so ridiculous, backed up against the wall and straightening his
hair with a rake of his fingers, a silly grin on his face.
"Look, Yanqui, I'm just trying to invite you to a party. And
if these particular girls don't work out, then maybe we'll
just go for a couple of beers, you and me, Yanqui. We ditch
Alejo who's way too young, get rid of El Gordo who keeps
scaring girls off and Manuel who's too much of a wimp and
I know a few places where we can't miss. Is it clear what
I'm saying?"

Alejo was watching me, and he could see what I was
thinking. Maybe Marelli was right. When else would I get
a chance to meet university girls?

"Go ahead if you want to, Yanqui," Alejo said. "Why
should I care worth a shit what you do?"

"Meet me at a bar called El Escolar, near the College of
Philosophy and Letters, at ten tonight," Marelli said. "You
know where that is?"

"I'm sorry, Marelli," I said, looking at Alejo, who was
pretending to ignore us. "I think I should buckle down and
study tonight. I'm in enough trouble already."

"Why should you buckle down and study if you're not
even allowed in school for a month?" Marelli asked; then
he walked away, shrugging his shoulders in disgust, and
started to bullshit with El Flaco Peluffo.

Alejo offered me a section of orange, then we both
stretched out against the pile of cement blocks to catch a
few minutes of sun. I left Alejo stretched out there looking
asleep and found Marelli as if to bum a cigarette. As I was
leaning in close to Marelli's lighter, I put a hand up as if to
shield the flame from the wind and said, "You swing by
and pick me up at ten o'clock on the corner of Junín and
Santa Fe. I don't want anybody to see it's you, so come by
way of Santa Fe just in case."

"All right, *che*, we'll have a real party tonight," Hernández-Marelli said. Then El Gordo looked in Marelli's direction, his cheeks bulging. El Gordo spat out a huge wad
of chewed up orange peels. Marelli jumped aside but too
late, most of it landing in a gooey mess all over his back.
Marelli started after El Gordo with a cement block raised

over his head but Father Vargas turned the corner around the little church and we all sprang back to our jobs. Hernández-Marelli passed me a rough cement block, the edges digging little blistered holes in his soft white hands (he actually had a manicurist who came to his apartment twice a week and did the whole family). As he passed the block on to me, he said, "It's true what I said about Perón a while ago. If you look closely enough over there, you can see the little dirt road that marks the actual line where Evita's bulldozers cut their engines. She wanted to rebuild all these slums with permanent little houses like those over there."

"So what gives with Father Vargas?" I asked.

"What gives with Father Vargas is that he spent three months under house arrest just before General Aramburu's big coup, *che*, the one when the Air Force bombed the Plaza de Mayo and Perón was thrown out of office. The San Andrés priests were agitating against Perón and some were arrested and beaten by the police. Father Vargas hates Peronists and Perón, but it's a strange thing, because he's like some of the Peronists himself in the way he cares about these people. Anyway, it's not good to mention Perón around Father Vargas, I'm just *boludo* enough to forget that and open my big mouth," Marelli said.

"How many layers is that now!" Father Vargas called to us, pulling out his measuring tape like a knight drawing his sword.

Later, we made the long ride home in the shaky Citroën pickup, all hunched up like monkeys under the canopy on a pile of tools and extra bags of cement. We drove through the chaotic traffic of Buenos Aires during the peak of the rush hour, the cars around us all talking with their horns, looking for a chance to jump the lights. We *compañeros* were riding in back like four corks rattling around in our little metal box filled with sharp shovels and huge bags of cement falling all over us, and we hung on to whatever we could each time Father Vargas slammed on the brakes. "Thanks be to God that Father Vargas has El Gordo riding up front with him," Alejo said after he flew forward over me and landed on a pile of shovels. In the distance behind

us, a traffic cop was forced to draw his pistol to get a line
of cars to stop at a major intersection, the traffic light
changing colors gaily overhead, unheeded in the jam as if
invisible in the wintry twilight against the smokestack-stud-
ded skyline, the sunset a dirty purple smear in the industrial
haze.

The evening had turned into night by the time we were
let off at home. Alejo and I labored up the steep marble
staircase to the second floor, our hands leaving little dusty
gray streaks on the black iron banister. We were tired,
breathing heavily as we passed the hallway mirror, and I
saw how covered we were with dirt. Our jeans and sweaters
were a mess, our fingernails black, a long splash of dried
gray cement across my forehead, my hair all stuck together
with dried sweat. I was struck by how quiet the flat was
even during the usually uneventful hours between teatime
and dinner. For some reason, Alejo and I were all but tip-
toeing down the hallway, our sneakers leaving trails of tiny
suction-cup markings in gray dust all over the dark wood
floors. It was as if we were trying not to get caught on our
way in.

Little Miguel was the first to notice we were home. He
called out from his bedroom, "*Hola*, Alejo! *Hola*, Diego!"
in a plaintive voice that was desperate for company. Miguelito had been nailed to the desk in his bedroom lately, a
family effort to try to help him pass his second and last
chance at his quarterly exams.

Mamá heard Miguelito's greeting and instantly appeared
at the head of the long hallway. "Leave Miguel study! He's
not to budge out of his room until dinner!" she said. "Now
both of you come and tell me about your day."

"*Hola*, Miguelito," I whispered as I passed his door.

In the living room, Mamá inspected Alejo and me as if
appraising any changes in our characters more than the
soiled condition of our clothes, hands and faces. "How did
you find the misery village?" she asked.

"I never knew people could live like that," I said.

"The charity project's not worth a fart," Alejo said. "It's
going to be sitting underwater with the next hard rain."

"Watch your language in front of your Mamá," Mamá said.

"I don't give a shit," Alejo said. "Anything's better than apologizing to that faggot music teacher," he said, then he turned rudely around and headed down the hallway for the shower. Mamá looked at me, a contract between us that we were going to ignore Alejo's little tantrum.

"Put some Noxzema on your face, my son, you've got a sunburn!" Mamá shouted down the hallway after him.

"Alejo has worked very hard today," I said.

"And how was working with Father Vargas?"

"I didn't mind it," I said. "I like working. I know how to jump in and get dirty. But Father Vargas is a hopeless architect. The new school building looks like it's going to fall over any minute."

"Father Vargas has been knocking on doors raising funds for that school I don't know how long. It will be a relief to everyone when he's finished. Now what are your plans after a shower, Diego?"

"I don't want to get too far behind in school, Mamá," I said. "El Gordo Rojo invited me over to study after dinner," I said before I realized my mistake. Now I would have to telephone El Gordo and make a deal with him to cover for me just in case.

"That's fine," Mamá said. "You'll come home early?"

"How do I know, Mamá? There's a lot to catch up on—civics, chemistry, the makeup exam for philosophy . . ."

"All right then, son, we'll expect you late. I've had Isabelita leave something out from tea for you and Alejo in case you're hungry."

"Thank you, Mamá."

"We'll all be glad when this is over, Diego. We never intended for our sons to become construction workers." Mamá spoke with an edge to her words, enough to remind me she was disappointed in me. Then she turned and went back to her art books in the living room.

I passed the deserted dining nook off the kitchen where I usually had tea with my brothers. Sitting out was Isabelita's contribution to the day, a small plate with a few stale toast rounds that looked as if she'd left them in the oven until they had turned into little brown rocks. Isabelita wasn't happy with me, either, having heard through the neighborhood maids' grapevine how El Rector's new young cook had lost her job because of my indiscretions. Her usually strong, flavorful Brazilian coffee was sitting cold in the cup, boiled and nasty, the milk in it forming a tough brown skin. I continued down the hallway without bothering anything else on the table. I brushed my clothes with my own hands in my bedroom, then I took them off and shook them out. Where were all the maids this afternoon? I rolled up my pants and stuffed them into the closet to wear again tomorrow. I picked up my shirt and sweater that I had left in a heap on the floor for the maids and put them in the dirty laundry bag myself. For a time at least, Mamá's construction worker sons would be treated just a little as if they were from a different class and breeding, that was clear.

I sat naked on the bed, the shades drawn across the windows. It was a restful darkness, a dim light in which objects seemed to reflect a kind of haze that was only barely visible. A long time passed, and my head ached, a dull throbbing in my temples from the day's labors under the wintry sun. I was tired, my back still feeling every cement block I had lifted. How long would I have to work like that? Such a small thing, I thought, wasn't it small what I had done? But the consequences weren't, and I thought of the poor girl, Cornelia, and how strange a world it was when one small mistake by me could so completely change her life. I imagined her out of a job, living in some wretched little muddy slum like the misery village where the trash was blown around by the winds, papers and wrappers and shreds of plastic scattered all over the place, hanging off the few bare wintry tree branches like miserable fruit. I remembered her beautiful face, her whole future wrecked in it with a few strong words, and how she had run out of the room, crying. But what had I really done? I had kissed her, and maybe a little more, but even so I had pulled her across an uncrossable line and that had been enough, and I felt rotten. Then suddenly all I wanted was to go home. I knew what some prisoners must feel, knowing they're guilty, the walls closing in, a heartsickness worse than loneliness because the time seemed to stretch out endlessly until I could kiss the ground of my own country again as if let loose from a life sentence. I wanted to see the old man, the old lady, my brothers, Carol, Harry, anybody. It was a lost feeling, knowing this was impossible, a sharp mood of self-pity that lasted until I was in the shower and feeling a little better, soaping myself all over, standing under the hot streams of water from the antique gilded showerhead shaped like a hungry codfish.

All of a sudden, I began hoping for a real boss time with Hernández-Marelli that night, all the valves turned open. I could already imagine my arm around one of those university girls at a café table at El Escolar, this time the kind of girl I could never get into trouble. It was easy from there to imagine her asking me up to her little student apartment for a drink. I'd select the music for her stereo and take her clothes off just like that—was that too much to wish for? I came out of the shower whistling a fractured tune, scrubbing the towel over my hair as I strode down the hallway past Miguelito's room ready for anything, a new Yanqui now with the dust of the day washed off, thinking if I could only once get a chance I was sure I could keep going until sunrise. Miguelito's door suddenly opened just a crack and the little scamp stuck his head out into the hallway. *"Psssst!"* he said. "This came for you today, Dieguito!"

He passed me a flimsy blue envelope, but one that was fat with pages. He grinned at me and I said, *"Che,* thanks for keeping a lookout," but it was too late. Mamá had a kind of radar out for Miguelito these days and she appeared at the head of the hallway.

"Back in that room, Miguel!" she shouted.

"Can't I even go to the bathroom?" Miguelito shouted back. "Do you want me to piss off the balcony?"

"You're going to be sorry when Papá comes home if you can't recite that lesson for him!" Mamá snapped back.

"What an intolerable piece of shit this is," Miguelito hissed at me quickly, then he shut his door loudly enough to express his anger at the situation.

"Pardon me, Mamá, it was my fault," I said quietly, bunching my towel together over my body and hustling to my bedroom with Harry's letter hidden under it. I sat down on the bed and opened the letter, eager for his news, the news of a real brother, and I resolved to answer Harry's letter that night no matter what. Out of a fold in the blue tissuey pages something dropped out. It was metal, shiny, like a misshapen, feather-light little coin, the elongated triangle of an aluminum flip-top broken off from its ring:

Dear James:

Just got over here and settled into our new base. It's a few acres of jungle slash near a village called Don Ba Tin. Everybody keeps telling me how much of a cushy duty being a grease monkey to a bunch of Hueys is going to be but this shit over here is bad. In your hands by now you've got a piece of the beer can that saved my life. I wanted to send you a part of it like a good luck charm. I'm wearing the ring part.

This buddy of mine named York and I and these spec threes White and Rezinsky were out on the perimeter drinking beer last night. York and I were on perimeter duty for a few hours, just leaning against the sandbags listening to the music turned real low. We were relieved by White and Rezinsky. We hung around drinking a few beers with them. Everybody was kind of tense because there was a lot of talk about some new offensive downriver from here. When there's that kind of talk, it gets across the river to the VC, and everybody was expecting to get mortared on. So we were all kind of hanging out near the bunkers, the hootches where we sleep were out of the question, man, quonset huts like big half-buried beer cans that make a big target. There was a lot of talk about some Arvons having trouble keeping it together down South, at LZ Betty Mike near a tributary of this river, the kind of soldiers not worth keeping in back of you, man, they just melt away. We could see the village of Don Ba Tin across the river, just the dark outlines of the cement blockhouses with their thatched roofs against the night sky. The Army rebuilt the village as a part of the pacification program after the old village was napalmed. Rezinsky said he could feel the rockets about to come in, like a sixth sense, if you can believe that. He said he could feel it by the way the water was moving, and in the winds he could read minds on the other side, like he could listen in on the gooks over there carrying a 60mm mortar between them, pushing the jungle back over a secret trail. They were setting up just across from us, he said, they were going to start in any second and then York stopped him. York is this big spade, I mean a really big dude. He just shut Rezinsky up.

Everybody wanted more beer. York said fuck it, he'd go. Then I said I'd go, too, I was uptight enough I wanted to go back to the hootch and get some reefer. The river was behind us, out there somewhere a kind of glowing electric blue under the moonlight. York and I went into the hootch and picked up a sixpack each. I got some reefer out of a stash under my cot. York said the refrigerator was fucked up, the beer was all warm, and he was in a real bad mood, so I started to fix the refrigerator. It's part of my head over here to fix things, so I fooled around with it a while until York said to leave it alone. We left the refrigerator lying there all in pieces. We were just out of the hootch, shuffling along with our sixpacks, and I don't remember hearing anything. We were just knocked off our feet, straight back on our asses in this white flash. I was eating dirt, man, and it was like I'd been struck by lightning. All the beer cans broke out of their plastic halters and were rolling around. Then all these rockets started landing everywhere around us, all at once, I could just hear them screaming in and then whump, whump, whump like that and I was out there trying to dig myself into this open ground hard as cement. Man, it was bad to be out in the open like that. I had to think fast. There were shallow slit trenches dug back near the hootch. Everybody back there was piling into them, but I'd have to stand up and run to get there and I was scared to stand up.

There was a perimeter bunker about a hundred yards
ahead, I remembered helping to build it the first few
weeks busting ass lifting sandbags in all this heat and
humidity but it was a small bunker, Schiller and Gold-
man would be over there, both officers, bad company
and taking up all the room. Then I thought of the
bunker radio shack where Garcia kept the communications going. He's got it rigged up in there so his
tapes of albums come through one side of his earphones and company communications through the
other. He's a pretty cool dude, he'd know what was
happening, and I wanted to get in on what we were
going to do, listen to Garcia get the firefight going in
no time, calling in a Phantom up there somewhere,
or a Skyhawk, if they could even find this shithole in
the middle of the night and rip the whole riverbank to
hell, napalm orange. Not that it would do any good.
They'd have to level the whole village all over again
for that. Somebody said they saw the rockets set loose
from over there, right in the middle of the village,
quick brilliant flashes like shooting stars. Don Ba Tin
was supposed to be pacified, nobody living there but
old gooks chewing on their beetlenuts. Then somebody started firing back from our side of the river
right into the village, fuck these gooks anyway, and
then over to the left of me somebody else opened up
with an M-60 shooting tracers like fireworks. There
must have been all kinds of hell to pay for him, nobody gave any orders to open fire, one of the lieutenants was screaming from his bunker to hold fire. Then
I looked up ahead of where I was crawling and there
wasn't anything left. York was on the ground up there,
too, and he was yelling that he'd been hit, he'd been
hit, then he started cussing like a street spade, moth-
erfucking this and that, he wasn't hit, one of his beers
had busted open and wet him all over. I lay there and
went through everything in my mind. All we had done
was step into the hootch a few minutes and get the
sixpacks. Only five or six guys had been asleep in
there, Olson nearest the refrigerator, I could tell by

the stink of his plastic sheets the way he's been pissing
his bed ever since he got here. I tried to take the
refrigerator apart by flashlight and left it all in pieces,
for which I caught hell this morning. I remembered
stumbling over somebody's boots left lying out. Then
York and I started back for our bunker and right there,
where our bunker was, that's where the first flash happened. I just stood straight up there when the rocket
came in like any asshole who's never been through it
before, and I was knocked on my ass. I was bleeding,
too, this big cut on my chin when I hit the dirt, it took
five stitches and Lieutenant Schiller is putting me in
for a purple heart, what a joke, man, I don't want
anything to do with any medals. White and Rezinsky
were dead. It was the impact that killed them. I always
thought it would be these big pieces of shrapnel flying
everywhere but it's not, it's the flash and the blast,
man, when the rocket lands it's instant death with the
shock. All that happened to me was that I cut my chin
open with this flip-top. I didn't even go on ahead to
look. I made it to Garcia at the radio shack to see
what might be going down as York was over there
trying to pick up White and Rezinsky. I didn't want
to see that, he could go look at the mess all he wanted
to but not me, we had medics for that. I opened up a
beer on the way and drank it and saved the flip-top.
I've hammered the ring into a good luck pinky ring
and am sending the other piece to you in case you
need it. Just think of me over here drinking beer
whenever I can, going back for sixpacks every chance
I get. I'm making this cool necklace out of flip-tops
with a hammer and some pliers that I'm going to send
Carol for her birthday. If the old man ever asks you
what I'm doing over here tell him that I'm keeping my
head down and drinking a lot to get through. I'm going to take some acid tonight with York, I've got some
windowpane I brought with me. I'm going to trip all
night and put the refrigerator back together. I really
think I can figure out that kind of machinery better
on acid, can see all the moving parts in it more clearly,

individually, like the parts are talking to me in terms of their pure functions. I've already fixed a film projector tripped out and by feel that way and it works great. I thought maybe you'd want to do some L too sometime, like nothing too heavy, cut it down the middle and split it with some Spanish chick you want to turn on. So here it is on the letter under my name. Take care of yourself and write me when you get the chance. I'm one of the guys in the company who doesn't get much mail. Got to go now.

Love,

Harry

·□·

One of the strangest things about this letter was the postmark date—I found Harry's first letter just to be sure—and I sat wondering how it was possible that the letter I had just received had been written three weeks before the first one. Was it the mails? Was it Harry? I read both letters over again, trying to form a picture of my brother in my mind. There was no doubt about it, the letters didn't sound right, his tone was unsettling, not at all as resistant to the war as I had expected. And why was he doing so many drugs over there? How could anybody handle that?

I dressed for dinner, which was quiet that night compared to most because Papá was off at an investors meeting to discuss the current political crisis. Mamá presided over the table with all the formality of a ruling duchess, buttering her bread a tiny mouthful at a time and lecturing Miguelito that it was bad manners to wolf down his food as if he were starving, the well-to-do class didn't eat like that, good education taught that one should be delicate about the food on one's plate and make polite conversation between mouthfuls. "The general principle of good manners is never to call too much attention to yourself," Mamá said. "And always leave a little of each portion when you're finished so your hostess knows she has served you enough and you're not a starving barbarian."

Alejo was describing the misery village and our chain gang crew to Martín Segundo, the three brothers laughing at his description of Hernández-Marelli actually lifting bricks. I sat there listening happily enough, watching the clock and thinking about my little secret to meet Marelli later. I also thought again about Harry's letter, and how I had stashed it in the bureau drawer under my socks. I remembered the three times in my life I had taken acid—once at an Airplane concert in the city, once just before the New York State Regents exam in chemistry on which I had scored an eighty-five after hardly opening the book to study, a miracle of filling in the multiple choices mainly by pure chance even with this girl in the seat in front of mine cracking her gum like cherry bombs going off in my brain. Then the last time, with my brother Harry. Christmas week just before I came to Argentina and on his last leave before he was shipped off to Vietnam. I hadn't been in the city with Harry since the bad night months before and I didn't want to go with him. But he kept asking me, he had this plan for us, and he had been invited to play a guest set that night at the old Gaslight Café, a dark basement bar and coffee house that was a hip place—James Taylor used to play there, and Mimi Fariña, and Linda Ronstadt before she became famous. It was an exciting gig for Harry even though it was a cold, stormy week between Christmas and New Year's when the West Village seemed deserted except for a few random shoppers up on Eighth Street exchanging gifts.

Harry wore his uniform that made him look skinny and ridiculous. His little cheap metal rifle and oakleaf clusters flapped against his chest in rhythm to his long gangly strides with his guitar. He thought it would be a cool thing to perform in his uniform, talking on at me that he was going to play mostly sweet love songs then announce through the microphone that he was going off to Vietnam and this was his last night before shipping out unless some peace-loving chick out there in the audience wanted to strip off his forest greens and talk him into Canada.

We dropped purple double-domes on the Long Island Railroad. The city at night was a fragmentary, kaleido-

scopic world with all its different colors and speeding cabs
that seemed jet-powered, everything screaming past at su-
personic speed. At the Gaslight Café, Harry couldn't keep
from laughing into the microphone, an ear-to-ear acid grin
even while he was singing, and sometimes the words of
his songs just dropped off as he went through complicated
riffs on his guitar that astounded all four lonely, rain-
soaked souls in the place. But there was a lot of applause
from them, and they were warming up on Harry, joined
by a waitress who called herself Sweet Eve, a cook named
Space, a dishwasher named Jesús. Harry sang one of his
love songs to Eve in the second set. He tried hard to get
her to let him take her out afterwards but it didn't work,
she was busy that night. There was some pleasant chatting
with everybody, a contact high all around. Somebody gave
Harry a card that would get him in to see the manager of
Max's Kansas City for an audition when he got out of the
service. In all of this, Harry never once mentioned he was
on his way to Vietnam.

We walked along the icy sidewalk to the corner of West
Third Street and toward the subway, past The Four Winds
coffeehouse that was already closed, where Harry remembered he used to play and the great waitresses the place
used to have. He told me how he once gave a waitress there
a bunch of yellow roses and made love to her for three days.
The rain had turned to ice that had already formed a glis-
tening sheet over the walks, our boots slipping and sliding
as Harry led the way, taking each long stride with the intense concentration of a sport—*sunshine dancing*, he had
called this kind of tripping once, rings on his fingers, bells
on his toes, the sidewalks a gypsy crowd in full bazaar,
*sunshine* in the ancient idiom of these streets. But Harry
knew there wasn't any sun out now no matter how much he
wanted to show his kid brother a good time in the big city,
the street glaring electric colors from halflit signs, colors
softened by the icy rain that glittered with a light all its
own. Then the world was suddenly blurred and going at ten
feet per second as we took the ice-rink pavement on the
running slide, Harry up ahead, catlike, a skater, the only
sound his guitar case slapping his knee as he caught himself

up and took the first clear patch of sidewalk with a stumbling jump like a paratrooper landing on his feet while I was falling with a high giddy laughter and a face turned upward into the cold-assed rain of a cold-assed city night and of this one particular night when it felt like there were no more tomorrows. My head hit the pavement with flashes of light, vibrating concentric circles, dizziness. Harry picked me up off the sidewalk with alarm, ''Are you O.K.? Are you O.K.?''

He helped me across the Avenue of the Americas into an all-night place run by Greeks called The Cube Steak House, Harry making his lame old joke, ''Here it is, the good old Cube Steak House, food from *grease*,'' and then saying to me, ''Hey, man, are you sure you're O.K.?''

Nothing was O.K. anymore. How could it be possible to have faith in anything if what you needed most only left you out in the cold like that, stuck out in the rain trying to make the best of things? If the one thing that could put the rest right, that could fix it all up again, only led you on by false hopes to cheat you in the end? Harry was the cheated one, that was clear—one of his last free nights in the World spent pouring coffee down his brother and getting hassled by the white-aproned Greeks who didn't like our looks. Then I made it all worse when I started blubbering, clutching onto Harry's green Army sleeve, trying to get my arms around him and hang on. ''Please don't go, Harry. Don't let them make you. The old man can go fuck himself. Don't go, Harry, I don't want you to, man, please, you're my brother, my *brother*, man, so don't, don't, *don't* . . .'' and I got loud enough that the police were about to be called.

Harry stopped this freakout by holding up a coffee spoon. ''Look at this piece of shiny metal,'' he said. ''What do you say about it? What is it for?''

Suddenly I didn't know, no idea at all, my memory short-circuited and this shiny thing twisting around in Harry's fingers like a chrome-plated snake. Harry was a magician, and magic was happening—the spoon slowly lowered, writhing around in Harry's hand like it knew what was coming next as it plunged into a dazzling vortex of hot black coffee and for a long time, a long moment fixed between

time, the spoon rested there in a dark universe absent of
stars before it moved, around and around, Harry's voice
calming me along with the measured consistency of this
movement throwing off fractured rays of light, "It's just the
acid talking. Don't let the acid make you scared. You can
control it just like I'm controlling this spoon, just you and
me mellowing out now, do you feel it? Hey, man, can you
feel your teeth? You feel how tight they are? I mean like all
hopped up on the acid all the way to the roots?" He took
my fingers and put them up to my mouth for me, and I felt
my teeth. "Drink some coffee now, that's it. Dig on how
your teeth can feel the coffee going past. . . ."

We drank our coffee, then Harry piled us into a cab and
we wandered around Penn Station for a while, breaking into
silly giggles at all the things piled up in the shopwindows
left over from Christmas. We cupped our eyes to the glass
and Harry said, "This is all the stuff nobody wanted to buy.
Dig it, man, those Mitch Miller records, posters of The
Monkees and Herman's Hermits, all those ugly dolls and
cheap plastic doodads made in Hong Kong. I mean, *look* at
all this junk," he said and we laughed. We had a Nedicks
hotdog and an orange drink. Then Harry bought us packs
of cigarettes and cashed all his one dollar bills into change.
We spent the rest of the hours waiting for our train by handing out one quarter and one cigarette to all the winos and
bag people we could find, one each to scores of them passed
out around the station. Harry even opened up filthy sleeping
hands and closed the fingers around the quarters, and he
talked awhile with others just nodding off in the plastic
chairs of the Long Island Railroad waiting room. He pointed
out a homeless madman who was mumbling to himself and
whispered, "Look at that one, he's really wise, man, can
you see that? He'd be a guru anywhere else, the things he's
saying, man, it's like Latin, like some kind of religious
language, man, just *listen* to him."

We caught the 4:20 A.M. train. I was coming down from
the acid by then and feeling burned to a crisp. I slept a lot
and snuck around quietly through the big house and avoided
my family as best I could for almost two days until my brain
felt rewired enough for speech, chores, dealing with the old

man and the old lady. Harry was gone by then. The old man had planned for us all to take a ride in the station wagon with him to let him off at the airport and watch him get on a jet bound for his base and then Vietnam but Harry slipped out early in the morning, vanishing in his typical fashion, not even leaving us a note.

Mamá rang the bell at the table for Isabelita to bring in our dessert and coffee. I had been quiet a long time, and I knew how to remain so, how to keep myself back as my new family went through their easy ritual of the evening meal. Thinking of Harry's letter at that moment, I was afraid for him. What kind of a fool was Harry to start tripping over there? How could anyone handle that?

I leaned my head through Isabelita's little cubbyhole and checked the wall clock in the kitchen, then rose from the table and bent over a little to let Mamá make a dry pass at my cheek. I collected an armload of books and called out, "Until a little while" to everybody. Then I was out and down the stairs to where our building's *sereno* sat, our night doorman, smoking and reading his paper. The headline in the newspaper read that the CGT was asking for wage increases, and across from that was another headline with front-page commentary, *El Gobierno Responde En Voz Alta*, about the military regime's appeal to the CGT union for austerity, and its call for cooperation from the Peronist labor organizations to save the economy of the nation. Toward the bottom of the page, there was a photograph of two U.S. soldiers under fire, running away from a helicopter carrying a heavy case of something between them, one of the GIs with a hand on his helmet as if holding it on. That headline read, *Nueva Ofensiva En El Mekong*. I left my pile of books with the *sereno*, the old doorman hardly looking up from his paper and giving me just one slow nod in the direction of the shelf and coatrack behind him. I stashed my books and told the *sereno* not to bother about the door for me. I used my own keys to open the building's front gate of heavy iron bars and to let myself out onto the street.

Hernández-Marelli was already waiting in his polished white beetle of a Saab, the sports car he used when his father's limo wasn't appropriate or available. One long arm was hung out over the driver's side window, cigarette between his fingers, his attention fixed through the windshield to see what kind of short-skirt action he could catch coming out of the neighborhood cafés and pizza parlors under the bright quartz lighting of the avenue Santa Fe, which was like New York's upper Fifth Avenue without a park and with more of a shopping district feel. Marelli was looking for a chance to *dar piropos*, to shout out something to the girls like, "Hey, beautiful, you want to go for a ride?" and lame things like that, his game to say something that made the girls look at him. I climbed into the car, Marelli waiting there a moment with his attention fixed ahead at a pair of legs in a red miniskirt down the street. "*Che*, look at that one," he said by way of greeting. "If that isn't enough to make you die, I don't know what is." Then like a real asshole, Marelli leaned his head and shoulders out the window and started to gesture at the passing girl as if already clutching her to his chest. "You make me want to die!" he shouted. "I'm dying, *che*, please save me! You're killing me!" and so on. The girl finally looked once over her shoulder and smiled at Marelli on her way down the street. I'd never understand it. How could an asshole like Marelli be popular with girls?

Alejo suddenly leaned his head through my window. There was a look of betrayal in his eyes, and an anger that said that betrayal was no small thing between brothers. It was a look I knew well, and it made me feel worse when he said, "Since when do you have to study when you won't be in school for a month?"

"*Che*, Alejo, we've got to get going," Marelli said. "These particular girls we're seeing don't like to wait."

"I'm sorry, *che*," I said.

"You're a pair of *boludo* bullshitters," Alejo said.

"Look, we'd take you along," Marelli said. "But it's hard enough for this Yanqui on his own, is that clear? These girls will think your stick's so small that if it were bronzed they could wear it on a keychain."

"You're such a *boludo*, Marelli, you don't even know the buttons are out all over the city," Alejo said. "Don't you read the newspapers?"

"What do you mean the buttons are all over the city?" I asked.

"Let's go, *che*, nothing's happening," Marelli said. He turned the ignition key and started the car, giving the engine a few revs that made an angry sound. "Nothing's happening. Your brother's crazy."

"Listen, he wants to go with us," I said. "So let's just take him along."

"Take him? Alejo? Are you crazy?"

"This is the way it's going to be," Marelli said after Alejo had already scooted into the backseat. I noticed how he had dressed to go with us, in sneakers and an old sweater. He pushed a box full of spray paint cans aside on the backseat. "If El Yanqui scores with this particular girl, and if I score with mine, which is already history, then you take a taxi home, is that clear?"

"Why don't you stuff it up your ass," Alejo said.

"This kid is really impossible," Marelli said. "You see what you've done to us now, Yanqui? Do you see that?" Marelli gunned the sports car. The box of spray paint cans with those little plastic balls inside rattled as the car laid a patch straight through a red light at the corner of Junín. Marelli then hung a broad U-turn that stopped traffic across the whole avenue and we sped off in the direction of the university. "Now listen," Marelli said. "There's going to be two, I repeat, two available girls there tonight, Gloria and Cristina. Gloria's a blonde, *che*, very good-looking. But Cristina is more of a radical. There's more of a chance with Cristina," he said.

"O.K., Marelli, you can take Cristina," I said.

"No, *che*, Cristina's the one for you," Marelli said. "There's more of a chance with Cristina."

"Why me? Why the radical?"

"Maybe she'll want to pump you for evidence of capitalist injustice," Alejo said.

"Look, *che*, I think Gloria and I might have a little thing going, that's all," Marelli said. "So there's really only one available girl for you tonight, Yanqui, and that's Cristina."

"I told you he was a bullshitter," Alejo said.

"In time of war, you jump into the nearest foxhole," said Hernández-Marelli, which was meant to cheer me up.

We neared the neighborhood where some of the University of Buenos Aires was located, its various colleges spread out all over the city. The UBA had once been a famous institution of higher learning until a general named Onganía had had most of the faculty thrown out and replaced by drones who wouldn't cause trouble for his regime. As Marelli pulled onto the narrow avenue in front of the College of Philosophy and Letters, just down from the restaurant called El Escolar where we were supposed to meet, it was clear right away that something was wrong. The rancid smell of tear gas hung in the air and something else, an odor like strong woodsmoke, clouded around lines of blue-uniformed buttons, all of them wearing blue riot helmets, their nightsticks sheathed and hanging at their belts. Books were scattered everywhere up and down the stone steps of the building, a heap of them still in flames like a dying bonfire, charred pages drifting over the sidewalk like fallen leaves.

"The whore," Marelli said. "It looks like an intervention."

Alejo explained that the word *intervención* was used when the police or the army broke the sanctuary of the university, invading in battalion strength to arrest radical students at their meetings and dissident faculty in their classrooms. From what he could see, the buttons had also barred all the doors of the buildings and sent squads through the library with blacklists in their hands to take out books found to be offensive to the military government. Then the buttons had piled the books on the library steps, one of them had emptied a can of gasoline on them and had thrown in a match. "It looks like Philosophy and Letters is going to be closed a long time," Alejo said.

"Something serious has happened, that's clear," Marelli said. He pulled into a no-parking zone at the corner near El Escolar. Before Marelli could get out of the car, a dark-haired, worried-looking youth in the blue blazer and blue jeans that marked him as a university student moved very slowly out of the doorway of the restaurant, a button with a machine gun standing just inside the place, watching him.

"*Che*, Marelli!" the youth said too loudly, then he opened the back door of Marelli's car and jumped in, falling all over Alejo and the box full of paints. "Let's go, *che*! Let's go!" he said in an intense, low voice, then he reached out and slapped the back of Marelli's seat a few times. "Hurry up, *che*! Let's go!"

The attention of the button in the doorway fastened on us. He looked like he was about to step out onto the sidewalk and maybe stop Marelli's car; just one wave of the machine gun in our direction would have been enough. But Marelli hit the gas just in time, whipped the car around in the middle of the street, and we were racing uptown.

"What's happened, *che*?" Alejo asked.

"Those assholes in the National Student Front held a meeting, that's what happened. It's like they invited an intervention, because everybody knew the buttons would step in if they held a meeting that big. It's almost like they advertised, so many people knew about it. So look what they've done. We're all fouled up now, *che*, can't they see that? Now we'll all have to start meeting underground."

"*Che*, what about Gloria and Cristina?" asked Marelli.

"What?"

"The girls, *che*, the girls," Marelli said. "I thought this was a party tonight."

"How can you think about girls at a time like this?"

"He's a bullshitter and nobody trusts him," Alejo said.

"In time of war, you jump into the nearest foxhole," I said, trying to make a joke, but the dark-haired youth made a noise through his teeth that was clearly a sound of disgust. My joke wasn't funny, and Marelli was making things worse by laughing.

"You're really fucked up, Marelli," the student said.

"Ease up, *che*," Marelli said. "You don't even study at Philosophy and Letters."

"Just drive, Marelli," the youth said. "We're meeting at this place I know in the movie district, up on Corrientes."

"The buttons are all over the city tonight," Alejo said.

But as we passed Azcuenaga and moved further uptown from the university district, the number of buttons suddenly thinned out. In the space of a few blocks, the city seemed

normal for a Tuesday night, the streets inhabited by a few
lone souls on their journeys back to their apartments. The
car reached the avenue 9 de Julio, named after the date of
the first official Argentine constitution, two wide boulevards
at the city's heart with a broad, long plaza between them
like the Chicago Midway. At its center was the obelisk, an
imitation of the Washington Monument. Standing high over
the twin avenues, mounted to the façades and rooftops of
the buildings that lined both sides of this thoroughfare, was
a billboard light show that was like Glitter Gulch in Las
Vegas. What was once the largest Coca-Cola sign in the
world flashed its elaborate white-and-red design on and off,
filling the streets beneath with a weirdly ominous glow like
a huge arresting police light, *Coca-Cola . . . Coca-Cola
. . . Coca-Cola . . .* Standing next to it, incessant blue lights
spelled out T-O-R-I-N-O, one of the Argentine national au-
tomobiles that cost ten thousand U.S. dollars a crack in
those days of four-thousand-dollar cars. Nearby were the
signs F-O-R-D F-A-L-C-O-N, R-E-N-A-U-L-T, F-I-A-T, P-E-U-G-
E-O-T, all of them like the glittering billboards for a bur-
lesque. It never grew dark on stretches of the avenue 9 de
Julio, BANCO DE LONDRES, MERCEDES, TORO TÓNICA, CRUSH,
I-B-M, and even a billboard cigarette ad that took up the top
four stories of a building and blew white smoke rings against
the cloud-darkened night sky above the slogan, *Winston
tiene gusto como un cigarillo justo . . .*

There opened up ahead of us a more discreetly lit street
filled with movie houses that had luminous entryways and
elaborately gilded lobbies like the movie palaces of the '30s
and '40s. There were enough people milling around to be
called a crowd, the Argentine love for *trasnochando*, for
nightlife, evident even on a weeknight of a dictatorship. It
was like daytime along stretches of Corrientes until four in
the morning, and along neighboring Lavalle Street it was
possible to see sides of beef roasting in the restaurant windows and crowds of people out eating their ribsteaks long
after midnight. It was said that the beggars and street musicians in this district played their harmonicas and accordions and tambourines in day and night shifts, hanging out
near the subway entrances or up on more active corners near

wealthy Florida Street, which was like a shopping mall half the city long, closed off to all traffic but pedestrians.

The dark-haired student, who introduced himself only as "Andrés," pointed to one of the expensive bars up on Corrientes. Hernández-Marelli circled the block twice looking for a place to park but there were hundreds of tiny cars, Fiat 600s and Renaults and others, packed against the curbs and not a space along the street anywhere longer than about four feet. Marelli was frustrated, pausing at a red light and banging his open palm against the wheel, honking the little anaemic horn of his Saab for an old smoky blue *colectivo* bus that seemed to take five minutes just to get moving. "Son of a whore, I'll show them how to park," Marelli said. He gunned his Saab around the block like a pace car, leaving traffic sitting at the light and making us all hang on. "Like this," he said. "Just watch me."

Marelli found a gap in a line of parked cars and positioned the front bumper of our Saab against the rear end of this little red Fiat, then gave our car some gas. Our car slammed into the Fiat ahead of us, moving it forward about a foot, making it in turn slam into the back of the little car in front, and that one slamming another, and so on down the line. Then Marelli threw the Saab into reverse and did the same thing to the car behind him, banging away at it like a kind of expert game of bumper cars, and steadily, working away like that, he began making the little parking space larger as we all lurched forward with a crash, then backward, then forward again, all of us whiplashing around in our seats until Marelli had made the space big enough to park in. This was sometimes a common tactic of parking in Buenos Aires, and most drivers left their safety brakes off knowing this might happen, lest they return to their cars and find them crumpled like crushed tin cans. Half a block ahead of us a tiny white Fiat was pushed nose-first into the intersection of Maipú and Corrientes. Then we all piled out of the cramped sports car, following Andrés into a big saloon and restaurant called El Facundo.

El Facundo was large and barnlike, with wicker tables and rattan chairs stretching into the smoky distance like shocks of weird grain standing in a vast open field. Thick

hanging plants left most of the tables in shadows, most of
them deserted. A few white-aproned waiters sat drinking
coffee and waiting for the night to get busy. The group we
were meeting was seated at a long boothlike table in back,
four girls and six guys, and we made four more males. The
expression on Hernández-Marelli's face showed his disap-
pointment—the odds were worse than he had expected, that
was clear—but as he neared the table, his shoulders slouched
a little and his stride eased up and a big easy smile shone
on his suntanned face as he said, all playboy, "*Che*, Gloria!
What's happening! What's everybody drinking?"

Alejo and I grabbed chairs from a nearby table so we
could sort of squeeze in at one end. Marelli introduced us
around. "This is the really cool yanqui I've been telling
you about, *che*, he's really great, a good type guy. This kid
over here is his friend from the Colegio who wants to get
involved in the struggle." It was clear we had just interrupted an argument. Everyone nodded at us briefly, then
introduced himself, Cristina, Juan, Jorge, Alberto, María,
Simón, Guillermo, Gloria, María Inez and Javier, giving us
only their first names.

Andrés showed an immediate proprietary interest in María Inez, calling the waiter over to order her another beer.
The other girls looked attached mainly to their argument.
The one named Cristina continued heatedly, "You're telling
me to sit down right in the middle of the Plaza de Mayo?
You're going to get up there with a bullhorn in front of all
those workers who are going to be drunk and crazy in the
streets and tell them to sit down and wait to be arrested?
Do you think you're Mahatma Gandhi? What are you going
to do when the gas bombs go off and the police start shooting?"

"What shooting! What shooting!" the one named Jorge,
a tall thin youth with braces on his teeth, protested. "The
whole world is going to watch what we do. There's not
going to be any shooting! And they can't arrest everybody!
This time, I swear it, we're going to cause such a mess that
the government is going to fall!"

"*Boludo!* Idealist!" Cristina shouted.

"You're a coward! An idiot pessimist!" Jorge shouted back.

"Listen! Listen to me!" said Andrés with an authority in his voice that overrode the others. "Everything is coordinated this time. Only a few of the old gangsters who have split from the CGT are going to sit this one out, Vandor and his bunch of traitors, and even then most of their union members are going to be with us in the streets. With this kind of general strike, the military is going to give in once and for all and announce the free elections."

"That's a children's story," Cristina said. "When have the military ever given in for nothing?"

"*Che*, this comrade is getting impossible!" Jorge said.

"Look, if they don't give in this time, then they will the next, or the next, or the next, is that clear?" Andrés said. "The important thing is that this is the first phase of the serious struggle, like the leader Cooke said, *la lucha seria*." Andrés repeated this phrase and banged his fist on the table. "And we have to be nonviolent in this demonstration whether we like it or not, because right now is the time for building, not for going out and getting our heads broken."

"That's just what's going to happen to us," Cristina said.

"Does anybody want a whiskey? Who wants a whiskey, it's on me," Hernández-Marelli said but nobody paid any attention.

"Building the base, a firm political base, Cristina, that's all I'm saying," Jorge declared passionately across the table. "We all know that the lesson of *el Che* Guevara in Bolivia was that going to guns and bombs before you've built a firm base just gets you killed. The same thing with the poor Tupamaros, who without a political base mainly ended up robbing banks in Montevideo."

"What base? What are you talking about?" Cristina answered him. "With the Peronists from the gangster unions? With the poor shirtless ones in the slums who can't even read their ballots? Where are we going to build this base you're talking about?"

"The alliance now, Cristina, and social revolution later," Andrés said. "That's been the plan and that remains the plan. We struggle for free elections now, Perón becomes president again, then we work for social reforms within the party. We demonstrate, we paint walls, we stop business as usual all over the country until that happens.''

"Your social revolution isn't worth a fart to Perón,'' Cristina said. "Not unless we prepare ourselves for a real revolution.''

"Whiskey? Beer? Anyone want to join Gloria and me in a little whiskey?''

"You're all so petty bourgeois and stupid at this table that we're probably sitting here being recorded by the CIA,'' Cristina said, then she looked quickly at me down the table for the first time as if testing my response. Something passed across her features, the thought that she might be wrong, maybe, but it wasn't enough to let the question pass. "So prove to us you're not in the CIA,'' she said.

"I'm not working for the CIA,'' I said.

"He's too much of a yanqui *boludo* to be a spy,'' Alejo piped in. "I can swear to that because I live with him.''

"Your saying you're not in the CIA makes me think you're in the CIA,'' Cristina said.

"*Che*, Cristina, he's a good type guy,'' Marelli said.

"Let it alone, Marelli,'' I said. "What can I do to prove it to you?''

"You can't prove it to me, that's the point,'' Cristina said.

Everyone watched me to see what I would do. There was a long moment when I realized how hopeless the situation was—I didn't know beans about their politics and, worse, I didn't care. This girl Marelli had left available to me wasn't worth making me care, it was like thinking about romancing a spider. So I stood up from the table, suddenly all playboy like Marelli, all laidback from the futility of going on. I said to Marelli, "I'll wait for you outside ten minutes, then I'll take a taxi home.''

Alejo started to get up and leave with me but Marelli gave him a little shove and sat him down. Then I turned and pushed aside the dangling tendrils of ferns as I made my way out from behind the table. On the avenue Corrientes, the crowd seemed even cheerful tonight, chattering away and stepping into the pizza parlors and bars for a slice or

for little beef, chicken or ham pies called *empanadas*. Didn't
they know what was going on? Even the lone police officer
down the street seemed subdued, quietly smoking while
leaning against a streetlight pole as if he planned to stand
that way until he earned his pension. Which version of
events was true? The one I could see on the street here or
the one they were all talking about in the bar? I was tired.
My shoulders ached from carrying cement blocks. I thought
of working out in the misery village the next day, of how I
would feel getting up at six in the morning to meet Father
Vargas' crew at six-thirty and of how many more days I had
to go to work out my sentence. I decided I wasn't going to
wait any longer even for Alejo and I began to search the
traffic for a taxi.

"*Che!*" Hernández-Marelli called out, catching up to me
as I was ready to climb into a cab. "Wait a minute, *che*!
That was a really cool thing you did. They just voted you're
not in the CIA and I'm supposed to bring you back in. Even
Cristina voted with you, Yanqui! It's like I told you, *che*.
You're going to have that girl's tits in your hands any minute, my stick's getting hard just thinking about it!"

"She's as ugly as a fetus, Marelli. Tell Alejo I went on
home."

"*Che*, Yanqui, don't mess up my thing with Gloria."

"So go with Gloria then! What does it have to do with
me?"

"Wherever Cristina goes, Gloria goes, *che*. Just one
whiskey, that's all I ask," Marelli said, and by that time,
he had an arm strongly around my shoulders and was already steering me back through the doorway of El Facundo.
"Alejo's having a good time, too. Alejo's getting along fa-
mously with everybody."

Alejo was listening to Andrés, María Inez and Cristina,
huddled with them at their end of the table. Andrés was
lecturing him, "It's a clear injustice the way those people
are living in the misery village where you're working. You
can see how Perón, as fouled up as he was, was the only
one to try and do something about it, at least to start building houses out there. With the military regime all we get
are new officers' clubs all over San Isidro."

"That's clear," Alejo said. "It's true. I've seen all the new military country clubs under construction."

"Perón is going to bring back his original program for social justice," Andrés said. "The Quinquinales plans that promised a total reform of this shitty system. And he's going to let the youth of his party work for our socialist ideals. That was the bargain he made with us when we started the serious struggle to get him reelected. We're the future of his party. And the old man knows he can't keep us down for long if he doesn't keep his promise."

"The power of Perón is the only way we can get free elections again," María Inez said. "Free elections is the first step."

"My family's for free elections but not for Perón," Alejo said. "My father tells stories of all the arrests and tortures under the last Perón government, and of how the economy all turned to shit. Perón even had some of the priests from our Colegio hauled off to the prisons."

"It was like a civil war back then," Andrés said. "Both sides were fighting dirty, everyone knows that. But now it's different. Perón has the workers, and the workers are sick of the military and want social justice. Perón has the intellectuals, because they want a chance to teach in their universities again and to do their work without censorship. And Perón has us, the students, because he's the only chance we've got right now to change this shitty system."

"It's like the song says," said Gloria. *"All we want is a nation with peace and justice."*

"Don't listen to these idealists," Cristina said. "Perón is so old and senile he mixes up the words to his speeches. And Andrés has left out something else Perón has, and it's something we should all think about. Perón has more friends in the army right now than the army has friends."

"For now, there's no other choice," Andrés said.

"Here's to a nation with peace and justice," Marelli said, moving one arm over Gloria's shoulders as he raised his whiskey with the other. We all toasted, to peace and justice, then there was some loose chattering, Andrés taking down our telephone numbers and asking us to think about joining in a street demonstration that was due to happen any day. I started to explain to María Inez about being an exchange student and that kind of thing, finding her the nicest girl at the table, already taken, of course, but it was easier to talk to her somehow because of that. Then Andrés looked at his watch and said it was time for us to go. Go where, I thought, where were we going now?

Out on the street, Hernández-Marelli looked up and down the block for a moment, Gloria standing behind him all too obviously keeping a lookout with hands working nervously at the clasp of her purse. Marelli pulled a screwdriver out of the back pocket of his jeans, leaned down to the Fiat parked in front of our little Saab and quickly took off the license plate. Marelli moved around to the back of his Saab, removed the screws, and bolted the stolen license plate over his own. Cristina was behind me, in the doorway of El Facundo, discussing further arrangements with Andrés when Marelli shouted, "*Che*, Cristina! Come on and ride with us!"

Marelli bunched up his fingers into an Italian gesture that meant *don't bust my balls* and Alejo took his hint, asking if he could ride with Andrés and Guillermo and María Inez. Cristina hurried across the sidewalk as Gloria was hopping into the front seat beside Marelli. I tried to hold the door open for her. "Let's go! Let's go!" she said with irritation, her hands formed into little scoops as if to shovel me in first, an awkward moment. Then she understood what I was doing, holding a door open for her, and she gave me a bored little look and scooted in. There was a problem with the box of spray paints. It was too big to fit on the floor of the Saab, too big for the shelf under the back window, and as I shut the door, Cristina was passing the box to me and somehow we ended up crushing it between us on the seat. I was trying to get the box out of the way so we could be more comfortable when Marelli took off like a drag racer to beat Andrés' and Jorge's cars to the intersection. Paint cans flew up and landed all over the car. Cristina and I spent the ride feeling around for them over the rubber floormats and under the seats as we circled down to the boulevard called El Bajo along the river, all three cars in tandem, Hernández-Marelli in the lead and waving the others on at every turn out his window, having himself a real boss time jumping in and out of traffic and going way over the speed limit. The three cars stuck together bumper to bumper in a dangerous kind of driving samba at high speed, dancing to the erratic rhythms of Marelli's foot on the gas.

The cars broke out of the center of the city like a jet formation, down and into the beginnings of Palermo and its huge system of parks called 3 de Febrero. Then Marelli slowed down suddenly to a normal rate of speed and made an easy turn past the College of Law, a huge building like the Parthenon, its columns and heavy doors standing like a monument at the top of a steep flight of concrete steps.

Marelli had managed to get his arm all the way around Gloria, pulling her close against him as he drove one-handed and felt for her tits with the other. Cristina and I were hunched up uncomfortably, the box crushed between us. On one of Marelli's wild turns, she lurched into me and I helped to lift her back upright by the shoulders, sort of leaning into her sideways and feeling the warmth of her black sweater under my hands and a little of the light weight of her body. She had a strong body, that much could be said, a long nose and big full lips, dark hair like a mussed but attractive fringe over a sharp face that was screwed up in anger as she said, "You idiot, Marelli!" Her hand came up and even grabbed onto my arm and squeezed it as the car slowed down. Then it was as if she felt me touching her in a different way, or she remembered how long my hands had stayed on her shoulders. She looked at me a little surprised and said quickly, "Here, take these, Yanqui," pulling away from me and handing me two aerosol cans. That was O.K. with me. We were in this together, at least, and I had the feeling there might be possibilities with this girl after all. "*Boludo!* Marelli!" she snapped. "You've just lost Jorge at the light!"

Marelli swung our happy little car into the half-circle driveway in front of the College of Law. "There's the button," Marelli whispered. A lone police officer in a blue uniform and with a walkie-talkie in his hand paced past a little phone booth of a guard station at the other end of the long driveway.

"Let's not sit here too long!" Cristina hissed.

"Why only one of them?" Gloria asked. "You sure there aren't more buttons?"

"No," Marelli said after a moment, "it's just him. Let's go," he said and backed down the street a little ways until we could turn around. We rendezvoused with Andrés and Jorge on the corner, all three drivers leaning out their windows in a three-car conference. "There's just one, *che*, so it's going to be easy," Marelli said.

Two of the others piled out of Jorge's car and into Andrés', which made a crowd of eight in his car, leaving only Jorge and María in the front seat of his looking like a nice little couple coming home from a dinner and the movies. Our car and Andrés' waited back on the corner under the shadows of the park's trees as Jorge drove his car along the boulevard just past the little guard booth in front of the College of Law. They stopped far enough past the guard to be out of sight, about a hundred meters or so, but still out in the open. Jorge turned out his headlights and pulled over, cutting his engine. He got out of the car and threw open the hood, then he reached in to twist the wires together to set off his horn.

María Inez hopped out of Andrés' car and ran ahead a little ways to watch what the police officer did. She ran back with a grin, waved her arms at us and hopped back into Andrés' car—meaning the officer had fallen for the decoy; hopefully he was on his way to stick his head under Jorge's hood. We sped up into the circling driveway in front of the College of Law. Our car doors swung open before we had even stopped as we pulled up in front of the main entrances of the building, lights off, engines running.

"Let's go! Hurry up!" Cristina whispered at us and she was out of the car on the fly with the box of paints and running up the steps with Gloria following.

"Come on!" said Marelli, springing out of the car to catch up to Gloria.

I was slower, behind all the others. Cristina was at the head of the steps, tossing spray cans to everyone and assigning us a letter. Andrés had already sprinted over to one side of the building and was making the upside down exclamation point used at the beginning of emphatic phrases in

Spanish. Guillermo beside him was starting a Q. Cristina said to Marelli, "Show this Yanqui and the kid what to do!" She gave Marelli three cans of paint. "U and R and A!" she hissed.

Marelli passed cans to Alejo and me with an excited grin, shaking his own with a rattling sound that seemed to me way too loud. "You paint the A!" Alejo said. "Let's go, Dieguito!"

"What are we painting?" I asked.

"Let's go! Just do it!" said Hernández-Marelli, and I moved in beside him, not able to make out the letters painted further down the line. All of us were moving our arms around like part of one big painting machine, making red letters as big as our bodies. "Like this!" Marelli said. "As big as you can, is that clear?"

I sprayed my tall, two-legged letter onto the empty stone wall just down from the last big door of the building. Both diagonal lines came first, as broad as both my hands, then the cross, the only sound that of our paint cans hissing. "Is this O.K.?" I asked.

"Hurry up!" whispered Alejo.

Andrés was suddenly on the other side of me, out of breath and working on an exclamation point, the last symbol to be painted. Then somebody shouted, "Son of a whore, it's the police! The police! The police!"

Spray cans hit the cement and rattled down the steps. Everyone jumped, stumbled, bolted for the cars with a shout as a black-and-blue Ford Falcon with flashing blue lights and the shrieking of an electronic siren turned into the driveway of the College of Law. I was the first to reach Marelli's Saab and dove into the backseat, Alejo falling in behind me. But where was Marelli? "Marelli?" I shouted.

Marelli was back up on the steps somewhere hanging onto Gloria's arm, even in these circumstances trying to argue with her to ride with him, which he did by dragging her along in panic until she gave in. It was crazy, and in the confusion, Cristina was down by Andrés' car looking around for Gloria. Then suddenly the police car was right up on them and everyone was blinded by lights.

Andrés car took off, leaving Cristina behind. She jumped

one long stride toward it and grabbed hold of the door but
too late. On the other side, somebody was diving into
Andrés' car through an open window, legs kicking out of
the window as it took off. Cristina reacted in an instant.
She turned on her heel and sprinted along the steps to the
end of the building, where she hopped a wall and disappeared into the darkness.

Hernández-Marelli jumped into the front seat from the
wrong side, precious seconds lost getting over the obstacles
of the gearshift and bucket seats so he could pull Gloria in
behind him. What saved us was that the engine was still
running. All Marelli had to do was shove the car in gear
and hit the gas, which he did before he had landed in his
seat. Marelli was laughing all this time, a high, crazy laughter that was a sound of panic. The police were only about
five feet behind us and already piling out of their car with
guns drawn. Our faces were lit like with strobes by the blue
flashing lights in which it was suddenly clear to me we were
all going to die. Then we were thrown back into our seats
as Marelli whipped the car out onto the boulevard. Through
the windshield, about three blocks ahead, we could make
out Jorge's car speeding away, its hood unlatched and flap-
ping up to blind him. We passed the open ground where the
first lone police guard stood with his pistol drawn, and talking on his radio. It was just a flash as we sped past him but
I saw the officer raise his pistol and point it after us and
then I was suddenly tasting the rubber mats and hugging
the floor of the Saab, covering my head with my arms,
somehow that was the most important thing. Being shot at
was like a new dimension—time slowed in an instant, an
eternity in a racing heart. All solid objects between me and
the bullet became the data of instinct, the information instantly passed across synapses doused with adrenaline, my
body moving as if involuntarily behind these objects. In this
case, I was low down on the floor trying to squirrel myself
under the backseat but what help could that be? The engine
on that model Saab was mounted in front, leaving only two
thin pieces of sheet metal—the trunk lid and the metal cowl-
ing behind the backseat—to protect me, the rest just loose
stuffing woven across the pitiful vacuums of wire upholstery

springs, no match at all for bullets. A crazy kind of panic took over as I heard the shots and I helplessly covered my head with the soft thin flesh of my arms and their bones made of glass as far as any bullet was concerned. I stayed all covered up like this with my mouth pressed and muffled against the bitter-tasting rubber floormats of Marelli's car. Alejo was on top of me, his instincts slower than mine, but managing somehow to get parts of my body between his and the bullets as he was shouting, "Watch out! Watch out! He's shooting at us! Son of a whore, he's shooting!"

Marelli knew all the streets in Palermo. Sometimes, he cut school and just raced around in one of his family's cars pretending he was in the lead at Monte Carlo. He was also a great driver. The police Falcon was only about two car lengths behind us, both cars swerving across the broad lanes of the boulevard and blindly running all kinds of lights, the siren's screaming getting louder as they gained on us. Then Marelli lost them with a high-speed maneuver. He used to go out on unfinished sections of the Pan American Highway to practice it late at night. He reached down and pulled the handle of the emergency brake as he simultaneously hit the clutch and brake pedals and threw the steering wheel all the way to the left. The car lifted off the pavement for an instant as it spun around on two wheels in a complete 180-degree turn, the trick being not to let the car stall out, to downshift right in the middle of this crazy, dangerous high-speed U-turn that raised a thick cloud of smoke all around us from burning tires. The blue-and-black police car flew by us in the middle of this turn. Its driver hit the brakes but stalled out as the police car skidded broadside about eighty or ninety meters in the wrong direction behind us. Before they could start up their engine and make a quick two-point turn, Marelli was already three blocks ahead, racing back in the direction from which we had come and against traffic on the boulevard. We were suddenly passing the College of Law again and Marelli shouted in excitement, "Look, *che*! Look at that!" He was laughing once more in that insane, panicky way. "It's pretty, no?"

I raised my head just enough to catch the high red letters

painted across the front of the building in the shadows behind its columns:

¡QUESEMUERALADICTADURA!

It flashed by in an instant as Marelli turned off the boulevard and headed up the hill onto a sidestreet somewhere in the neighborhood of La Recoleta. Marelli was all playboy again, relaxed enough at the wheel to pull little Gloria up from her side of the car's floor. Marelli whipped across a street, up a hill again, around a block, and across the imaginary line that divided La Recoleta from El Barrio Norte, then he continued on deeper into the narrow streets of the city, nice dark empty streets I didn't remember existed.

"Did you see that?" Alejo kept saying. "Son of a whore, they were shooting real bullets. Did you see that?"

Marelli pulled into a parking place and jumped out quickly to take off his stolen license plate and leave it lying in the gutter. We all shared one of Gloria's cigarettes as he did this, since the few in my own pack had broken into pieces in my shirt pocket. "Is that what you paint on walls?" I asked Gloria. " 'Death to the dictatorship'?"

"Sometimes it's something else," she said. "Like if we're advertising a demonstration, we'll paint just the date and a slogan. Or if there's only a few of us, maybe we'll paint just 'Perón.' Or maybe 'Peace and Justice,' or whatever Andrés tells us to paint. I don't know, I'm really not that political."

"You're not political?" I asked.

"A few walls, a few demonstrations, nothing serious."

"You don't call back there serious?"

"They were shooting at us, che," Alejo said. "Since when do the sons of a whore buttons shoot at students out painting walls?"

"I don't know," Gloria said. "It's never happened to me before."

"Didn't you hear them shooting at us, che?" Alejo asked, more as if he couldn't believe it than as a real question.

"It's getting too risky, that's clear," Gloria said. "And

they say if you're caught painting walls now they can get you thrown out of the university."

"That was real shooting back there," Alejo said. "Do you know what that means? Those were real bullets!"

Marelli climbed back into the car and turned to us with a self-satisfied expression after doing his little job. His eyes were lively, his speech coming out of the side of his mouth in the cool, macho way Carlitos Gardel used to sing tangos. "*Che*, Yanqui, what time do they pick you and the kid here up to go work in the misery village?"

As if he didn't know, I thought, but I didn't say anything. Marelli's eyes were filled with the possibilities of the rest of his night and it was clear they didn't include anybody but Gloria. But first, Gloria wanted to cruise around and look for Cristina. Hernández-Marelli protested that it wasn't worth our taking the chance. He finally gave in, and we cruised around through the dark labyrinth of the 3 de Febrero parks, in around the College of Law, then past the statues of Alvear, Mitre and Urquiza, on further by the huge bunkerlike U.S. embassy, all of us searching out the car windows into the shadows of the parks for signs of Cristina. "Let's go, *che*," Marelli finally said. "She's probably home right now sitting in her big bathtub. Besides, El Yanqui and his brother here have to get up early in the morning, don't you, *che*?"

"Too early, *che*," I said. "What a barbarous hassle."

Alejo gave me a look that confirmed again what a bullshitter Marelli was as Marelli started to explain to Gloria in his slow cool playboy voice about this school the priests were building in the slums that had once been planned by the Peronists, wasn't that a kick? And how the church jumped in years later like it was trying to finish Perón's work? In his explanation, Marelli left out any reference to himself, as if a guy like him had too much pull and too much money for something like actually working, even on a charity project, as if he'd just as soon give a big donation every month. We were cruising into El Barrio Norte toward home through quiet, sleeping streets. I wondered how I had ever gotten involved in such craziness, thinking of Alejo's real bullets and how lucky we all were to be alive.

Marelli let us off. He leaned out his window and offered his left hand limply, foppishly for me to shake. "Ciao, Yanqui," he said. "Wait until you hear from one of our friends." There was mischief in his voice, and in the smug way he was treating Alejo and me like we were all spies who had just completed a dangerous mission—the microfilm was safe in friendly hands and now it was time for James Bond Marelli to take off with his little girlfriend, that was clear. We watched them drive away, Marelli pulling Gloria closer to him as she tilted down his rearview mirror and looked at herself in it, shaking out her hair.

"Look at this paint all over me," Alejo said. I noticed for the first time all the smears of red on his pants, his hands, his face. "What am I going to do?"

"Where did you say you were going tonight?"

"Over to a friend's to study, the same as you," he said.

"Say you were painting something with him, a science project or something like that, or a map of Russia," I said.

"We don't have science projects at the Colegio, and we don't paint big maps."

"Then say it was a piece of furniture, a chair or a table, I don't know," I said. "Say you were painting something."

"Maybe I should just tell them the truth," Alejo said.

The *sereno* of our building was asleep behind his little mail table, chin on his chest, arms hanging limply at his sides. Alejo snuck around him quietly and got our books. Slowly, both of us tired and talking in whispers, we climbed the stairs and let ourselves into the apartment. Papá was still out, and Mamá and the others were sleeping. Alejo took this as a sign that he could fix things by throwing his paint-stained clothes down the old incinerator, Mamá would never know they were missing. He looked for a can of acetone and an old rag in the utility closet for his hands and face. We said goodnight as he was heading into the bathroom. The paint remover caused red blotches that he would have to explain to Mamá the next day was a heat rash from playing *fútbol*.

As I was pulling the change, keys and wads of colorful pesos out of my pants pockets that night getting ready for bed, I felt it sharply in my hand. I held it up and considered its frosty gray reflections of light, and it made me feel lucky. I was alive, safe, climbing into my bed a changed person, swearing I would never again in my life do anything more dangerous than take the airplane home. And all through the next day, as I was working sleepily alongside Alejo, José, El Flaco Peluffo, El Gordo Rojo, Father Vargas and the others, everybody out there but Hernández-Marelli, who had somehow managed to get his old mother to hand-deliver to Father Vargas an excuse that he had come down with a sudden incapacitating flu, I kept reaching into my pocket from time to time, as if to make sure my new charm was still there, my new good luck from my brother Harry. I could feel it sharply in my pocket against my thigh, something better than a rabbit's foot, better than any medal of St. Christopher, a charm that was like an odd and feather-light little coin, the kind of luck that crossed oceans.

# 4

## State of Siege

Alejo put in another week working in the misery village then went back to school, and I missed him, his easy good humor in the mornings, the way he could put Hernández-Marelli in his place. I labored another few days with Father Vargas' crew, the mornings and evenings growing steadily darker with the coming of winter. Then just as I was beginning to see an end to my sentence, all work stopped on the school in Villa Hendaya.

Work stopped all over the country. Not a factory or a shop was open, save for maybe a kiosk or two on the street corners for necessary cigarettes and newspapers. Many of the newspapers began to be seized by the police even before they were unbundled, or their editorial offices were suddenly shut down to keep news from getting out about the crisis that was developing in the North. In the streets of Buenos Aires, armored cars and trucks, full of federal police and khaki-uniformed soldiers, suddenly appeared by the hundreds. Rumor had it that tens of thousands of steel and industrial workers in the North had walked out on their jobs in defiance of the military regime's demands. Joining them were many thousands of students—workers and students striking together—and an angry mob of these workers and students took over a large sector of the industrial city of Córdoba. They turned over buses in the streets to make barricades. They tossed Molotov cocktails that landed in happy little splashes of flames. They took potshots at the police and set the turned-over vehicles on fire to block the certain approach of tanks and soldiers. A news blackout was imposed. Special radio-jamming devices were rumored to have been flown in all the way from a CIA base in Panama and set up around the city so even ham radio messages were impossible to receive.

Despite the news blackout, within hours the Northern uprising was joined by as many as a hundred banned trade unions and political parties around the country. The political life of Argentina was made up of at least twice this many factions, no one group of them seeming able to make up a majority. Argentina in those days was like a hundred armed Mafias, in the familial rather than the criminal sense, all fighting for political power, and when they weren't allied and struggling against the military regime, they quickly took to attacking each other. During the Córdoba insurrections, alliances were struck once again, and some of these factions became involved in an uprising that resorted to bombs and machine guns. Trotskyist E.R.P. guerrillas attacked military bases in the interior and blew up public buildings in a half-dozen cities. What was left of the Guevarist Tacuara guerrillas in the poverty-stricken sugarcane province of Tucumán, thought to have been wiped out to a man scarcely two years before, suddenly showed their faces again in skirmishes with police. In Buenos Aires, the Peronist urban guerrillas who called themselves Montoneros, named after a renegade band of gauchos on horseback that had roamed the *pampas* almost a century before, were arming themselves for the first time and helping to organize mass demonstrations across the country. In all of this, it seemed that every political group, every armed trade union action wing, every student committee had a separate goal for the nation, mainly its own vision of prosperity and power.

What later became clear and confirmed by historians was that Perón himself was directing most of these actions from his exile in Spain. It was by Perón's personal command that the uprising in Córdoba almost became a revolution. It was Perón who ordered a change in tactics for his supporters in Argentina to those of violent confrontation, orders that he sent secretly from his exile by means of dozens of personal messengers. These orders to begin strikes and violence were eagerly received by many workers in the Argentine labor movement who simply wanted twenty or so more dollars a month in wages; that much might have satisfied many of them. But Perón and his lieutenants wanted much more—the dictator's return and nothing less. In those days, Perón was still widely referred to by the common worker as the Chief, the Leader, the *Caudillo*—the one charismatic demagogue of the nation. And the violent demonstrations that Perón personally ordered were just beginning. It soon became clear that strikes, demonstrations and indiscriminate terrorism would continue without end until most Argentines got what they thought they most wanted—Perón himself returning home to save them.

Over the city of Córdoba in the North, the military government unleashed its paratroopers, thousands of them dropping from wave after wave of circling airplanes, parachutes opening like exotic green blooms in the cloudy, wintery skies over Córdoba, the Pittsburgh of Argentina. An armored division was brought up. Very little was known about this military response in Buenos Aires but there was an emergent sense that something had to change. The people were reaching their limits and the nation deserved better than what it was getting; its workers merited higher salaries for one thing, and its students wanted to meet freely at the universities without the threat of soldiers or of the police closing in on them and tossing them into jail, or worse, merely for discussing in open assembly the ideas of free speech, fair wages and democratic elections.

From the back rooms of labor union and student safe houses in Buenos Aires, hundreds of printing presses from each of the disparate factional groups began to spill out leaflets, position papers, posters that were stapled to walls and telephone poles, taped to the seats of the *colectivo* buses all over the city, calling for a national general strike in sympathy with the workers of the North. The newspaper *El Clarín* was shut down for its Peronist sympathies, a company of secret police breaking into its editorial offices with guns drawn and pulling all copies of the day's edition off the shelves, suspending its publication for weeks to come. The same thing happened to the weekly newsmagazine *Primera Plana*, a kind of *Time* magazine of Argentina. But the news of the national strike still got out; the voices of so many labor and student groups couldn't be silenced, not as long as the exiled dictator Juan Domingo Perón himself could not be silenced—an old and partly senile man with a penchant for marrying chorus girls and gripping fast to his last chance to regain the power he had lost a decade and a half before. Hundreds of thousands of workers and students took to the streets all over Argentina, either directly or indirectly for the cause of Perón. Others in these demonstrations also contributed to the cause, those like Hernández-Marelli, for example, who acted as if the whole thing was happening for the really boss time of it all. It was one way to let out all the stops and to show his love for his country, in defiance of the lousy military, by taking to the streets, especially if there were a few special girls involved, *che*, university girls with little apartments where it was possible to hide out afterwards and hope for the government to fall, yet one more of the many violent falls everyone could remember since he was born.

No accurate count of casualties from these uprisings was ever possible, no firm data even by which to guess how many souls were shot down in the streets or lined up against walls, stripped of all identification and simply made to vanish off the face of the earth. Little would be mentioned in the history books of the next decades because the confusion was so great amid the chaos of so many political factions like a hundred sled dogs pulling in different directions at their harness, snapping their jaws at each other by its end.

In the city of Córdoba, from rooftops, behind walls, from the high windows of buildings, the military regime was using what were called *francotiradores*—snipers who struck terror in the general population by shooting at anyone or anything that moved through the streets, a kind of terrorist named after General Francisco Franco of Spain, the man who had invented this tactic during the Spanish Civil War. *Francotiradores* were soldiers or secret police dressed in civilian clothes and armed with high-powered rifles, murderers from a distance. No one in the streets was safe from them, and it was an effective tactic to scatter crowds during demonstrations, for example, or to prevent even three or four people from assembling in a park for days afterward. Anyone with any sense at all locked himself in his apartment and stayed off the streets because of these snipers who fired once or twice from a particular location then moved, active especially at night in cities under siege, unseen murderers who snuck around the burning buildings and through the barricaded streets filled with smoke and tear gas. The scattered corpses they left behind have since been largely forgotten, unheralded, a mere footnote in a much stormier and more chaotic history to come.

Few people in Buenos Aires knew exactly what was happening at the time. But often each man's outrage at his own perception of the injustice done to him, his own condition as he saw it and not only as it was told to him by any union or political party, was enough to move him to take to the streets. So he joined his brothers in a mob that grew to tens of thousands strong. They gathered in the center of the city like a soccer crowd on a championship Sunday but twice as wild, with flags and banners, with clouds of leaflets and gaily colored streamers tossed up into the winds as they joined in the uproar of chanting voices, *Death to the dictatorship! Death to injustice! Long live Perón!* As the mobs grew in force and numbers throughout the first day of national strikes, groups of workers and students running through the streets playing catch as catch can with police, there was one most consistent outcry, a two-toned chant that echoed through the deep canyons made by the buildings high around them and along the broad avenues at the city's heart, a sound that rose up like a single breathy voice on the river breezes and with the volume only achieved by so many thousands of voices crying out all at once, making a storming wind of the single chanted word, *Pe-rón! Pe-rón! Pe-rón! Pe-rón! Pe-rón! Pe-rón!* . . .

* * *

At the home of the Beneventos, the French windows stayed shuttered and locked with all of us inside. Papá spent much of the morning in his study listening to the radio and rattling the pages of the few newspapers Isabelita had been able to find in the streets and buy for him. By mid-morning the military government had declared a state of siege throughout the nation—all constitutional rights were suspended, and the whole country was now living under martial law. Every five minutes on the radio and television, the regime was calling for an end to the strikes and a return to order. But the shops, factories and businesses stayed closed and crowds began to gather uptown.

Papá made phone calls from his study, changing appointments, putting off currency transfers, doing what most of Argentina did during one of its frequent general strikes—trying to conduct what business he could over the phone, hoping for a cooling down of the situation before the losses grew any worse. The telephone was essential for this. During the best of times, Intel Argentina's service frequently broke down. But it was characteristic of the military that the phone exchanges were guarded as closely as the national vaults, and during the strikes most of the lines were kept open. Papá did what business he could from his study, today in the peculiar absence of his music. The day seemed even more like an emergency not to hear Papá's records playing, in their place the sound of news-radio static with frequent reports on conditions in the city and in the interior—the official government version of events from which Papá could interpret the true situation, the one the people are never told about but that finally drifts to them in bits and pieces, even if it takes years.

What was soon clear was that the military had been set loose on tens of thousands of workers in the North, and the police and army were out in full riot gear all over Buenos Aires. Knowing this took something out of Papá. It took away some of his optimism for the future of his nation, and of his children, and he was soon in a fury over the stupidity of it all—one of the richest countries in the entire hemisphere once again going down the tubes because of its internal squabbling, its quick replacement of good sense by violence and its childish lack of political discipline. Couldn't people see what was happening? Couldn't they see the many gifts now torn from their hands because of *el caudillismo*, the demagoguery of these Peronist mafiosi, armies and naïve student gangs that had turned once again to living outside any laws?

"If their beloved Perón ever does get back into power, he'll have the leaders of every underground army he ever inspired taken out and shot," Papá said at our noon meal. "Then he'll throw the rest of them into exile or into the prisons. And why don't they know that? How can they be so stupid? Don't they see that that son of a whore Perón will only give them the very same forms of oppression they think they're fighting?"

"Please, Martín, we're at the table," Mamá said.

"This is important, and they should know it," Papá said. "And I want to be sure that our Diego here knows that most of Argentina is not out in the streets. Most of us are huddled like this around our cold-plate lunches hoping that the state of siege can put a stop to this fucked-up nonsense before it's too late."

"So now you're betting your chips with the military?" Mamá said. "Workers don't have the right to strike? Newspapers shouldn't print the news?"

"What I'm saying is that the Peronists are serving up a bigger mountain of shit right now than the military, isn't that clear?"

"Please, Martín," Mamá said.

"All the *fútbol* games are canceled until the end of next week, *che*, what a hassle," Miguelito said.

"If you thought about school as much as your *fútbol* teams, maybe you'd pass the sixth grade," Mamá said.

"The boy and I have already settled this," Papá said.

"I'm just glad I'm not out there lifting bricks for Father Vargas today," I said.

"That's stupid," said Martín Segundo. "You've only got six more days to go and you're back in school."

"So what idiot would want to be back in school?" Alejo piped in. Then he turned to Miguelito and said, "*Che*, look at the positive side. Maybe this strike will go on another week and they'll have to cancel the make-up exams until after vacation.''

''You think so?'' Miguelito asked brightly.

''You're going to study until your ass is flat whether they do or don't cancel them,'' Papá said. ''That's what I want all of you to do. No television, no music, just books opened on your desks until I tell you to close them. Nobody goes out of the house but Isabelita or me, is that clear?''

''*Sí*, Papá.''

''*Sí*, Papá.''

''*Sí*, Papá.''

''But Papá, I always watch *The Three Stooges*,'' Miguelito said. ''Can't I just watch that one program? *The Three Stooges* can't hurt anything.''

''For a half hour and that's it,'' Papá said. ''You tell me when you're turning it on and when you turn it off.''

''*Gracias, Papito.*''

''Listen, Papá, I really had planned to go over to El Gordo Rojo's to study,'' said Martín Segundo. ''El Gordo's brother is supposed to tutor us in math, *che*, Papá, and trigonometry is a real hassle without El Gordo's brother to go over all the theorems.''

''It's a state of siege outside!'' Mamá said.

''But Mamá, nothing's happening in this neighborhood. It's all uptown! And El Gordo only lives three blocks away!''

''A lot can happen in three blocks,'' Alejo said, crunching away on a heel of French bread. Martín Segundo gave him a look that implied the consequences of another word. Alejo quietly reached across the table for more bread.

''Listen, Martín,'' I said. ''Maybe it would be a good idea if I could tag along with you to El Gordo's.''

''Nobody's leaving this house, is that clear!'' Papá shouted loudly enough to make Isabelita jump as she cleared our plates off the table. She served us a small hunk of cheese and a few pieces of old fruit for dessert.

''But Papá,'' said Martín Segundo. ''Without El Gordo's brother to help me with this exam, I might as well head for the sidelines right now!''

''I could use some help with math, too,'' Alejo said.

"Martín," Mamá said suddenly, smoothly, a diplomat's tone of voice she sometimes used to settle commotions in her house. "It really would be safer if three of them went than one alone. And it is just down the street."

"Don't I have a voice in this house anymore? Doesn't anybody hear what I'm saying?"

"Yes, Martín, we're listening," Mamá said.

"Very well then." Papá let loose a frustrated breath like letting air pressure out through an uptight valve. "You can go to El Gordo Rojo's but no farther. You are to telephone as soon as you get there. And you are to leave for home well before six because there's a curfew on tonight, is that clear?"

"*Claro*, Papá," said Martín Segundo.

"*Claro*," I said.

"*Claro*, Papá," echoed Alejo.

"Get out of my sight and over there before I change my mind. This dessert isn't worth eating anyway," Papá said. "And get back before dark or I swear that none of you will be able to sit down when you take your exams!"

We were just about out the door when the telephone rang.

"Diego!" Papá called out from this study. "Don't tie up the phone!"

Near the door, I picked up the hallway extension.

"*Sí*," I said. "Who's speaking?"

"*Che*, it's Marelli. We're supposed to meet the gang at three this afternoon at the Once subway station. Don't be late."

"What are you talking about, Marelli?"

"The demonstration, *che*, haven't you heard? We promised them we'd be there!"

"Well they can count on somebody else," I said. "And if you're smart, you'll stay home today and pull your stick off all by yourself, *che*, they're shooting out there."

"Don't be ridiculous, Yanqui, there isn't any shooting in Buenos Aires! It's a demonstration! Thousands of people will be there! It happens all the time!"

"Then it can happen without me," I said. "I'm not going."

"*Che*, Yanqui, I can't believe you're doing this, I really

can't. Who's going to take Cristina off my hands? I show up without you and I'm sunk with Gloria tonight!"

"You're sunk anyway, Marelli, and I don't give the littlest shit for you and Gloria. *Che*, you want me in trouble forever?"

"You promised me, Yanqui, you really did."

"I don't care what I said, count me out," I said. "Besides, it's too late now. I've already told the family I'm heading over to El Gordo Rojo's to work on math. I've got to phone in from there and leave from there and I'm going to keep my nice little yanqui ass sitting safe over at El Gordo's all day today."

"Diego!" Papá called out from his study. "I'm waiting for an important call!"

"I've got to get off the phone, Marelli. Ciao."

"I'll meet you over at El Gordo's in five minutes."

"Marelli!"

Alejo was suddenly there beside me in the hall as I slammed the phone down. He stopped chewing on his apple and looked at me as if sharing the mischief of a secret. "You're going to the big demonstration with Marelli today, isn't that right?"

"No, I'm not," I said sharply. "You see these? These are real books. I'm going to take these real books over to El Gordo's and this time I'm really going to open them, is that clear?"

Martín Segundo joined us outside the door of the apartment as we were starting on our way down the stairs. He had a perplexed look on his face, an expression of frustration. "Listen," he said, "do my brothers have to follow me everywhere? I couldn't talk at the table, but what if I had some other plan?"

Martín waited until we were all walking down Arenales Street to explain more clearly. "This afternoon, El Gordo and I were going to play a few records and telephone a couple of girls who live in his building and invite them over. El Gordo's parents are away, and we've got the whole place to ourselves, do you understand what I'm saying? But now that you two are coming along, I had to phone El Gordo and tell him you're coming. El Gordo decided to forget all about the girls and wants to set up his projector to show El Yanqui slides of the trip he and his mother took to Tierra del Fuego, what a *boludo*," Martín said. "*Che*, Diego, I'm sorry, but sometimes two friends just have to go off on their own."

"Sorry," I said. "I didn't know you had a hot date."

"Everything's clear now," Alejo said. "We'll just leave you two alone, won't we, Diego?"

"Come on, don't bust my balls," Martín said.

"We'll just head home, Martín," I said. "We'll tell Papá we changed our minds and decided to stay home and study."

"It's too late now anyway," Martín said. "Once El Gordo gets the equipment set up, it's all over."

"That's all right," said Alejo. "We won't get in the way. You can sit in the back row and feel up El Gordo all you want."

Martín had just shoved Alejo up against a building and was about to lift him off his feet by his jacket collar when Hernández-Marelli pulled up in front of El Gordo's in the little white Saab. Both Gloria and Cristina were in the car with him. How had Marelli managed that so fast? Had this been his plan all along? Cristina was dressed strangely, wearing a man's shirt with a kind of ascot around her neck, and a blue blazer almost like a student's from a colegio, only her silver loop earrings and the tilt of her red beret making her stand out as different. And the most surprising thing was that she was smiling at me, leaning out of the car window and waving at me excitedly as they pulled up to the curb.

"Who's that funny-looking girl with Marelli?" asked Martín. "*Che!* Marelli!" he shouted, glad to see him, and waving back at the car as if Cristina had been waving for him.

"That's a particular friend of mine, Martín," I said. The way Martín looked at me gave me a sudden feeling of power. "*Che*, Cristina!" I called out. "What's happening, sweetheart?"

As we reached Marelli's car, it felt as if I had been dating Cristina for months. I was suddenly leaning my head down to her window meaning to kiss her politely on the cheek, just a friendly little Argentine kiss, and I put my hand be-hind her head to pull her face closer to mine. The girl didn't know what to make of this at first but she played along, then she turned her face toward mine and we kissed, not all that quickly, on the mouth. It was wonderful to kiss a girl that way, casually on her lips, as if we had been lovers for a long time. Cristina opened the car door and scooted over to make room for me, and what else could I do? "Ciao, Martín! Be a real brother and cover for me," I said, hand-ing Martín Segundo my books.

"Where are you going?" Martín asked. "*Che*, Marelli, why didn't you let me in on this?"

"Because you're too much of a jerk-off, Martín," Alejo said, then jumped into the backseat of the car beside me. "Isn't that right, Marelli?"

Marelli made a lewd gesture with his fist out the window at Martín and hit the gas in that way he did that ended any chance of an argument. The feeling I had as I watched Mar-tín's shocked expression fading behind us, his eyes wide behind his glasses, his upper teeth biting into his lower lip at the sinful prospects he was undoubtedly missing in the company of Marelli making him green, *che*, it was one of the best feelings I had had for months to get the drop on Martín that way. How long had he been making me feel like a martian? Like a pariah he was shackled with that stood to ruin his social life for good? Like an alien yanqui presence he would never quite adjust to as long as we shared the same home? Alejo saw it, too, and was punching me on the shoulder and laughing at Martín. It was hard not to laugh, and there was a spirit in the car that promised the rest of this day was beyond any talk, far past my ability to question it. This was a real adventure, *che*, and here was a beautiful woman I had just stepped up and kissed like we were going to be lovers for life.

Hernández-Marelli reached a leather-covered pocket flask filled with his father's scotch toward us in the backseat. I passed it to Cristina, then I drank down two big gulps and passed it on to Alejo. The look in Marelli's eyes told me we were outlaws now, that was clear. It was like we were crossing the border into the territory of the *federales* on our way to rob all the gold in the dusty little towns. We were going to take care of this one big job today, then take off with the saloon girls for a hot bath, a bottle of whiskey and throwing dust until we couldn't stand up. "You see how Cristina is all dressed up like a boy, Yanqui?" Marelli said. "Isn't that really boss? Like a kind of unisex Che Guevara just out of a fancy prep school?"

"The thing is that the police always single the women out of the crowd. They go after them first," Cristina said. "You can't be too careful."

"*Che*, how did you get away from all the buttons the other night?" I asked.

"I just crossed through the parks and took a taxi home. A button did stop me to check my identity card as I was getting in the cab, and that was a close call. I had to keep one hand in my pocket. It had red paint all over it," she said. "Does everybody have documents? Everybody should be carrying his documents."

"I've got my good little passport from *la USA* right here," I said. I pulled my passport out of the back pocket I always carried it in and flipped it open to my picture. My hair was longish in the photograph, a dark scarf tied around my neck, the epaulettes of a strange-looking band uniform coat making me look like one of Sgt. Pepper's Lonely Hearts Club Band. I hadn't looked at that picture in a long time, and it was hard even to recognize myself. There was a distant, stoned glaze in the eyes as they stared off to one side of the tiny photograph as if expecting a drug bust might be coming from that direction.

"*Che, heepee,*" Cristina said. "You show that to the police and they won't believe it's the same person."

"This doesn't look like me? How about this," I said, and held my fingers up in a V and said in English, *"Peace now, baby,"* and everybody laughed. "Free love, too, that's my thing, everybody doing it with everyone else in the parks."

"That sounds like my kind of demonstration," Marelli said.

"Decadent hedonists," Cristina said. "Castro says you *heepees* are just a passing phase."

"I can't find my documents," Alejo said. "Son of a whore, I've checked all my pockets. I can't find my identity card!"

"Nothing?" Cristina asked.

"We'll let you off at the next block just to be safe," Marelli said. "It's against the law not to carry it, you know."

"Son of a whore, I can't find it," Alejo said, squirming around checking all his pockets again. "I'm always losing that shitty thing!"

"What happens if he doesn't have his documents?" I asked.

"It's not serious. Just don't get arrested," Gloria said.

"Arrested? What do you mean, get arrested?" I asked.

"Nobody's getting arrested," Cristina said. "My advice to Alejo is to stick with you. You've got that good yanqui passport and they probably won't want to arrest you if you're caught. But just in case some of us are, take these phone numbers, Yanqui." Cristina dug into her jacket pocket and handed me a little slip of paper with three numbers on it. "If you see any of us get arrested, find the nearest pay phone and keep dialing until you get hold of someone. Tell them when and where, anything you can, do you remember everybody's name? There's Andrés, Juan, Jorge, Alberto, María Inez, María, Simón . . ."

"It's all right, I remember them," I said.

"Just the first names are enough. The people who'll answer will know us. They've got the kind of connections that can spring us in no time," Cristina said.

"I know everybody's name, and I'll stick with El Yanqui," Alejo said.

"Do you really think you might be arrested?" I asked.

"Don't bother yourself about nothing," Marelli said and tried to pull Gloria closer to him by hooking an arm around her neck. She slipped out from under it and pulled away. "*Che*, Yanqui," Marelli said. "These girls are really tough ones. You go out and risk your lives for them and they probably won't even give you the courtesy of a good slow dance."

"It's unjust exploitation, that's clear," I said.

"Maybe we're fighting on the wrong side," Marelli said. "You ever think of that? What would a general do in this situation?"

"The generals can't get it up, that's their problem," Cristina said.

"Maybe they didn't practice enough when they were young," Alejo said.

"It's a shame, Yanqui, a real sad shame . . ."

Marelli pulled the Saab into a parking place somewhere near the Plaza Once, close to one of the main entrances to the subway that runs along the avenue Santa Fe and eventually connects up to other lines that run into the center of the city. Most of the gang was waiting at the Once subway station, all of them except for Alberto and Simón, who had apparently chickened out.

What seemed odd to me as I joined an anonymous knot of souls descending the old, crumbling concrete stairway was that the subways should be running at all. But then it was clear—they were run by the military regime, and the government was making it a point to keep functioning whatever services it could. Federal workers would surely be fired for any complicity with the general strike—though most state employees called in sick or didn't show up at work out of fear for their own safety—but the subways were running and there was no excuse. Anyone who wanted to get to work could get there at least that way. The contradiction in this was that tens of thousands of people from all over the sprawled-out city would also be able to join in the demonstrations.

I checked and rechecked my pockets for the list of Cristina's phone numbers as our train lurched off. Alejo was happily crammed in a group with Andrés, Jorge and María Inez, talking conspiratorially with them. Hernández-Marelli was still trying to get an arm all the way around Gloria. We stopped at a station and the crowd around us grew thicker, most of them men looking as if they were off to a Sunday *fútbol* game. What was different from a soccer Sunday was that even this far from the Plaza de Mayo, where were the police? Why hadn't I seen the usual button or two on the subway? When had I last seen a subway station without police since I'd left New York?

"So what happens after this?" I asked Cristina. Hernández-Marelli was lurching into my back at intervals and it was a fight not to knock into the girl as she stood fitted under my arm that reached up over her, hanging onto a strap of the rocking subway car. "Am I really going to get to see you tonight, beautiful?" I asked.

"Sure we will," Cristina said. "Don't worry. Nobody's getting arrested. And if we do, we're almost always sprung from this kind of thing by evening. We'll all meet at my place and we'll have a party," she said, but before I could think fast enough to ask her for her address, the doors opened out onto the station just up from the avenue 9 de Julio and we were all pushed out onto the platform. "Talk to you later," Cristina said, and she gave me a quick kiss on the cheek; then we were suddenly lost and fighting our way through a crowd that was thicker even than the one that spills out of a sold out stadium when the game is over.

Andrés took the lead of our little snake of students, behind him María Inez, followed by Cristina, then me, Alejo, Marelli and the others. Cristina turned in line and showed me how to hook my fingers through her belt and grip her around the middle, my fingers sinking into the little soft roll of flesh just above her waist. Alejo hooked his hands through my belt, and so on down the line, until we were all moving together, snaking our way through the crowd. Then all I could see was the back of Cristina's blue blazer and in a kind of jerky motion, pressed and shoved up against her back, we began to squirm our way through the crush. I could feel her firm, shapely behind moving and pressing tightly against me and I kept thinking dear God, dear God not now, as we were pulled along. Our blue snake climbed, or rather was carried along in the mob, up the station steps and out into the overcast afternoon on the avenue de Mayo. The capitol building's high dome shone in the gray distance at one end of the avenue. Up ahead, toward the Plaza de Mayo, I couldn't see anything but the crowd.

Tens of thousands of striking workers held banners spread out overhead. There were signs on sticks, and streamers,

and people everywhere handing out leaflets proclaiming
their allegiance to various organizations. C.G.T. was the
most prominent, a general workers' union, like an Argentine AFL-CIO. There was also the F.G.B., the printers'
union, and the S.M.A.T.A., the auto workers' union. Mixed
in with the unions were all the Peronist groups, the J.P.,
Peronist Youth, the J.S.P., the Peronist Trade Union Youth,
alongside the J.U.P., the University Peronist Youth, and so
on, dozens of different factions. Communist groups were
there, too, the O.C.P.O., and the P.R.T., the Workers'
Revolutionary Party. Maybe half of the trade unions and
political organizations in the nation were represented that
afternoon, half of the hundreds of political splinter groups
that were stubborn and aggressive enough to make the conduct of any new democracy, if that could ever be achieved,
as tough as it would be to run a family with a hundred
armed and contentious teenagers under the same roof.

In the stumbling, packed crowd, I kept looking down at
my feet. Though I could feel Alejo's fingers through my
belt, I sometimes wasn't sure and checked to see if his
sneakers were still following mine. Most of the men around
us wore cheap or shabby shoes, polyester shirts, some with
cheap paper caps from their Sunday *fútbol* games. Most of
them looked so poor—*los descamisados*, the shirtless ones,
Evita Perón had called them. But the men around me did
wear shirts, many of them the dark blue with bright yellow
stripe of Boca Juniors—the working class team of Argentine
*fútbol*. Boca Juniors had so many notoriously Peronist fans
that an Air Force general had once joked that he could take
care of the Peronist problem in Buenos Aires by means of
a single precision bombing raid on the Boca stadium any
sold-out Sunday.

"Look at this crowd!" Alejo said in my ear as our snake
of students writhed along through the mob. "There must
be half a million people out here!"

"Stick with me, *che*," I said. "Don't let go."

We slowed down, Andrés in the lead up against an im-
penetrable crush of bodies. The crowd around us had begun
to chant various songs. It was hard to make out the words
above the general uproar of so many souls all packed be-

tween the high buildings along that section of the avenue de Mayo. Most of the singing sounded like the Peronist Youth song. And faint strains of *L'Internationale* sung in Spanish floated in from behind us. Loudest of all was a one-word chant of solidarity, *A-se-sinos! A-se-sinos! A-se-sinos!* It was because most of them knew that at that moment, around the steelyards and foundries of Córdoba, the government's paratroopers were moving in and arresting everyone or, worse, blindly shooting at anyone who was out of doors. In Buenos Aires, it wasn't so much a demonstration march as an immense mob that had begun to mill around, oddly festive with its angry outbursts at the police and the soldiers that it seemed no one could see. Where were the police? Where were all the soldiers? But they must be here, I thought. They were probably waiting for us all in a line somewhere up ahead.

*"A-se-sinos! A-se-sinos! A-se-sinos!"* the crowd began to chant louder. Cristina picked it up, raising a fist in the air like the thousands around us as we snake-danced along. She was cheerleading us on to join in, and I found my own voice suddenly filled with shouts at nameless assassins, in my mind the ones who were at work everywhere in this world, my throat and mouth filled with this hoarse shouting of outrage added to the great human noise, *"A-se-sinos! A-se-sinos! A-se-sinos! A-se-sinos! A-se-sinos! A-se-sinos! . . ."*

Khaki army uniforms suddenly appeared all around us, some of them on sidestreets but others *above* us, over the avenue, the heads of soldiers with dark green helmets poking out the second-story windows and waving their nightsticks and machine guns down at the crowd.

"Look! Look up there! They've got guns!" Alejo shouted behind me. At the same moment, a wave of angry emotion moved through the crowd and the chanting grew louder, *"A-se-sinos! A-se-sinos! A-se-sinos!"* Everyone seemed to be shouting at the soldiers as hundreds of snakes of demonstrators weaved in and out of each other like a jammed-up parade of Chinese dragons.

The mob up ahead suddenly halted against a police line, the crowd behind them not catching onto what had happened in time to keep from crushing into the mass of hu-

manity ahead of them. My face was smashed into Cristina's
back. It was hard to breathe. I was so pressed in I couldn't
raise my elbows or use my arms. I tried to shout something
about this to Cristina but nothing could be heard over the
sudden screams and outcries rising up all around us. By the
faces of the soldiers perched above us along the high can-
yon walls made by the buildings, it was clear we were
surrounded, we had been lured into a trap designed for
tens of thousands. Glass shattered. To the left of me, a dark-
looking man had been crushed against a shop window so
forcefully that he went right through it. The rest of us were
carried along by the mob, not hearing, not seeing, jostled
ahead by the force of it, out of control. I was beginning to
panic in the crush. Where were we going? How in hell
could we get out of this?

"The subway!" Alejo shouted into my ear. He had to
repeat it several times before I got what he was saying.
"The subway! The subway!" I turned a little and saw the
stricken look on his face. "Let's get over there! Over there!
Make for the subway!" he screamed and tried to use a free
arm to wave toward a nearby subway entrance.

A tear gas canister popped with a muffled explosion in
the very subway entrance where we had decided to go. No
matter the gas, we would have run for it if we could. We
would have shouldered and shoved our way through, anything to keep from getting crushed by the mob, because
that was what was happening, people were still massing in
behind us until nobody could move or breathe, and at the
same time the whole crowd up ahead was trying to turn
back and run but came up against a solid wall of their own
kind. A burst of machine gun fire rang out. All hell broke
loose in noise and smoke.

The soldiers above us fired off tear gas grenades into the
crowd along the avenue like kids dropping water baloons
on innocent passersby, the soldiers laughing at this, having
themselves a real *joda* picking individuals out of the crowd
as though to see if they could land the gas bombs on their
heads. People were coughing and choking and trying to run
but there wasn't anywhere to run to, nobody seemed able
to move. Everyone was blind, gagging, trying to fight ahead

as if we were a dammed-up river of souls waiting for a floodgate to open, jamming up in the only direction gravity would allow, while a block ahead of us, lines of blue-uniformed federal police wearing riot helmets had already started in on the crowd, cutting people down with their nightsticks as if scything down a field of grain. More and more gas bombs were going off through the crowd like fireworks, and the crowd was breaking apart, everyone panicking, everyone trying to find someplace to run.

The police had set up traps along all the little sidestreets, all the way up to San Martín Street. Blue police buses and gray armored cars stood like barricades across the narrow streets, waiting for their human cargoes bound for the emergency prisons. These dammed-up sidestreets were the only outlets, the only places to run. The military had made a perfect plan for our demonstration. Even using all our strength, wrestling and fighting people in the crowd around us and still hanging on to each other, we couldn't make it through, couldn't get over to the subway entrance. We were carried along helplessly in the powerful currents of the street. Then the machine guns went off again and nobody could hang on anymore.

"It's over our heads!" Alejo shouted. "They're shooting over our heads!" he screamed. In the crazy panic, his hands were ripped loose from my belt and our snake broke in two. He was leading his half and I was trailing mine, but we were spreading further and further apart as Alejo raised both fists and started screaming, *"A-se-sinos! A-se-sinos! A-se-sinos!"* with an unbelievable force and volume. For a moment, everyone around him, hundreds and hundreds of people, rallied behind him and took up their outraged chant again. His part of the crowd stopped moving, fists were raised, and for an instant it was as if so many thousands were going to rise up in such violent shouting that the police would melt back, the soldiers would retreat from the sudden murderous spirit of the mob that was screaming until they were hoarse, *"A-se-sinos! A-se-sinos! A-se-sinos!"*

I was suddenly coughing and completely blinded. Tear gas was everywhere like a thick, soupy fog and I was carried along by the mob at a speed that approached running.

With one full gulping breath of pure tear gas, my head
wanted to explode. All the valves were wide open, snot
running down both nostrils, my eyes like spigots, and in
my blindness it felt like somebody was scrubbing my eyes
with steel wool. The inside of my windpipe caught fire and
white-hot coals settled into my lungs. Before I could see
anything again, everyone had scattered. My fingers broke
loose of Cristina's belt and waist and I was shouting and
coughing, "Cristina! Cristina!" after her as if that could be
any help, as if anything could help us now.

Temporarily blinded, I lost all sense of direction. I didn't
know which way to go to make for the subway, even if I could.
Trying somehow to rub my eyes back to sight with the heels
of my hands, I was carried along onto a sidestreet where groups
of federal police played catch as catch can with clusters of
terrorized demonstrators. I ended up crushed against a building, hugging against it and trying to make myself small. I
started to be able to see again. On the street around me, unleashed police dogs were now running after demonstrators,
tearing at the cuffs of their pants, backing them up against
walls and holding them there until teams of buttons could
gather them up. The buttons gave even the most cooperative a
quick blast on the head with their sticks or shoved them
straight into the crotch or diaphragm. Workers and students with
blood running down their faces were dragged into waiting
police buses, some of them just pulled along like limp dolls
by their feet, heads battered along on the pavement.

Somewhere on this street, the crowd thinned a little. In
one of the sparse knots of demonstrators, I thought I could
make out a familiar figure being arrested—it looked like
Andrés. Two buttons dragged Andrés to the other side of
the street, taking their time, and Andrés was smart enough
to go completely limp as they pulled him along by one arm
and the collar of his jacket. Then I saw the shape that
Andrés' arm had been formed into, twisted into three crazy
angles like a bent-up coat hanger. I started to shout down
the street at Andrés, then stopped; it was pointless, he
couldn't have heard me anyway. All I knew was that the
crowd and the tear gas had thinned on this sidestreet just
enough so that I could run if I wanted to like all the other

people running past, though there was no place to go but into the clubs of the waiting police.

I ducked into a doorway. It was amazing that nobody else had found this doorway yet, a steel cage drawn across it. It was the entrance of a shop called *Ciudad de pelucas*, City of Wigs. Arranged in the tall barred shop windows were tiers of styrofoam, faceless heads with cheap synthetic wigs on them looking like a bizarre arrangement of shaggy flowers. Two students ran past at full speed, whipping past the doorway in the opposite direction from the police line. Two buttons were hotly after them. That was the way it happened in these demonstrations—it seemed as if the police picked some of their victims one by one, then took off after them. Others ran right into their clubs, but if they spotted you shouting too loudly or making too violent a gesture or cussing them out, even at the center of the crowd, some button might notice you and that was it, he picked you out, he focused on you, hunter and quarry. Pity any demonstrator who got caught after a hard chase.

The buttons giving chase ran past me in the doorway, so closely past me I could have reached out and tripped them. I waited a moment, then stuck my head out of the doorway and looked down the street. A fog of tear gas was dispersing over the scene. Two blue buses were turned broadside across the street like barricades. Some demonstrators, the ones who were fast enough or strong enough or just damned lucky, ran straight through the police lines. They seized their chance and broke away from the buttons near the buses and dodged through and around the police or bulled their way through. That was the only way out that I could see. But what to do now? Should I try it? I looked around for somebody, anybody I knew, but I had lost them all in the crowd.

Three buttons trotted down the sidewalk, searching out victims. One of them fastened on me. He raised his nightstick up and pointed it at the doorway where I was hiding. On impulse, I slipped out of the doorway and started calmly walking *toward* them—no way was I going to make them chase me. After all, I was just a poor yanqui, a guest of their nation lost in this crowd and trying to get back to my apartment. I was a good little yanqui and didn't know anything about their politics, wasn't that clear? My story was that I was trying to get back from a workout at the downtown center for club C.U.B.A.—the University of Buenos Aires gymnasium and health club all of the Benevento family belonged to and that was located somewhere nearby, if I could only just remember the exact address. After my workout at the club, I had tried to catch the subway home because it was so hard to find a cab on a day of national strikes, that was the story I made up just as the buttons reached me. Their faces didn't look good, too grim-looking in their pretty blue riot helmets. They had been made to work too hard today by all this hassle. They were soaked with perspiration and their faces showed the strain, that was clear even as I sort of smiled and held up my hands to them like a tourist might who was asking directions on the street.

"Documents!" one of them said, maybe noticing that I was a foreigner. It was a privilege that he had spoken to me, I thought. I hadn't seen anybody else on the street who was that lucky. Then another button raised up a long nightstick like a baseball bat and shoved it under my arms from behind, making them into big chicken wings. Both my hands suddenly went numb but I smiled at the nice button, glad to see him. I was lost, that was the situation, and could the nice police officer help me get out of this mess?

"*Norteamericano,*" I said, overdoing the yanqui accent, my mouth opening wide and chewing on the word like on a wad of dry cotton. "*No comprendo.*"

"*Norteamericano?*" the one behind me asked. He sounded confused, checking out the reactions of the other two officers with him. They were already looking down the street into the thinning crowd for more victims.

"*No comprendo,*" I said and smiled at them, trying to move my shoulders in a little shrug until the pain of the nightstick stopped them. "*Norteamericano,*" I said.

"Passporte pleees," the older-looking button of the three interjected. I nodded my head quickly, letting them know I comprehended now. The one with the nightstick let my arms go long enough for me to reach into my pocket for my beautiful green passport. How long had I been carrying it in the back pocket of my pants just in case I ever needed to show it to the buttons? I was glad to show it off, the nice signature of my powerful secretary of state right there on a page before my picture, for example, and the American eagle with its arrows in one claw and its olive branch in the other, what a great seal that was, I was glad it had something to do with me, that and all the pretty writing telling me it would let me travel anywhere in the world but Cuba, North Korea and North Vietnam. I wasn't any communist, that was clear, and weren't nice yanquis like me best friends to the military regime? The button in front of me examined my photograph, looking from it to me then back to it again, maybe a little skeptical, uncertain. Couldn't he see that I was the same person? He flipped my passport closed and dropped it into his shirt pocket—a very bad sign.

"My passport?" I asked, all humility. Wasn't the nice policeman going to give it back? Then my cheeks were suddenly hot and flushed, my palms were breaking out in a sweat and I was trying to stall somehow. The button saw this, even as I was pretending to look away from him and scrutinize a window somewhere behind him, next to the Wig City window, and windows further down the street, a leather goods store, a stationer's, a pizza joint. It would be nice if the pizza joint were open for business, I thought, I wouldn't mind sitting down with these buttons over a little espresso to talk the situation over like gentlemen. I remembered all the pesos I had in one of my pockets, nice big red-colored bills all of them, maybe forty-five dollars' worth of nice Argentine money, at least a week's wages for a police cadet. The button in front of me had an expression on his face like he knew now what I was, where I had come from, everything about me, everything he needed to fuck me over as much as he wanted.

"Maybe you captains would like to split a little tip," I said in perfect slang Spanish, the accent even surprised me it sounded so Argentine. Why had I done that? Fear, clearly, and the sudden absence of a better idea. "Just let go of my arms," I said slowly, "so I can get into my pockets. Let go of my arms and I promise to come up with a little something extra to have with your tea."

The button behind me let go of my arms at the signal of

his partner. The third button with them spotted a student running on the other side of the street and suddenly jumped off the sidewalk and gave chase, a bad sign, didn't he even want his share of my little bribe? All the signs had turned very, very bad, that was clear, and I was going to cry in a moment, I was going to start bawling like a kid if nothing else worked.

"Very well, *flaco*," the buttons said. "Show us what's in your pockets."

"A thousand thanks, *capitán*," I said. "You won't regret it. I'm innocent, not a part of anything like this. I was just on my way home and got caught out here. I'm an athlete, see?" I said and tried to point to my sneakers in a kind of jerky motion that made one of the buttons jump back. I froze there in response and thought, why had I done that? What good would pointing at my shoes do me? "I was trying to get home from my gymnasium. I didn't want to miss a workout, you understand?" My left hand was slowly reaching under my jacket into my pants pocket but it must have been too slowly, because the button behind me drew his pistol in a single quick movement, a big square black pistol that he pressed into the side of my head. My breath was caught somewhere between the barrel and my mouth, a sound of panic coming out of my nostrils in an involuntary, high-pitched nasal squealing, "All I have is money! Nothing else! Nothing else! Only money, señores, please look at it!" I said and brought my fist ever so slowly up out of my pocket, inching it up to my belt, my breath escaping in a rush as the button covering me lowered his pistol and replaced it in his holster. The other button grabbed the wad of bills out of my hand and shoved them into the same pocket as my passport without even counting them. "A thousand thanks. A thousand, thousand thanks, señores," I said, slowly trying to take a step off to the side, a little nearer the open pavement. "You've been a very big help. A thousand, thousand thanks, I can't tell you how grateful I am. Can you please tell me where Arenales Street is from here?"

Nobody was going to answer my question. I was suddenly thrown against the building, legs and arms spread. One of the buttons whipped through my pockets, turning them out, and my wallet, coins, the good luck charm from Harry, cigarettes, phone numbers, everything I had with me was hitting the sidewalk in a rain of coins. This frisking was so fast I couldn't get anything out of my mouth but, *"Por favor, señores! Por favor!"* before the buttons turned me back around again and shoved me roughly off the building. One of the buttons hauled back with his nightstick. There was a sick flash in which I saw the future, my head rang out, and then I was on my hands and knees, that much I knew, the sidewalk reeling under me like a storming sea. Was that my blood? That was a silly question, there were splatters of it, sprays of it, somebody was shaking a paintbrush full of blood and whose else would it be?

The buttons grabbed me under the arms, one on each side, and I felt my knees dragging the pavement. My knees were sled runners along the street and the cloth had burned through on my pants, I could feel that much. It hurt my knees the way they dragged me along and I tried to push up on the toes of my sneakers to save my knees but somebody kept slamming me back down. Somewhere ahead, a blue bus rose up out of the street like an Andean mountain. It looked like the bus I used to ride in to high school games back home, a big Ford schoolbus, only it was painted two shades of blue, a nice big American bus and I wanted to help the buttons get me up into it, it looked like a good place to be compared to being dragged along on my knees. Then I was suddenly landing face-first at the top of the flight of bus steps. The buttons sort of bundled me up and shoved me by my legs into the bus. My vision blurred, my ears ringing, my mouth filled with blood as the guard at the top of the steps kicked me along until I was in the aisle. Then all these other hands reached out for me. Who were these people? I had a hard time making them out in the deep shadows of the bus, these faces and hands of other demonstrators all around me who were reaching out, helping me to move my big heavy yanqui legs, my clumsy yanqui body that felt like a big sack of mashed potatoes toward an empty seat in back. "Another one," somebody said. "Son of a whore, *che*, they really gave it to this one."

Somebody sat me down in a seat at the back. Sitting down felt better, my head felt smaller somehow, it had shrunk to the size of a basketball by then and was still throbbing as if with a pressurized gas but no pain, the real pain hadn't started. The landscape was just beginning to slow down enough for me to make out the people around me in the fading light of the afternoon and I tried to move my mouth to make sounds. I wanted to say something to all these people around me but nothing came out that sounded anything like words. A man across the aisle from me bunched up a piece of old banner, a rag of white linen with the bottom half of a red *P* painted on it. "For your head, *che*," the man said and I did what I was told and tried to bunch the cloth up to my head but somehow it wouldn't stay in my fingers, it kept falling from my hand. A man behind me picked it up and gave it back to me but again no go, it slid down my face and dropped away, the bus turning around and around, faster and faster like I was drunk, and I had to hold onto the seat to sit steady. The man behind me pressed the little strip of bloody cloth to my head for me and held it there, his other hand on my shoulder to keep me from falling over. I tried to thank him. My mouth moved and made a word that sounded like the one for thanks, what was that word again? Who were all these kind people, anyway? Where was everybody going? Where was Alejo? Where was Cristina? What was happening here? I wanted to ask all of these questions as soon as I could and I tried to move my mouth to make the words but I couldn't talk yet, I had to close my eyes first, just once to get the bus to stop whirling around and to keep my head from bursting. My eyes were going to close for just a little while and then I was going to ask them, I might think of the right Spanish words by then and somehow I would find out, one of these kind people would tell me what had happened.

# 5

## Why Can't You Live Pretty?

The police bus pulled into a long narrow avenue that was lit with blue flashing lights reflecting like strobes off the ranks of helmeted soldiers standing all around the buses and armored cars parked to make a gauntlet of the street. I opened my eyes to an intense throbbing pain behind them, my stomach queasy and heavy, a metallic, nauseating taste in my mouth.

I recognized in the gray evening ahead the big soccer stadium called River Plate. It stood past the northern reaches of a system of parks that stretched into the city district called Belgrano. The stadium rose up over the river en route to the posh suburbs of San Isidro, where the armed forces had built their expensive country clubs. It was the newest stadium in Argentina, designed to hold perhaps fifty or sixty thousand people though sometimes, on a championship Sunday, the stadium packed in as many as eighty or ninety thousand, *la negrada*, as they were called, the big black mass hanging out over the upper decks, jamming its concrete stairways and entrances. Dictators everywhere are fond of building stadiums like River Plate. In times of national emergency, when a dictatorship blacks out the press and carries on its state terror to keep order in the streets, the beautiful bowls of the stadiums with their spiraling ramps, their labyrinths of concrete caverns behind the seats, the limited access with all the gates and turnstiles and the big barbed fences all around make them easy to transform into the biggest prisons on earth.

River Plate was a beautiful new stadium, home of the professional *fútbol* team of the same name, the second most popular soccer club in Argentina and clearly the favorite of the middle class. Miguelito, Alejo, Martín and I had all cheered for the River Plate team, had jumped up and down and shouted ourselves hoarse at the games in this stadium, feeling the concrete floors quaking under our feet from the pounding of so many fans. The four of us had jumped up and down and sung the team songs, linking ourselves together arms-over-shoulders to keep from tumbling down the steep cement stairways of the upper decks, tens of thousands of us, many wearing the shirts of our team—white jerseys with broad diagonal stripes the color of blood. I was thinking dimly of this on the police bus, surprised to be at River Plate stadium. It felt like there were two hot soccer players using my head for their *fútbol* as the police bus ran the blue-flashing gauntlet and pulled into line with other buses and army trucks parked in the shadows of one of the stadium's cavernous entrances.

Two soldiers dressed in camouflage and wearing riot helmets busted through the hinged bus doors and up the steps like they were on some kind of commando raid. Machine guns aimed at our faces, they pushed the police officer who had ridden with us out first, then they started kicking the rest of us out, shouting, "Let's go! Let's go you sons of whores! Let's go!" and waving their machine guns at us, everyone on the bus hustling out as fast as he could. One of the soldiers stood behind the driver's seat and gave each of us a fast painful shot in the back with his boot, sending us flying down the steps. Somehow, the soldier missed me, or maybe I ducked out of the way and took the steps in a jump, I don't know. Out on the paved area in the shadows of the stadium, two lines of the same kind of soldiers were shoving us along between them, using the wooden butts of their automatic rifles to keep us trotting along with our hands on our heads. I felt two of those shots hit me from behind, one sharp on the shoulderblade, the other like a kick on my backside. Every step I took, it felt as if my head were going to come off. Just getting a hold on the dizziness took everything in me, and I was moving too slowly, these soldiers around me were going to fuck me over if I didn't hurry along faster, that was clear. We all trotted past an armored personnel carrier that looked deserted of soldiers, a big green elephant of a thing with its guns uncovered and aimed at the stadium gates. It had felt like my stadium once, but it wasn't mine now, I thought, hurried along past these lines of soldiers. I looked over in the direction of the river and saw an open area in which other soldiers stood, dressed differently, in khaki and with billed caps like the Afrika Korps, hundreds of them spaced evenly under the floodlights, legs spread wide, both hands presenting their automatic rifles with military rigidness. I fought off a sudden insane desire to break into a run in that direction, as if I were capable of running, out across the open floodlit field where maybe I could dodge around the soldiers and make for the riverbank, but as I was imagining this I was rudely shoved along into the ticket booth and turnstile area and it was too late. The sound of the turnstiles was fast, like some kind of crazy factory noise as we slammed through them. An officer stood to one side, watching his aide clicking off numbers on a hand-held counter, and I stopped a moment. There was a little clear area of guards around this officer and I stepped into it and said politely, "There's been a mistake, *capitán*. I'm a North American. I want to see my consul."

The officer game me an oddly friendly look but at the same time, with a movement of his hand, he ordered one of his soldiers to shove me along. There was a look in this particular guard's eyes that told me not to draw too much attention to myself, there would be chance enough for explanations inside.

The wind under the shelter of the entrance was stronger than outside the stadium, as though all the air were being sucked out of its interior in a blast from its concrete lungs, and it cut through my shirt. What had happened to my jacket? I couldn't remember taking it off but there it was, gone, and I was shivering all over suddenly, teeth chattering. I tried to lean over and throw up. I felt that if I could just get sick I would be all right, but nothing came.

A prisoner behind me put a hand on my back. "Are you not well, *che*? Come on. Come on with me, *che*," he said quickly and helped to move me along that way a few steps. Then a knot of soldiers made us turn to our left and start up some stairs onto one of the stadium ramps, which had the feeling of a long dark tunnel. Voices echoed ahead. The sound of our feet scraping along the rough concrete was like a crashing in there, and there was another sound, made up of all the little noises we were making, of sharp breaths, groans, whispered cussing, a sound that was like an intense, growing pressure in my ears from an underwater dive. The guards along the ramp were spaced about every twenty feet, and they stood back and let us alone as long as we kept moving. Up ahead, in the darkness lit only by the gray, cloudy dusk coming through the side of the ramp that was opened to the winds above its concrete and wire-mesh retaining wall, one of the guards shoved a rifle into the line of us and stopped us. We were all made to kneel down, our faces ten inches from the dark concrete wall. I scooted a little closer so I could lean my forehead against it. The cement was cold, and it made my head feel a little better.

After a number of quick glances down the ramp, I finally began to figure out what was happening. At the base of it was a network of offices for stadium administration and a subterranean labyrinth of dressing rooms, store rooms and passageways. This was where the Army was doing the processing. Guards were moving slowly along the line of prisoners below me, taking all identity cards and making sure all pockets were empty. They assigned a number to each prisoner and marked it down on a clipboard list. Then a number would be called out and a prisoner was led down to processing. It was a slow, slow system. But I could see that after receiving their numbers, the prisoners below me were allowed to turn around from the wall and sit more at ease. Cigarettes were tossed back to some of them, and one prisoner at a time was allowed to piss over the side of the ramp into the wintery dusk. The guards seemed more restrained there, too. They were in a bad mood, that was clear, it was a hassle for them to have to be there. This resentment showed in the rough edge they maintained toward us, but other than that, they seemed relaxed enough. After the guards had done their number assignments, groups of prisoners down the ramp from me settled into the sad, expectant atmosphere of a refugee camp.

I could make out voices around me rumoring that the government was going to be lenient this time, everyone would be let go with a little matter of a fine. How soon might depend on who could turn up enough pesos at the stadium gates, that was the situation—if workers were taking to the streets because they couldn't live on fifty-three dollars' worth of pesos a month, then how could all these soldiers make do on forty-five dollars a month in pesos? And who was going to pay them for all this overtime? But the system was moving too slowly. It seemed like I would have to kneel with my head against the wall all night, seeing the world through eyes partly blinded as if by blue sparking wires, taking breaths in big gulps in between throbs of a headache like high-voltage shocks. The guards finally worked their way up to me, and as they were turning out my empty pockets, I said, "There's been a mistake. I'm a North American student, señor. They took my passport when they arrested me. Please tell them to look for my passport and they'll see that it's a mistake that I'm here. *Capitán*, please . . ."

"Without documents," the guard said to his partner with the clipboard list, ignoring my pleas. "You're number fifteen forty-four," he said, as if he wasn't going to repeat himself. "Step back and wait your turn."

A part of my dizzy brain started chanting in a little interior voice, *fifteen forty-four, fifteen forty-four, fifteen forty-four*, panicked that I would somehow forget this number even as I said, "*Capitán*, please, I'm sick. I need medical attention. And I've lost my jacket. I'm freezing up here."

"Back against the wall," the guard said with irritation and I immediately stepped back as the two of them moved on down the line. In a moment, after the guards were almost finished with our particular group, a salt-and-pepper-haired, dark-eyed prisoner in our group shrugged his shoulders and carefully moved close to me, a cigarette hanging out of his mouth, a clever little smile on his face.

"Here, *che*," the man said, taking off his leather jacket with relaxed, slow movements that wouldn't draw attention from the guards; then he peeled off the blue and yellow soccer sweater he was wearing underneath that. "I'd let you have the jacket but it's the only one I own," he said. "I have another sweater on under this one, so I won't be cold, *che*, so take this," he said.

"*Gracias,*" I said. I pulled the sweater on as slowly as he had taken it off, both our backs pressed against the wall so we wouldn't stand out too much from the others around us.

"What I want to know is how come a yanqui needs my shirt?" the little man asked in a voice loud enough so that a few of the prisoners on either side of us could hear him. "Unless he's a yanqui shirtless one," he said, using the Peronist term for the poor. The others laughed quietly as I finished pulling the *fútbol* sweater over my head. Then everyone was talking in my direction at once.

"*Che*, are you really a yanqui?" somebody asked.

"What's a yanqui doing here?"

"Look! He's rooting for Boca Juniors!"

"Are you a friend of Rockefeller's?"

"*Che*, how do you find it in Argentina? Does this kind of shit go on in the United States?"

"I got a brother in New York, he runs a restaurant, a Blimpie's restaurant, his name is Mauricio Martínez on the corner of Second Avenue and Twenty-first Street in Manhattan, you ever heard of him?"

"*La USA*'s got all the money but Argentina has the best women, don't you agree?"

"You heard that the yanquis went to the moon? Is that true?"

"Of course it's true, *boludo*. They spent millions and millions of dollars to build a big rocket ship, count down, blast off and *pow*, before you knew it, they put yanquis on the moon.''

"You know that Argentina's got a moon program, too? We're going to take all the generals and admirals in the country and stack them one on top of the other until we get there.''

"We'll have plenty of them left over to run the moon, too, after we've landed.''

I tried in monosyllables to answer these questions coming at me too fast to comprehend in the dizzy, pressurized fog of my senses. That little voice was also still repeating *fifteen forty-four, fifteen forty-four, fifteen forty-four* until it felt as if it had been stamped into my brain like into iron under thousands of pounds of pressure. All I managed to say was that I was with some students, that's why I was there. "I'm an exchange student, in a colegio," I said and that was about all. Nothing moved me more than an intense desire to get back down the wall again, off by myself, so I could sit and lean my head against it, using the huge cold stadium as an icepack. I tried to find a clear space of wall away from the others but the little man who had given me his Boca Juniors shirt followed me a few feet and sat down beside me.

"*Che*, it looks like they really gave it to you," he said. He took out a handkerchief and spit a huge ball of saliva into it. "You're going to have a scar on your forehead," he said. He leaned in to try and wash off some of the dried blood. I tried to wave my hand at him not to bother but what the hell, his spit felt good. "It would be a shame, a scar like that, except a few athletic scars are really attractive to the girls. I'm witness to that. Just look here," he said and pointed out several small white gashes on his cheek and up to his temple on one side of his face. "I work in metal sheeting, in construction," he said. "We put up roofs. One day, a piece of a roof came down on me. But it hasn't hurt me with the women, *che*, not one bit.''

"*Gracias*," I said. "Give me your address and I'll see you get your shirt back.''

"It's an old rag of a shirt, *che*. I've been afraid to let my wife wash it since April in case she might try to throw it out. It's gone through a lot of *fútbol* games, that shirt, ripped off and waved around like a flag. It's my battle shirt,'' he said. "It's been through many, many battles in the stadiums. Have you seen an Argentine *fútbol* game?''

"Of course. Right here. The family I'm living with all cheers for River Plate. I'm not sure I will anymore, not after this," I said.

"Why not? It's a good team," he said. "The team doesn't have anything to do with this. But River Plate is not as good a team as Boca Juniors. Boca is hungrier. River has just got a few stars, like that forward Daniel Onega. You ever seen him play?''

"He's a phenomenon, that's clear," I said.

"He's phenomenal, but he's too much of a star player. He doesn't pass enough. He can take the ball all the way down the field himself and miss the shot sometimes when if he passed, River might have won the game.''

"That's true," I said. "I saw that happen the last game I was here. That was only a month ago, *che*, and it seems like all my life.''

"This your first time arrested?''

"What a hassle, *che*. I didn't know this could happen.''

"Nobody knows what can happen in this country. Most people just go about their lives as best they can, good people, you understand, a little lazy, most of us, but still very very good types, we Argentines. Many of us have quit giving much thought to politics. Everything comes out the same for us no matter what. With a democracy or with a military government, our wages come out about the same. I swear to you, the only real difference is that the military keeps banning our unions and it's a lot harder to fight back under them. But either way, ever since I can remember, the people of this country have been living despite their government, do you understand what I'm saying?''

"It looks to me like a lot of people give a thought to politics," I said. "Why else would so many be here?''

"I'm here because I have a union," the man said. "The Construction Workers Union of the Argentine Republic, the U.O.C.R.A., *Uocra*, we call it. Even when our union is made illegal, when our leaders call for a strike and a demonstration, I go on strike and show up at the demonstration, it's that simple, because the situation can change tomorrow and if I'm not a member in good standing, I could lose my job. But most of the time, it's not like this. When our union is legal, we go on strike and gather at the Plaza de Mayo. Our leaders make speeches. We dance around and sing Peronist songs, then we all go off somewhere for a few little beers and we're back on the job the next day. It's like a long weekend, *che*, most of the time, like a big union party. Maybe we get higher wages and maybe not. Maybe we can meet openly in public again. Or maybe we have to continue to meet in small groups in somebody's living room. This is only the second time I've been arrested. The first was under *presidente* Illia, a democratic president, *che*, the one who made the promise to bring Perón back during his election campaign so all the Peronists would vote for him. Illia went back on his promise once he was in office, and the unions held a lot of strikes in protest. Then the economy went straight into the shit and the military took over again and cracked down on everyone. You yanquis are lucky, really lucky. You yanquis don't have to wrestle with this shit all the time.''

"It can be bad in my country, too," I said.

"*Sí?* In North America? That can't be true," he said.

"You don't think it can be bad but it can be bad," I said. "You think we're all rich but we're not. It's a struggle for my family in its own way, a big Catholic family. Then with our *presidente* Nixon, I don't know, my friends and I have been to some demonstrations. We wore black armbands when he was elected and that kind of thing, to try and stop the war in Vietnam."

"That's a terrible war in Vietnam."

"That's clear," I said.

"But maybe communism for them is worse, no?"

"You think so? Really? Do you think your Peronism is any better?"

"It's a completely different thing, you can't compare," the man said. "And it's clear, Peronism is just as fucked up as anything else, *che*, I don't fool myself. But under Perón, everything in this country changed. He was the first president to favor the unions in this country since Yrigoyen way back in the twenties. He gave Argentina its first labor laws, retirement plans, health programs and that kind of thing. And for the first time in factories, unions could negotiate grievances strongly with management. Our wages went up. And Evita's social reforms built almost half the public grade schools in this country. There was work everywhere for a good long time, and Evita raised money for national charity projects and housing for the shirtless ones, and she got the voting for women. Women weren't even allowed to vote in Argentina before Perón. We're never going to forget what Perón did for us, never in our lives. There wouldn't be a single peso for our old age if it weren't for him. And we older ones who can remember what it was like will tell you that the workers in this country felt like we had a chance for the first time. We knew what we wanted, just a little piece, that's all, a tiny piece of this country we could take home with us. Perón gave us that much for a good long time."

"But *che*, wasn't he a dictator?" I asked. "I've always heard he was just as bad as a military regime."

"Of course, he became a dictator after Evita died, that's clear. But a lot of what he did was from outside pressure. The old families and old military wanted their power back and the yanquis had just arrived to help them, so it was really like a war for a time. But any Argentine worker will still tell you it was better under the last years of Perón than it ever was when that son of a whore general Aramburu took over, *che*. He bombed the Plaza de Mayo. You can still see the shellholes in the Casa Rosada. Even then, Perón wasn't forced out of power. He stepped down from power of his own free will, thinking it was for only a short time, that's clear, to avoid a bloodbath. You know what he said when he left into exile? He said, 'Can you imagine what would happen in this nation if I hadn't taken all the guns from the unions? We could fight a great civil war and win against the forces of the military and of imperialism, but at what price?' "

"Perón said that?"

"Sure he did, I wouldn't lie to you. Then General Aramburu came in and slaughtered all the Peronists he could find. And maybe worse than that, something this nation will never forget, Aramburu stole the body of Evita from where she was still lying in state in her glass coffin and hid her away. Beautiful Evita, who belonged to all of us! All these years went by and none of us has forgotten it. Someday, somebody's going to make old Aramburu pay for that. Her body should be returned. And I don't think you could find many people in this country who would grieve if Aramburu's body was found someday in a ditch,'' the man said.

"What's so important about Evita's body, *che*?"

"What's important about her is that the military is still afraid of her. They're afraid of what she means, all the best that Perón ever meant. And *che*, she was still beautiful, nobody can deny it, as beautiful as the day she gave her final speech, her blonde hair around her head like a saint's halo. She was one of us, we were her family, and we want her back just as if she were our mother, wouldn't you?''

"I don't know, *che*, it's got nothing to do with me," I said. "I don't know anything about politics in this country. I got involved in this demonstration because of my friends, and maybe because there were some girls along, to make a certain impression on them, I don't know . . ."

"And that's clear, yanqui, that's what it's all about, isn't it? First you get your little job to earn a little money to be able to take your nice little girl out on a date. It's got to be a nice expensive date, very romantic, with flowers and music, all the right things. After that you work like a dog in hell to save up all the money you're going to need to get married, *che*, and you do that, thinking you're going to have this woman for life, this nice little girl is going to be all yours. Then after you're married, you have to work overtime at your shitty little job in order to put food on the table for all the kids, the Mamá, the aunts, the uncles, everybody, and to keep a roof over all their heads. You sure aren't going to keep your little wife if you don't, and that's the way it goes. When things get bad and no matter how hard you work it's not enough, you go out into the streets and shout the government down. That's when you listen to your union's leaders and do just what you're told, because nobody else is looking out for you. Nobody else in this country cares a shit if you're kicked out of your house and you die of hunger, that's the situation. Even when you know you're going to get arrested and maybe somebody is going to get killed in the streets, you still have to go, because at least that's doing something, you can show your little family that you've taken enough. My wife always treats me like a hero when I get home, *che*, I'm looking forward to it. My wife is very beautiful, and the last time I got arrested, we just shut the bedroom door on the kids and the in-laws and we hardly came out again for almost three days. It's like after the war is over, you get to come home.''

"I wish we were home," I said. "I've never wanted to be home so much in my life."

"You got a nice home?"

"Sure, very nice. Five brothers and a sister, a big family, seven kids in all, *che*, you've got to be fast at the table. You've got to pitch in and do everything around the place, too, no way the old man and the old lady can handle all of us. We've got a nice house, and a good school, everything. A nice little town outside of New York, right on the water, it's beautiful any time of the year. I miss it, *che*. Most of all, I miss all my brothers."

"And where are you living here in Buenos Aires?"

"In the Barrio Norte, with a family of the well-to-do people, very very rich, I've never seen so much money, believe me. One roomful of this family's furniture would cost enough to buy everything in my own family's house. Two maids, a doorman, two cars in the garage, and every little thing for the Mamá."

"It must be pretty, *che*, to live like that," the man said.

"Pretty? I don't know. It's maybe prettier at home. My mother at home can't stand to have anybody else come in and clean her house, you understand?"

"*Che*, I think your problem is that you're not looking around you enough. You don't appreciate the finer things in this country. Take advantage of the opportunity! If you don't do that, it's a sin. Learn to live pretty, *che*, if you're given the chance."

"I've tried, believe me," I said. "I swear to you I have.

That's what I thought I've been doing, I don't know," I said and I couldn't talk anymore suddenly, my throat just shut down. My nose and eyes filled to bursting and all the valves in my head just blew open with the pressure and everything was coming out. My body was shaking, and I was crying, I couldn't help it, and trying to stop made it worse. "I don't know . . . I don't know . . ." I was crying. "It's all my fault. My family here is going to kill me, and my brother Alejo, if he's been hurt, I don't know . . ." Most of what I was trying to say was incomprehensible through the big rushing bellows of rasping breaths that sputtered in my mouth and choked back into my lungs with heavy sobs, "I don't know, I just don't know . . ."

"*Che, che, che* . . ." the man said, reaching out with both his strong hands and grabbing me firmly around the shoulders. "It's all right, *che*! Everything's all right! It's going to turnout A-O.K., Yanqui," he said, and I closed my eyes and let everything out, all the wretchedness in my head. If there were saints on this earth, this man was one. He had the best gift of all in him and he gave it freely, without wanting anything in return. I might have freaked out like on acid right then and gone over the edge, but I recovered myself a little, mumbling to him how sorry I was, I'd send his shirt back after I had seen that it was cleaned.

The man sat back from me a bit and bummed a cigarette from someone next to him. It was someone's last black tobacco cigarette, and it ended up carefully broken into thirds, one stub of it placed by the man between my lips. It was the best cigarette I had ever had, the best tasting smoke, that little harsh nub of white paper dribbling black tobacco flakes all over my chin before the flame touched its end and the smoke rose all around me, warm blue comforting smoke. The man was smiling at me now, and he wanted me to buck up, things weren't that bad when there was still this nice cigarette to smoke. I took a big harsh draw of tobacco so strong it felt like I was burning up inside and I was, I was burning up, on fire inside sharing in that one phantom body of smoke, everyone around me filled with it, men on down the line lighting up, too, as many cigarettes as there were. Maybe all the cigarettes I have

smoked since in my life have been to try and get the taste
of that one back in my mouth. Further down the ramp, a
guard even, a guard lazily shouldered his walkie-talkie and
reached into a pocket to toss a few cigarettes across to the
prisoners in front of him, their knees drawn up to their
bodies against the wall. I was starting to see clearly again,
and the pain was leaving my head. It was a burning pain in
my chest that I felt now, a pain that expanded with every
breath, a beautiful pain, as if everyone together was sharing
in this *ite, humo est* in one big united breath I hoped I would
never lose.

There was a long silence in a light so dim by now on the
stadium ramps that the gaily lit cigarettes shone like flares,
faces glowing behind them for brief instants in the smoke.
Everyone was quiet, long enough that I finished my cigarette and closed my eyes and was almost asleep by the time
the harsh white glare of the guards' flashlights raked over
us. We could hear them calling out numbers in the section
of prisoners just down from ours. We all sat up, listening
more closely, getting ready to jump out and present ourselves. A number was called with a sound so muffled I
didn't recognize it as my own.

"Fifteen forty-four!" a guard shouted again. "Fifteen
forty-four!"

"*Sí!*" I was on my feet, shouting. "Here I am!"

"*Che*, what an injustice," somebody said. "They're taking that yanqui before any of us!"

"The buttons don't put their fingers on yanquis."

"How much of a bribe did you have to pay, *che*?"

"Shut up!" the man next to me said. "Any one of you
says another word and I'm going to make shit out of your
face with my fists!" He stood there in front of the others
with his dark fists clenched, an angry tempo of steady
breaths drawn through his nose like a boxer's. After a moment, he turned to me and said with emotion in his voice,
"You go on now. Learn to live pretty, *che*, and stay away
from demonstrations. None of this shit should concern
somebody like you."

"A thousand thanks for everything, brother," I said.

"Give me your name and address so I can send a new shirt to you."

"No names and addresses in here," the man said. "I think the less anybody knows, the better off I'll be, you understand?"

"I understand," I said, then we embraced strongly like brothers, the man slapping me on the back with his tough little hands like hammers. "Thank you, thank you, thank you," I said. "May all go well with you."

"Equally with you, *che*," the man said. A guard was beside us now, impatiently motioning at me with his night-stick like he was ready to step in and use it any second to get me moving. The guard motioned for me to move along down the ramp to processing. Everything would be simple there, I thought, and I wasn't afraid anymore, now that I was moving. There might be explanations, stories to tell, a phone call to Papá if I was lucky, but I was confident that soon all the arrangements would be clear, my family would have me sprung out of there in no time. I started to move fast enough that I had to slow down to let the guard catch up as I was leaving the little section where I had been de-tained. Then I had to slow down a lot more as I passed the row of prisoners from my bus group lined up against the cold cement wall. The breeze coming off the river had now turned into a chilly wind with a bite in it that had these men turning their collars up and huddling close to one another to stay warm. Even so, hands reached out at me, pulled out of jacket pockets to try and grip my hand quickly and shake it, or they wanted to touch me as I passed them, reaching up and brushing my pantleg or the sleeve of my sweater. I moved down the line that way, touching them, not stopping to grip each hand but shaking one or two, taking little pats on my arms and shoulders, little touches all along the ramp of my section as they called out to me, *"Ciao, flaco!"*

"Good luck, *che*!"

"Come to Boca stadium sometime, sit in the northwest sector of the bleachers where I always sit, we'll have a little drink together and I'll teach you all about the game!"

I still remember the sound of their voices.

*"Que tengas cuidado, che!"*

*"Váyate con Dios!"*
*"Que te vayas bien, che!"*
*"Dios vos guarda a vog!"*
*"Adiós!"*
*"Hasta siempre!"*
*"Adiós!"*
*"Adiós!"*

What first struck me about the processing area was that there could be so much light. In the deep rooms under the stadium, fluorescent bulbs ran along the ceilings with a brightness that was blinding until my eyes adjusted. Then I saw all the folding tables that had been set up, ranks and files of them each with an army clerk sitting behind them and a prisoner before him, many of the prisoners sitting there bloody, in pain, around them mounds of arrest forms and file folders piled as high as their heads. So many manual typewriters made a noise as loud as machine guns, a steady roaring in my ears that made my headache start pounding again, so many of them in the large room with its low ceiling that the ringing of the carriage returns never stopped. Interrogations were going on everywhere. Voices were raised, answers shouted above the noise by the prisoners, some of whom were handcuffed to their folding chairs. As I was led along the wall of the room by the guard, I heard a series of interrogations, *Name? Address? What union action group called you to the demonstration? How long have you been a member of this group? Who is its leader? Answer me now and things will go much better for you, is that clear?* and that kind of thing.

All the answers were recorded on sets of similar looking forms, then placed into file folders of a peculiar salmon pink color that were piled everywhere around us, so many high stacks of them on the tables that it was possible to look out over the room and imagine a scale model of a futuristic city of high pink buildings. A soldier with a cart moved around between the tables collecting piles of these folders, then he rolled them out of the big room through a passageway in back. Some of the prisoners were being led out that way, too, all of them handcuffed, as opposed to most of the others who were free of shackles and seemed more docile and cooperative. It was clear that the signs were bad for the handcuffed prisoners they were leading out that way, shoving them roughly through a one-way door, it seemed, because nobody was led back in, at least not during the short time I was in processing.

A system was at work all around me and it was clear—what the army was after was information, and lots of it, full reports on every prisoner, then he was let loose with a fine or a bribe and that was that. These were easy years, relatively, in Argentina. The military seemed like a troop of delinquent boy scouts compared to what they became a few years later, and the point of our arrest and detention, it seemed, was all these file folders, ten of thousands of them.

The Argentine Army had been trained in the thirties and forties by crack instructors from the German *Wehrmacht*. It had an officer corps modeled on pre-World War II Germany's, with principles of absolute order and discipline, loyalty and sacrifice that went beyond most other armies'. It was widely known in the streets of Buenos Aires that many officer cadets slept with photographs of Adolf Hitler over their bunks and were openly trained to revere him. Something else the Germans had left behind was the Argentine military's obsession for archives and records—pre-computer-age systems of information that were carried from one huge depository to another by soldiers in knee-high polished boots. It was an extremely efficient system nonetheless. After decades of keeping files on everyone ever arrested at student and union meetings or out painting walls or at street demonstrations, there must have been a central library of file folders that rivaled the depositories at Nuremberg, and the military was growing subtler about its records all the time, spawning subsections of files on family members of the detained, for example, and on their friends, their businesses, their real estate and wealth, the kinds of cars they drove, their homes, their lives. Fascist repression was built on such foundations of paperwork, it seems; the more the military knew in its records, the greater was its possibility for abusing its own people. And time would prove what the generals would do with the people recorded in these files.

As I was being led through a large interrogation room, it was clear that my own case was special. I wasn't questioned in the big room but led into a small office to one side, where a captain of the army seemed to be in charge. What I remember most is the sense of immediate joy I felt when I saw my beautiful green passport sitting on his desk, and the way he stood up for me in a friendly manner when I came in. He gave me my passport immediately, apologizing all over himself. "I regret very, very much that a North American student has been treated in this way, I assure you. It's a regrettable mistake," the captain said. He was a young man, prematurely bald, with strings of black hair pulled across the tight skin of his scalp in stripes. "If I only knew the officers who had arrested you, I'd have their heads, I swear to you. Vincente," he said to an aide standing by the door. "Please get this yanqui here a little cup of coffee and some aspirins. Wouldn't you like that?" he asked me and I answered yes quickly. "But you must understand how confusing it is in these demonstrations, how hard it is to tell the innocent bystanders from the criminals, isn't that clear? Now what can we do to get you safely home as quickly as possible?"

Everything was understood in a minute. I gave the captain the address and phone number of the Beneventos so his aide could call them to let them know that a police escort would be driving me home. A police escort! I couldn't believe it—he was treating me as if I were suddenly a visiting VIP to be spared any inconvenience. The captain seemed ashamed enough that a yanqui student had ended up detained that he even gave me my arrest record, all three copies of it in the salmon pink folder on which was written only my name, nationality, passport number and detention number, with no need for anything else under the circumstances. "You wouldn't want a record like this to get into the wrong hands," the captain said. "It might be misunderstood and cause you problems with your student visa. It's better if we just consider this situation as if it never happened, don't you agree?" Of course, I agreed immediately. "By the way, you speak admirable Spanish," the captain said. "I wish I could speak English so well. I was a student once in your country and loved it very much, a very wonderful country, the United States. I attended a six-week course in crowd control at your country's national police academy in Washington. I was speaking very good English by the time we finished but I've forgotten it all by now because it's so hard to find chances to practice.''

The aide came in with my coffee and aspirins. The coffee was a thick syrup, it had so much sugar in it, but the aspirins were like a miracle. The captain started to practice a little English on me but he spoke it terribly, and it was hard to respond to; then his aide rescued us both by saying a police car was waiting outside to take me home. ''Gooodabya,'' the captain said. ''Etaka-ita-eeesi,'' he said and grinned. I shook hands with him firmly, this captain was my best friend by then, that was clear, with no hard feelings, mistakes can happen, that was my attitude as I was led out of the stadium.

In the open area outside, clusters of army troops in riot gear looked like they were packing up and getting ready to leave the scene, their workday over, their cigarettes lit and their mood much improved over others I'd seen that day. My army guard turned me over to a pair of blue-uniformed federal police in their black-and-blue Ford Falcon patrol car, one of a line of them parked just outside the stadium gates. I was told to scoot in behind the wire-mesh cage in the back seat, then the police car took off at a fast speed.

It was the second time in less than a month that I had been driven home like in a taxi by the federal police. The first time was after I had banged up the family's Peugeot and wrecked a part of the low wall of the fountain pool across from the statue of General Bartolomé Mitre. I thought of this on the fast ride home, how I had mostly blacked out in the backseat after telling the police who I was and where I lived and that I was a yanqui, trying to shovel the money I had left in my pockets at them. The police had decided to deal directly with Papá—and they must have seen that the little matters of both the car and the fountain might be taken care of without them having to take the trouble of writing out a ticket. I was carried up the stairs and allowed to get sick again in the bathroom before Isabelita saw to it I had been put safely to bed, even as Papá was talking over my situation with the two police officers. How much had he had to bribe them? And who was it who had to pay for the municipal crew out repairing the fountain pool the next morning? Papá had never told me. It must have taken hundreds of thousands of Argentine pesos and maybe more, and here I was again, disappointing him, dealing out another blow to all of them, and both times somehow I had gotten off without so much as a parking ticket.

It was a sad ride through Buenos Aires, and I felt lousy, the officers in the front seat indifferent to me as I looked out the windows at a city all but deserted that night because of the curfew. Truckloads of police and soldiers were still out in force but the streets were quiet. The victory of the military had been so swift and complete almost everywhere in the nation that day that Buenos Aires looked as if it would be back to normal by morning. As we turned a corner onto dark Junín Street, I almost wished I hadn't been set free, not if I had to return again to them like this, in trouble and fucked up and nothing but a worry to them. I would almost rather have been back in the stadium than here, pulling up in front of my family's house in a police car again at this late hour, well after midnight, and to see the lights still burning in Papá's study, spilling out across his balcony through the blinds of his closed French windows. I swallowed hard. Would Alejo be there? What would I do if he wasn't? What was I going to tell the family we were doing?

Mamá and Papá were both waiting up, and so was Martín Segundo, alerted that I was coming home. Alejo had made it back—somehow, he hadn't been arrested. Martín told me Alejo had managed to get to the subway entrance and walked out through the tunnel to the next station down the line with most of the others in our little group. When he saw that I hadn't made it home, Alejo had told Mamá and Papá exactly what had happened. He had been confined to his bedroom for the night, and was grounded for a month in punishment. Papá had been on the phone to police stations, to friends he knew in the military, even to one of the de facto president's cabinet ministers, frantically trying to locate me in all the hassle of the state of siege. As I entered the Benevento flat, Martín told most of this to me, Papá still on the the telephone, calling off searches for me, turning off all the alarms he had raised.

I came in led by Martín and sat down in the living room. When Mamá saw my wound, she became very dramatic and sent Isabelita off to the kitchen for a basin of water and disinfectants. "I'm sorry, Mamá, Papá, please forgive me," I said as Isabelita was washing off my cut. "I'm a stupid *boludo*, I know it. It's all my fault. I should have listened to you and stayed home."

"It's all that son of a whore Hernández-Marelli's fault, Papá, I swear it," Martín Segundo said. "He's the one to blame."

"Shut up, Martín," Papá said. "Go to bed now."

"I'm so ashamed of myself, for this, for everything. I wouldn't blame you and Mamá if you just want to send me back to I.S.E. and let them put me on a plane straight home."

"Don't say another word, my son. Just look at this," said Papá, inspecting the gash on my forehead after Isabelita had cleaned it with gauze. "Are you sure you're all right? Did the police do this to you?"

"Sure, Papá, it was the police," I said. "I was just trying to get my passport out of my pocket then *pow*!"

"Martín," Mamá said. "I think you should take him directly to the doctor's with a nasty cut like that."

"Those sons of whores in the police are going to have to answer to an official protest, believe me, my son," Papá said. He noticed the file folder I had brought in with me and picked it up. "What's this? Your arrest record? But there's nothing on it!"

"That's clear, Papá," I said. "A nice captain let me take it out with me. He said nothing would show up on any official records because it was all a big mistake."

"Of course they would do that!" Papá said with frustration. "Now if I want to lodge an official protest, or if you wanted to call your embassy and make a formal complaint, the police will say they've never heard of you! They'll have no record of your arrest!"

"But this is the record, Martín," Mamá said.

"It's blank except for his name! This doesn't prove anything! Anybody could have gotten hold of blank forms and written this!"

"I'm so sorry, so very sorry, Mamá, Papá," I said. "I'll never not listen to you again."

"You'll have to risk a little ride down the block to the doctor's," Mamá said. "If this cut isn't stitched up soon, it's going to heal looking like a big ugly gash."

"No, please," I said. "I've caused enough trouble."

"Quit saying you're sorry or you're going to make me angry," Mamá said. "Don't be more of a *boludo* than you've already been!"

"But it might be dangerous, Mamá," I started.

"Do what I tell you!" she snapped. "Take a jacket and go with your Papá, it's just down the street. Martín, you go get the car out of the garage, it's safer to take the car," she said.

"I'll go with Papá, so he won't have to drive around the block," I said.

I grabbed up a jacket and joined Papá in the entryway of the building. Looking up and down the street for police, we ducked out of our building entrance and across to the garage. The posh Barrio Norte seemed as deserted of police that night as it usually was of demonstrations and other turmoil. The garage attendant wasn't on duty, on strike too, probably, so Papá used his own set of keys, and we opened the high barred gates on our own. We found Papá's car close by, on the first level. He hustled us both inside and we drove off cautiously down the street without the headlights on. Then Papá said, "This is so stupid, nothing's happening," and turned the car lights on with a jerky movement that made me feel his irritation.

"You're not angry at me, Papá?" I asked. "You're really not?"

"Look, Diego, I'm a lawyer and I don't really ever get that angry. At this idiocy that we have to live through in this country, yes, sometimes, and sometimes I pretend to be angry, sure, to discipline you boys. But one of the beauties of practicing the law is that you learn that anger has no real place in a civilized society. Reason and conscious action, legal action, that's always much better than anger, always the best and surest ways of ever achieving your goals. Believe me, because I know. Anything else just gets your head broken and you're thrown into jail if you're lucky, and if you don't have luck, you just get yourself killed, that's what happens.''

Papá pulled into a parking place and shut off the lights. I started to get out, but he stopped me. ''Listen, my son, because I know,'' he said. ''When I was a young man, my brother Frederico and I got so impassioned about the congressional elections of 1940 that we ran around with guns hijacking the trucks that carried provincial ballot boxes in for counting. We stole the boxes and stuffed them with ballots all marked for the Conservative party candidates, then somebody else delivered them with forged identification. We were part of a conspiracy. This kind of thing was happening all over the province, and I'll tell you, Ortiz and Castillo's Conservative party friends won by a landslide that election. Anyway, my son, my brother Frederico and I were turned in for it. Witnesses from the other parties demanded we be arrested and made enough of a stir that we finally had to turn ourselves in and ended up serving sixty days in the provincial prison. And if our party hadn't won that election, we might still be in prison. Our family couldn't have raised the money to buy us out in those days.''

''You were in prison, Papá? I can't believe it!''

''A poor miserable *boludo* hanging on the bars, and the lowest I've ever felt in my life, believe me. I've felt like an idiot ever since, too, because it's clear now that Frederico and I had made a big mistake and we were working for the wrong side. The Conservatives ran one of the most corrupt and unjust political parties in Argentina's history, but what could we know at eighteen? That experience made me very, very careful in the future, I swear to you, because I will never again risk my life or reputation for something unless I'm sure that it's right, and maybe not even then,'' Papá said.

The Benevento family doctor had an office in an apartment on the first floor of the building where he lived, about three blocks from the Benevento flat. His name was Dr.

Giezeman, a third-generation German-Argentine Jew who was among Papá's best friends, a tennis and card partner from club C.U.B.A. Dr. Giezeman was a good doctor, and we almost never had to wait very long for him. He was ready to see us this time, too, padding around his clean office in his bedroom slippers, white lab coat thrown hastily over his pajamas.

Dr. Giezeman took his time, washing the cut, examining everything, even looking over the other parts of me, shining lights into my eyes and asking me if I felt like throwing up, then listening to my heart with his stethoscope and banging my skinned knees and elbows with a rubber hammer. After a tetanus shot, he injected a local anesthetic into the skin of my forehead, and swabbed it with antiseptic. In all of this, he didn't once ask how the injury had happened, as if Papá had told him what was what and not to ask. He chattered away to Papá, speculating on when Argentina's stock market might open again and what shares he should dump or buy because of what the yanqui dollar might do against the peso with the new state of siege and that kind of thing. Papá and Dr. Giezeman joked about these things, a world hardly part of my comprehension as he made eight slow stitches, stinging even through the anesthetic. There was a strange tugging of the sutures through my skin that made it feel as if it weren't thread he was using but something fifty times as thick, like big, rough cords. Then he finished, assuring me there wouldn't be too much of a scar, I'd still be pretty enough for the girls, and not to worry, the headache should be gone by morning. Then he showed me his work in a little mirror. I was amazed at how small the cut looked, up the right side of my forehead and running just over the scalpline, tiny compared to what I had imagined it was from all the blood. And my right eye had turned purple, a real shiner and a real surprise since I couldn't feel and couldn't remember any pain there. Dr. Giezeman gave me a bottle of antibiotics to take for a week, just in case. Papá made arrangements for the bill and we were back out on the street it seemed in no time. On the ride back home, the streets of the Barrio Norte seemed completely deserted, and it was a strange, exposed feeling to be riding in the only car in sight.

"Our family has a certain reputation to maintain, you know that by now," Papá said. "And political agitation can be very damaging to a family's name. One agitator alone can possibly endanger even the lives of everyone else in his family, is that clear?"

"It's not clear, Papá," I said. "What do you mean?"

"The kind of thing you and Alejo did today is dangerous for all of us, that's what I'm saying," Papá said. "And what if your people at I.S.E. knew about this? First there was the car accident, when it's against I.S.E. rules for you to be driving at all. Then there was getting suspended from school. And now this arrest. Do you get what I'm saying? If we had let I.S.E. know about these things, I'm not sure but that your scholarship might even be revoked. Nobody wants to see that happen, least of all your Mamá and me, so my advice is to tell everyone that you got that cut and that black eye in a game of *fútbol*, is that clear?"

"That's clear, Papá," I said. "I'd never let I.S.E. know about this."

"I don't mean just I.S.E., my son," Papá said. "You have a name and a reputation to protect, along with this family's, and even to spread something like this around Colegio San Andrés would make this mistake of yours very much bigger than it is, very very much bigger. You're in trouble enough with the school as it is, and who knows what the other students might tell their parents?"

"But Papá, how can I lie about this thing when Hernández-Marelli is going to spread it all over the school?"

"I'll take care of Marelli then," Papá said. "I'll give his father a call as soon as we get home. And as for Alejo, I'll talk to him, too, and explain. At least he knows the value of discretion."

"Listen, Papá, Hernández-Marelli walks all over his father and mother. He's famous for it," I said. "Phoning Marelli's father won't do any good."

"You just leave Marelli up to me," Papá said with irritation. "That son of a whore has caused enough harm. You should learn when people are using you, my son, when they're going to use you then leave you standing there to pay the price. Marelli is one of the users of this world. I cringe to think of the times he's used Martín Segundo because Martín is *boludo* enough to want to go to those parties with him."

"I don't know if I can lie about this, Papá," I said. "Don't get me wrong, I would if I could get away with it. I just don't think the others are going to let me."

"Then maybe you can learn something much more useful," Papá said. "Maybe you can learn to avoid the truth without lying."

"It's not clear, Papá. What do you mean?"

"I mean just what I said, my son, and if you think about it, you'll see how much sense it makes. Rule number one for any guest is not to draw too much attention to himself. But number two is that if you know the truth about your host and it's not very nice, avoid it at all costs. Get around the truth without lying. When asked a question to the point, give the answer to a different question, do you understand what I'm saying? Let this be a lesson in diplomacy and an education in discretion, is that clear?" Papá asked. By this time, he was turning the recently repaired Peugeot into the big parking garage. "And don't you worry one bit about Marelli," he said. "Just leave Marelli up to me."

"Listen, Papá. Maybe you should let me try talking to Marelli first," I said.

"You listen to me or you'll make me angry," Papá said. "You're not to talk to anybody about this thing, not a word, not without clearing it with me first, is that clear?"

"Sure, Papá. Whatever you want me to do," I said.

Papá parked the car, and I helped him close and lock the big iron gates of the garage. We looked up and down the street for police again, then I followed Papá at a normal quick walk across the street and into the entrance of our building.

"All I'm saying is that this is a lesson for you," Papá said as we were slowly climbing the stairs, "that's all, a harsh and painful one, but it could be much more painful for you if you go broadcasting it all over the place, do you understand?"

"It's clear, Papá," I said. "I understand."

"That's good, my son, I'm glad," he said. "Then we don't have to say anything more about it."

The next morning, all of us brothers were confined to the house until school would open again the next day. We were supposed to remain alone in our rooms, but after lunch, I found a few private minutes with Alejo. We spoke in whispers.

"*Che*, how did it happen? How did you ever get out of there?"

"Through the subway, Diego. If we could have stuck together another five minutes, you'd have made it out with me and we wouldn't be in such trouble, what a hassle. I'm sorry you got it so bad, *che*."

"And Cristina? Was she with you?"

"No, *che*, she wasn't. Gloria was giving Marelli a hassle about it the whole time. Andrés, María Inez and Cristina didn't make it into the subway with us, but don't worry, *che*, she'll be all right."

"But *che*, we don't know! She was probably arrested! And I don't even know where she lives!"

"Marelli would know," Alejo said. "Or he could give you Gloria's number and she could tell you."

"I'm going to phone Marelli," I said, already starting for the hallway extension.

"Wait, *che*!" Alejo said. "Don't try it with Mamá and Papá in the living room!"

"You're right," I said. "I'll try Marelli later."

"Listen, you'll probably see him out at the villa tomorrow anyway. It's safer that way. Or at least wait until tomorrow when you can call him from a public phone. Martín is around, and Miguelito, and Mamá isn't planning to leave. We're in enough trouble, *che*, and just mentioning Marelli's name in this house is going to make it worse."

"Maybe so, *che*," I said. "Maybe it would be best if I wait until tomorrow."

The next day, when I began to work again on the Villa Hendaya school with Father Vargas and El Gordo and the others, putting in my last few days before returning to classes, the issue of my black eye and the stitches on my forehead was settled with an easy lie. The big news at Colegio San Andrés was that Hernández-Marelli had been suddenly drafted into the Argentine Army. According to Marelli's friend, José Ugarte, the buttons had shown up in the middle of the night and had literally dragged Marelli out of his bed with a draft notice dated three months before and a warrant for his arrest. Marelli's father wasn't at home, and his hysterical mother hadn't been able to stop them. Inside of a day, the Argentine Army had shaved off all of Marelli's long thick playboy locks, made him swear the oath of allegiance and induction, then had shipped him off to a basic training camp more than a thousand kilometers away in the cold southern desert of Patagonia.

I learned of Marelli's news from El Gordo Rojo, working alongside him on the wall of the school, the two of us by then the real veterans out there and knowing how to get to work the easiest jobs. El Gordo said that José Ugarte had received a frantic phone call from Marelli from his basic training camp asking José to spread the news that he had been drafted but not to give up hope for his return because it was all a big mistake. Marelli expected his father, the judge, was going to use his influence to clear the whole thing up as soon as he could. I checked El Gordo's story out with Alejo, and Alejo confirmed most of the details. Marelli's getting his head shaved was a hot topic of conversation between us brothers at our meals, whenever Mamá and Papá were away from the table. "They almost drafted him last year," Martín said. "The *boludo* is lucky he got out of it this long."

Maybe this was true—maybe Marelli really had been legitimately drafted. He had flunked senior year enough times, that was clear, and he was surely old enough, and maybe the Buenos Aires draft board knew somehow that Marelli had been suspended and was on his way to being expelled from Colegio San Andrés any day. Maybe that was the real story, and I quietly considered it. The other possibility only Papá could have affirmed or denied, and I knew that Papá was going to avoid any such questions, so I didn't ask them. What could I have done about Marelli anyway? I had enough problems of my own, and the Argentine draft was a common government tactic for getting rid of troublemakers. Rumor had it that during one general strike, fourteen thousand auto workers had taken to the streets in the colonial city of Rosario, on the banks of the River Plate to the North. Almost all of the strikers were arrested and of those, ten thousand of them had had no military service. The auto workers' strike was solved by drafting many of these ten thousand workers into the Argentine Army, ripping them from their homes and making them into *pelados*, shaved heads, then shipping them off to basic training camps in the South—just like what had happened to Marelli, hard to believe but true.

So what could somebody like me possibly do for Marelli, anyway? But without him, how would I ever find Cristina again? I telephoned Marelli's household, hoping his mother might have his address book and be able to give me at least Gloria's number, but nobody answered at the Marelli apartment for two days. Then I got hold of a maid who said that the judge and his wife had gone off to their country house for an extended stay and she didn't know when to expect them back, and no, she didn't know where he kept his address book. That evening, I waited on the steps of the College of Medicine, where Cristina had said she was a student, hoping to catch sight of her or Gloria, and I even asked a few young doctors-to-be if they knew a girl named Cristina that fit her description, but it was pointless, I wasn't even sure she had given me her right first name. I walked slowly home, hands in my pockets, one of them still searching for the charm from my brother that had crossed oceans, and that was no longer there. I felt my luck had already begun to change.

All that week after school I went back to the university hospital district at different times of day, searching the little plaza in front of it and combing the benches under its scruffy palm trees, then I worked my way through the student bars and coffee houses nearby but found nothing, not a trace. Even after I gave up looking for Cristina, I lay awake nights wondering about her, my mind filled with fantasies. The only chance I had was to wait until Marelli's family returned home and get his boot camp address from them, if they would even give it to me. Until then, my best instincts told me to get myself back into classes at Colegio San Andrés as quietly as I could, to study hard and to get myself through, and to stay mostly at home, keeping as low a profile as possible while I learned to live pretty, as the man had said.

# 6

## The Big Ranch

It was Papá who first suggested that I take a trip into the country to visit his brother Frederico and to see the family's large *estancia*. He presented the trip to me as a learning experience but it was clear there was also a certain tension in the Benevento family after five months of close living with El Yanqui, because of my troubles at school, my scrapes with the police, and the possibility that I was leading Alejo into the wrong crowd of friends.

I finished out my sentence at Villa Hendaya and started back to classes at Colegio San Andrés. I only had a week to make up my work there until I left again for the family's big ranch before the term was over and winter vacation had officially begun. I made arrangements with my professors to take make-up winter exams, with phone calls from Papá to help explain my situation. Everything was settled for me easily, and everything was clear. As I moved through my daily routine of school, meals and homework, I felt my family's need to put their house in order after the chaos I had brought into it. Alejo was still grounded for going to the demonstration with me, lying in his bed after school and in the evenings, feeling low even as he devoured his books and his heels of bread. Sometimes we got together over the newspaper and followed what we could about the nation's events. The Peronist agitation was continuing in random bombings and armed raids by groups like the Montoneros and the E.R.P. These acts were strongly countered by the military, who also used them to justify continuing their state of siege. We compared their mentality to that of the U.S. government, which was stepping up the bombing in North Vietnam, and we agreed that neither policy was working. But mostly, Alejo was confined to his room. Martín Segundo was off to various parties and social events to which I was also invited. I wasn't officially grounded like Alejo but I respected what he was going through and preferred to stay home, keeping my low profile. Without a date, and with my black eye turned a jaundiced green and the stitches like an ugly caste mark on my forehead, I wouldn't fit in with Martín's class of girls in any case, and I probably would only have hung around the imported scotch or the champagne and strawberry punch, and I wasn't going to take the chance. Maybe it was Papá's formal tone of voice when he proposed the trip to Tío Frederico's, without his usual invitation to sit and listen to music with him, that made me feel somehow like an exile in his house. Mamá's cheerful attitude at the prospect of my prolonged absence from her fold also made me feel a little like a troublesome dog who was being sent to the country, sparing its family the more radical solutions.

Mamá gave me wads of money to shop for my trip, and I bought expensive handknit sweaters from Uruguay, imported Levi's and a cool pair of black riding boots with flamenco heels. When the day came, Isabelita packed my things in a new leather suitcase with DIEGO tooled across its strap, a gift from Papá for my birthday, which was still a month away. The Beneventos saw me off in a taxi bound for the Retiro station, little Miguel carrying my bag down for me and chattering away, "Let's make a deal, Diego. You write me letters from Tío Freddi's, and I'll give you personalized service to see the mail that comes for you is forwarded, is that all right? Meanwhile, Alejo and I are going to work on Mamá and Papá to get them to send us out to the ranch to join you for our winter vacation. *Che*, it's a great time out at Tío Freddi's. The three of us get out there and we'll have ourselves a real boss time, that's sure. I have a horse named Porotos out there that I ride. He's a very fast horse. Write to me and tell me how Porotos is doing. And get Tío Freddi to write to Papá and Mamá and invite Alejo and me to join you. Martín never likes to go. He always gets into trouble with the horses and ruins everything. But with the three of us out there, it's going to be great.'' The little guy saw me into my cab like a gentleman, repeating my destination to the taxi driver so he was sure the man had gotten it right. He stood on the sidewalk in front of the building, waving at me and shouting, ''*Adiós, che!* Have a great time! See you out there in two weeks! Ciao, Dieguito! Until a little while!''

My first good look at the pampas out the windows of the train confirmed what I had studied in school and what everyone had told me—this was a rich land, with wheat fields that stretched far off into the horizons and pastures where the grasses stood taller than a man. Every fifty kilometers or so, there was another dusty cow and farming town with its cement-block houses and little tile-roofed train station where freight cars waited on the sidings to be loaded with beef and grain. It was easy to imagine how the fifteen or so skinny cattle and ten horses the first Spaniards had released on the pampas had increased on such land to the millions of head that were running wild on it three centuries later.

It was easier for me to understand Argentina's history as I looked out the windows of the train and saw the glaring difference between the opulent port with all its culture and the impoverished, dusty little unpaved towns of the provinces. There was almost a physical boundary drawn two hundred kilometers or so from Buenos Aires, after which I entered what seemed a completely different country—the people were darker, for one thing, many of them dressed in baggy and drab clothes. And it seemed that as far as I could see, there was nothing but ranches, wheat farms, more ranches; I was only to see a few paved roads, all of them major highways, during the entire trip. There was a lot of the country I didn't see then, and I knew it—the colonial Spanish city of Córdoba in the North where steel mills and discontentment were still smoldering away, and the deep and natural port of Rosario upriver where there were auto factories and a strong trading center with Paraguay and Brazil. There was Tucumán, like one vast sugar plantation with its *indio* laborers who managed to get along on a standard of living perhaps a little better than colonial slaves. There was the quaint provincial capital of La Plata, and the Andean city of Mendoza with its prize-winning vineyards, and San Carlos de Barriloche in the high mountains that was like the San Moritz of South America. Nor did I see the prosperous German colonies in the central hilly mountains near Rio Cuarto, nor the booming oilfields of Commodore Rivadavia in the southern desert, nor the beautiful fruit-growing region of Chubut, nor the fancy beach resort town called Mar del Plata built by Aristotle Onassis to be a kind of Miami Beach of Argentina. There was a lot I didn't see then, but it was still coming clear to me what Papá had said and what Professor Herrera had been trying to teach us at Colegio San Andrés all along, that no matter the ruling politics, the military, Peronism, even the most lenient of democracies, the history of Argentina was still one of unjust geographical divisions. Whatever development there was in the interior was always second to what had been illogically spent on the gigantic sprawling city of Buenos Aires, which held nearly half of Argentina's population and still treated the country's vast resources, one-fifth of the total landmass of South America, as if it were one big ranch at its back door.

The train continued, hour after hour, into the sunset across an unbroken landscape of fields and pastures that dropped away into haze if I squinted and tried to see to the end of them. Being on a ship and leaving land for the first time must be something like this, I thought, feeling so diminished in size. There were immense stretches of empty land, then wheat fields after harvest, close-cropped expanses of stubble as far as I could see. There were cattle-herds at railheads that looked like great migrations, drovers on horses herding them into corrals and up loading chutes onto freight cars. By the time I got off the train at a town called Henderson the next afternoon, it was hard to believe after the sight of so much standing food that it was possible for anyone on the continent to go hungry. It was easy to see the truth in what Papá had told his sons one evening in his study: "The real hope of this country is still its rich land. Argentina has the potential perhaps to feed one quarter of the world's population. And it's a comfort to us to know that no matter how bad things might get, unlike other countries in Latin America, nobody in this country is going to be starving. Even the poorest of Argentines still eats. We eat more per capita even than you yanquis do, more kilos of meat, and more calories each day per person than any other country in the world."

Tío Freddi was blond, a kind of broadchested, Nordic version of Papá, and he wore a black Basque beret cocked at an angle over one eye. He was waiting for me in a maroon Chevy pickup truck at the small train station in the town of Henderson, named after the bastard son of an English count who had been sent to Argentina to establish a family trading station for the British railroad. He was murdered in his first year by a raiding party of Araucanian Indians, as Tío Freddi explained to me, leaving only his name behind on the pile of smoking rubble that would become the town.

Tío Freddi was accompanied by Rudolfo Churro, whom everyone called Rulo, a cousin of the Benevento family who managed a chain of provincial pharmacies and happened also to be visiting the family ranch. Rulo was a lanky, olive-skinned type in his late twenties who wore sunglasses and kept his black hair long enough to be considered radical. Rulo stood back acting cool as Tío Freddi crushed my hand and slapped me across the shoulders. "So! This is my brother's yanqui cowboy! The way he described you, I thought you'd be bigger! We have to get you out to the ranch and put some meat on your bones, *flaco*!"

We had work in town to do first, loading boxes of veterinary supplies into Tío Freddi's pickup. The supplies had arrived on the same train as I had, and Rulo and I labored for a while passing the big cartons down off a loading dock to Tío Freddi, most of the boxes marked *Fiebre Aftosa*, which Tío Freddi explained was vaccine for hoof-and-mouth disease. "Big work out on the ranch every six months. Every single beef, *whapa*, injection!" He made a gesture with both hands, pantomiming giving a steer the needle as if I hadn't understood him. "It costs a mountain of my money every time, but who cares? We haven't had a case of hoof-and-mouth disease in this whole district for twenty years. I love my cattle, sometimes more than my family. I want to see them nice and fat and healthy, you'll see."

We all piled into Tío Freddi's pickup and took off. I sat between the two men on a seat that was like a bucking horse once we had driven through the few blocks of dusty streets that was Henderson. The road to the family ranch was really a muddy track with ruts and potholes that extended in a straight line into the pampas ahead. We passed tens of kilometers of barbed wire fences along one side of the track, and on the other side the country was open, a landscape of tall grasses brown in winter and with a few distant patches of dark green eucalyptus groves that marked where there might be houses. On one side of the road, the grasses grew higher than the truck, tall and thick-stemmed, filled with seed at the end of autumn, the tops spread out into frondlike heads that made them look like a dense field of straw-colored peacock feathers. On the other side of the road there were large herds of cattle grazing, most of them bunched up near the wire—fat-looking black cattle or brown ones with white faces, serenely poking their noses into the brown tufted grass under the warm sun of a mild winter day. We passed a chapel built almost on the road, a tiny building of whitewashed adobe, deserted in evening, a glimmering bronze bell hanging silently in the little Spanish arch of its steeple. Every few kilometers, a dirt track suddenly appeared and turned off at a sharp angle from this main road, but otherwise we passed no buildings, just open grassy fields with these tracks that cut through them into the distance. Far ahead of us on our rutted track with its mane of grass that was the major road, what looked like dozens of brownish-gray snowballs suddenly sprouted legs and started to run.

*"Ñanduces!"* Tío Freddi shouted, then he laughed and gunned the pickup to catch up to the birds but they were fast. The Chevy was doing sixty miles per hour by its yanqui speedometer, and it took a long time before we were suddenly on top of the panicked flock of rhea ostriches, hundreds of brownish flurries of running birds with huge black doll's eyes scattering all around us. "We'll remember this place and come back on horses Saturday for a little hunting. With the *bolas*, yanqui, do you understand?" Tío Freddi asked, whirling one hand in the air as if it held an imaginary set of *bolas*. He laughed crazily out the open truck window at the ostriches, wildly gesturing at them with one arm and swerving the Chevy around on the little mud track of the road as if trying to hit one. When we had almost left them all behind, an ostrich suddenly went down ahead of us and the truck flew over it with a thump that made Tío Freddi laugh. A cloud of dust and feathers rose behind us as the birds disappeared against a darkening sky.

"*Che*, Yanqui," Rulo said. "Have you ever made love to any of the blondes that are all over your country?"

"What did you say?" I asked.

"To the blondes, *che*, in your country?"

"No," I said.

"In this country?" Rulo asked.

"I don't understand," I said.

"He asks everybody the same thing," Tío Freddi said with a mischievous smile at Rulo that made me feel like they were sharing a joke at my expense.

"I keep thinking there's a basic difference between blondes and brunettes," Rulo said. "Don't get me wrong, I love all kinds of women, and I never turn a good woman down. But I prefer the blondes, like the ones you have all over in *la USA*. You see them all over in your yanqui magazines, and in the movies, and I've always thought *la USA* must be a paradise because it has so many blondes. Dark-haired girls have a stronger smell, a thicker skin, they're like good strong liquor. Blondes are like a taste of something very very sweet, have you ever noticed that?"

"I've never really thought about it," I said.

"Tonight, after you're settled at Tío Freddi's, we'll take

a drive into town to La Correntina's. You and I will experiment on this problem and you'll tell me what you decide,"
Rulo said.

"What are you talking about? What's La Correntina's?"

"When my brother Martin tells me to show somebody a
good time, we show him a good time," Tío Freddi said and
laughed. "You know, Rulo, I haven't been to La Correntina's in maybe two months? This year, it's been one thing
after another. So tonight's the night. I'm in a mood for a
celebration, how about you?"

"Suits me," I said, still not catching on. "What kind of
clothes should I wear for this place?"

"Not a stitch, if you're ready," Rulo said and they
laughed.

The truck slowed down, jolting and bouncing around over
potholes. My head hit the roof of the cab a few times, then
suddenly this rollicking motion of Tío Freddi's driving
changed and I had to put my hands out just in time to keep
from smashing into the dashboard as he slammed on the
brakes.

"Nuns!" Tío Freddi said. "Son of a whore, Rulo, look
at them! Nuns!"

Ahead of us, a dark gray Citroën car that looked as if it
were designed to resemble a species of giant insect moved
slowly, head-on, in our direction. "It's the Three Marías,"
Tío Freddi said. "We named them the same as the constellation. They come from the chapel school down the road
and they're all named María." He stopped the pickup and
hopped out, leaving the engine running. Rulo and I watched
as Tío Freddi checked the soft ground on either side of us
and the problem came clear to me—it was muddy on either
side of the road, and there wasn't room enough for us to
pass.

"Would you believe it?" Tío Freddi said as he hopped
back into the truck and shifted gears impatiently. "Nuns!"
He hit the gas pedal with a slam of his boot, hanging onto
his open door and looking behind us as he backed the pickup
fast, about thirty miles an hour in reverse. The Citroën in
front of us slowly approached, and I could make out the
nuns' dark habits bouncing around inside. Tío Freddi had

to back up almost to where we had come upon the ostriches before he could turn out onto solid ground and let the nuns pass. As their little gray car pulled by, we all waved at them and smiled when they waved back, their car pausing a moment as it passed Tío Freddi's open window, and he called out to them, "Is the priest coming to the chapel this Sunday?"

The nun who was driving nodded her head and answered in a shout, "A new priest from Villa Tosco! And the Pérez-O'Reillys are bringing their new baby in to be christened the following Saturday!"

"We'll be there!" Tío Freddi shouted, then he waved to them as they passed by. Tío Freddi idled there a moment, then he looked over at Rulo and me with amusement and said, "Do you have your left nut in your fist?"

Rulo laughed and said, "Here, Yanqui," and made a show of reaching his left hand down to his crotch and squeezing. "When you pass nuns, you do this," he said. "You grab your left nut, like getting rid of a curse, so you won't have bad luck in all the bad things you're planning to do, you understand?"

"Come on now," said Tío Freddi. "Everybody. I'm superstitious about nuns." He reached into his crotch and squeezed. Slowly, feeling ridiculous, I imitated this gesture and gave my own left testicle a tiny pinch. Rulo and Freddi broke up as if this were the funniest thing they'd ever seen. Freddi hit the gas again with a high, giddy laugh, slapping his open hand repeatedly on the dash and saying, "We're going to have a great time tonight, you'll find out! A really famous time!"

The Benevento *estancia* was made up of four large ranches put together over a century by three generations of my new family. They measured their land in hectares, and the Beneventos had added to their holdings a thousand hectares at a time; they owned seven thousand of them by the time Tío Freddi took over management of the land, something like seventeen thousand acres, or about twenty-six square miles of fenced-in pampas that bordered a deep creek called Henderson, named after the same unfortunate British trader as was the town. There were groves of eucalyptus trees that grandfather Benevento had planted all over the original home place. Along the creek bottom, on another section, was the ranch that had been added by Tío Freddi and Papá's father, where the rich, humid pampa soil yielded some of the most profitable crops of sunflower seeds ever recorded in Argentina. Tío Freddi boasted that he had personally added more than two hundred hectares of new level fields for crops, and he had married into a vineyard, a honey house and, just as important to him, a polo grounds and stables left over from the nineteen thirties.

The sun was setting fast, and I had to try to imagine the lay of all this land that Tío Freddi was describing to me as we turned off the main road and passed through a large wrought iron gate with the name *María Consuela* in welded black iron letters, the name of the first grandmother Benevento, the one Tío Freddi's grandfather had returned to Naples for from his seasonal wheat harvesting jobs and had brought back with him after a marriage arranged by the family.

The pickup rose up out of the rangeland suddenly onto what might be called a very low bluff. The shapes of eucalyptus trees appeared in the headlights, a long tunnel-like passage through the grove with its minty atmosphere that seemed instantly cooler, almost chilly, some of the trees in the grove with trunks as big around as fifty-gallon barrels. Then the surface we were driving on changed, paved with crushed stones, and we came out of the grove through a collection of white buildings that resembled a tiny village— a large barn and corral with the eyes of horses and cows glowing in the quick rake of the headlights across them, then bunkhouses, machinery sheds, a pumphouse and other outbuildings, and a small whitewashed chapel just like the one we had passed along the road. Off to one side, in its own grove of shade trees, a modern ranch-style house sprawled out over a well-mowed lawn. At the sound of the truck approaching, three or four men in baggy shirts, pantaloons and rope-soled shoes appeared out of the near darkness. Tío Freddi followed their directions into a storage shed, where the medicines we had brought were going to be unloaded, then we all walked from the shed across the open yard to the main house, its windows cheerily glowing in the night.

Tío Freddi's wife was waiting in the main doorway for us, a maid at her side, and Freddi introduced me to his wife quickly, as if she were simply another part of the vast holdings he had described to me. I gave her the formal Argentine handshake and little kiss on the cheek as Tío Freddi was saying, "This is my beautiful Inez Benevento Reynal, of the famous Reynal family of this district. When we married, we added another thousand hectares to the ranch from her father's land. He was the one with the polo grounds. Inez' father was one of the most famous polo players in the world. A veterinarian, too. All the men in her family prefer to work as veterinarians or lawyers in towns rather than live on their ranches, so the Reynals were lucky Inez found me, weren't they, my love?"

"You've probably discovered my husband has a very egocentric view of himself," Inez said, smiling at Tío Freddi. "But we tolerate him in the family anyway."

"Our yanqui nephew," Tío Freddi said. "What do they call you? Diego?"

"Very happy to have you here," Inez said. "Now if you'll excuse me, I have some things to see to, so we can talk later."

Rulo watched Inez walking down the hallway to her kitchen and whispered loudly over my shoulder, "Did you ever think you'd see a woman who looks as good as she does this side of Buenos Aires?"

"Out here in the province, we've got the richest land and the most beautiful women," Tío Freddi said. "Inez has the heart of the Irish and the passion of the true *criolla*, the true native girl. She needs her little trip to the beach at Mar del Plata once a summer, and two times a year to Buenos Aires for shopping, and she's happy. Of course, I hardly ever go along. Pah! Buenos Aires stinks! The air! The swampy climate! All the noise! And it's run by a bunch of gangsters in uniform, that's clear. Out here in the province, the life is much cleaner. It's a better life, don't you think?"

"Sure," I said after a brief awkward moment in which I

was thinking that I had only been on the Benevento ranch about ten minutes. "It's a marvelous life," I said.

"Out here it is," Tío Freddi said.

"That's it, a marvelous life, no?" Rulo said.

"Much better than the cities," I said, agreeing with him because it seemed to be what Tío Freddi wanted. He put an arm around his new nephew's shoulders in an emotional embrace that felt like one of Papá's big Italian hugs.

"This one's a gaucho yanqui," Tío Freddi said.

"Surely," Rulo said. "And tonight, like gauchos, we're going to take our lances to La Correntina's for wine, music and throwing our dust around."

"Then let's go," Tío Freddi said. "Let's wash up and get dinner over with! Conchata!" he shouted to the maid, who had been waiting there with her arms stretched out, a mound of fresh linen in them held in place with her chin. "Take these two here to the guest house," he ordered. "If you need anything, I've assigned one of my men to you," Tío Freddi said to me. "The one called Casimiro. Just open the back door of the guest house and Casimiro's window is the one facing you from the bunkhouse across the yard. He doesn't hear so well anymore, so you might have to knock on his window until you wake him. He's going to pick out a horse for you in the morning."

Tío Freddi moved off down the hallway to wash up, and we followed the maid out of the house and across the starlit yard to a tiny white cinder-block cottage where the dim yellow glow of kerosene lamps shone through the curtained windows. Conchata informed us that the electric generator would only be running for another hour—it was always turned off at dinner, so we should bathe before then if we needed to. The guest house had two sets of bunkbeds against the walls, a bureau and a mirror, a pair of red-checkered armchairs to match the curtains, and a tiny sink, toilet and shower stall in a closet-size space in one corner. "I love this little house," Rulo said. "I used to pick up girls in town and bring them out here when I was a boy. Just about every boy in the family has had an initiation in one of these bunks. The bottom ones are best. It's like having them in a steel trap built for two and then *pow*, you spring the catch!"

The maid was bulling her way up and down the ladders of the bunkbeds, making up all four of them, for some reason, and changing the linen on Rulo's already rumpled one, her arms working like stocky pumps, making the clean sheets crack as she spread them out. Rulo flopped down on the first made-up bunk and folded his arms behind his head. He was so tall he looked ridiculous up there on top, his legs bent at the knees and dangling off into space. "It's going to be a good night tonight, I can tell," he said. Rulo reached into the pocket of his leather jacket and produced a small bottle of pills. "*Che*, would you like one of these?" he asked, popping a white capsule on the end of his tongue and sticking it out to show me.

"One of what?" I asked.

"Nothing serious," he said. "Just a little amphetamine from one of my pharmacies. You better take one, Yanqui. After the long train ride, you don't want to be falling asleep at La Correntina's, do you?"

"Don't worry about me," I said. The thought hit me that it had been almost half a year since I had taken any drugs stronger than aspirin, and it amazed me that I had gone that long without missing them and was even a little suspicious of them now.

Unlike Rulo, I waited until the maid was out of the guest house before showering and changing for dinner. We had a few minutes before we were due to be called to the table, and I followed Rulo's example in flopping down on my bunk, a bottom one across from his top one, and I closed my eyes for a little rest. I was sleepy, that was clear, and I began to daydream of myself falling asleep sometime later in a smoky palace full of alluring gypsies. On our way into the house for dinner, I thought what the hell, and I asked Rulo to give me one of his little white pills.

The smoke of beef barbecuing filled the night but because of Rulo's pill, I suddenly wasn't hungry. Inez's salad course tasted like burned paper, and her brothy soup filled me after two spoonfuls. I felt like I had about sixty cups of coffee pumping in my blood and the thought of steak and fried potatoes to follow made me queasy. I spent most of the dinner apologizing to Inez that I didn't have an appetite,

Tío Freddi leaning over me from time to time to show me
how the best Argentine beef needs no steak knife, it can be
cut with the edge of a fork. I choked down several mouthfuls of the biggest, tenderest rare steak I had ever seen. As
Inez went off to see about coffee and dessert, Tío Freddi
had the electric generator turned off and we all leaned in a
little closer over the table in the lamplight. Tío Freddi
winked at me as a maid cleared my unfinished plate and
said, "You should have eaten more. You're too skinny.
There's no need to be nervous! La Correntina is the best in
the province, I swear it!"

"Does she still refuse to show anybody her tits?" Rulo
asked.

"La Correntina hasn't changed since you saw her last,"
Freddi said. "But her girls are better now."

"La Correntina always wears something to cover her
tits," Rulo said. "They say she had a husband once, a lazy
gigolo who lived off her earnings. She promised him she
would never show anyone else her tits."

"That's a lie," Tío Freddi said. "She just wants certain
customers curious enough to pay extra."

"I don't believe it," Rulo said. "La Correntina's tits are
a legend. She'll never show anybody what belonged to
him."

"Let's just skip dessert and get going, what do you
think?" Tío Freddi said. "Inez!" he called out. Inez appeared in the doorway with the young cook, who was bringing in a platter of French crepes filled with hot *dulce de
leche*, a kind of caramel. "I'm going to take these two into
town," Tío Freddi said. "Carlos and Joaquín are waiting
to play cards with this yanqui at the recreation center," he
said. By Inez's expression, a certain tightening at the corners of her mouth, I could tell Tío Freddi's story was for
the sake of propriety toward his wife and she knew it, she
was long on experience with his so-called card games, his
guided tours of local color for his guests. She nodded once,
a gesture of acceptance. She waved her young cook back
into the kitchen with the nice dessert.

"I hope you have very good luck at cards," Inez said to
me sweetly.

"I've never really been much good at card games," I said, and I could feel a heat breaking out all over my face.

"Well then I hope you're dealt all the best hands," Inez said and smiled a little, a brief crack in the reserved tightness of her face that looked like the only part of her body not tied down by her modest clothes—a long gray dress with high collar and gray lacework at the sleeves. She offered her cheek for Freddi, Rulo and me to kiss, then retired to her bedroom.

Tío Freddi, Rulo and I all piled into the Chevy pickup and sped off into the pampas night, rocking and bucking along in the perilous darkness on our way to La Correntina's. Rulo's speed was pumping full bore through my system at a high enough pressure that I felt as if the top of my head was ready to blow off. I realized how fast Tío Freddi was driving along the potholed track, seventy or eighty miles an hour, hard to figure how he even knew where the road was the way the tall grass on either side seemed to leap up into the headlights in fantastic shapes. Speed paranoia ran through me. It felt as if any second Tío Freddi was going to skid off onto the soft shoulder and probably kill us all in the tumbling fireball of his Chevy. Thoughts were racing through my mind, like which side of the cab to throw myself toward if we started skidding off the road in order not to take the long stickshift through the chest, my hands gripping the dash, teeth clenched, my feet automatically reaching for imaginary brake pedals and slamming against the empty floor. All at once, like a wild animal jumping out at us from the tall grass ahead in the eerie light, a humped-over gray shape appeared. Twin red reflections looked like glittering eyes in the headlights as Tío Freddi hit his brakes going sixty and nearly spun us broadside into the grass. When we had finally stopped, I looked out and recognized a little gray car—it was the one that belonged to the Three Marías.

The Citroën was sitting crossways in the narrow road, one of its front-wheel-drive axles pulled out and its tire sunk into the mud at an odd angle. I sat in the cab of the pickup as Freddi and Rulo surveyed the situation, the three nuns piling out of their car and conferring with the men with happy expressions on their faces. They had run into trouble and we had arrived miraculously to save them, that was clear. Freddi crouched around in the mud in the deep shadows cast by the headlights and I got out of the truck to watch. "Maybe we can jack it out," Freddi said. He waved at me to go back to the truck. "Get my jack out from behind the seat!"

I found the pickup jack, unshackled it from its place behind the seat, and carried it over to Tío Freddi. Rulo was looking for something solid to rest the jack on. He took a scrap of board from the back of the pickup, then a burlap sack to go over the board, and finally they used Freddi's spare tire as a base. Nothing worked. Every solid object they put under the jack sank into the soft ground at the edge of the road. Tío Freddi strained at the jack handle as Rulo and I grunted and lifted up on the back bumper as if that would help but it didn't. Jack, tire, burlap sack and board sank out of sight into the mud. Rulo put a soft playboy shoulder against the front of the car and I joined him. The Three Marías started heaving their small bodies against the car with us—six people in all, our combined straining just about lifting the little French compact into the air, but it wasn't enough, we couldn't even manage to push it off the road. Tío Freddi tried the car, just to see what might happen. He started the engine, but when he tried to put the car into gear, there was a sick screaming of disintegrating steel and none of the tires was spinning.

We were covered head to foot with mud. One of the nuns was on her hands and knees in the grass, and I crawled around helping her search for her shoe that had been sucked off in a swampy tire track. Rulo stood by the pickup and slammed his fist into his open palm, turning his face to look up at the starry night as if asking it how such a thing could have happened. Tío Freddi seemed more stoic, pleasantly lowering the tailgate on the Chevy and like a gentleman helping one of the nuns up into the back to ride with Rulo and me. The other two nuns slid into the cab to ride with him. As Tío Freddi was getting in behind the wheel, he shrugged his shoulders at us in an exaggerated way and asked us in a loud voice, "Confess it now, which one of you cheated this afternoon? Which one? Which one of you cheated?''

Tío Freddi laughed as he began to back up at about fifteen miles an hour a good part of the way to the ranch. The nun riding in the pickup bed with us occasionally pounded on Freddi's window and shouted at him, ''Be careful! Watch out! Slowly, please!'' Every time she was bounced and jolted by the bumps in the road. At one point, I reached out and grabbed her to hold her steady but she shoved an elbow into my ribs and pushed me away, clearly embarrassed. I didn't try again. Considering where we had been going, it didn't feel right that I should have put my arms around a nun.

There was a hubbub when the little sisters arrived at the main house. Inez got out of bed and called servants out to help settle the sisters in their guest rooms, to light their kerosene space heaters and to find them something to eat. Tío Freddi led us away from the turmoil and into his large ranch house living room, where he lit a fire in his big fireplace and served Rulo and me each a stiff scotch. He was still laughing, saying things like, ''Don't take it so hard, Rulo. Some nights are good for sinning and some nights aren't, that's just the way it is.'' Ribbing Rulo until it lost its humor, Freddi finished his drink and marshaled us off to bed.

Rulo was disappointed. Monday marked the beginning of work with Tío Freddi's herd down on the piece of land furthest from the main house, the thousand hectares called San Ignacio because the Jesuits had once established a mission nearby. It was a long ride on horseback to San Ignacio, and we were going to sleep a few nights out there during the roundup. Since it was Saturday night, and since La Correntina's was closed on Sundays and Rulo had to leave on Tuesday to be back at work making deliveries to his pharmacies, his part of the expedition to La Correntina's would have to be put off until his next visit. As we lay in our bunks in the little bunkhouse, Rulo was complaining about our bad luck that night, *mala leche*, he called it, spoiled milk, and his complaints were starting to get on my nerves by the time he rolled over and started to snore. I tried to do the same but I was too wired on Rulo's pill to sleep. My eyes wouldn't stay closed no matter how much I forced them, so I pulled a jacket on over my pajamas and stepped outside into the night.

I stood in the Benevento yard, at the center of its little village of white buildings surrounded by tall eucalyptus trees. I looked up at the sky, a deep cobalt blue that was glowing like the paintings of Henri Rousseau. It seemed to be curving overhead, lit up by the stars and a quarter moon. I realized I hadn't noticed the stars in a long time, maybe not once since I had been living in Buenos Aires. I remembered the sky at home and this one seemed strange to me— it seemed there were far fewer stars in the southern hemisphere, millions fewer, but because of that, each one seemed all the brighter, standing out more alone in its dark space. I identified the Southern Cross, looking as if it might duck down into the trees, then I found the three identical stars in a line almost at the center of the inverted blue bowl of the sky that made up the constellation called the Three Marías. A thought stirred, the sense that something mysterious had happened that night. I realized that it might be the smallest things that determined lives, the minuscule unremembered words, the most minor mistakes of movement that were able to change anyone's destiny. People traveled along, slipped on a muddy path, thought nothing of it, but everything in the world suddenly changed in its own small way. A star dropped from the sky, streaked, extinguished in a flash, and who knew what had altered in the universe? I was amazed for a moment that the world might work that way, that a single action or word, either made or unmade, done or undone, unknown or unremembered, might already have decided for me if I would be lost or saved. This thought wavered in my mind vividly for an instant, a sudden grasp at a larger meaning I almost understood, at my own significance and insignificance in this world, then the thought just as suddenly vanished, burned away and scattered under the stars.

I found my way back into the bunkhouse feeling tired and confused, crashing from Rulo's speed, and I tossed and turned all night. The next morning, the sisters would men-

tion all our names at Sunday mass at their little chapel down
the road. They said a blessing for us in gratitude for our
kind assistance. My name was particularly singled out by
the María whose shoe I had pulled out of the mud, this
incident sung aloud to the congregation in her devoutly
cheerful voice, "Much thanks and many blessings, dear Señor, for the nice North American student who is visiting us
on his vacation, and who took the time to find my shoe."

The next day I was turned over to the charge of Casimiro. He was the oldest gaucho anyone could name in the
district around Henderson, though nobody could remember
the year he was born, least of all Casimiro, who claimed
that he had already had a wife and child by the time Grand-
papá Benevento drove his first wooden-wheeled cart and
oxteam onto the ranch he named María Consuela. Casimiro
was stooped and broken-looking. One of his arms was
weirdly twisted and seemed useful to him only while bending down or performing chores below his waist like stirring
up the fire for barbecues. He actually kept this arm tied to
his waist by the wrist with a leather string, which seemed
to help its movement—he picked things up, a feed bucket,
for example, with his injured arm moving around like a
crane arm suspended from its leather cable. "Just look at
him," Rulo said. "He's so old he's actually held together
by strings."

Casimiro said he had broken every bone in his body over
his years of *domas*, the gaucho horse-breaking roundups.
His face really did look as if every bone in it had been
broken, a sharp *indio* jaw hanging crookedly under a bul-
bous nose as big as a baked potato, and not a tooth left in
his mouth. His hands were as tough as tree bark, his fingers
like thickly jointed stubs of dark bamboo. The morning he
picked out a horse for me, Casimiro's famous big nose was
already red, and his breath reeked of the cheap red wine
that could be bought in the village for the equivalent of
about eight cents a bottle. Casimiro was drunk every day
before the sun fully cleared the horizon.

The morning I first met him, the sun was an eerie white
light burning through a blanket of chilly winter fog. I fol-

lowed him out through the tall, wet grass into a pasture behind Tío Freddi's stables, a long, low barn with its tin roof reflecting the first silvery sunlight cutting through the mists. My English riding clothes were soon sopping from the tall, dripping grass. I stood watching Casimiro clucking to a small herd of horses somewhere nearby in the foggy pasture, then they appeared out of the mists, stamping around him, snorting at the grain sack the gaucho carried from his partly useless arm and swinging from the end of it like a hobo's provisions. *"Ayeeeeeeo! Inglés!"* Casimiro called to me. "This spotted mare here, this pretty little *yegua* is the one for you!"

I liked the new name Casimiro had given me—*Inglés*, or English—after Rulo had introduced us. Anyone who spoke English was an *Inglés* to Casimiro. No matter what I told him about the United States, I was still called Inglés, and because Casimiro introduced me to the rest of the gauchos as Inglés, that became my name, even to Rulo and Tío Freddi after the first day. And I felt like an Englishman in the getup I was wearing—my knee-high riding boots with blunt silver spurs on their flamenco heels, jodhpurs, khaki shirt, and the Argentine Army sweater and jacket from Tío Freddi's two years at the national military academy. With a black Basque beret cocked on my head in Tío Freddi's style, I looked like somebody out of the British cavalry as I posed in the guesthouse mirror, complete with riding crop under my arm.

I strutted around like this, watching Casimiro lead the mare called Manchitas into the corral. Four or five other gauchos were already saddled up by the gate and waiting to begin the day's long ride. Rulo was having trouble with a young gelding he had chosen for himself in the corral, one of the gauchos yanking at the reins to get the horse to stand still long enough for Rulo to mount up. Casimiro put the smallest-looking saddle I had ever seen onto the back of Manchitas—it looked like a jockey's saddle to me, nothing more than a little oblong pad of leather with a cinch and stirrups. I put a boot in one of the stirrups and tried to step up onto the horse as if I had been doing it all my life. The horse took a long stride forward and I ended up bellying on, almost making it into the saddle before Manchitas kicked up her heels once and I went ass over teakettle into the wet grass.

I pushed up off the ground and wrung the water out of my jodhpurs, waving off Casimiro's questions if I was all right. Then like a true greenhorn, I reached out for the reins, threw a boot into the stirrup and whipped up onto the mare's back too fast. She jumped off on a hell-bent gallop out into the pasture about fifty meters until I pulled back on the reins and went sailing over her head.

Tío Freddi joined us from the main house, and he decided the English saddle didn't give me enough to hang onto. All the gauchos by now were sitting up on the whitewashed corral fence, enjoying the entertainment. "It's better to ride *criollo* style anyway," Tío Freddi said to me. "Why didn't you tell Casimiro you didn't know how to ride? He would have given you this native *recado*," Freddi said, the both of us watching Casimiro cinching up a gaucho saddle on the back of Manchitas—a polished wooden frame like a pack saddle with a thick sheepskin fitting over it, and with a set of *bolas* tied to the little wooden A frame that stuck up in front like a saddle horn. This *criollo* or native saddle had plenty to hang onto, that was clear, and I appreciated this as we all mounted up and Tío Freddi saw us off on our long ride, staying behind to see to some business and planning to join us at San Ignacio later with his truck full of medicines.

It was a four-hour ride across the Benevento ranch that was grazed down in places. In other fields, its long brown grasses were as tall as the shoulders of my horse so that it was like journeying through a jungle of grass. Rulo galloped around wildly through it, the sides of his horse and his own legs torn and scratched before long. We raced across the grazed-over pastures a few times, his horse always beating mine by about thirty lengths. Then our group came up on a small brick and adobe house with a huge garden that took up almost a hectare.

In the garden was a lone *chinita*, as Rulo called her, a beautiful dark woman with two tiny dark children crawling beside her, on her hands and knees digging winter vegetables. This was the gaucho named Joaquín's place. We had taken a little detour on our way to San Ignacio so that Joaquín could pick up some extra ropes and several more big jugs of wine that were tied by their necks behind his saddle. After he remounted, Joaquín leaned down from his horse and kissed his wife quickly, then he bounced both his kids up on the horse's neck a few times, showing them off, and then handed them back down again. As we rode off, Rulo explained that most of the gauchos on Tío Freddi's ranch lived this way, as tenants on the big ranch, each with his little house and garden, some of them located more than two hours' ride from the main house. He said there were about fifteen of these little places spread out over the forty-two square kilometers of the Benevento hectares. Some of the gauchos had been born on the ranch, and a few had never been further from it than Henderson.

We rode on, the sun coming up brightly by midmorning and burning off the few remaining patches of fog. We reached San Ignacio a little before noon. It was marked by a eucalyptus grove in the distance with a few native *ombú* trees, like huge open umbrellas growing around a collection of weathered buildings that had once been white with green trim. One of the buildings was long, an old stables that had been made into a bunkhouse on one end, its other end converted into a small warehouse. As we rode in, a gaucho nearly as old as Casimiro was processing honey into big steel barrels from the rows and rows of white rectangular beehives that stretched out under the grove of trees like headstones in a cemetery. Just as we came up a little rise into the trees, one of the gauchos rousted a small animal out of the tall grass and galloped in a circle around it, shouting, "Look! A *peludo*! Don't let it get away!"

Without his horse breaking stride, the man jumped off and smashed the little animal on the head with one of his *bolas*, and then leaped back up into the saddle, holding it up by the tail. It was a kind of armadillo, about the size of a small turkey, and it became part of our lunch, turned over on its back in the fire and cooked in its own shell, a meat that looked a little like chicken and tasted like a kind of sweet pork.

But before lunch, there was work to do. We took off after a part of the herd that was grazing in a nearby pasture. It was an improved herd of Angus-type cattle, Rulo explained, the product of sixteen generations of bulls descended from prizewinners imported from Scotland. The gauchos whooped and hollered, galloping after maverick steers that tried to break off into the tall grass. In an hour we had herded about five hundred of the fat black cattle into the large corral at San Ignacio. Alongside the corral was a system of wooden chutes that led out to two deep concrete dipping tanks already filled with a white foaming bath.

Before we finished, Rulo had grown tired of herding cattle and broken off from the group. Since I seemed to be either chasing the cows in the wrong direction or losing the steers I galloped after, I also turned my horse and spurred it after Rulo's up into the trees and through the ranks of beehives, the two of us heading for the bunkhouse.

Rulo was feeling burned out and wanted to lie down. We tied our horses outside, and Rulo led me through the dark, long warehouse room that held maybe a hundred big steel drums full of processed honey. An ancient gaucho he called Don Morales was taking apart and scrubbing pieces of an antique machine. Rulo and I stood watching as he put it back together and then showed me how the thing worked. He turned a crank and paddles broke up the wax honey-comb, a system of screens inside filtering the honey. It looked easy, but when Don Morales let me turn the crank, it was like trying to pull a canoe paddle through super glue. "When the gauchos are no longer able to do the strenuous work, Tío Freddi doesn't send them away," Rulo said. "He retires them to the jobs like this one, or to keeping the buildings painted, or like Casimiro does, taking care of the horses."

I tried to converse with Don Morales after Rulo went off to take his nap. Outside, the whoops and hollers of the gauchos could be heard getting closer as they finished filling San Ignacio's corral that had once been a polo grounds. "I'm from North America, the United States," I tried to explain in my clearest Spanish. "Do you know where that is?"

"Can you get there on horseback?" Don Morales asked, his accent thickly gaucho and hard to understand.

"I don't think you'd want to try," I said. "It would be as far as riding all the way to Buenos Aires and back fifty times."

"I've heard Buenos Aires is a long trip," Don Morales said. "I've never been there. You'd need a very good horse then to get to your country," he said. He finished churning away at his honeymill. "Try our honey. We make very good honey here. It's because of Freddi's sunflowers," he said. He moved the collection drum away from his honeymill and dipped a small ladle in. I tasted a fingerful, a thick, clear honey the color of sunflowers, then I followed Don Morales about his chores. I helped him fill a big drum with the broken honeycombs, then we carried it outside. A cloud of bees immediately gathered around our heads like locusts. I ran back inside, slapping at my head and shoulders. Don Morales continued on, unbothered, carrying the barrel until he reached the first rows of white beehives, then he set the drum down and pulled the lid off. A swarm of bees started flying hungrily into the barrel, a gathering cloud of them all around it, reclaiming what was left of all their labors.

Tío Freddi arrived in the Chevy and signaled that it was time for the *asado*—the long lunch of barbecued meat and *galleta*, round loaves of featherlight bread, which Joaquín produced from a big sack. Everyone sat around a fire Casimiro had built under the eucalyptus trees and watched the Inglés learn to eat with a gaucho knife. A piece of steak was slapped between two light slices of *galleta* bread, a bite of meat and bread was gripped between the front teeth, and in one quick upward slice with the knife the piece was cut off; the trick was to do this without taking off the end of one's nose at the same time. Gauchos did everything with these knives that they carried in their sashes and belts, usually at the middle of their backs. They chopped firewood, cleaned and trimmed their horses' hooves, used them like cleavers to crack the ribs of beef, then they wiped the knives off on their pants and ate with them. The peludo killed that morning was eaten with knifepoints dipped into its shell like into a cooking pot. Jugs of wine were passed around, and bitter *maté* tea was sucked from gourds through nickel silver straws. Then everyone stretched out under the trees.

After a short siesta we rode back out of the trees to the San Ignacio corral. The work was running the cattle out of it and through a system of chutes, where they were vaccinated for hoof-and-mouth disease, then sent through the dipping tanks. The dipping was the hard part of the job— poles and rope ends were used to move the cattle out of the chute and down a slippery concrete ramp into the deep tanks that were foaming over with foul-smelling pesticides. The cattle swam through the long, narrow tanks, one or two of the gauchos up on the fence, following them alongside, poking them with their poles to make sure the heads went under and were well soaked with the solution. Twice, a cow's flaring nostrils didn't come back up to the surface and everything stopped while the gauchos felt around in the deep bath with weighted leather ropes until they hooked a leg or the head. They used their horses to drag the drowned animal up out of the tank and then far off into a field.

My job was to help drive the dipped cattle into a small fenced-off pasture, where most of them rolled around in the dry grass with a deep, plaintive bellowing. Now and then, on Tío Freddi's instructions, I closed a gate at the end of the chute system and helped to drive certain animals into a holding pen, the older cows and two-year-old steers Tío Freddi had somehow missed last month when he had sent his cattle off to market. It was good work. I liked the dust kicked up around me and the contact with the cattle, watching the gauchos riding around whooping it up like *indios* on the warpath. Tío Freddi was making calculations about everything; he personally checked each animal, supervised its doctoring, then registered it in his records that would enable him to estimate next year's income by the condition of this year's herd, "provided this country's crazy economy ever settles down," as he put it. By evening, we had run nearly six hundred cattle through vaccinations and dippings. Another *asado* was smoking over the fire as the gauchos rolled out their bedrolls in the bunkhouse. Casimiro stretched his poncho out near the fire, at the edge of the pasture where our horses were hobbled and grazing. We gathered around the fire for the evening meal, huddling close around the coals to stay warm.

I stayed near Tío Freddi—the *patrón*, the Inglés and Rulo making up a little group to ourselves further back from the fire. I was amazed to learn that Tío Freddi didn't know exactly how many cattle he had. "Somewhere over nine thousand cows," he said. "Maybe another five hundred steers held off the market last month because the price was too low. We're not even getting the equivalent in pesos right now of thirty dollars a head for a four-hundred-kilo steer. Can you imagine beef that cheap? We should be putting steaks on every table in Europe, but now that the English have been courting those sons of whores in the Common Market, Europe isn't buying very much of our beef. They're paying eight yanqui dollars a kilo for French steaks in London. And look around you! Look how many there are! What can this country do with so much beef?''

"Our ranchers wouldn't get a price even if they did have the markets," Rulo said. "It's the gangsters who run the big international companies who would still make the money. Take the case of Aristotle Onassis. Did you know that a lot of the fortune of Onassis, his billions of dollars with which he caused your country national shame by marrying Jacqueline Kennedy, did you know that a lot of it was originally earned on the backs of Argentine ranchers? When Onassis was a young man, he started a shipping business in Buenos Aires. He overcharged for every pound of beef and grain he shipped like a racketeer. He got so rich that he even built and owns huge parts of the beach resort at Mar del Plata. A lot of people in this country will tell you what a gangster he was when he started. Now tell me how a beautiful, beautiful sweet lady like *la Jacqueline* could marry a gangster like him?''

"All it shows is how much crooked gangsters run the world," Tío Freddi said. "Consider my situation. All the animals on this ranch, all nine thousand cows, the two hundred sheep we keep for fleeces and meat, the twenty-five good Arab and native horses we keep in the stables and the other two hundred horses that are running wild all over the place, aren't worth the price of a small-size business, not even a good Burger King franchise, in the United States or in England. But what can I do? Do we ranchers run the world? We have to sell cattle every year whether the price is low or high or we'd run out of grass to feed all of them. It's only my sunflower seeds that are making me money in times like these, when the shipping costs are high and the foreign markets are so closed to all our beef.'' Tío Freddi stared for a moment into his fire. ''*Che*! Casimiro! We should have a *doma* for this yan—for the Inglés!'' he said in a loud voice across the fire. ''A *doma* is really something to see. We round up all the horses on the place. We save some out of the herd for our own, and we break them to ride, then we send others off to the meat markets. We have a *doma* every year about this time or the horses breed so much they'd take over the whole ranch like rabbits.''

''My father, the one the family calls Tío Churro, fought for the price of beef all his life,'' Rulo said. ''When you yanquis quit importing Argentine canned corned beef, it nearly killed him. It was hard for him to believe that it suddenly wasn't popular anymore. He watched the price of it drop lower every year, the number of cans he could sell dropping with it, until he would have lost our side of the family's whole fortune if I hadn't convinced him to sell some of the canned beef interests and invest in drugstores. Then you yanquis quit importing any of our beef at all, supposedly because of hoof-and-mouth disease.''

''What a lie that is,'' Tío Freddi said. ''Look what we did today! There hasn't been a case of hoof-and-mouth disease on my ranch in twenty years, and hardly one in the district. Besides, any trace of the disease is killed off in the canning process. A lot of the fortunes in this country have gone straight to shit because of that lie, not that I blame you yanquis so much that nobody wants to eat our canned beef anymore.''

''My family in North America used to eat canned beef,'' I said. ''We used to eat it for breakfast. I don't really remember when we stopped, but we don't anymore.''

''That's clear,'' Tío Freddi said. ''Who can say? Tastes just change, that's all, and suddenly there's more beef in this part of the world than anybody knows what to do with.''

"It's all the fault of the yanquis, that's clear," Rulo said. "If the yanquis would ever open their doors to our products, this country could be something again, a potential, the force to deal with in Latin America like we used to be. I'm sick of the way the yanquis treat this country. I don't like yanquis," Rulo said.

"Rulo forgets all the good things you yanquis do," Tío Freddi said. "Like making the Chevy I'm driving, or my good Ford tractor, and all the new seeds, the miracle weed killers and pesticides. And your good yanqui technology, the airplanes, the new computers, even electric toothbrushes . . ."

"Sure, sure, technology," Rulo interrupted bitterly. "And with every machine that crosses our borders, the generals collect twice its value in import duties. Everything's fucked with on the way into this country and fucked with on the way out, that's the situation, because the whole system is corrupt. If anybody ever asks you why things are so fucked up in Latin America, you just tell them that," Rulo said. He flipped the tea leaves out of his *mate* gourd with an angry quickness. "Too many palms to grease, and too many yanqui banks taking their percentage of everything. I really don't like yanquis, no offense meant to you, but I don't like them. Let me give you an example. A yanqui company once tried to put vending machines all over Buenos Aires. Argentine consultants warned them against it, they said it would never fly in our culture, but the yanqui company convinced an Argentine company to take out a big bank loan and buy thousands of yanqui vending machines anyway by greasing the right palms. They set the machines up all over the city of Buenos Aires, you know, selling cigarettes, candy, sodas, all kinds of things, and do you know what happened? We Argentines just kicked the machines to pieces. Good people, lawyers, doctors, clerks, secretaries, policemen, students, everybody all over the city just kicked out all the little glass windows and took their nice little packs of cigarettes and their candy bars. Do you understand what I'm saying? It's a matter of culture. We Argentines would rather go to the corner and give the old man at the kiosk a few pesos for our cigarettes. Or we'd rather buy candy from the kids in the street, and rubbers are much better if you can go back to the pharmacist who sold them to you in case the tire goes flat, do you understand? So we Argentines just kicked all your yanqui vending machines to shit just like that. We showed them in *la USA* how much we hate to do business with yanqui machines, and maybe also how much we hate yanquis," Rulo said. "And if you want to know something else . . ."

"Please, Rulo, I can't listen anymore," I said. I took a long breath, my whole body tense. I realized I had been holding my breath the whole time Rulo was speaking. "None of what you're saying has anything to do with me, is that clear? My family in *la USA* isn't getting rich on the backs of South America," I said. "Let's just change the subject."

"You're right," Tío Freddi said. "Let's talk about something else. Nothing really compares, anyway. You just can't compare this part of the world with the United States."

"That's just the point!" Rulo said. "Nothing compares!"

"Lay off, Rudolfo," Tío Freddi said.

"All over the world, it's buy on the yanqui installment plan, don't you know that? Roads, bridges, phone companies, computers, auto assembly plants, drug factories, jean factories, everything you can imagine, and they shove all this shit down our throats without knowing anything about us! They find some corrupt government official who will sign all the son-of-a-whore yanqui contracts for his little pension in Miami or Los Angeles and the whole country has to pay off in son-of-a-whore yanqui installments . . ."

"That's enough, Rulo," Tío Freddi said; then to me, "My apologies for your cousin Rulo. His mother died when he was young, and his father didn't teach him any manners."

"I don't want to make problems," I said. "This kind of talk is just making me feel a little crazy right now, is that clear? I'd be grateful if we talked about something else."

"I just don't like your country, that's all," Rulo said. "You don't find us in an unjust war like the one in Vietnam. We Argentines don't go around murdering innocent people so we can keep selling bullets and Coca-Cola. It's a shame and a crime, that's what it is."

"Just shut your mouth, Rulo, or I'll have to shut it for you," Tío Freddi said.

"Come on, Freddi! Everybody knows this! Yanquis are building their business on murders and lies, but especially lies! Take the case of Muhammad Ali, for example. You know why the yanqui government took his title from him? Do you really believe it had something to do with him not letting himself be drafted into the army and go off to that shitty war in Vietnam? Every Argentine knows that Ali was set to fight the Argentine champion Oscar Bonavena in his very next fight, or pretty soon, anyway. Don't you think it's strange that the title was taken from Ali just as he was set to lose it to Bonavena?"

"That's a lie," I said. "A dirty lie, Rulo. I've never heard such a stupid thing in my life!"

"Enough! Enough!" Tío Freddi said. "Maybe we should all just go off to bed now, what do you think?"

"Sounds perfect to me," I said.

"Listen, my yanqui nephew, I want you to know that I love your country," Tío Freddi said. "Inez even keeps a photograph of your *presidente* Kennedy in our bedroom, hanging right beside her portrait of the Sacred Heart. *Che*, Rulo, did you know that the yanquis launched another Apollo today? What do you think of that?" Rulo didn't seem to be listening. He moved across the fire from us and spread his long body out on the ground. "It's a miracle, it really is, to think of men walking around on the moon," Freddi said. "We should be rejoicing that a free country is the first to do it."

"Really? Today?" I asked. I looked out away from the fire toward the dark, misting horizon of the pampas at night, where an oddly shaped quarter-moon seemed to be caught like a dim beacon in the gathering fog. "I forgot that was going to happen," I said.

"*Che*! Casimiro!" Tío Freddi called out. "Do you know that the country this Inglés comes from is landing men on the moon?"

"That's a lie, Freddi," Casimiro answered him. The old

man stood up, wavering around from too much wine. "I heard about that recently, and I think not a word of it is true. The moon is made out of light and that's all there is to it! God made it that way so good gauchos like me can take a piss in the night and not wet all over their boots!"

Everyone laughed at Casimiro as he clownishly turned his back and took a step away from the fire, then at the sounds of pleasure he made letting loose like a horse.

"Casimiro is turning into a drunk these days," Freddi said to me in a low voice. "I'll have to talk to him about his wine if he wants to stay around."

We all sat for a moment, staring into the fire. Casimiro had walked away into the darkness and we could hear him singing something incomprehensible, the word *luna* sounding hoarsely a few times. He was singing a little song in dialect about the moon, walking away under the trees toward the bed he had made for himself with his poncho and the thick fleece from his saddle, where he could sleep all night near his horses.

"We should all go to bed now," Freddi said, but he didn't have to, most of the other gauchos were heading off to their bunkhouse as if at Casimiro's signal. I stood up, stiff and sore from the day's riding. Tío Freddi threw an arm over my shoulder and kicked dirt at the fire to smother it. "Don't you think this is the life out here?"

"It's a great life, that's clear," I said.

"My brother Martín hates the life of the ranch," Tío Freddi said. "Has he ever talked to you about it?"

"No. He hasn't," I said.

"Sometimes my brother Martín doesn't have any sense. He could have been a rich man ten times over if he had only jumped in and done a few generals some favors. Anyway, he's not a good businessman. And he wouldn't know the first thing to do with the family's land."

"The family is lucky to have you to manage all this land for them," I said.

"I don't understand why Martín won't sell his share to me," Tío Freddi said. "He doesn't like it out here. Yet he won't even sell his part to his brother, not even if I agree to include his sons in my will and make sure of their inheritance. It's like a wedge between us, and it's hard to understand.''

"I wouldn't know," I said. "Papá and I have never really talked about the land.''

"Well, there's no other life than this for me. I don't care whether I'm making mountains of money or not. You think I'd trade a big fortune in money in that dirty city for all the good air out here under the moon and the stars?''

"Before long, the yanquis are going to claim they own the moon,'' Rulo said. There was a malevolence in his voice that stopped all movement around the fire. "They'll probably own the stars someday, too.''

"Enough! *Por favor!*'' I said in a sharp tone. I was rocking back and forth in my boots, the wine from dinner causing a hot, intense throbbing in my head. I watched the shapes of two of the gauchos move in closer, as if ready to step in between us.

"*Che*, don't get so bothered,'' Rulo said. "Everybody knows you son-of-a-whore yanquis already think you own the stars.''

That was enough. I launched across the fire meaning to pick Rulo up off the ground where he was lounging and maybe shout into his face. But he moved, and I landed with both open hands on the top of his head and ended up giving him two loud slaps across the face. Rulo grabbed at my ankles and threw me off my feet. We were rolling around, the rage I felt turned into a kind of desperate flailing of my fists all over Rulo's back, then my boots were kicking at his tall, heavy body that was suddenly pinning me to the ground. We wrestled, strained, rolled, Rulo somehow getting me into a headlock and mashing my face into the dirt. Then Tío Freddi was on Rulo's back, pulling him off me, which made things worse, since Rulo wouldn't let go of my head while Freddi was wrenching him around. Freddi was shouting, "Son of a whore, Rulo! Enough! Let him go!'' and that kind of thing. Then one of the gauchos jumped in and finally peeled Rulo's locked fingers open from the butcher's grip of his headlock.

"Let him up! Let him up!'' everybody seemed to be shouting at once. My ears were on fire from the headlock and my head was ringing. I could see the dark shape of one of the gauchos now holding Rulo in an armlock. It was my only chance, and I jumped at it on impulse. I reached out into the fire for the first charred branch I closed my fingers around, then I launched into Rulo, swinging my heavy stick like a bat while the gaucho was still holding him. Rulo screamed and sank to his knees, both hands over his head as I broke the stick over it. Tío Freddi finally wrestled me from behind, one beefy arm enough to lift my whole body off the ground with me still swinging what was left of my stick through the air.

Rulo was crying like a kid, on his hands and knees and bleeding from his mouth. His fat, sensuous playboy lips weren't going to kiss any girls for a while, that was clear. He was humiliated, and outraged, it hadn't been a fair fight. Luís held Rulo's arms back as he tried halfheartedly to get up and start in at me with his fists, but Rulo wasn't really trying, maybe he knew he had pushed too far, that he should have shut his mouth before it was too late. Tío Freddi dragged me back behind the honey barn and bunk-house, once a gay stables for a polo grounds. Tío Freddi let go his strong hold on me behind the bunkhouse. He slapped me across the back and shoulders, laughing and saying, "That was great! Good move! That son of a whore deserved it, that's clear! There isn't a single man in this family who hasn't had to shut Rulo up that way at least once!"

Tío Freddi led me around the building and into a part of the dark bunkhouse that was lit by a single lamp with the wick turned low. Don Morales appeared in the doorway of this little room that was off by itself, with two beds in it, and motioned for me to come in. Don Morales lit another lantern and filled a basin with water, then found a bottle of hydrogen peroxide.

"Listen, I'm sorry about this," Tío Freddi said. "But I should head back to the main house in the truck and take Rulo with me to see about him. I'll be back by the time you're all up in the morning." Tío Freddi turned to Don Morales and said, "You take care of this Inglés, you hear me, Don Morales? See that he gets what he needs. He's staying here, in the room for the *patrón*." Then he said to me, "This is the room where I always stay. The smell gets pretty strong trying to sleep in the big room with those gauchos all night. Isn't that true, Don Morales?" The old man laughed and nodded at Tío Freddi, then started to try to get me to let him wash the scrapes on my face. "You make sure to get all the dirt and gravel out of your scalp," Tío Freddi said, inspecting my forehead. "It's nothing. The cut you came with opened up a little, that's all. A little peroxide and you're all fixed up," he said. Then Tío Freddi said goodnight to us, and to the others in the big room.

I told Don Morales not to bother, to go back to bed, and he reluctantly said, "As you say, little *patrón*," and shuffled out of my small bedroom. I listened to the gauchos stirring next door in their big room, boots hitting the floor as they were taken off, the sounds of the last of the men getting undressed and turning in, still talking over the fight; they seemed happy enough about the way it had turned out. For a moment, I wished I were staying in the big room with them. But then this room for the *patrón* had everything, real beds, a table, an ornate commode with Chinese designs, even a mirror on the wall.

I stood in front of the mirror, washing my face and scalp in the basin, carefully picking out tiny bits of dirt and gravel from the little scrape that had opened on the healing cut on my forehead. I doused it with peroxide, then I stood for a moment inspecting my features in the mirror in the dim yellow lamplight, my blue eyes looking fierce whenever I thought about my ridiculous fight with Rulo. My left eye was a little swollen, I noticed, but I wasn't sure if that was from the fight or a bee sting. My face was sunburned from the long day. A really good day, all things considered, I thought, as my fingers, black with dirt under the nails, swollen and blistered from handling ropes and leather, were running over the light stubble of a beard that was starting to grow.

The rest of my nights were spent at San Ignacio by choice. I turned down Tío Freddi's invitations to accompany him to the main house each evening in the pickup, only going once to pay a polite visit to Inez, who Tío Freddi said was lonely for conversation. Inez was the kind of woman who fit a description I had once heard Father Naboa use in philosophy and religion class at Colegio San Andrés, *la perfecta casada*, the perfect wife, who seemed to be following in a slightly modernized way the rules of devotion to her husband and duty to her household set down by Fray Luis de León in the sixteenth century. Inez was modest and reserved, her life taken up mainly with managing her servants and raising her children. She played this role to her chattering maids as a benevolent elder sister might, assisting as well as guiding them in running her impeccable home. The only break in her isolated life was the month she spent in Buenos Aires with her family late each spring. She took her three toddlers with her, and all the women and children in her family went on a shopping spree together, then spent two weeks at the beach resort at Mar del Plata.

She kept a battery-operated phonograph going with popular records—sambas and tangos by the great tenor Roberto Carlos, romantic songs of heartbroken lovers sung by Leonardo Favio in his emotional baritone. Her latest discovery was *los Beatles*. The one night I spent at her table, sunburned and with a sparse beard starting to show on my chin, we discussed the White Album, which one of her cousins had sent to her from England. Otherwise her style was reflected by the twin canopy beds in white lace dresses of her bedroom. It was hard to imagine Tío Freddi sleeping in a bed like that, *los Beatles* playing in the background one last time before sleep and Inez on her knees, praying to her tiny shrine of the Virgin on her nightstand under her icon of the Sacred Heart and the glossy smiling photograph of John F. Kennedy. Inez and Freddi had three children, two boys and a girl, all under four years old. "The perfect number," she said at the table. "I wouldn't want to deal with any more."

Tío Freddi cut her off with irritation. "We should have as many children as we can, or one day the world's going to be nothing but the blacks and the Chinese!"

Inez looked quickly across the table toward me. Embarrassed, she drew herself up more erectly in her chair. A tension fell over the table which lasted through dessert and even through Tío Freddi's cheerful explanations as he dealt out cards, showing me the system of hand and facial gestures I had to know to play the ancient Spanish game of *truco*. I was glad to pack up my things and move out to San Ignacio again in the morning.

The days there were taken up with the work of dipping cattle. Occasionally I would ride off on my own through the pastures, or up through the thick eucalyptus grove that provided a momentary illusion of being enclosed, harbored, a relief from the overwhelming feeling of smallness out on the pampas, where I was like a chigger on a leaf in a Pacific of grass. Casimiro sometimes followed me on these rides, and the old gaucho taught me some of his lore, such as how to use the *bolas*. It was made of three round stones wrapped in a rawhide, each on a short rope with the ends braided together in a kind of knot. You gripped one of the heavy, leather-covered stones while swinging the other two overhead on their short rawhide ropes until they were whipping around like helicopter blades. The trick was to aim the knot, the center of the three ropes, at the target, then to let go with a certain snap of the wrist. I practiced with the *bolas* on horseback, wrapping them around trees, clumps of tall grass and bushes. I missed the snapping of the wrist sometimes and ended up nearly knocking myself out with one of the hard stones. Once, I let go of them too soon, and the *bolas* spun down under the feet of Manchitas and wrapped up three of her legs. The horse dropped to her knees in a panic under me, then she kicked around wildly trying to get untangled after I jumped off. Casimiro rescued us, wrestling the *bolas* free of the kicking hooves. He told me that without knowing it, I had discovered the way gauchos lasso animals. They aim the *bolas* at a horse's or a cow's legs, wrapping them up in a single shot. Casimiro kept the others laughing through that noon's *asado*, describing to them how the Inglés had lassoed his own horse.

We broke off dipping cattle early one evening, and Casimiro showed me how to butcher a steer. There was the strange, gory moment when the knife was used and a life was gone in a rush of blood, all of us looking on with a kind of celebration, a certain feeling of human power. Then came the methodical work of skinning, and of cutting up the carcass mainly into long strips in the gaucho style, then the parceling out of the meat to all the men to take home to their families. We ate the organs with our *asado* that night, the heart, liver, kidneys, fat tripe and sweetbreads.

I went to sleep early each night and woke up at dawn to a gourd full of bitter *mate* tea. I began to feel that I could live this life forever. The men around me seemed like happy people, and they loved Tío Freddi's land. Their talk was of horses, cattle, the work to be done and of their families somewhere nearby in the pastures surrounding us. After the first few days, most of them started to ride home on their horses each night, unless Tío Freddi stayed on with us for the evening *asado*, in which case they stayed late and slept in their big room in the bunkhouse. They each earned an equivalent in pesos of about twenty dollars a month. The rest of their salary was paid in a few horses, whether to ride or sometimes sell, as much meat as they and their families could eat, and a little tenant house and garden. They considered themselves well-off to be working for Tío Freddi; he was known as the kind of *patrón* who would keep them on if they became disabled or too old. This was an important consideration because their work was dangerous. I often saw a gaucho, galloping hell-bent across the pampas, take a spill when his horse was tripped up by a chuckhole. They were also kicked by the cattle, and slammed up against the chutes and the fences.

Sometimes the air swarmed with thousands of small green and brown beetles that looked something like leafhoppers. Clouds of them seemed to follow us around through the grass, sometimes landing on exposed skin, on bare arms or on the neck. Occasionally, one of them would bite, a stingless bite that left only a faint pink dot if any mark at all. "Don't let them bite you," Tío Freddi said. "Keep your sleeves rolled down. One out of every ten thousand of these beetles carries a disease called *Mal de Chagas*. It's a very rare paralytic disease, but a very bad one. I don't think we've had a case of it on this ranch ever, but I'm always careful anyway. In Henderson, there's a man who's now a spastic from *Mal de Chagas*. Just seeing him's enough to make you careful." From then on, I wore a scarf around my neck and kept my arms covered in case a cloud of the beetles rose up chattering out of the tall grass, and I spurred my horse to outrun them.

One night, I tried to explain to Casimiro and the others about the moon, how it was possible for men to land on it. I had asked Tío Freddi to bring me an issue of *Life* magazine from the main house, but Casimiro wouldn't even believe all the color pictures of the astronauts, or of the insectlike Apollo landing craft. He finally understood it to be a kind of huge tractor the English were shooting on the tip of a gigantic bullet straight into the sky. But to land on the moon? "The moon is a plate full of light," Casimiro insisted. "God fills the plate once a month. He spills the light out of the plate, then he fills it again. It's all a lie they're telling us in this magazine."

There was no way to convince Casimiro. I tried again, but this time he turned from the fire and walked off indignantly. I continued my explanations to the other gauchos, and they seemed to agree that old Casimiro didn't know what he was saying. But I went to sleep that night with the impression that they had looked at the pictures in *Life* and then back up at the moon, and even as I demonstrated with three fingers just how the spacecraft would touch down, they nodded their heads only out of politeness to a foreigner, or because I was in tight with their *patrón*. I used my set of *bolas* to explain planets, orbits, the sun and the moon but it was no use. To them, the sun still rose up from the ends of the earth and plunged back down again and that was day. They would never believe that a man could walk on God's plate of light.

Tío Freddi held a *doma* one Friday after I had lost count of my days on his ranch. It began with a long ride to one corner of the ranch, where we flushed out a huge herd of horses. They were mostly wild and flew away from us through the tall grass before we could get very close, but the gauchos knew their business. They rose up suddenly around the hundreds of stampeding horses, waving blankets and grain sacks full of old tins cans to turn them. The horses were a mixed and colorful herd of browns, blacks, grays and paints, all looking shaggy with the long hair of their winter coats. The gauchos eventually turned the herd in a big, wheeling circuit across the flat plain, heading them in the direction of San Ignacio's corral and dipping tanks. More than a hundred horses were finally gathered in the corral by late morning, the rest escaping in small groups up into the trees, where Don Morales ran around waving a blanket to turn them away from his rows of beehives.

Tío Freddi and Casimiro looked over the horses together, some of the animals so wild they repeatedly threw themselves against the fence rails trying to get free. The *asado* was eaten in shifts that day as gauchos took turns scaring the wild horses back from the fences so they wouldn't break through. Tío Freddi pointed out certain horses to Casimiro that should be cut out and broken, young ones he would add to his riding stock back at the main house and begin the work of training. Others would be sent off to the dog-food and glue factories. Before the *doma* began, about half the herd was run through the loading chutes, vaccinated and dipped like cattle. Then they were set loose again, forming a small herd off in the distance that circled around in a dustcloud all afternoon.

The dust the horses raised in the corral made it hard to see. The best riders among the gauchos whipped their *bolas* around and began to lasso horses in the corral. The animal went down hard with a groan. The gauchos were suddenly on top of the horse and working as fast as they could while dodging the wildly kicking hooves. They got a rope on the horse and tied it to a post at the center of the corral. One of the men used a short stick, pushing it between the horse's teeth, working its mouth to make it a little raw and sore so the rider would have a better chance of getting it to respond to a bit and bridle, which they put in the horse's mouth right away. After bridling, they strapped a kind of leather rigging with a handgrip and stirrups on the horse's back instead of a saddle. One of the gauchos gripped the little handle, leapt on the horse's back and they were off and running, bucking like cowboy and bronco around the corral. Or the horse suddenly bolted like a runaway, with the gaucho on its back hanging on for his life.

The *doma* was tough on the gauchos, and on the horses. Three horses broke legs going down with the *bolas* wrapped around them and had to be shot. When this happened, the gauchos took out their knives and cut off both rear hooves. They cut around the horse's hind legs just above the elbows, then they peeled off the two long sleeves of raw horsehide. These were later made into what the gauchos called *botas de potro*, or bronco boots. All that was required in their manufacture was to shave the hair off the hide, work the leather until it was more or less soft, then to sew the toe ends closed and pull the boots on, the elbows of the horse's hind sleeves making perfectly fitting heels.

Tío Freddi made presents of particular horses to his hired men. He told me that the ranch produced a good breed of horse; Grandfather Benevento had bought imported Arabian stallions and had bred them with the native stock. The mixture of *criollo* and Arab strains produced a good breed for working cattle, and they were widely known to be the best polo ponies in the world. But how to choose among so many horses? I circled the corral and marveled at the spectacle of them stampeding around during the *doma*. I watched Casimiro supervise the shooting and dragging off of a young mare that had broken its leg. The old gaucho did this work with real sadness. "That's a shame. She was a fine one," he said many times, drinking down half a bottle of cheap wine in the process. There was a sadness as well as celebration about the *doma*, and a sense of victory whenever one of the gauchos rode up on a newly broken horse, its coat foaming, its eyes showing white around the rims with fear but the gaucho grinning, making the horse do turns, spurring it to a gallop then reining it in. It was a miracle of horsebreaking. Twenty minutes in the hands of these gauchos and a horse could seem tame. Then the broken horse was branded with an iron, vaccinated, dipped and let loose in another section of the corral.

\* \* \*

There was a party our last night at San Ignacio. By then
I regretted the prospect of returning even to the relative
civilization of Tío Freddi's home and family. There was
to be an ostrich-hunting trip, and a drive into Henderson
for "card games." I could also discuss with sweet Inez
the lyrics from "Dear Prudence" and "Why Don't We Do
It in the Road?" But I would just as soon have stayed on
in my little kerosene-lit bunkhouse room kept spotless by
Don Morales the beekeeper. I even had all my things
moved into it, arranged neatly in the little chest of drawers, Tío Freddi having driven my suitcase out to me when
it was clear I planned to stay on at San Ignacio as long as
I could.

At the *asado* that night, the gaucho named Luis brought
out his guitar, but he had trouble playing it because he had
sprained his wrist taking a spill on one of his *doma* rides.
But his voice was nice, a high tenor in the gaucho dialect
that rounded out the endings of Spanish words and mixed
them with slang expressions I couldn't understand. This
music had echoes of *indio* laments, sad melodies in epic,
rhyming verses. Listening hard, I could make out ballads
about journeys, or about living alone out on the pampas
with nothing but a horse, a poncho, a knife and a guitar,
pronounced *guitaja* in his dialect. There were songs of the
loneliness of being away from a wife and children, and of
the pride of following the gaucho's life, which was considered freer and more honorable than any other. There were
also verses about being misunderstood, and sometimes mis-
treated, and violent descriptions of knife fights to defend
pride or women or both. The songs invoked God often, in
almost every other phrase, as if these men shared a kind of
churchless religion of songs, as if the songs themselves had
become a kind of celebration of the Mass of the lone soul
out on the pampas, hosts served up with reverence on their
guitars, like some verses of the one long song I understood
the best: *I was born like the fish are born/at the bottom of
the sea./No one can take from me that which God gave me./
What I brought into this world/from this world I'll take
away. . . .*

Tío Freddi offered to drive me to the main house to spend

the night, but I preferred to stay on at San Ignacio and ride in with the gauchos in the morning. I saw Tío Freddi off and rejoined the *asado*. It had been eaten down to the last tender strips of ribsteak when two headlights shone in the distance. Casimiro noticed them and reeled up close to me by the fire. *"Ayeeo! Inglés!* Everyone's sorry to see you go from San Ignacio!" he said. "We want you to remember this place as long as you live!"

"I promise you, Casimiro, I'll remember San Ignacio. And most of all, I'll remember you."

"I don't think it's going to be Casimiro that you remember the most," he said. He looked around the fire at the others with an amused expression. Everyone watched me to see how I would react, and I laughed with them, trying to share in their joke that I didn't yet understand.

Casimiro flipped his thumb up out of the neck of his wine jug, where he had been using it like a cork. He took a long drink and wiped his mouth with the back of his hand. Then he gestured with his arm, swinging it weirdly at the end of its leather thong in the direction of the still-distant headlights. I saw the lights were slowly approaching us, bouncing around across the dark fields. "This is going to be a memorable night!" Casimiro said to the others and laughed. *"Inglés* has got firsts. But who's got seconds? Who wants thirds? I always say it's best to parcel out the mares according to age, the oldest of us first in line! Ramón? Luis?" he asked, and both Ramón and Luis shook their heads. "It's only justice that married men should go last!"

I looked more closely at the approaching headlights, bobbing in the eerie black Sahara of grass, and I realized the yellow foglamps were in the wrong places, this wasn't Tío Freddi's pickup coming back as I had thought it was.

"Inglés!" said Casimiro, taking me firmly by the arm. "Your cousin Rulo told me to say to you that this is the very best gift he could think to give you. He wants to make up for that fight you had. He told me to send you his regrets that he can't be here himself!"

"What are you talking about, Casimiro?" I asked. By that time, the pickup was just reaching the other end of the grove of trees. I watched it for a few minutes, taking a deep drink of the terrible wine Casimiro offered me as if in answer to my question. Then I could make out the features of the gaucho named Carlos behind the wheel. Beside him was the figure of a woman, her face round as a cabbage in the glow of the dashboard, which both her hands were braced on to steady herself in the pitching, bucking pickup moving along the rough track of road. I experienced a rush of panic. The gauchos all around me were getting to their feet, laughing and saying to me, "Let's go, *Inglés*! Come on, boy! Look! Here's La Correntina!"

The pickup passed through the grove, lurching up out of the trees and coming to a stop at the bunkhouse door.

"Let's go, *Inglés*! Let's give it to her! Look! There she is! La Correntina's here! It's La Correntina!"

They pushed me out from behind the fire like a crowd of drunken brothers, Casimiro moving ahead of us and singing out her name, "Correntina! Correntiiiina!" An empty wine jug dropped off his thumb and fell to the path. He led the way as the rest of them pushed and dragged me along over the rough grassy trail and through the long, dark honey warehouse with its big sticky drums that we kept banging into in the darkness. Don Morales was sitting in the doorway that led from the honey room into the bunkhouse. He was cleanly shaven around his shaggy moustache and chewing on an unlit *cigarro*. He wore a bright pink scarf around his neck and a wide gaucho belt studded with silver coins held up his cleanest pair of baggy pants; he looked like a sad old gypsy at a carnival. A hot fire was going in the old metal stove of the big bunkhouse room. *Truco* cards were spread out on the table under the only lamp. The other lamps were all arranged around my little room, the door to it standing open by the time we all filed in past Don Morales, each of the gauchos ahead of me respectfully removing his hat as he looked in. A crowd gathered in the narrow hallway as if reluctant to move too much further on. Casimiro ushered them all out of the way and into the big bunkhouse room, then he grabbed me by the arm and pushed me through the doorway to meet La Correntina.

She was short, round—fat is the only word. Her face was pretty though, not gaudy with makeup but healthy-looking, with nice big brown eyes under dyed red hair cut into the shape of an overturned bowl. She stood in black high heels, no stockings, wearing only plain blue-green panties that bulged out over her stomach under a bright red sweater with the sleeves pulled up to her elbows. She stood in the middle of the room like a squat red bull, in a posture as if deciding whether or not to charge.

The furniture in my little room had been rearranged. The two beds had been pushed together to make one big one, and there were several more lamps, one by the bed and one on the small table that hadn't been there before. The table was covered with a gay checkered cloth, and somebody had put checkered curtains up on the only window. The commode and basin with their Chinese designs sat full of water on the shelf by the mirror. "Correntina, it is my proud obligation to introduce you to this young Inglés," Casimiro said. "And here is La Correntina," he said to me, then made a lewd gesture with his finger in his fist and closed the door behind me with a laugh.

Without a word, La Correntina moved over to the pitcher in a businesslike way, pouring more water into the basin and wringing a cloth out in it. I froze there, staring at La Correntina in front of me, who held out her wet cloth toward me as if I should know what to do with it. "Come on now," she said, frowning. "Come here and show it to me. The first one shouldn't keep the others waiting. Let's go. I don't want to spend all night out here with the cows."

"That's all right," I said, my mouth dry, my mind suddenly having trouble finding the right words in Spanish to say what I meant. "This must be some kind of joke by my cousin Rulo," I said.

"A joke? How do you mean?"

"I mean, well, ah, you don't have to do it. I mean with me. Is that all right?" She didn't get what I was saying, and I sensed resistance. "Look. I'll tell the others you did a great job and send them in, you understand?"

It took a moment for La Correntina to comprehend this,

a gradual bovine shift of her features into a hurtful expression. "Are you a faggot, or what?" she asked.

"No, no, señorita, I assure you," I said. "It's simply . . . ah, how do I say it? We just don't do it like this in my country."

"Not in your country?"

"No, señorita, I assure you," I said.

"Show me how you do it in your country," she said.

"No, no, you don't understand! We just don't do it . . . well, all right, how do I say it? Please pardon me for saying it but we just don't do it . . . I don't anyway, ah, with . . . ah, *putas*," I said. "We just aren't used to doing it with *putas*."

The way I had said the word *whore* had a violent effect on her. She let out a sound that was partly an incredulous laugh. She tossed her wet towel with a slap back into its basin and bulled her way over to the little chest of drawers where she had draped most of her clothes. She was rattling off a streak of Spanish with the Corrientes accent, something like, "If you think I'm going to give back your cousin Rulo's pesos after coming all this way out here I'll make you all the joke of the town! He's a son-of-a-shithead brute, that cousin of yours! Once before he did this to me and now he did it again! Another one of his stupid shitty *boludo*-with-the-brains-of-a-parrot arrangements!" La Correntina was tripping over her high heels trying to get into her skirt. "Here he pays me a mountain of pesos to do the thing with some *Inglés* all the way out here and the stupid faggot of an *Inglés* turns out not to have any stick at all!"

"Please, please, please, señorita, keep the money! Keep the money! It's me that Rulo's made the joke on! *Por favor*!" I said, raising my hands up at her as if to calm her down, a lame gesture that had no effect. "Shhhh! Please! The others!" I said, making a kind of chopping motion to indicate the gauchos waiting in the big room. "Quiet down and you can keep all the money! Look! Here's more," I said, starting to reach into my jodhpurs, then I realized I didn't carry any money in them.

La Correntina stopped dressing and looked at me more

closely. Her small, lipsticked mouth formed a shape as if sucking on a plum pit while a thought formed in her mind.

"It's all right," I said. "The others are waiting."

"I think I understand now," she said. "This is your first time, isn't that right?"

"*Sí*," I said in a blast of tension rushing out of my chest. "My first time."

"Nobody told me it was your first time," she said.

"Well it is," I said. "And I'm not sure if I want the first time to be here, like this, do you understand? Not that it has anything to do with you," I said, afraid she might get the wrong impression, and I added quickly, "You're very pretty, of course. And I can see how the others all admire you and find you so desirable." I saw my mistake immediately when La Correntina grinned at me under her bowl of bright hair, her skirt falling around her shoes in a swirl.

"I still don't think you understand," I said.

It was too late. She already had me backed up against the closed door and was reaching for the buttons of my pants, nicely, all smiles, chattering away at me, "Ay, a nice boy like you, so handsome, so young, with the good little beard like this should be out throwing dust with all the girls he can! If I ever got you to my house, all the girls would be after you, all the young ones would be begging me to let them. An Englishman! Rich! Beautiful! You could have all the girls," she said even as I tried gently to push her off of me but one of her hands was already under my shirt and what she was doing felt good, running her hand over my chest, my stomach quivering under her fingers, her other hand sinking into my pants and finding home. I stopped moving. I let go for a moment, closing my eyes. Maybe it was just the idea of La Correntina that was somehow repulsive, because when I closed my eyes, her big fragrant pillow of a body was moving sensually against mine and it wasn't bad, not bad at all. Her hand stroked, slowly, a hand that knew the economy of touch, the exact pressure, just the right moves. I threw my arms around her thick little body. I leaned awkwardly over her and rested my head on the soft pillow of her sweatered shoulder, my pants falling around my boots. She was still sweetly chattering at me, "What a pretty boy! What a nice pretty stick! How nice! Not too much! We don't want it to go off in my hand! How pretty! How nice!"

After some clumsiness with boots, jodhpurs, shirt buttons, La Correntina pulled me over to my bed. My eyes closed again, hands braced on either side of the generous pear shape of her body. She was nice, and I wanted her now, no question. I let myself go, directed by her expert hands until suddenly all was movement, a shock of sensation, colorful visions in the dark, closed rooms of my eyes as I wanted to move faster, to dance to a rhythm like speeded-up rock 'n' roll, harder and faster until the bed was stomping against the floor, the room was quaking, a herd of horses was stampeding around us in rhythm to the high-pitched rumba of her voice saying, "Pretty! Pretty! Pretty! Pretty!" until it felt like she was screaming it in my ears and she was right, it was pretty, nothing had ever felt as pretty as this, then it was suddenly over just as fast as it had begun.

I lay there a moment flat against her, breathing hard, my cheek resting on the soft red wool sweater that covered her breasts. She let me lie on top of her that way for a while, coming to my senses, the voices of the gauchos at their card game in the other room filtering through.

"Are you finished?" she asked softly. There was something in the distant tone of this question that made me raise my head and look at her. I was still inside her, something was there, and I flew off on impulse, this time with both eyes open and looking directly into hers. The bed started slamming the floor again. I pressed her beefy round shoulders hard into the bed with a violence that made her laugh. She was laughing whenever she could take a breath, eyes alive with my good time, laughter at the beautiful violent joy I had found in her as if she knew that it would stay with me for the rest of my life.

Later, I joined the party in the big bunkhouse room as La Correntina spent time with Casimiro, Don Morales and some of the others. I sat at the table with a glass of wine and did my best at a game of *truco*, but I mixed up the sign for the six of clubs (a pinch on the nose) with the ace of coins (a tug of my right earlobe) and was causing poor Luis to lose big to Joaquín and Carlos. Luis quit the game and started to play his guitar again. We drank wine and waited for the others to finish with La Correntina, who was impatient to get going. I don't know when the idea struck me that I should go with her. It wasn't only my idea. Carlos let on that there would be a big party in town at La Correntina's place, after the bar and the movie theater had closed in Henderson. I thought it over, sitting in a kind of daze in front of the sheetmetal heating stove.

When La Correntina started to go home, looking as full as a sail in her red winter poncho, I made the sudden decision to leave San Ignacio. Casimiro could lead my horse back to the main house in the morning, and I could catch a ride back to Tío Freddi's with Carlos and Luis later on. Afraid to be left behind, I hastily dumped my gear into my suitcase, just emptying the drawers into it. I rushed into a pair of clean jeans, shirt and sweater, then grabbed up my rolls of money. I took a little more time combing down the disheveled peaks of my shaggy hair, regretting it because by the time I was running after Carlos' truck, Luis had already taken the seat in front next to La Correntina. I threw my suitcase in the bed and climbed in, huddling with my back against the cab and bracing myself the whole way as the pickup pitched and bounced over the rough grassy track that led straight across the flat pampas to the town of Henderson.

At La Correntina's that night, half the weekend sinners in the district must have been clustered under the tin roof of her barnlike cement-block bar and dance hall. There weren't enough chairs to seat the crowd nor even enough clean glasses to go around. Though at first I decided to limit myself to talking and drinking, after the second glass of wine I got the notion to order another drink and then stand in line to wait for La Correntina's next available girl to take me off to the courtyard in back for a little *tiro*, as they called it, just a little shot, then I would come back into the bar, drink another glass of wine and stand in line again and so on, until all the big colorful peso bills in my pockets were gone, also all the larger denominations I had stashed in the shaving kit in my suitcase, five or six hundred thousand pesos, a small fortune, enough that it would surely take days until I ran out of ammunition.

This decision took hold with a resoluteness that caused me to force my way through the crowd at the bar to where La Correntina was sitting. She was watching her bartender pour drinks and pull in the money, and I kept thinking Rulo must have paid a fortune to get such a woman to drive out to San Ignacio. She was the queen of the town, the one who owned the whole shooting match. She was happily drunk by then, wavering around on her high stool with a half-dozen of the older men standing around her like court jesters. I pushed my way through until I was standing next to her, then I pulled some of the big dark-red bills out of my pockets, the nice ten-thousand-peso ones, spilling them out like so much useless paper on the bar in front of La Correntina. I was trying to get my message across, shouting above the noise, all my vowels mixed up in my mouth. She couldn't hear anything I was saying. Then she saw my money lying there and a spark of drunken communication was exchanged. La Correntina grabbed my face with one of her hands and kissed me on the mouth. The noise of men's voices rose louder around us and she let my face go, my money now wadded up in her other hand.

"Dolores!" La Correntina shouted across the room. She slapped her hand loudly on the bar to get some attention. "Dolores!" she shouted again, and her troops were suddenly moving. The bartender, a small, dark man, gave orders to a big fellow wearing the top half of an old army uniform and blue jeans, a nightstick and a revolver stuck into his belt. "Dolores!" La Correntina shouted.

There was a big commotion from the back of the room at the door that led into the courtyard. Three or four young men nearest the door were trying to talk to La Correntina's guard, who already had his nightstick out. La Correntina, as if tuned in by a kind of radar to everything going on in the place, swiveled around on her stool and faced them. "We say we're next in line!" the men shouted. The music stopped and a quiet settled over the room. "You shouldn't let anyone go ahead of us!"

"Nobody in my house gets what he deserves!" La Correntina shouted back at them and the room was instantly so noisy with laughter it was like a rain drumming on the tin roof. Glasses went over, card games scattered to the floor and, somewhere in this chaos, the guard with the nightstick bulled his way through the line of men with me behind him, making way for me to cut ahead of them all and into La Correntina's inner courtyard with its rows of little tin shacks.

The girl named Dolores was also called La Cubana, because she had been born in Cuba, a sad black girl with long legs and the most beautiful breasts I had ever held in my two hands, seldom having held any before and certainly not like those sharp, cone-shaped bitter chocolate breasts that thrust up from the dark, hot landscape of her exotic skin, smooth and blue-looking in the dim lantern light. After our first quick jolting *tiro*, I was busy trying to make this beautiful girl feel less bored, and I had finally made her laugh by starting to shower her body with all the blue bills I could find in my jeans pockets, all the pretty five-hundred-peso ones. I was dancing around naked in front of her, pulling more money out of my bunched-up jeans, when the gaucho named Carlos knocked on the door of our little shack and called in to me that it was time to start back to Tío Freddi's.

I looked at La Cubana, laughing and collecting all the blue paper money, folding the bills lengthwise with her sharp red nails and spreading them into a fan in a game of hide and seek, now you see it, now you don't. I told Carlos to go away, I'd make it back on my own. Then I opened the door just a little and held out a few bunched-up bills as a small tip for him.

In a moment, Carlos was back. The door of our little shack flew open and the gaucho's shadow took up nearly half the room. He threw my suitcase into the shack, landing half-unzipped the way I had left it, clothes and things spilling out. "And here! Take this too!" Carlos said in a rough, low voice, tossing in the rainbow-colored wad of pesos, still bunched up in the same shape as when I had handed them to him. The door slammed. La Cubana and I listened to the sound of the gaucho's bootsteps fading in the courtyard.

La Cubana didn't want to talk much about herself. For a few extra pesos she was a princess or a madonna, a panther, a spider, a dancing girl from La Habana, anything men wanted her to be. After our second quick *tiro* in a bed full of scratchy paper cash, she ordered drinks sent in to us from the bar, watered-down domestic scotch at thousands of pesos a glass for which she was paid a commission. When I tried to talk about myself, that I was from North America, an exchange student from Buenos Aires and that kind of thing, she asked me if I had any grass. "Don't you smoke a lot of marijuana in your country?" she asked. "Do you by chance have any marijuana with you?"

I scrambled through my suitcase for a few pills Rulo had given me the night of the nuns and I held them out to her like diamonds, hoping they would interest her. "I have a personal friend who owns some pharmacies, and I've got plenty of those," she said, stretching her long shape out on her bed, her eyes half-closed.

There was a thin packet of cards and letters in my suitcase that I had been meaning to answer. The packet was buried in the mess of dirty socks, shirts and riding clothes at the bottom of my bag. An impulse struck me and I followed it, tearing the rubber band off the envelopes and flipping through them quickly until I found the right one. I unfolded Harry's letter and held it up to a kerosene lamp. I carefully tore a strip of its paper off, then I used a razor blade to divide the tiny dot on the paper that looked like a miniature Japanese flag of the rising sun in its little shiny windowpane. "Have you ever heard of LSD?" I asked.

"I think I read about that in a magazine," La Cubana said. "Is it good?"

We washed our halves of acid down with our expensive scotch and sometime later, just as we were really getting off, I tried to climb into bed with her for one more little *tiro* but we were both too doubled over with insane giggling, a thin haze of light from the lantern slicing the room in half between us. When I tried to touch her, she jumped

away with a crazy, jittery laughter. Somehow the idea
formed that we should try to find the bar—it was just possible to remember there was a bar out there somewhere in
the night. The strange, prolonged time spent putting on our
clothes to walk out into the chilly courtyard was like a jour-
ney that took light-years.

By the time I reached the door back to La Correntina's
bar, which was glowing blue-white under a cloudy sky in
which a moon shone like a faint frosted bulb, like a car-
toonist's idea of light, I had somehow lost track of Dolores. After we had giggled at the moon, La Cubana had
been struck by a shift in plans, always dangerous on acid.
One of the neighboring little shacks had its door standing
open and she had a friend inside she said she had to step
in and see for just a moment. I tried to find words to tell
her to come with me but I wasn't sure the sounds I made
were actually in Spanish, then she was suddenly gone.

The barroom was alive, too alive—I had an awareness
that it had become a huge, living beast made up of music
and noise, black tobacco smoke and threatening movements. For a moment, I was no longer able to distinguish
between pattern and humanity. The night became a rau-
cous parade of La Correntina's, with tambourines and
wooden flutes, with guitars and weird stringed instruments
made out of armadillos strummed so fast the musicians'
fingers looked like the wings of hummingbirds. For a moment, everything was a part of this music made up of
strings, whistles, shouts and hoots, and of the bandmem-
ber who started dancing the *malambo*, his bootheels hail-
storming on a small wood stage in a gaucho flamenco gone
mad. He took a set of *bolas* and began a *malambo* rope
dance with them, whipping them around like helicopter
blades that seemed to lift him off the floor. The room went
up in cheering and applause that was like a herd of horses
stampeding in my head.

I pressed myself through the crush toward the bar, halfway there losing track of where it was I was going and
having to tell myself I was a liquid, I could flow, the surface
tension of all my cells was as strong and smooth as oil. The
noise was loud, pulsing, and there wasn't much oxygen in

the air anymore but luck was with me, always there, and in
a battle like this, victory went to those who least deserved
it—just as I slipped through the crowd to the bar, a heavyset
man hitched up his pants and scooted off his barstool. I
landed on it like a shipwrecked sailor tossed to the shore.
*Lucky, lucky, lucky*, I thought, the bartender serving me up
a whiskey without my even asking for it, scooting it along
the bar's zinc surface that reflected the world in a silvery
fuzz. *Lucky you, lucky you*, I thought, watching a distant
oily figure it took a moment to recognize as myself drinking
whiskey in the mirrors behind the bar, all of them cracked
or fissured and splitting up the world that moved in them.
*Luck . . .*

La Correntina moved in the colorful mirrors, borne
along by the drunken crowd in a chaotic parade. A voice
started talking in my head, *Listen and look, look and listen, this is her train, her court, carrying along all her
possessions. Don't you know who she is? Don't you know
where you are?* In the mercury windows behind the bar a
multitude was passing in a dusty, smoky whirlwind with
whistles, hoots, shouts, drums and tambourines and I
didn't know I was me anymore, it was as if I were sitting
on the high steel tower of my barstool that had once been
a tractor seat and I was unable to move, caught, trapped,
fixed there like a stuffed hunting trophy watching it all
with my big glass eyes. First came the beasts of burden,
the rich ranchers, cattle merchants, bankers and lawyers,
bearing along their big chests full of yanqui cash and their
green felt gambling tables piled high with rectangular
chips, the color green pulsing all around them like strobes;
hanging around their necks were heavy harnesses made of
beef, grain and leather, the kind of men so weighed down
by their wealth that they thought they were resting. After
them came an innumerable troop packed tightly together
on the dance floor, shoulder to shoulder in a smoke thicker
than any pampas dust, all of them men who made their
livings from open mouths—gauchos, tractor drivers, field
workers, packers, truckers, bartenders, grocers, bakers,
cooks and servants and mobs of everyone else who stuffed
bellies, the smell of them heavy, as strong as a jungle's,

all of them poor and though they were laughing, they were the kind of men so tied to the seasons that they always feared the worst. Then came the lackeys among that rabble, on their little low stage with their guitars and flutes and stringed instruments made of armadillos, La Correntina's musicians, the only real geniuses in the place, and they were suddenly like great poets, like Homer and Shakespeare and Luis Vélez de Guevara, like the Beatles and Dylan and Hunter S. Thompson, dressed in uniforms of white felt ponchos, so squeezed together on their tiny stage they could hardly play their mad fast music that was wild with words, kicking with hoots and whistles and magic flutes for a crowd so thick they couldn't move, the ones that needed good music the most; they kept on playing, princes of songs passing hats for their meals. And who were the ones dressed up in such brilliance that it looked like they were decked with silver and jewels, uniforms so rich it seemed they were dripping with gold and pearls, the ones who had so many shaven-headed privates around them that they stood out all the more, most of them so padded with fat they looked like stuffed exotic birds, the ones who were riding along using great statesmen as their horses and with such twisted shapes under their gold braid crusts that they were really hairless hunchbacks and amputees, one-eyed lame deaf babblers, toothless dogs with the bones of innocent corpses, the rich and powerful through violence, the bloody princes of this world, the ones who with shrewdness and hatred and pure luck had stolen all their wealth with the weapons of fear and were the most miserable souls on earth? Brass, bangles, epaulettes, red, blue and green ribbons, caps worn straight and only taken off when they were talking to women were the officers, some of them from the army and some from the police. One of them was gray and bald and wore his uniform as if he were dressed in the crown jewels and he was the drunkest, so La Correntina doted most on him, calling for her youngest girls and her finest whiskey, tipping his hat to a clownish angle on his head as she pushed him to the front of the samba parade on its way to a table that had been liberated just for him while his comrades in arms and

the rest of the crowd looked on, waiting their turns knowing that promotions and women always favored the wrong
men. Somewhere among them was a one-eyed priest who
was teaching himself about sin and carrying before him a
huge tree branch hung all over with canes, miters, laurels,
medals, red cardinal's caps, crowns, crests, tiaras and
honoring speeches tied up into little scrolls, all the human
dignities he was parceling out to the crowd with his good
eye closed. La Correntina's girls came and went through
the crush of souls with ease, carried along like they were
princesses riding on the backs of elephants, hard to tell
the bargirls from the ones who worked in the courtyard,
and it seemed they were always changing places. There
was a stool at the end of the bar three down from mine
reserved just for them; they appeared from the courtyard
and joined the parade at times as if they were taking coffee
breaks in a factory. The first was dressed in an orange robe
and gaudy red heels and sat at the bar the longest, full of
complaints; she was too hot, her drinks weren't right, she
needed aspirins; whenever she opened her mouth to speak,
her words were all jumbled into nonsense with a silly expression on her silly pitted face, a scar at the corner of her
silly mouth, none of the attentions of the men ever pleas-
ing her, and though she was the ugliest, she seemed the
most favored. The one who took her place was called La
Felicidad, a moody girl whose face kept changing with
anger, tears, boredom and laughter one moment to the
next; she wore a wide band of gold on her right hand that
showed she had made all the promises of marriage but had
never kept a single one. Another girl called La Lisa was
as squat and fat as La Correntina and wore her oily hair
in a French twist, her face painted like a carnival doll's,
an iris behind her ear, a whore who spent her time ranging
through knots of men in the crowd telling them how handsome they were and soliciting dates; when she sat on men's
laps and spoke with her hands, her fat fingers grew long
and huge and multiplied in the air and looked like hundreds of wagging tongues. The memory of La Cubana
flashed into mind, the little voice in my head asking what
she was doing, why wasn't she here? Then the flash that

she must be alone somewhere and crying, on a bummer trip, the pretty black girl who didn't wear a single jewel, the only real beauty in the place forgotten by everyone. I tried on impulse to turn away from the mirrors and make my way toward the courtyard to search for her but I couldn't move, I couldn't handle even turning my face toward the crowd. Then the oldest-looking whore, in a green grass skirt, sat down on the bar stool and asked into the mirrors at me where she could find La Cubana in an angry, envious tone. I was unable to answer her, all my languages were suddenly gone but to raise one hand in a gesture that seemed to say I wasn't sure; the old whore's face turned green and into a beaklike shape with sharp fangs when she opened her mouth, then she spat something at me and glided off through the crowd like some kind of monstrous green falcon, on her way picking up scraps of meat off of plates and stuffing them into her mouth. The girl in orange came back again, riding on the shoulders of a rich man with horns on his head who looked like a minotaur, and she complained about a girl called La Esperanza, pointing her out loudly in the parade and saying she was keeping all the best customers for herself; La Esperanza was standing on a green felt gambling table, bleached blonde and looking pregnant, waving a lit *cigarro* over a crowd of rich men, then smoking it for them under her skirts with a laughter gone insane. Other girls came and went, in and out, up and back, some huge and some tiny, some drunk and some sober, some jeweled and greedy-looking, others joking and profane enough to sell the crosses from around their necks; some were in slippers and robes, some in dresses, some wearing glasses, all different kinds, one who was stealing the tips off the tables, one who told on the one who stole and caused a row with La Correntina; some who gossiped, others who were histrionically crying with too much drink and overwork, and there was one who kept serving drinks and leaving change on the wrong tables. They were all dissolving in some kind of colorful pool, pieces of them breaking away and flying across the room to be searched out by intelligent-looking men in groups of three, doctors and undertakers who picked them up and tossed them into black boxes; provincial administrators, bureaucrats and even a few teachers were skyrocketing around behind them, holding pens in hands shaped like mortar-boards and writing on the hairy sides of skins of beef. Worshippers surrounded La Correntina's girls in noise and smoke, all of them looking hungry, desperate, some laughing, some crying, some singing, some quiet, all of them in his own way resigned to this madness—this one a petty liar, that one a small-time cheat, the one over there who married for riches alone, the rancher fast asleep over his last hand of cards because he was afraid to go home to his wife, some of them gluttons and some of them drunks, some just there for the music, but all of them fools for La Correntina's girls, stewing and mixing over them in the thickening dust of her parade, leading them off in the shrill screaming noise in which everyone had lost his senses and which was building up to a pressure that was going to crush my brain. I was riding on a golden ass that pulled a cart with square wheels, a square glass to my lips, and all around me were demons and giants, dancers and dwarfs and hucksters with drums and wooden flutes; I saw them in hundreds of fracturing windows, each of them for an instant pressing his face to the glass then pulled along past me on his toy wheels. At their center, billowing up at times like a huge hot-air balloon filled with drunken maniacal laughter, was La Correntina herself, standing apart from all of them, a woman in red and blue-green, the woman who I didn't think was very bright at first but who everyone around me was still listening for above the noise; La Correntina was surrounded by her petitioners, never alone, picking them out like the random choices of lightning bolts, men who looked as sad and hungry as coyotes, all of them raising up their voices in hope, and in their confusion, not a one of them understanding the others. . . .

I couldn't take it anymore, but I didn't know what to do; then the big guard who wore the top half of an army uniform turned up at the bar for a drink. I tried to speak to him but I couldn't, and I kept laughing crazily, then fell off my stool and finally, after he shouted a question above the noise to

La Correntina, the guard led me out into the courtyard to the little shack that La Cubana and I had shared it seemed a lifetime ago. She was gone, no trace of her there but the odor of her jasmine perfume. It was cold and I lit the small kerosene heater that soon had the little tin *cabaña* like a sauna. I took my shirt off and sat on the bed, leaning against the wall. I tried to close my eyes and rest but couldn't stand to keep my eyes closed because I kept losing my balance and tipping around. There was an eon of panic in which I was sure somebody was outside the door ready to burst in and kill me while I kept telling myself it was just the acid talking. Then that feeling slowly passed, replaced by a confidence that I could handle anything, that all I had to do was wait the acid out until I crashed. Finally, I was able to close my eyes, the bed bobbing around like a life raft adrift on a quiet sea. The first shadowy light of a rainy day showed through the crack under the door. By the time it was fully day, I decided to get up, change my clothes, pack up my things and walk down the street into the new universe of the morning.

It was then I discovered my suitcase was gone. Nothing was left. All my clothes, my books, my shoes, my nice shaving kit, my good German camera that the old man had carried with him through World War Two, and all my money, more than four hundred thousand pesos, maybe about three hundred yanqui dollars, everything was gone. But worst of all, my passport was missing, my visa and vaccination papers, all my identification it was illegal to go without. I thought of all the hassle to come, of the bribes Papá would have to pay at the *Oficina de Extranjeros*, the Argentine immigration agency, for sets of new papers, and all the waiting I would have to do at my own crowded yanqui consulate, of new photographs, interviews, everything.

The bar at that hour of the early morning was deserted except for a maid who was washing down the floor and knew nothing about my suitcase. I looked at my face in the mirrors behind the bar and saw someone deranged. I finally awakened La Correntina's little bartender. How would he know about my suitcase? He followed me back into the big room and had me uselessly write down Tío Freddi's name and address on a piece of paper in case somebody found it. Just as I had finished doing this, Tío Freddi actually pulled up in front of La Correntina's in his pickup.

I explained the situation to Tío Freddi and tried to make clear to him how much I needed all my things, my money, my camera, my passport, everything. He was sympathetic at first, and strong with the bartender, telling him what a good friend of La Correntina's he was, and he kept saying, "That's a shame. We'll do everything we can to find it. But listen, don't get your hopes up," he said; then he laughed ironically and said, "You know if you lose something here, *che*, you never get it back. Isn't that the truth? Come on now. Don't worry. You can straighten out your documents in Buenos Aires, and until then, you won't need them out here. So let's get going. We have another two thousand cattle to start working on the María Consuela ranch today, though if you want, you can rest in your room. I just thought as long as I was in town, I'd round you up and get you to help me load supplies. So let's go. We don't want to sit in the bars all day!"

I looked around La Correntina's helplessly, as if my suitcase might somehow materialize on one of the tables, then I followed Tío Freddi outside and into his truck. On the long ride home, Tío Freddi kept laughing suddenly and turning to me, saying, "La Correntina really is a fine one, isn't she! Wasn't she a good time! You know she was!" He slapped me across the shoulders and laughed. I stared out ahead through the windshield across an ocean of grass. "It's a good life out here, Yanqui, don't you think?" Tío Freddi said. "Out here, it's the best life there is!"

Two days later, there was a letter for me in the mail Tío Freddi brought back from town. Miguelito had been as good as his word. There was a single large envelope from him with a short angry note inside it saying Mamá and Papá had decided to keep the boys slaving away in Buenos Aires their whole winter vacation, and how was his horse Porotos doing? Enclosed with that was a flimsy blue airmail envelope from Harry. The letter from Harry had a strange postmark—it was only three weeks old, incredible to think it had come all the way across two hemispheres, through three countries and the whole province in such a short time, the quickest letter I had ever received from overseas. I eagerly went into my little guesthouse and sat down, anxious to read Harry's news, and tore the envelope open. With the first glance at the one rumpled blue page, I caught my breath. For a moment, I thought I was still hallucinating from the acid, looking to the page and away, then back to the page again quickly with a shock of panic:

*Fevertree*

# 7

## Fevertree

I remembered a certain beat-up apartment in the East Village. Harry and I were sitting crosslegged on the floor inside, members of a big circle of ragged souls with long hair and painted faces. The Cream was blasting "In the Sunshine of Your Love" from somewhere down a long hallway. There was nothing much in the place but old bleeding mattresses and pillows, in one corner a TV set that was flashing a continual silent movie of colorful snow, its back removed and its guts exposed. A dirty window looked out over Avenue B onto a Puerto Rican grocery with a speaker horn over its door playing *piña colada* music, as Harry called it, songs in Spanish with a Caribbean jungle beat. An old Puerto Rican who was known as Camacho in the neighborhood was leaning against the grocery's window, posted there selling nickel bags. A joint of his good Caribbean grass was being passed around our circle.

A really big dude with a full beard and dressed in a white linen sari and a necklace of shells, the street freak who had invited us up to his pad for a toke, started talking to my brother Harry. "We're all in this thing together," he said. "Can you dig what I'm saying? If we form the right kind

of movement, we can beat this life," he said. "If everybody
who's dodging the draft right now, and don't get paranoid,
man, because I'm in the same situation. And I don't mean
just you and me, I mean like a mass movement. Like all
the kids out there burning draft cards. I mean, if everybody
just throws all his I.D. away, like his driver's license, birth
certificate, social security card, especially the fucking social security card, man, I mean everything, and if everybody starts going by the *same name*, and living by that
*name*, hundreds of thousands of young people all over this
country, the entire Selective Service system would collapse
overnight. Can you dig it? Wouldn't that be far out? So
that's why we call ourselves Fevertrees. All of us, man,
we're all Fevertrees," he said.

The people in the circle nodded their heads at us and
began to introduce themselves with warm hugs and hand-
shakes, all of them calling themselves Fevertree as a last
name. There was a Dorothy Fevertree, and a Dawn Fevertree, Billy Fevertree, a Frank and a Sky and all the rest. It
was like an alias they had all agreed upon. If it was some
kind of code for a small community or only the product of
a stoned night, it didn't matter to them. According to them,
Fevertree had started as a name they used whenever they
took part in antiwar rallies and might be arrested, or when
they spoke up at open meetings to promote nonviolent protest when everyone was sure the FBI was listening. Within
a few short months, thousands of people in the peace movement, coast to coast, would supposedly start using the name,
even people who weren't dodging the draft. The idea was
that with so many thousands openly using the same name,
they might be able to cover for the ones who were in hiding,
something like the thousands of non-Jews in Denmark who
wore yellow Stars of David during the Hitler years. With so
many people using the name Fevertree, some with forged
and some with legitimate identification to back them up,
maybe the FBI and the police wouldn't be able to tell one
Fevertree from another. There would be Fevertrees with
homes, families and straight jobs as well as the Fevertrees
hiding out in the streets or in the countryside.

"Hey, man," this big dude with the beard who called

himself Speed Fevertree went on. "There's even a rock band that calls itself Fevertree now, have you ever heard their albums? And I know a Fevertree who works as a beekeeper in Oregon, and a Fevertree who's been dodging the draft for three years and is somehow working in East Africa on a government grant. Uncle Sugar doesn't even know who he's sending the checks to, man, and they think he's black, isn't that far out? And I know all kinds of other Fevertrees all over this country. Now you, man," he said. "You and your kid brother here. You're Fevertrees now. Tell everybody you can. Pass the good word along and get as many people as you can to use the name, you dig what I'm saying? It's like it should spread on contact, from one brother and sister to another, like something . . . ah, man, I don't know." He stopped talking to take a big hit off the joint. His chest filled. He held the smoke in his lungs, his eyes bugging out a little and turning red, a grin on his face that was like a primitive grimace of pain. Then his cheeks puffed out and he let the smoke out of his nose and mouth in a rush and said, "What was I saying, man?"

He had said enough. Harry had heard him, and had already taken on the name, putting John and Jacob in front of it. My brother Harry started calling himself John Jacob Fevertree as a stage and street name, and he talked of little else for some time after that. He even went into raps to people on the sidewalks, the ones who had gathered around to listen to him play his guitar and maybe to flip him some spare change. "It's like the same idea going around and around in your brain," my brother said, "in everybody's brain, like a Buddhist prayer wheel, or a universal mantra, something like that. I mean, we can do it. We can make it happen. We got to make this kind of commitment, you know, or else we'll all get sucked into this country's bum trip. And I don't only mean the stinking war, man. I mean all the power trips and the commercial trips, the fucking money trip especially, and most people will just continue to free associate with all those bummers while the rest of us live in fear, you dig what I'm saying? I mean heavy fear, paranoia, World War Three, man, and some of us will still be dropping out and hiding out and living these helpless

lives. I was taught that we were all born with something
like this inside ourselves, like the way a Jew might sense
his Jewishness in the cradle, or hey, I was raised a Catholic,
and I was taught all Catholics are born with certain obligations, have you ever thought of that? Obligations! I grew
up thinking countries were like that, too, like a newborn
American kid might carry something like a specifically
American genetic code, like we were all born different, sure,
but where we were born really meant something. But it's
not like that. That's a silly dream, man. The truth is that
we all got to make a choice, and we got to find that choice
inside, to make it work *out there*, a code of values, man, if
you want to put it in establishment terms. But to me it's
more like a chant, or a song, something that reminds you
what you are, and something you can run over and over in
your brain to stop your own self from going over the fucking
edge. The world's been doing things pretty much like it
since the beginning of time with crap like flags, kings and
queens, and patriotism, man, the communists with their
fucking privileged bureaucracy, or this country's idea of
loyalty to Nixon's Amerika, if you can dig what I'm saying.
That's nowhere, man, really nowhere, because all of these
things started as ways to bring people together to live their
lives in peace and here they are, making them tear each
other apart. That's why we need the name, a universal name,
can you dig it? Fevertree. That's it. It's like a family tree.
We're all in the same family, man, and we might as well
make the choice right now or there's not a prayer in hell
that all these people are going to survive, man, if you can
dig what I'm saying. Hey, thanks for listening. Thanks for
the spare change. Be cool. Take it easy, man. Later.'' My
brother tipped the rawhide hat he had started to wear when
he had changed his name as if to go along with its frontier
sound. Then he took up his guitar again and started playing
another song. He went on and on with this, for a time. He
sang a song, a few people gathered around, then he went
through version after version of his Fevertree rap as deeply
launched into it as any monk in his meditations until the
people were no longer listening.

Cold weather hit the streets. My brother lost girlfriends,

was kicked out of crash pads. In winter, still dodging the draft and now with a warrant out for his arrest, he had a harder time finding under-the-table jobs or scaring up enough spare change to survive on. Then he got an unexpected break. One of the managers of a West Third Street baskethouse helped my brother get an invitation to sing professionally at a place in Chicago called The Earl of Oldtown, a famous bar for folksingers. Donny, Tommy and I pitched in and helped Harry buy a bus ticket. In Chicago, Harry made the acquaintance of a so-called "talent agent," who managed to get The Earl of Oldtown to extend my brother's invitation to play there. The talent agent got twenty-five percent of my brother's earnings, and Harry also moved into the man's apartment. Money was short. The agent cashed the checks made out to the name of John Jacob Fevertree while my brother was allowed to sleep on the couch in his living room.

One night, the agent brought in a very young girl, a runaway, and disappeared into his bedroom with her for a couple of hours. My brother went off to The Earl of Oldtown to play his sets for the night. Later, he was a guest on disc jockey Ray Nordstrand's famous *Midnight Special* program, along with the Chicago folksinger Fred Holstein. My brother returned from the radio show just in time to be arrested along with his "agent." The agent was charged with statutory rape, and my brother was brought in on the same charge, though it was changed to contributing to the delinquency of a minor when it was clear that he was only sleeping in the same apartment. According to my brother, it was a set-up. The girl had been involved in several other statutory rape cases in the past. She let herself be picked up as if she were a runaway, stayed with a man for a night, then she telephoned her mother, who in turn telephoned the police. Then the mother made it clear she would drop all charges for a certain cash sum made payable to her, and my brother was also sure that Mayor Daley's police got some kind of cut out of the deal. My brother was arrested in Chicago under the name John Jacob Fevertree, then fingerprinted and held in Cook County jail. Somehow, and he never knew how, the police discovered his real name, maybe through fingerprints taken one time my brother was arrested during a sit-in and the charges dropped, or maybe through the "agent," who knew my brother's story. In any case, nobody made bail in time for him to blow town before his real name turned up on an FBI report that he was being sought for draft evasion.

Harry placed a collect call to the old man, who raised about two thousand dollars to pay for the bribe and a lawyer. The old man flew to Chicago to sit in the courtroom where my brother pleaded guilty, though he stated he was ignorant of receiving any draft notice and claimed extenuating circumstances. A kindly federal judge gave Harry the choice of going either directly to jail or into the Army. My brother flew home with the old man after signing papers that in effect enlisted him into the Army, though he had about a week's "grace period" before he had to present himself for swearing in and basic training.

"I don't think I could make it through five years in jail. And I don't want to have to leave this country forever," Harry told his brothers. He was skinny, starving, in rags, and his eyes showed something more than defeat, a fatalism, I think, that his life was just never going to work the way he had planned. "I was running out of places to crash, anyway, man. And I just couldn't make it anymore out on the streets." Besides his bad luck, there were too many others out there like him, all making music and living off the same sources, all still going by different names.

The strange lines of chicken scratchings signed with the name Fevertree really scared me. At first, I thought it must be a message written in some kind of Vietnamese code, then I realized it was gibberish, the kind of thing Harry did on acid, making up his own private language, like the words *say* and *tan* put together the way they were reminded me of the kind of word jokes Harry played sometimes when he was tripping. It seemed pretty clear to me that my brother had blown his mind over there. But what could I do about it? What could anybody do?

I asked Tío Freddi to drive me into town, where I stood in the Henderson postal and telephone office and tried to

make a long-distance call to the old man and the old lady.
I didn't know what I was going to say to them, so maybe it
was a mercy that all the international lines were busy at
Intel Argentina. Then I tried to send a telegram but that
didn't work, some of the public employees for the nation's
telegraph service had just gone out illegally on strike, sab-
otaging important equipment. And what would I say to the
old man anyway? *Dear Mom and Dad. Bad letter from
Harry. Please advise.* What could they possibly do with
that? It would only worry them, and they would be as helpless as I was under the circumstances.

Ever since getting Harry's first letter, I had been replay-
ing a terrible scene in my imagination. Harry was up in his
helicopter, firing his machine gun into a bulletstorm from
the ground, then the helicopter was hit, bleeding dark smoke
into a pale blue Vietnamese sky like a wounded guppy trailing its guts in a fish tank, then it exploded in a tumbling
fireball into the jungles below. Praying that would never
happen was somehow better than not knowing what to think,
that maybe Harry had tripped out completely and had gone
through the barbed wire and into the jungles and had deserted and was sending me a message in code that he was
in hiding again, gone underground. Or maybe something
else had happened that I couldn't imagine.

Harry's letter brought me unexpectedly home. It recalled
a frame of mind I had shared with Harry out on the streets,
thoughts of nonviolent rebellion, of protests, of his songs,
and of how ill equipped either of us was to effect any real
change, least of all Harry, who must have broken down in
the conditions of war. Suddenly, I wanted to get someplace
where I could make a phone call all the way to Vietnam if
I had to in order to find out what had happened to him. I
decided to cut my stay short at Tío Freddi's ranch. The day
after I received Harry's letter, I packed what I had left of
my things in a paper bag. I borrowed the fare from Tío
Freddi and took the early train back to Buenos Aires.

I arrived at the train station without telling my family I
was coming home, and as it turned out, the timing of my
return couldn't have been worse. I found the apartment
strangely empty just before the noon meal, Mamá and Isa-

belita the only ones at home. Isabelita answered the door and called out to Mamá that it was me. Mamá rushed into the hallway and said urgently, "What are you doing home! What could have happened to bring you back so soon?"

"I've had some bad news about my brother," I said. "The one in Vietnam. It's unclear what's happened, and I want to find out."

"I'm very sorry to hear that," she said. "Are you sure it's bad news? What kind of bad news? My God, but you gave me a fright coming home without telling us! Why didn't you telephone?"

"I'm sorry, Mamá. I just had to get back," I said. "In any case, it was really nice at Tío Freddi's but I started to miss all of you. It seems like a miracle to be home again," I said, giving her a son-to-mother hug and kissing her cheek.

"But is that your luggage?" Mamá asked. "This paper bag? Where's your suitcase?"

"It was stolen on the train," I said. "Last night while I was sleeping. Everything's gone, my camera, my money, the nice clothes you got for me and worse, my passport and all my identification, what a hassle, Mamá. I've had a terrible, terrible night on the train," I said.

"Look at those clothes you're wearing! And that beard! It's just like your Tío Freddi to send you home looking like a savage. What bad luck! It's been a week of bad luck," Mamá said. "Martín Segundo got his news from I.S.E. yesterday that he was rejected. Rejected! No year abroad for him, you understand?"

"No, Mamá," I said. "I didn't even know he had applied to go abroad with I.S.E. Nobody ever told me."

"Well of course you knew! Hasn't Martín been talking to you about it?"

"No, he hasn't," I said.

"Well, maybe not. He completed all the interviews months ago, just before you came. And naturally, why should he talk to you about it? What could it have to do with you? Like all of us, he probably didn't want to make you feel uncomfortable."

"I'm sorry, Mamá," I said. "I'm sorry for Martín Segundo."

"There's nothing to be done," Mamá said. "I.S.E. in New York said the reason Martín was rejected was that they couldn't place him in a family that matched his personality and background. Can you imagine that? Why would a good boy from a good family like Martín be so hard to place? This house is in an uproar over it. And the I.S.E. decision is final, your Papá and I have already gone twice to see them. We're very, very sad. It's been a big blow. Your Papá and I were hoping you wouldn't be home for another week or so until things calmed down, but here you are!" Mamá took a step back from me and regarded my appearance, wrinkling her nose. "What a mess you look! Like one of Tío Freddi's gauchos! Now go off and change out of those clothes, my son, the others should be home any minute. After we eat, I'll give you some money and you can go to the barber's. We can't have you looking like a savage back at school."

"But Mamá, it's the style these days," I said. "It's just starting to grow."

"You can go around like an *indio* at Tío Freddi's but not in my house," Mamá said.

"Seriously, Mamá, I don't want out cut off my hair and beard," I said.

"I don't want an argument, Diego! It's been hard enough this week!" Mamá raised her voice sharply. "What an injustice! Martín has the best grades, the finest background, and his test scores for the I.S.E. were very high! And think what a support for I.S.E. we've been all along, giving them contributions, and even hosting our own exchange student! Having you here with us! It's an injustice, that's clear, a terrible, terrible injustice for everyone. So we don't need any more friction in this house, is that clear?"

Her words cut deeply, partly because they hit me with a possibility I had never imagined—that the reason I was living with my new family at all was that they thought it would help to get Martín Segundo an I.S.E. scholarship to the United States. How could I not have guessed? All that member-of-the-family stuff when I was nothing but a tool to gain influence, an insurance policy for Martín's year abroad. It was possible that everything we had lived through together, their calling me their son, giving me my name, their taking me in stride with all the trouble I had caused them had been nothing but a sham, a big lie, a con job, placing bets on Martín's future and using me as one of their chips. The effect of Mamá's words must have shown on my face. She started to say something to explain herself when I cut her off. "If you wish, señora, I can apply for a transfer from this house. There are temporary families I can stay with even tonight."

"No, no, my son!" Mamá said. "It doesn't have anything to do with you! We love you very much! Miguelito and Alejo have been looking forward to having you back home!"

"It's not my fault, Mamá," I said. "I've hardly even met the people at I.S.E. And what you've just said suggests that . . ."

"I know, Diego, and I'm sorry. I didn't mean it. I'm just upset," Mamá said. "Martín Segundo knows it, too, that none of this is your fault. It's the fault of the terrible administration of I.S.E. ! I'm writing a letter, your Papá is writing, and Martín, and I want you to write to them, too, as soon as you can, to make clear to them what an injustice this is for everyone."

She was trying to smooth things over, the same charming smile on her face as when she entertained Papá's clients at one of her parties. Behind this, I sensed a new tension between us. She knew she had been indiscreet, making me aware of an uncomfortable possibility it would be hard to ignore and now here I was, a means to an end that would never be reached.

"I'll go and change my clothes, Mamá," I said. "I've had a hard night on the train."

I handed my dirty clothes to Isabelita, and went down the hallway to my room, maybe the best bedroom in their house. I began to think it was petty to feel the way I did, but that still didn't change my view of the family. Didn't a lot of things work that way in Argentina? Wasn't it who you knew, what influence you had in the right circles that determined who made it and who didn't in this country? What use could I possibly be to my new family now?

I felt sad and lonely, changing out of my muddy jeans and the puff-sleeved gaucho blouse Tío Freddi had given me that smelled like a barnyard, untying the grungy *paisano* scarf from around my neck. I found my good gray school trousers and a clean shirt, that much I would do for Mamá's sense of propriety at lunch. As for the rest of it, if I was going to stay on with the Benevento family, my beard was staying, too, and my hair was going to grow as long as I wanted even if I had to catch the next flight straight out of the country.

Martín Segundo and the boys came in with Papá, who had taken them out shopping. When little Miguel discovered I was home, he ran down the hallway and burst into my room with a big embrace. Alejo brought in a pile of interesting books he wanted me to read, one of them the paperback edition of Gabriel García Márquez's *Cien Años de Soledad*, which he had just discovered. Martín waited at his customary place at the table in the dining room. When I came in for lunch with Miguelito and Alejo, he hardly greeted me, only a brief *hola* as if I had just returned home from a walk. Papá was cheerful enough, shaking my hand and giving me one of his warm Italian hugs, telling me how strong and sunburned I was; "Look at this one, coming back to us half-gaucho," he said. He asked me how his brother Frederico was, and how the ranch was, and he made pleasant small talk. The matter with I.S.E. wasn't mentioned, no doubt Mamá had cautioned them. It was as if they were all avoiding the subject for my sake, which made it seem even more as though something basic in my relationship to them had changed. They plied me with questions about Casimiro and cousin Rulo, and about the *doma* and the *asados* out on the pampas. Miguelito, of course, asked me about his horse, Porotos. Tío Freddi had told me that one of the gauchos had made a mistake at a *doma* and Miguelito's horse had been sent off to be made into dogmeat. I lied to Miguelito and told him I had ridden his horse, Porotos, and what a fine horse he was. Mamá mentioned that I had come home carrying a paper bag, and I told them how the nice suitcase Papá had given me had been stolen on the train. Papá began to outline a plan for me to go to my consulate to apply for a new passport, and how he would take care of matters with the right government office to replace my visa. I told a modified version about the Three Marías, as if Tío Freddi, Rulo and I had planned to go gambling the night we ended up rescuing the nuns instead. For a moment, as they were listening, it started to feel like it used to at the Benevento table, as if I were still one of them. I finished the story and everyone laughed but Martín Segundo, who was morosely pushing his food around on his plate. "*Che*, Martín," I said. "Mamá told me about the rejection from I.S.E. and I'm sorry. You can believe I'll let them know how wrong they are. They're a bunch of stupid *boludos* to let this happen, that's clear," I said.

"I don't care a shit for I.S.E. or anybody connected with them," Martín said, letting me know I had been tactless—as if he needed me to buck him up or defend him. "I'm better off anyway. I'd rather study in France or in England any day than in the United States."

"Listen to me, you two, I've got an idea," Mamá said, breaking the silence that had fallen over her table. "Martín, you could use a trim, and it's clear that Diego needs a haircut. I'll give you the money, you go get haircuts, then maybe you'd like to go to the movies. Go out to the movies and for a pizza. Why don't you two go get a haircut and then have a good time?"

"Listen, I'm sorry, but I've made a decision about this hair," I said. "I've decided to let it grow long, as I would in my own country, to show my protest of the war in Vietnam," I said. "It's something very personal to me, something very important to me. Excuse me for a moment," I said and on impulse, I went to my bedroom and fished out Harry's latest letter, then passed it around the table. I realized this was wrong, to use my brother's situation as if to politic my way out of a haircut. I hadn't been in Buenos Aires three hours and I was already doing things that made me hate myself. "Something's happened to my brother, that's clear," I said. "When I go to the consulate to see about my passport, I want to make an official inquiry about him. I hope you understand."

"As far as I'm concerned, it's your decision, my son," Papá said. "But you must realize that nobody in this country is going to know what you mean by it."

"I have enough trouble introducing you at parties without that beard that makes you look like a goat," Martín said.

"I'll make my own parties, thank you," I said. "I haven't been to one of your boring parties in months. You can take them and your boring friends and stuff them up your ass, *boludo*."

I shoved my chair back from the table rudely and left the dining room. I grabbed my overcoat in the hall, the good one of camel's hair Papá had bought for me, then I slammed out of the flat with Mamá's voice calling after me, "Wait! Come here, Diego! Diego! Come back here, please!" But I was already out and down the stairs.

My plan as I walked fast down Junín toward the avenue Santa Fe was that I would catch the first taxi that passed and ride straight to the I.S.E. offices, where I would request an immediate change of families. But on a busy corner that was just then shuttering down for the siesta, I realized I had hardly any money in my pockets, just loose change. I wasn't sure I even had enough for bus fare all the way into the Barrio Once where the offices of I.S.E. were located. The day was cold and clear, the *plátano* trees along the streets bare and tinged with black exhaust. Cabs were letting out their last passengers for lunch and sleep, and the *colectivo* buses were moving sluggishly along the fashionable avenue. I chased after a bus of the yellow 69 line but before I got to it, I realized it was going the wrong way.

I waited on the corner in front of the new, modern Banco de Londres building, which squatted in the elegant Barrio Norte like a concrete bunker designed by the Bauhaus. By now everything was closed, the streets mostly deserted. The I.S.E. offices would be closed for lunch, too, I realized, I'd have to wait until three if I wanted to phone them. An old, fat man in a white apron was packing up the flowers he sold on the street, locking them away in a big metal trunk he pushed along on bicycle wheels. Where was I going to go? I fingered the few coins in my pocket, hardly enough to buy myself a coffee. I walked aimlessly in the direction of the

Plaza San Martín, the riding boots I was still wearing heavy
and uncomfortable on the sidewalk. I looked at the reflection of my face passing in a shop window, messy and gaunt.
Martín Segundo was right. My face looked like a starving
goat's.

Later, I ended up sitting on a bench in the Plaza Vincente
López, which was usually full of old men reading their
newspapers but was deserted that afternoon. The grass was
brown, and worn to dust around the benches. It was a sad
little plaza in winter during the siesta. The bronze bust of
the bearded composer of Argentina's national anthem looked
out sternly across the little park at the surrounding buildings, many of them old and with French facades, once rich-
looking but faded now. There was a sense of elegant failure
all about this little park, an atmosphere that the old men
who sat there most of the day had left behind them, bench-
fuls of forgotten grandfathers who passed their mornings
under the composer's glare, a man who had written a song
about liberty for a country so often locked in dictatorship.
The expression of military severity on the bust made me
think of the generals of his time, San Martín in particular.
San Martín who had won his war for independence with the
best expectations, only to turn gray in the exile of his regrets. And I thought of Simón Bolívar, powerful liberator
of the North, and of his last words on his deathbed, *I've
plowed the sea. . . .*

I felt increasingly lost and alone, and as if I had also
been through a kind of war. I wanted to go home, back to
my fine yanqui hometown of Port Washington by the water,
back to my big, crowded house where the old man and my
mother and my sister and brothers would be waiting, good
ol' Donny, Tommy, Carol, Kevin and little Will, where
could they be now? What were they doing? I subtracted an
hour to figure the time in New York and placed each of my
brothers exactly in my imagination. The only one I couldn't
picture was Harry. What was Harry doing now? What had
happened to Harry? To Harry, Harry, Harry, Harry . . .

I decided the best thing to do was to cash in the whole
trip. According to the I.S.E. rules, I had that choice. I would
wait until an hour or so after the siesta, then I would take

a bus to the I.S.E. offices, pick up my return plane ticket
and that would be that, I'd be out of this country on the
next jet. Then I wondered what I would tell my North
American brothers. I thought of the sense of defeat it would
mean, how the old man and my brothers would be disappointed in me, as would my teachers and the kids at the
high school. How would I ever explain coming back before
my year was finished? Then I realized I would miss getting
my degree at Colegio San Andrés and I would probably
have to spend another six months at least going to high
school to make up the credits, there was also that point to
consider . . .

I couldn't go home, not now, that was the situation. I
lowered my head to my knees and cried bitterly, pounding
my fists into the bench, and crying out *I can't take it, I
can't take it anymore, I just can't take it, can't take it, can't
take it* . . . Anyone looking out his window at the little
plaza might have mistaken me for an unfortunate beggar
gone crazy with grief. Then whoever was watching would
have seen another, younger boy wearing an overcoat that
looked two sizes too small for him trotting across the street
to approach this crazy one, a sensitive-looking kid with long,
thin arms that reached out to the boy on the bench. It was
Alejo, and he was patting my back and saying, "*Che*, Diego! What are you doing here? Everything's all right! I swear
it! Martín is just acting like a baby, and he's been a real
*boludo* all day! Can you hear me, *che*? Are you all right?"

"I'm fine, *che*, it's all right," I said, regaining some
control so Alejo wouldn't see me crying. "I just needed to
be alone. Please leave me alone now. I'll come home later,"
I said.

"But I've hunted all over for you," Alejo said. "Look.
Mamá gave me all this money. She thought maybe you and
I would want to go to the movies since Martín is acting like
such an idiot. Do you hear me? Look at this, *che*, we've
got all kinds of money." He held out a big sheaf of pesos.

"I don't want any more of their money," I said. "I've
cost your family mountains of pesos and it's against the
I.S.E. rules. I'm supposed to be living on the allowance
from my scholarship and not spending their money."

"*Che*, forget about I.S.E. ! It's not important! Martín can sit home and sulk all he wants to, he'll get over it!" Alejo said. "You and I are going to the movies, Yanqui, what do you think? There's a really great movie playing, all the kids at school are talking about it. It's the uncut version of *El Vaquero de la Noche*," Alejo said, meaning *Midnight Cowboy*, which he said had just opened at a theater in the central business district. "There's a great place right next door to where it's playing that's got the best banana milkshakes in the city, and I'll bet it's open all afternoon. Come on, *che*, let's go. We don't want to just sit here like a couple of old men."

There was no way to turn Alejo down, and we spent the afternoon together. I sat across from him in an expensive *confitería* near the Plaza Constitución as we waited for the next showing of the movie. Some of the places in this business district never closed during the siesta, too much quick commerce was being done everywhere. Men in ties and business suits were rushing around, grabbing fast sandwiches and coffees in the background as the two of us slowly drank our good banana milkshakes and talked over Alejo's books. He was on a magical realism and fantasy craze that had started with Gabriel García Márquez and had gone rapidly through Jorge Amado and Borges, then completely over the edge into science fiction like Ray Bradbury and Arthur C. Clarke. Alejo talked about books with the same excitement most boys talked about *fútbol*. I had read some of the books he mentioned. We laughed together and shared our frank admiration for the wonderful details and moments of certain stories, like the one from *El Aleph*, by Jorge Luis Borges, in which the narrator is amazed each time he closes a book that the words don't mix themselves up.

The time came for the movie to start. I bought both tickets, and we waited for a small crowd to go in with because Alejo was under seventeen and the military government was starting a crackdown on theaters that showed restricted films. All through the movie, Alejo punched at me on the shoulder or in the ribs, talking all the time through the explicit sex scene as if in ecstasies that lifted him half out of his seat, "*Che*, what a beautiful little ass she's got, you have to admit it. And nice tits, too, son of a whore, *che*," he said. He also joked about the subtitles in Spanish that had cleaned up the dialogue way too much. It had turned into a fine afternoon, good to sit in a warm, dark theater listening to my own language being spoken, and it was great to see a woman's ass and breasts filling the whole screen, and to watch the Cowboy and Ratso playing their lives out in the city neighborhood I knew so well, and to have Alejo there, punching me fraternally on the arm and tugging at my shirtsleeve, "They're really not saying that, are they, *che*? What did Ratso just tell him? *Che*, come on! Tell me what they're really saying!"

At the consulate on Monday, after taking care of the paperwork for a new passport, I waited to speak to an assistant Public Affairs officer. He resisted at first, then agreed to send an inquiry to the embassy in Saigon concerning my brother, Specialist E6 26251606, asking for a telegram in response from the U.S. Army describing Harry's whereabouts and his condition. The officer told me not to hope for a quick reply. He had made such requests before, and the U.S. Army was notoriously slow in finding its own people; then he advised me that if nothing happened soon, I might try the International Red Cross, which was usually faster. He shook my hand and said, "We're glad to have you here. You exchange students really make a difference for us in this country. Keep up the good work."

Three days later, a national holiday, Alejo and I went to the military's big parade. Miguelito had been caught for shoplifting chocolate bars from the corner kiosk, one of his mischievous pranks, the kid had his pockets full of coins and he was just showing off for his friends, and so Miguelito was grounded. Martín Segundo had made other plans that didn't include me, so I joined Alejo and two of his new older *compañeros*, Manuel, whom I hadn't met before, and Jorge, the student who had driven the decoy car for our little wall-painting expedition. When I saw Jorge greeting Alejo like a buddy, I realized how much he had come to know the university crowd during my stay at the big ranch. I was excited to see Jorge, and as we walked down to the big boulevard that ran through the Palermo parks, I tried to find

out about Cristina, "*Che*, you remember Cristina?" I asked.
"Whatever happened to her? Do you know how I can find
her?"

"I don't know," Jorge said. "Nobody's seen her since
the big demonstration. Andrés thinks she just dropped out
of the movement, *che*, she probably didn't want to screw
up her studies at the university. I don't really know her, and
anyway, she was too crazy and hotheaded. We're better off
without her in our little gang."

"But who would know her? I'd really like to see that girl
again," I said.

"I'll pass the word on to Andrés that you asked," Jorge
said. "You know Andrés really had it bad after the demonstration. The police kept him five days and broke both
his arms. He's still got both arms in casts."

"Look," Alejo said, pointing at the large crowds gathering on both sides of the boulevard. "You'd think all these
people would have seen enough of this military shit," he
said.

"Maybe they're like us," said Manuel. "They want to
get a good close look at the enemy."

Papá had recently borrowed a good Nikon camera from
a business associate for me to use the rest of the year with
my new family. I was anxious to try it out, and because of
this, I took a lot of slides at this parade. It was the famous
parade of the 9th of July holiday commemorating the day
in 1816 that the cities of the interior first joined with the
rich families of Buenos Aires to create a new republic that
rejected Spanish rule. The 9th of July was also the traditional day for the military to show its strength. This year,
fully half of Argentina's armed forces were paraded through
the streets, no doubt to reinforce the government's state of
siege in the minds of the people. A military parade on this
scale was in itself a symbol of the suspension of constitutional rule, ironically staged on the day that celebrated Argentina's first constitution.

Truckloads and truckloads of armed troops passed us,
some of them the Army *de la frontera*, the border patrol
corps of the North that wore the exact same cut of helmet
as the Nazis. They made a sharp contrast with the tradi-

tional *granaderos a caballo*, cavalry dressed in blue coats
and blue hats with feathered crests like soldiers of Napoleon, sabers raised to their shoulders in salutes, eyes left to
the long reviewing stand that was draped in sky blue and
white streamers. Here all the generals, the admirals, the
important government bureaucrats and foreign dignitaries
could be seen standing at attention, returning the salutes of
this cavalry corps that had been the alma mater of half the
generals who had ever seized political power in military
coups. The regiment clip-clopped by on their tall horses,
braids and ribbons trailing from the tails and manes, a bu-
gler sounding calls from time to time as several riders at
the rear of the formation executed daredevil maneuvers with
their horses, a spectacle as colorful as any queen's guards,
moving with pomp and circumstance down the boulevard.
Following them were tanks with guns raised high, mounted
88 mm antitank guns on their motorized caissons, then shining white Hawk antiaircraft missiles in batteries of three on
their big army trucks. Directly above, dark camouflaged jets
were rocketing low over the avenue, their sound so loud
that the packed crowds along the boulevard started covering
their ears.

One slide of the parade showed Alejo turning to face the
camera, his hands over his ears and his face showing a
startled expression that seemed to say, who had ever seen
so many tanks? So many riflemen in tight goose-stepping
formations? So many police marching in riot helmets, ready
for action with their nightsticks at their shoulders like rifles?
Behind him was passing a kind of light tank for fighting
with demonstrators in the streets that had a huge firehose
nozzle instead of a cannon.

The same reaction as Alejo's could be seen all over
Buenos Aires that day, people awed by the sheer power
displayed yet clearly ill at ease. It wasn't that Alejo or any
of us were vessels of pacifist feeling—we wanted to see all
the big tanks, the colorful missiles, the sharp-looking gren-
adiers. We wanted to experience a little of what it must be
like to stand under loud, shrieking jets coming in low on a
bombing run. That was what everyone seemed to be there
for, whole families who spread blankets on the wintery grass

of the parks. They drank their wine and ate their broiled chicken or cold fried beef *milanesa* sandwiches while they cheered at each new military achievement of their nation, a voice like a sportscaster's calling out to them over a system of huge bullhorn speakers lining the streets, "And here comes the famous Antarctic Brigade! That snow tractor there doesn't always serve to pull antiaircraft cannons! Usually it is pulling supplies for the many research scientists who explore the vital resource of the nation that is Antarctica . . ."

Behind the gaudy, orange and yellow tanklike snow tractor that was pulling a battery of futuristic cannons marched files of soldiers dressed in white snowsuits, goggles over their faces, machine guns carried on straps over their shoulders. A few paces behind and walking along in a little informal group like pompous sea gulls, five or six scientists in open labcoats grinned and waved at the crowd, then up at all the generals and dignitaries as they passed the reviewing stand. Not far behind the Antarctic Brigade marched about a thousand cadets from the military academies. "And here come the future chiefs and leaders of Argentina!" the loudspeakers sang out. "Let's hear a round of applause for these brave young men whom the people will look to to save them in times of national crisis!"

Just as in the present crisis, no doubt, when the military's state of siege had settled over the country like a permanent smog. Most of the courts were overseen by the military now, and there was no longer habeas corpus, not even the need for any charge or public notice at all to put people in jail. Most political parties were declared illegal, as were almost all the trade unions, especially those with leftist Peronist leanings. Press censorship was completely in effect, and even more newspapers and magazines were shut down. The military now controlled the state-owned industries like the public utilities, the railroads, auto factories and some of the slaughter yards, which amounted to about one-third of all the industry and commerce in the nation. And here again the military was showing its strength, an effort to impress the people enough to put off free elections for months or years in order to avoid the inevitable return to Peronism.

On the reviewing stand, the de facto *presidente* general

himself was standing, soon to be congenially replaced by
the general next to him, and so on, it seemed, forever. All
of the lower-ranking generals were around them, the ones
who would later take their place in this line to power, gold
braid laurels already on their caps and shoulders; they were
already saluting the parade like emperors. All around them
were the ranks of civilian government officials and their
wives, and the ambassadors of France, of England, of Spain
and the Soviet Union, of Mexico, Peru and Brazil, and
numbers of other, more junior statesmen, all arranged, it
seemed, by the importance of their countries. Next to the
de facto *presidente* general himself stood Ambassador John
Lodge, younger brother to Henry Cabot of *the* Lodges,
personal friend to *presidente* Nixon. The United States ambassador stood up and politely applauded each passing close-
order drill, each sharp army corps that was goose-stepping
past with stiff salutes.

I tried to drag Alejo through the thickest part of the crowd
to get closer to the reviewing stand and snap pictures of
Argentina's rulers. "Come on, *che*, haven't you taken
enough pictures?" Alejo asked. We came up against a line
of blue-uniformed federal police in front of sawhorse barricades. I was about to try to pretend I was a member of
the press and talk my way past them for a photograph.
"Let's go, *che*!" Alejo said, cautious at the way the police
seemed to respond to my inquiries, and I let him drag me
back through the crowd.

I caught up to Alejo at the fringes of the crowd. His back
was turned to the parade, the khaki hunting jacket he had
borrowed from Papá making him look a little like a soldier
in blue jeans. Jorge and Manuel were back there with him,
and it was clear they had seen enough. A dark humor af-
fected them all the way home on the packed *colectivo* bus.
Alejo kept turning to the others and saying things like,
"*Che*, did you see all the arms! Son of a whore, *che*, have
you ever seen so many military police?"

He was overwhelmed; so were we all. A certain battle
line had been drawn, that was the situation. All over
the country, men in uniform had been parading through the
heart of every major city. In Buenos Aires, the troops, the

tanks and armored personnel carriers from the big parade were returning to their bases and military camps in the suburbs, ready and waiting to strike back in the streets in case of any future actions by the Peronists.

Perón was at that very moment sitting in his big fortress in Spain near Barcelona, attended by his new former—chorus-girl wife, Isabel. The old Turk, as people like to call him, was at that moment sending out messages to his new terrorist army that had gone underground, living by the gaucho name Montoneros. "Against brute force, only intelligently applied force can be effective," he wrote to them. It was his signal, his personal blessing, his direct order that a campaign of violence should begin.

All over Argentina, the Montoneros began to study the manufacture of terrorist bombs. This was the only way available to fight back, it seemed, to youths like Jorge, Manuel and even Alejo, the only chance they had to try and change the existing military repression. The Montoneros, the E.R.P. and F.A.L. revolutionary armies had recently carried out popular raids on army prisons in the interior, pitched battles that had involved hundreds of guerrillas belonging to various Peronist action wings. At least one of these actions was successful—holes had been blown through the barbed wire of one large concentration camp, and after intense fighting more than a hundred political prisoners were set free to join the resistance. And in the minds of many young people, what the *Montes* had done with General Aramburu was also proof of their strength and that their victory was possible. The old general who had deposed Perón had been kidnapped and tried in secret by the Montoneros for his many misdeeds against the leaders of Peronism, the least of which was the desecration of the tomb of Evita Perón and the stealing of her remains in order to smother Evita's hold on the national imagination. The old walrus of a general had been plucked from his rich retirement and was later finally executed for his crimes.

"Look at this! Isn't this great! Isn't this fantastic!" Alejo exclaimed when the official government version of the story about Aramburu's execution came out in the newspapers. "The Montoneros are really out doing something, that's

clear! They're really fighting back against this shitty government!'' Even Martín Segundo celebrated this news with
Alejo. It was as if the new youthful armies of Perón had
finally proved to the whole country that Aramburu was mortal and therefore all generals were mortal. With this, and
with some vengeance for the desecration of the grave of
their Evita, whom they revered as a kind of political saint,
the first important steps in the exhumation of Peronism had
been taken. Many years later, Aramburu would be kidnapped yet again, his bones stolen from their grave and held
in ransom for Evita's remains.

Alejo's real involvement started, I think, that afternoon
we were coming home from the 9th of July military parade.
I witnessed a certain change in his eyes, a kind of hardness
coming into them. ''Somebody has to do something about
this situation, don't you agree?'' Alejo said to Jorge, Manuel and me on the crowded *colectivo* bus. ''Son of a whore,
I swear it, *che*. Something has got to be done before the
military crushes out everything.''

How Alejo's new political awareness was expressed later
that year after I had left, I don't know. What I did come to
see was that Alejo's friends were in the first stages of entering the militancy of the Montoneros, meeting out at
country estates and ranches for bomb and weapons training,
and that to be a *Monte* was becoming a popular thing to do
in his crowd.

An unusual visitor came to Argentina—Nelson Rockefeller. At that time, he was being considered as United States
ambassador to the U.N., and was on a tour representing
*presidente* Nixon in Latin America. He was particularly
talking to the military regimes that then ruled Brazil, Uruguay, Bolivia and Peru, as well as to Argentina's, no doubt
bringing word of *presidente* Nixon's new desire to strengthen
trade relations and to assist them in their struggles to keep
leftist political movements, including the new breed of Peronism, from disturbing the status quo. Rockefeller, of
course, was a symbol for a revived policy of yanqui busi-
ness-as-usual all over Latin America. For decades, his family and its Chase Manhattan Bank had poured billions of
dollars' worth of investments into Latin America, including

a profitable chain of new supermarkets called Minimax. Minimax supermarkets were all over major cities of Latin America, and there were at least fifteen of them in Buenos Aires—big warehouse-size stores designed on the U.S. models of Safeways and A & P's complete with modern freezer displays of all the most advanced twentieth-century packaged foods that were just being introduced, and with soft Muzak serenading Argentina's shoppers down the aisles.

Like many sober thinkers in Buenos Aires, Papá regarded Nelson Rockefeller's visit with alarm. He often talked about it in our little sessions in his study. It wasn't that he objected to Rockefeller's involvement in the nation's development. On the contrary, he considered all the money American banks and multi-national corporations were investing in new factories, stores, products and marketing techniques to be the best possible solution to the problems of the continent. Papá was even a lawyer for one investment firm, a *Sociedad Anónima* (an apt Spanish term which best describes the word *corporation*). This particular *Sociedad Anónima* had a deal with a group of United States banks to match soft pesos invested by its wealthy members with loans in hard dollars at a fabulously low interest rate. It was in effect a means for the society to purchase dollars at budget prices, then to roll over its investment capital at a profit, and to keep on doing this at a steadily escalating and inflationary pace within the fragile monetary system many Argentines called *la bicicleta financiera*, the financial bicycle on which it seemed the nation's whole economic future was suddenly riding.

Papá had faith in this system, given a little political stability and provided the generals didn't steal too much from the economy, and he made his living from its legal manipulations. But in such a delicate political climate, why did Nelson Rockefeller now have to come in person? Couldn't he be more discreet, and meet with the nation's de facto leaders somewhere else, in Geneva, for example, or even in Mexico? Didn't he know that police and army divisions all over South America would have to be mobilized, that tear gas grenades and machine guns were going to be fired in the streets once again? Didn't he even know that his own chain of Minimax supermarkets made easy targets for terrorist bombs? It seemed to Papá that Rockefeller's visit made no sense at all, and the timing couldn't have been worse, unless Rockefeller was meant as an official gesture on behalf of the United States publicly to rub in the face of the people their growing dependency on its capital and markets. "We all know in this house that the first rule of good manners is never to draw too much attention to yourself." Papá said. "Nelson Rockefeller visiting us at such a time is simply bad manners."

The day Nelson Rockefeller was due to arrive at a big military ceremony at Ezeiza International Airport, Alejo and Martín Segundo both woke me up before dawn. I dressed quietly and followed them out into the street. The city seemed unusually quiet that morning. A few demonstrations had been planned, but nothing the size of the huge ones in the months before that had brought on the state of siege. "What is this? A demonstration?" I asked. "You've both got to be crazy! I'm not going, *che*, look what happened to me! Forget it, please, and come on back home."

"Nobody's going to any demonstration," Martín said and laughed. "We're going over to a friend's apartment to watch the show, *che*, so don't get all heated up."

"What show?"

"You remember Jorge? Jorge Gallo, from the wall painting and the demonstration? We're going to his place," Alejo said.

"So what's so big about his place? Listen, brothers, it's four-thirty in the morning. Why don't we get smart and go back to bed?"

"Jorge lives about a half a block down from a Minimax supermarket, you understand?" Alejo said.

"Now I know you're both crazy. Son of a whore, Martín, you should know better than to get involved in something like this!"

"Who's involved? Who said we were involved?"

"Jorge Gallo has this great balcony, a real grandstand seat," Alejo said. "All we're doing is going to watch the fireworks."

"I told you we shouldn't have invited him," Martín said. "Any yanqui is bound to get all heated up about this."

"I'm not heated up, you idiot," I said. "I'm just staying out of it." I turned away from them on the street to head back home.

"*Che*, Yanqui!" Alejo said. "Trust me, Diego, there's not a chance we'll get into trouble this time. And didn't you say only yesterday how much you hated the idea of Nelson Rockefeller's visit? Didn't you, *che*?"

It was true. I hated the idea of Rockefeller making it that much harder to be a yanqui in this country, and that because of his travels, hundreds more people were going to be arrested or even killed in the streets all over South America. At the same time, I was curious. Also, the fact that Martín was with us made me think it had to be safe. "Tell me how it's safe," I said to Martín.

"Look, Yanqui, we have nothing to do with it. We're just going to sit on Jorge's balcony. Probably nothing is even going to happen, all right?"

We sat out on Jorge Gallo's fifth floor balcony, where his family's maid had set up a folding table with a big pot of coffee and steaming milk, sweet rolls, cookies, hot croissants, marmalade and butter. We ate breakfast with Jorge's books opened on our laps so that each time one of Jorge's parents, who were early risers and who looked ancient enough to be his grandparents, padded past in their slippers and robes, we started reading out of the books to each other and pretended to take notes. Now and then, Alejo hung out over the side of the balcony that looked directly down the street to the gay, red-lettered sign that spelled MINIMAX over the plate glass windows that took up half the block. Martín and Jorge were talking politics, discussing the students they knew who had joined up with the *Montes*, and the pros and cons of the left-wing Peronists versus the more violent E.R.P., the Trotskyist People's Revolutionary Army, or the Guevarist F.A.L., Armed Forces of Liberation, agreeing that all of them viewed Peronism as a mere first step toward pure socialism by somehow reforming its fascist roots. Martín was using terms like "the people" and "the proletariat" and "dirty capitalism" and "the leftist vanguard," words

I had never imagined could come out of his mouth. During the past few weeks, since coming back, I had stayed at home and studied or read books, or had walked alone all over the city. Meanwhile, Alejo and Martín had gone out a lot together as if to the movies or over to a friend's. Now I wondered, where had they really been going?

I sat quietly on the balcony, sleepily listening to the others. In my mind was the absurdity of what we were doing, waiting there for a bomb to go off as if it were some new form of entertainment. A misty dawn was rising over the tops of the buildings. Deep purple and rose-colored clouds shone overhead, letting in the first light of morning.

"Look! There it is!" Alejo hissed, pointing down at the street. "Do you see it? Right in the doorway!"

We all looked at once at a small plastic bag that seemed to have something bulky in it, set on the sidewalk just inside the entryway to the Minimax. Could that be a bomb? Right out there in the open? Why weren't there any police around to see it? If everybody knew this was going to happen, I mean everybody who had any brains at all, why weren't the police guarding all the Minimax supermarkets? It would have been easy enough, I thought, one or two officers sitting in a patrol car might have prevented it. And why weren't the bomb squads with their trained German shepherds sniffing the building? Why? It didn't make sense, and I thought it must be nothing, the police would be the first to know if that plastic bag held a bomb.

An old man crept past on his way down the sidewalk, right in front of the Minimax. Martín started to call down to warn him but Jorge stopped him. "Don't be stupid!" Jorge said. "If there are any police around, they'll come looking straight for us!"

"Where are the police? That's what I'd like to know," I said. "I don't see any police."

"A patrol car stopped there just before you came, but nobody even got out and looked," Jorge said with a little clever laugh. We waited tensely, watching the old man turning a corner down the street. Another ten minutes passed. By then full sunlight had broken through the mists into the street.

"Let's go, *che*, nothing's happening here," I said. "That can't be a bomb down there."

"Another few minutes and we'll go, Yanqui," Martín said disappointedly, checking his watch.

At exactly twenty after six, the bomb went off. It wasn't a huge bomb, just a small one, and poorly made, it seemed, because all that happened was a big yellow flash that lifted the front doors off the supermarket and shattered five of the big glass windows in a muffled explosion. Nobody was working in the store, luckily, and nobody was passing by at that moment on the street. Then suddenly, as if they had been waiting just around the corner, the street below us filled with police cars, fire trucks, news crews from national television, and people from all over the neighborhood started gathering around barricades that were quickly set up. People on their way to work stopped at the barricades, looking on at the minor damage as if it were nothing more out of the ordinary than a little electrical fire, then they continued on about their business. All over Buenos Aires that morning, similar bombs went off in front of fifteen of Rockefeller's Minimax supermarkets, most sustaining only minor damage. There was also one casualty—an unfortunate woman crossing the street in front of one of the markets was cut by flying glass and taken to a hospital.

Jorge, Martín and Alejo were celebrating around me, laughing into their cups of coffee as the street was closing up beneath us with police. People up and down the block were hanging out their windows or on their balconies just like us to watch; Jorge's parents came out to the balcony and Jorge innocently explained what had happened. Once the parents were gone, the little party the boys had been sharing started up again.

"Did you see that, *che*! It was perfect!"

"You see how it didn't damage anything but the market? The *Montes* really know what they're doing, don't you think? Just the right size bomb!"

"I'm not sure this one was the *Montes* or the F.A.L., but who cares? It worked! It really worked!"

"What a boss time, *che*, that was great! I wonder what that son of a whore Rockefeller is thinking now?"

"You're a bunch of *boludos* to think this is any good,"
I said. "You think this is great? You really do?"

"Come on, Yanqui, don't get all heated up," Martín said.
"It's not like it was your supermarket!"

"That's really fucked up, Martín," I said. "You should
know better. This kind of thing is just going to get you
killed. All of you," I said. "What would Papá have to say
about this?"

"*Che*, you wouldn't tell Papá!" Alejo said.

"To the shit with all of it," I said. I wanted to say something more, to grab up both my brothers by their shirts and
shout into their faces, then drag them home. They were my
family, and I loved them, and it was like I could see them
cut loose in some madly careening vehicle that was tumbling straight for a cliff, but what could I say? How could
I possibly get them out of this? "Count me out," I said. "I
don't want to know it, I don't want to hear it. I've never
seen anything more stupid in my life. From now on, count
me out of it, is that clear?"

I left them sitting on the balcony. I dodged my way
through Jorge's parents, took the stairs down because they
were faster, then pushed my way through a small crowd
that had gathered on the sidewalk. I headed for the subway
down the block, already forming a plan to make the best of
this terrible morning and try to join in with the early courtyard *fútbol* game before classes for a change.

On the corner, near the subway entrance, I was picked
out of a small group of pedestrians on their way to work by
a lone police officer, probably because of my long hair. He
ordered me to stand up against a building. He frisked me,
going through all the pockets of my newest Colegio San
Andrés jacket, my gray pants, my wallet with its temporary
national I.D. card. I submitted to this calmly, without a
word, waiting for the officer to open up my nice new passport. When he saw it, the officer apologized to me and let
me go. "I'm sorry to bother you, but with this," he made
a vague motion back down the street, "you can see how it
is," he said. I thanked him and continued on my way to
school.

* * *

Over the next few months, I was shaken down by the police like this with some regularity. It happened about twice a month, maybe nine or ten times in all. I would be walking down a street, would pass a blue-uniformed button, and I could tell with one look into his eyes that it was going to happen. I learned to stop right there, smile, and get out my new passport to show to the *capitán*, as I respectfully began to call even the lowest-ranking officer. I did all of this even before he had taken a step toward me and ordered me to spread my arms and legs out for a good frisking. This was suddenly nothing out of the ordinary—it began to happen to students all over the city, especially those with long hair, but also to anyone who might strike a button the wrong way.

Weird blue laws had gone into effect under the state of siege and were being personally enforced by the military. Women were hassled for wearing "immodest" clothing in public, often accosted at bus stops and ordered back home to change. Unmarried couples were no longer allowed to walk with their arms tightly around each other in the parks, or openly to kiss one another in public places. There were rumors of goon squads of the military who broke into the apartments of unmarried couples who were somehow known to be living together, perhaps informed on by a jealous spouse or former lover. The mere accusation of illicit sexual behavior could lead to a conviction on a morals charge under the military's state of siege. The military began to shut down movie houses that were showing objectionable films like *Midnight Cowboy*, as well as tightening up the usual press censorship, all in the name of preserving moral values. El Rector of San Andrés began to give regular sermons on the new morality, stressing every citizen's obligation to support the efforts the military was making to clean up the wayward youth of the nation that had long been considered the most Catholic in Latin America.

Meanwhile, the military was busting into secret union and student meetings. They were closing down restaurants where leftists were known to meet. Shaking down students all over Buenos Aires became a regular part of this new military program, so much so that, as I said, the shakedowns no longer bothered me. They were a hassle, sure, but I had learned to handle that kind of situation, that was all, I knew just what to do. It was a little like playing the goal position in *fútbol*, my regular position—when the ball had been kicked enough times at forty miles an hour straight at your face, well, you learned to put your hands up just in time.

# 8

# Reckonings

Spring in Buenos Aires came early that year. One day in September, the air was suddenly warmer and thunderclouds gathered over the city, carried in by tropical air currents, a change in atmosphere from the northern jungles. A heavy, pleasant heat caused all the plazas to explode with flowers and the trees to leaf out with their new green fans almost overnight. And the girls, the beautiful girls all over Buenos Aires began to experiment with the briefest cuts of mini-skirts as if in open rebellion against the conservatism of the military regime. All over the city, I noticed that people were actually walking faster, dawdling less, picking up the pace of their lives. As the temperature rose, there were suddenly longer lines at shops, at movie theaters, at banks. *La Bolsa*, the stock market of Buenos Aires, was going wild with new speculations. About the third or fourth day of spring, it struck me what was happening. All around the neighborhood of La Plaza de Mayo and along the big diagonal boulevards I watched the afternoon rush hour begin, and I realized how fast everyone seemed to be spending money, throwing high-figure peso bills around, wads and rolls of them, counting off hundreds of thousands and even millions of pesos, emptying shops downtown of everything they could find—radios, televisions, books, clothing, jewelry, anything they could carry, anything that had an exchangeable value, and new auto sales figures were going off the charts. The restaurants were also suddenly full all the time, as if people were splurging as much as they could to get rid of all the pesos in their pockets.

The military government issued an order that many people in Buenos Aires had seen coming. The Argentine peso was to be devalued again. All *old pesos* were to be turned in to banks by a certain date and exchanged for *new pesos*, with a face value only ten percent of their former denominations. An almost worthless one hundred peso bill, with old General San Martín's pessimistic expression on one side in blue and mauve inks, would be reprinted with the figure 10 stamped in crude black ink on the blank space directly across from his picture, a figure more in line with its real value, the numbers boldly visible against the white embossed profile of the young General San Martín's hopeful expression on the reverse side that shone like a kind of ivory cameo when a clean bill was held up to the light. In response to the military regime's announcement, the black markets were suddenly flooded with tons of old pesos, bales of them that were losing value overnight, and everybody in Buenos Aires was trying to buy *los verdes* with them, the greens, as many good yanqui dollars as they could get. The black market price of dollars rose much higher than the official government rate of exchange. Exports priced at the official rate began to freeze because of the fictitious higher value of government prices compared to black markets, the military using the situation to milk huge profits from imports pegged at the official rate. Before the devaluation, prices started inflating so quickly that chalkboards began to replace price signs, and shopkeepers were changing price tags almost every day. Monetary reform was desperately needed. Argentina's financial bicycle was once again pumped up to so high a pressure and moving so fast that it was throwing its riders off.

Papá started wearing a money belt, because he was buying dollars anywhere he could. He traded with clients, and with friends overseas, rolling over loans and converting investments in pesos into foreign cash. He collected many of his fees at a discount in black market dollars, just as anyone in the nation who was in a position to was doing. He worked sixteen and eighteen hours a day that spring, going half-crazy with work, meeting clients at all hours and rewriting old contracts. Each night before his late dinner, Papá locked himself in his study, exhausted, took off his money belt, then pulled out the family account books. It was a sign of the times that he started to keep large amounts of his yanqui cash in a strongbox rather than deposit it in any bank. "I'm making money, lots of it, and that's the shame, in a way," Papá said to me with a sad smile one night. "Better that way than to lose my shirt, of course, and I'm as happy as if I'd rolled the big seven to be doing it, don't fool yourself. But I keep wondering how much longer this can go on. The worker down the street can hardly fill his grocery bag on the old pesos he earns, and here I am stuffing my pockets and holding up my pants with your good yanqui dollars."

The Benevento family made investments with their dollars. They went into a partnership to buy an apartment house, a building into which Mamá also sank part of her inheritance from her father, converting a large sum of soft pesos at the last minute into hard French francs and so able to become a full partner in the enterprise. For Mamá, this also meant a change in her life. The two classes she had started to take at the University of Buenos Aires had been discontinued because the professors had been barred from teaching, accused of being socialists. Because of the new faculty shortage, university students had to draw lottery numbers to see which ones could get into the few available classes. Others became *estudiantes libres*, free students who were issued student numbers and only permitted to use the decimated libraries and to turn up during the semester to take exams.

Mamá seized on the new investment she and Papá had made in the apartment building. She shopped for business outfits and began to go off in the afternoons to consult with architects about the renovations, using her art education and good taste to help modernize interiors. With one of her friends, Beatrice, she picked out a ground floor apartment to convert into an art gallery for Argentine painters who were finding it hard to exhibit under the military regime. This idea of the art gallery was unpopular with Papá, at first, because he didn't see the profit in it and there might be some political dangers. But Mamá won the argument; starting a gallery for dissident artists was a firm decision in her life.

Sundays, the city was taken over by a traditional hysteria. After morning mass and the midday meal, armies of fans eager for the new season of professional *fútbol* filled the buses and subways. Hundreds of thousands of them, mainly dressed in something with the colors of their team, bore pennants and hats aloft; gangs of youths ranged through the streets carrying their team's banners and folded them up awkwardly on the packed buses and trains. Taxis with colorful streamers on their antennas cruised the streets with radios on full-blast. All four Benevento brothers joined in this mass celebration of the game. We didn't usually sit in the comfortable mezzanine seats. Ignoring Papá's warnings, we preferred to stand up the whole game on the steep, bare concrete galleries in the *popular* that was packed so tightly with fans we could hardly move, watching the game with the tens of thousands of *negros hindúes*, as Alejo named the big black savage crowd. The four of us were caught up in the full-throated enthusiasm of forty or fifty thousand fans singing to the tune of the Beatles' "Ob-La-Di, Ob-La-Da," "Let's go Ri-, Let's go Ri-, Let's go Ri-ver! La-lala-lalala-lahhh . . ." over and over again, chanting it to the opposite side of the stadium at the sections of stands reserved for the visiting team, who would sing back at us, trying to outdo our enthusiasm.

The most spectacular singing duel was always at the games with Boca Juniors. Across the stadium, the packed masses in blue shirts with broad yellow stripes would begin to move like a strangely uncoordinated monster, the song's rhythm making them rock back and forth in different orders and directions, their one huge voice singing to the tune of the Peronist Youth marching song, "We are the boys of the Bo-oh-ca . . ." in answer to every refrain of the River Plate song we sang. When a goal was made, the huge stadium broadcast a joyous roaring that could be heard on the winds all over the city on Sundays and on almost every radio and TV. When River Plate scored, the four of us jumped up and down together in the crowd, brothers all in a line and linked to each other with our arms over each other's shoulders to keep from falling in an avalanche of fans over the upper deck, the crowd all around jumping up and down with us, the stadium quaking under our feet as if the whole structure was in danger of collapse.

After the big game, if there was still enough sunlight, we took a soccer ball to the long grassy strip of park next to the College of Law, its big Parthenon of a building now sandblasted clean of slogans. We formed two teams, two-on-two, usually Martín and Miguelito versus Alejo and me. My team was handicapped from the start. It was something about the way I had trouble kicking a soccer ball correctly, somehow it always rose too high, its ribbed leather globe turning as lazily as a knuckleball, so that a player on the other team had plenty of time to take it on his head or chest or bounce it once at his feet and then dribble off for the opposite goal, with me having to take risky hookslides to try and stop him. Because of these unorthodox tackles, I developed a reputation for being a rough player. I was always kicking shins and drawing fouls, and about twilight, poor Miguelito and Martín would have to find a pharmacy that was still open and buy themselves Band-Aids. When we stopped for Cokes and pizzas at a restaurant near home, Martín lectured me, "*Che*, you were a real barbarian today! Look at my knee! Look at Miguelito's lip! Your problem is that you're playing *fútbol* too much like your North American *fútbol*, where the whole point is to beat up on the other players." We walked home in the fresh breezes that come in off the River Plate in spring, our bodies tired, our voices hoarse from shouting and singing at the game, and once home, we flopped into chairs in front of the television to watch the evening rerun of the match we had been to that afternoon.

One day at school, history class broke up in chaos. Llamas-Pérez was due to be called next to recite the history lesson on the era of immigration, but he had failed to memorize it the night before. Fearing that one more zero in history meant he might not graduate, Llamas-Pérez sat at the back of the crowded class and quickly used a penknife to cut his gray trousers off above the knee. When the teacher, called El Mono, "The Monkey," because he looked like a hairless ape, called out his name, Llamas-Pérez stood up from his desk and his cutoff trouser legs dropped to the floor, leaving him in a pair of ragged shorts. He shuffled up the aisle between the desks with his gray flannel pantlegs bunched around his feet like weird moon-shoes. When the class broke up in laughter, El Mono launched into angry shouting and sent Manuel Llamas-Pérez to the office to register three demerits against himself. It was a stroke of genius. Llamas-Pérez had bought for himself with three demerits an extra night to cram for El Mono's class the next day.

I ducked out into the corridor after history class, on my way to the latrine for a quick little cigarette. El Negrito was clumping fast along the archway, a clipboard under his arm, his hair an oily mess, his gray shirt soaked through with perspiration. El Negrito hadn't been seen around the school for a while, and he said, "*Hola*, Yanqui," at me as if I had seen him the day before.

"When did you get back, Negro?" I asked. "Why were you gone so long?"

"A little vacation," he said. "We went up North at first, then we stayed with my wife's sister right here in Buenos Aires."

"There was a rumor going around that you had quit," I said. "Everybody said you had told El Rector to stuff it and were living on all the money you've saved."

"I wish it were true, *che*, but it's not. Nothing changes for me. The lame always have to run like the wind."

"You know after El Rector's dinner, I wanted to kill you," I said. "I kept looking for you to kill you but you were gone."

"It was a long vacation, and we hadn't taken one in years," El Negrito said. "But I explained everything to the Monseñor before I left, that it was all the girl's fault, *che*, and she was really love-crazy, isn't that true?"

"That's a lie, Negro, and you know it," I said.

"Don't mention it," El Negrito said. "Listen, *che*, I was just saving you the embarrassment. Anyway, that was a long time ago. And the girl came out all right, they put her in the San Andrés convent school in Tucumán as a cook, so why make problems? Here I am again, and you're still here, back to the same old thing. If I had stayed away any longer, the work of this place would be so fouled up it couldn't function. So what can one do? I'm the hungry ox that pulls the cart home, and I'm busy. I have to get these lists over to Professor Montiel, so see you later." El Negrito started to limp off in his cockeyed way a few steps, then he turned back to me abruptly. "When it comes time to fix up your papers for graduation, you know, anything you need, you just tell me," he said and was off again with his fast-paced limping across the courtyard.

I started to shout after him that I wouldn't need his help to graduate but I stopped. Along with most of my classmates in senior year, I had grown superstitious about graduation. Just looking around our classroom, it was clear that at least a quarter of the seniors were going to repeat the year for the second or even third time. The bell rang for the start of the next period. A throng of students in their blue blazers shoved their way around me along the archway, coming in from their quick courtyard *fútbol* game or their cigarette breaks, streaming into class. I was so much a part of them now that nobody even noticed that I was different. I wondered what it would feel like to leave.

I began a campaign of postcard writing to everyone, to the old man and the old lady and all my brothers, even a few to uncles and aunts I hadn't seen since I was a child. I had been lazy about writing letters for months, and it was guilt that moved my pen. On my daily walks through the city, I picked up various postcard views of Buenos Aires, of its statues, parks, its ornate theaters, and just after the city opened up again after lunch, I sat in the bright sidewalk cafés along Corrientes and the avenue 9 de Julio and penned brief communications to the folks:

Dear Mom and Dad:

   This is the big statue in a park near where I live. I'm
having a great time here. I'll graduate with all A's
except for Chemistry. I love you and miss you. Have
you heard from Harry?

                                        Love,
                                        "Diego"

   I signed all the cards with my new name, as I had started
to do in the first letters I had written home. And to my
brothers Donny and Tommy:

Dear Don and Tom:

   Say hey, bros! Things really rock down here! The chick
in the red feathers shown here dances at the theater
around the corner! I have my own car to drive! Say,
Don, please talk to Bob at the rivet factory. I'm going
to need a job when I get back.

                                        Ciao,
                                        "Diego"

   I also wrote another of the several notes to Harry I had
sent off since his last cryptic letter. I kept trying the consulate, too, but they hadn't yet received any news. In my
letter, I told Harry again about my rich family and not to
worry about me, and to get himself home in one piece, and
I begged him to write me an answer as soon as he could. I
finished the note, then bought postcards of city sights—the
bright lights of its avenues at night, Florida Street with its
elegant shops and crowds of people window-shopping in its
galleries, as well as all the cards showing beautiful girls I
could find, and one of a soccer game. I sealed the cards in
the envelope and posted it, my concern about Harry steadily
growing.
   Hernández-Marelli turned up at school one day. He was
in army uniform, standing around the courtyard *fútbol* game
and talking to his friends between classes. Shaved nearly
bald, he was thin and pale and had a boyish look in his

cheap green private's uniform, but he had still kept some of
his cool. "*Che*, the training was hard, very hard, and that's
when the army found out about my bad back. I'm here in
Buenos Aires for a few little medical tests. You'll see I'll
get out of this hassle in a few days and be with the team,
playing wing like always," he said. From the way the students flocked around him in the courtyard, it was clear that
he was still a school hero if he wasn't one anywhere else.
The ball came his way and he took it, demonstrating his old
*futbolísticos*, as he called them, bouncing it on his head and
chest, then doing little backwards kicks with his heels,
keeping the ball in the air for thirty or forty kicks, a long
time. Then one of the younger students snatched the ball
from him and took off on the run.

"*Che*, Yanqui! You've turned into a hippie!" Marelli
shouted with a big laugh when he saw me. Everyone from
our gang gathered around, El Judeo, El Gordo Rojo, José
Ugarte, El Flaco Peluffo, Llamas-Pérez and the others. Only
Martín ignored Marelli, showing off in the courtyard by
doing *futbolísticos* while reading a magazine at the same
time, a very funny trick except that his glasses kept falling
off.

Marelli threw his arms around me in a friendly hug, but
I felt something desperate in it. Then he turned from me
and made a fist in one of his intense cheerleading gestures
and started chanting, "Yan-qui! Yan-qui! Yan-qui! Yan-qui!
Yan-qui! . . ." and students hanging out in the courtyard
watching us took up this chanting for a minute, a tribute to
Marelli's enthusiasm as much as to me. Then somebody
kicked the ball at my feet and I took off with it, shouting,
"Let's go! Let's go!" to start one of our frequent two-
minute games before the bell rang for our next class.

"Over here!" Martín shouted, and I saw he was open on
the other side of the courtyard and passed the ball over to
him. Then Martín was in trouble and the ball came whiz-
zing back across to me, easy to stop against my chest. Hernández-Marelli was suddenly on top of me, one on one.
Marelli was all feet at times like these, a crazy dance, and
I was trying to work the ball behind my feet so he couldn't
steal it, looking for a shot at the goal. I got ready to foul

Marelli if I had to, my elbows out and ready so if he tried
to hookslide under me he'd get one in the face; then Marelli
lost his rhythm and I kicked the ball past, beating him out,
and I took my shot. The ball slammed into the wall just
wide of the goal, but the noise it made was loud, the courtyard echoed with it, a good hard shot nobody would be
ashamed of. The bell rang and the gang said "Ciao" to
Marelli and headed off to classes. Marelli threw his arm
around my shoulders. "*Che*, meet me at the Café Singular
after school, what do you say?"

"The one just up on Callao?" I asked.

"That's it, *che*. Nothing serious. We'll have a little lunch
together and a few little beers."

A cousin of the Benevento family was coming over to
lunch that day, and I was generally expected to be there at
such times, but something in Marelli's intensity made me
say yes. What harm could a little lunch be? I told Martín
Segundo to tell Mamá and Papá I was out with Marelli, and
that I would be home in time to visit awhile with this cousin
I had never met and would probably never see again.

The Café Singular was a tiny place, with a bar and about
six tables. Marelli was sitting at the biggest table by the
window, wearing sunglasses and looking as if he were a
spy, a ridiculous pose since it was obvious that he was a
poor shaved-headed draftee. Yet he was all gentleman to
the waiters, acting like a real *patrón*, his hand still manicured and heavy with gold rings as he gestured at the waiters to bring him another expensive imported scotch. He
stood up when I entered, pulling my chair out and gesturing for me to sit down. He had draped his army jacket
over his shoulders like a cloak. He snapped his fingers for
the waiter, and I ordered a beer. I didn't know what to
say, feeling like I might be partly responsible for what had
happened to him. "I'm sorry you ended up drafted like
this," I said.

"Why should you be sorry? They were trying for two
years to draft me, it's just that this time, my father didn't
have the influence to stop them."

"Really? That's true?"

"Of course, *che*! I've probably flunked senior year more

times than anybody else at school, and this is what happens
when you get old enough to be drafted. A real hassle, I tell
you." Then he said, "*Che*, I almost forgot. I talked to
Andrés on the phone yesterday and he has a message for
you. He said you were asking about that crazy girl Cristina
and to tell you that she's disappeared."

"Disappeared? What do you mean, disappeared?"

"How do I know? I'm just giving you the message.
Andrés is pretty upset about it, but *che*, she's probably just
gone underground or left the country for Cuba or something. Nobody's heard a word from her since the demonstration, not even her parents."

"That doesn't sound like her, Marelli," I said. "I didn't
know her that well, but it's not like her. She had a loud
mouth, she was always talking, and if she were going underground, she would have said something about it, don't
you think?"

"*Che*, she was the craziest one of the bunch. Don't worry
about her. She probably found some radical with a big stick
from the E.R.P. and is off happily making bombs with him.
That's why she hasn't even told her parents."

"You think so? Really? She was that radical?"

"Sure, don't worry. Besides, she was too much of a communist to be your type, Yanqui. But what do I know? I
haven't seen any of that bunch, not even Gloria, since I was
drafted. I've got enough problems already without politics.
What a hassle, *che*! I'm ashamed even to tell you what I'm
doing in the shitty army."

"What are you doing in the shitty army?"

"Waiter!" Marelli called out, raising an arm languidly
and motioning to the man behind the bar. We focused on
our menus for a moment, and as we both ordered, Marelli
seemed to be feeling on top of things, his old self again, as
if we were two young gentlemen involved in the ritual of
drinks, wine, beefsteaks and salads, parceling out our day.
After the waiter left, Marelli said, "My father used to go
out to lunch all the time with a particular friend, a rich
lawyer from the Echeverría-López family, a very good friend
to him. Sometimes my father took me along, and I sat with
the two old men watching them drink their whiskeys and

smoke their cigars. One time, this lawyer said to my father, 'Roberto! Don't you ever get bored with all of this? We drink, we eat these big meals, we take our naps then we go to work a little and come home to drink, eat big meals then sleep again. Don't you ever get bored? I think I am, Roberto, I think I'm getting bored with lunch,' he said. And my father sat there for a moment looking at his friend, this friend he went out to lunch with almost every day, then he said, 'What else is there? Can you think of anything better?' Those two old men laughed about that all day," Hernández-Marelli said, laughing a little himself. "Can you think of anything better, Yanqui? What I want to say is that I'm thinking you're a very good friend to me and there's nothing better than this," he said.

"You're crazy, Marelli," I said.

"You don't think I'm talking seriously?"

"All right then, *che*, we're very good friends. There's nothing better than this," I said.

"Do you think I've changed?" he asked, his cool little smile suddenly gone. "Do I seem different to you?"

"You look like a bald ostrich," I said.

"You wouldn't believe what I'm doing in the army," he said. "I don't believe it sometimes. I'm driving a garbage truck, out in Quilmes, in the suburbs. I asked my father to use his influence, and he said it was the only way the army would station me close to Buenos Aires. So here I am, a garbage truck driver, on regular ten-hour shifts. I was in a barracks for a while, but now I'm even allowed to sleep at home, and I wake up at three in the morning and go to our base, then drive around all day sometimes to finish my route. A garbage man. That's what's happened to my father's influence. The worst of it is that he's retired from the courts and gone totally alcoholic, and he's cut me off. Not one more peso until I get out of the army and finish school. No money, no cars, no clothes, nothing, absolutely nothing. I don't even know if I have enough with me to pay for my part of this check. You're a very good friend of mine, Yanqui, and I wanted to tell you this before they put the plates on the table."

I reached into my pockets and started counting my

money. I wasn't carrying much money anymore. It wasn't worth as much as it used to be, and I only had about three hundred new pesos. "If you quit ordering whiskeys and kick in about a hundred new pesos, I think we can pay the check," I said.

"Agreed," Marelli said, chewing on an ice cube from his glass. He was quiet a moment, disappointed at the small pile of bills and change I had counted out on the table then put back in my pocket. I had never seen Marelli this way, subdued and depressed, not even looking out the big window to see what kind of girls were passing by. The steaks and salads came, and I changed our order to the house wine instead of the expensive vintage bottle from Mendoza that Marelli had already ordered. I told Marelli about my night at La Correntina's, and how it ended up, and other things that had happened. That and the food picked Marelli up a little, but there was something strange about the way he was eating, shoveling his food in fast, as if ready to jump up and make formation any second. He drank glasses and glasses of wine, almost the whole liter in about five minutes, then he stopped eating suddenly. He took off his sunglasses and fastened an intense, pleading look at me with his tired eyes and said, "*Che*, I'm half crazy, I really am. I need money, all kinds of it. I'm in love. This time I really mean it, it's not any ordinary thing like with Gloria. This one's a classy girl, and a very rich one, the daughter of the Paraguayan ambassador. Think of it! And me with nothing to work with! Not a single mango in my pockets! My mother even thinks I should be living on the salary of a common truckdriver, son of a whore, *che*. Twenty thousand new pesos is all I need and I think I could get things really going with this girl. And listen, Yanqui, it's only a little loan I'm talking about. As soon as I get new X-rays, I really do stand a chance of getting a medical discharge . . ."

"Enough, *che*!" I said. Marelli stopped talking with a hopeful expression. "Look, I don't have any money. Not any more. My scholarship only gives me seven hundred new pesos a month. The rules are that I'm supposed to get by on that and I'm trying to follow the rules."

"But that's a scandal!" Marelli said as if all sympathy for me. "Who could get by one week in this city on seven hundred pesos?"

"That's the way it is," I said. "Is that clear?"

"I see how it is then," Hernández-Marelli said. He drained the last of the wine and set the glass down hard. "You mean all the money you used to carry around wasn't yours? It came from the Beneventos?"

"Where else would it come from, *che*? The Beneventos have spent mountains of pesos on me, for fees at the school, all my clothes, food, books, medical bills, tickets everywhere, and I don't know how many hundreds of thousands of old pesos Papá had to spend to fix things up when I wrecked the car. Do you think I'm rich, Marelli? Is that it?" I said. "Listen, a lot of things have changed since we last met. I don't want their money anymore. I don't think I could live with them anymore if I took their money."

"You're crazy, Yanqui! Do you know how rich the Beneventos are? It's like saying you couldn't live in Rio if you had to go to the beach!"

"I'm not going to do it, Marelli," I said. "I'm not going to ask Papá for twenty thousand new pesos so Hernández-Marelli can date a new class of girlfriend."

"But you didn't let me finish. It's not only me, *che*. This lovely girl has a friend, also a Paraguayan, a very dignified and beautiful girl. There's going to be a big dance at the Hotel Alvear, a posh debutante party for a friend of these girls, very high-class. My idea is that you work it out with Martín to take the car that night . . ."

"I've given up driving," I said. "It's against the rules of my scholarship."

"All right, all right." Marelli's hands were in front of my face, making quick gestures like a marketplace trader. "We can rent a limo. We put on our nice tuxedoes, I'll even loan you my burgundy tie and sash, then we pick up these nice girls, bringing armfuls of flowers for them and for their Mamás. We take them to the Alvear and start to dance. We dance disco, sambas, tangos, and those really slow dances, *che*, one arm around their waists and the other hugging their tits right up against you . . .''

"Quit wasting your words, Marelli, really . . ."

"Listen. Just listen. The genius in this plan is what comes next. We're all at the Hotel Alvear, right? And we've rented rooms upstairs, you see? It'll cost tons of mangos, I know it, but it'll be worth it, I promise you. Believe me, Yanqui, I know how these things go. We get them really tired, then we ask them up to our rooms for a little drink. They won't want to go home just yet, and as long as we stick together, they'll take us up on our little invitation. Then once we get them up to our rooms, we're on our own.'' Marelli grinned at me, his old self again, reaching for my pack of cigarettes and helping himself. "Well? What do you think, Yanqui?''

"Look at me, Marelli,'' I said. "Take a good close look. Am I the kind of type you expect to see at debutante dances?''

"Sure! The hippie look is getting to be very *in* these days.'' He punched the word *in* in English. "And look at me. The two of us together somehow balance out.''

"Then sell your fancy stereo!'' I raised my voice. "Sell your personal television! Sell your Rolex, your rings, sell anything!''

"My stereo and television fit into future plans,'' Marelli said.

"Son of a whore, Marelli . . .''

"Haven't you ever made love watching television? There are all kinds of fantastic things you can do without taking your eyes off the screen,'' he said.

"Marelli!''

"All right, all right, Yanqui,'' Marelli said, raising his arm and calling for the waiter as if he were the one paying the check. "I've got to be going now. But think about it, *che*. If you just tell me you'll think about it, I'll be satisfied. I'll give you a call before the end of the week. Ciao,'' he said then, holding out a limp hand for me to shake, which I did. I was biting my lip, afraid to say a word. Any sound at all from me would have been the same as saying yes. "Or you call me anytime. Marelli's back in town now,'' he said. He left a hundred new peso bill on the table, put his sunglasses on his face, and was out the door before the waiter reached me with the check, somehow also managing to pocket my cigarettes.

I pulled my money out of my pockets, counting the last few pesos of my tiny allowance for the month into a neat little stack, hating to see them go. I wished Marelli well, good luck on his X-rays, that he made it out of the army, that he made it with his girls, whatever he wanted, and I knew that he would. He wouldn't telephone me at the end of the week, or ever again, probably. I knew he would find his tens of thousands of new pesos somewhere, or from somebody else, that he was lucky that way. Some rich people seemed born not able to be poor, their fate defied their best self-destructive efforts and they landed on their feet every time. And still, they complained. Like Marelli, as rich as he really was and would always be, in the army only four months and already sleeping at home and he was complaining. A revolution was brewing, that was clear, and smart nice girls were going underground with machine guns, or vanishing, disappearing without a word and who knew where, and here was Marelli, griping about being short for a date. If nuclear bombs ever fell on Argentina, God forbid, Marelli would find himself at the bottom of the deepest fallout shelter in the country with the prettiest girl and the best bottle of scotch and still be complaining about his life. Goodbye, Marelli, I thought, stay well and take it easy. What could be better than this?

About a week later, a letter arrived from my mother, long before any of my postcards could have reached the States. It didn't come by regular post. The old man had a photographer friend on some kind of an assignment that brought him to Buenos Aires, and this photographer hand-delivered the letter to Isabelita one morning while I was at school. We four brothers came home in a group that day, and Miguelito and Alejo stood around watching me read this important-looking letter:

Dear "Diego":

You haven't written in so long we don't know what to say. The last letter said things were fine and that you had learned the language. We presume you are having too much fun with your "new family" to think about the one that has put up with you since you were born. Well, things aren't very nice around here right now. Harry is home. He's in the hospital. They sent him from Vietnam to Japan, where he was lost in transit for a while and nobody knew. Then he was transferred to an Army hospital in Jersey. He was in Jersey only a couple of weeks before he was sent directly to the Veterans Hospital in Northport, the closest one. Your Dad made sure the Army gave your brother an honorable, not a medical discharge, though Harry wasn't grateful for that. He won't even talk to us. The doctors say Harry has a mental illness, that he hears voices and sees things. We went to visit last Saturday and he called me "Joanie" and your father "Bobbie." Then he just started talking nonsense to himself and wouldn't answer your father's questions. Dad even slapped Harry to try and shake him out of it and Harry had to be restrained. Who is Joanie? Who is Bobbie? The doctors continue to work with Harry, but it's pretty grim. Your Dad read the records and it says "gravely disabled" on all of them. His doctor said Harry was suffering from a number of delusions, among them that he had a brother who was lost in South America. I laughed and told the doctor that part of it wasn't so crazy, we do have a son in South America right now. The doctor thinks Harry is a danger to himself and others, and wants to send him to a longer term hospital because the V.A. is crowded and is changing its rules about cases like Harry's. He wants to send Harry to the state facility at King's Point for a long term commitment. That means they'll keep Harry at Northport only a month or two until he is "stabilized"

and can be legally committed for the treatment he
needs. The Veterans Administration will take care of
moving Harry as long as we sign the papers. Anyway, you know your father. He's not going to sign
anything until we're sure what it means. The doctor
would have had us sign right then but your Dad is
going to consult a lawyer. He's very upset about
Harry. I have to keep reminding him that at least
Harry's alive and out of the war now. I told Father
Brautigan about it and he agrees. I said now he's got
only one of my sons to think about in his prayers for
travellers.

Another thing, and maybe I shouldn't tell you, but
for a few days it even had me as down in the dumps
as Harry's illness. On a Thursday morning a few
weeks ago, I arrived as usual at the office and was
told I was no longer needed. Why? No answer. But
why? A mumble about a new image—a new president was taking over the company—then another
mumble about not being able to keep anyone who
had worked with the old president. The following
Monday, I filled out the required forms at the New
York State Unemployment Office and I was able to
fill out all the blanks in English, thank you. (The
forms are in English and Spanish, and Spanish translation is available on request. You can sure find a job
with your new language when you get home!) The
clerk asked me why I had been dismissed. It didn't
say on his report. He phoned the office and somebody there said to put on my forms "inadequate performance." Inadequate performance? After eight
years? I'm only getting half the salary I used to earn
every two weeks now from unemployment, and I'm
looking for a new job, but that label really hurts. I'm
fighting it, trying to get them to change it. I'm so
furious I'm cleaning the house more than ever, which
I hate. Donny quit working at the rivet plant and got
a better job, as a waiter at the North Hempstead
Country Club, so he and Tom are chipping in to the
kitty now. We're on a tight budget but we're O.K.,

so don't worry. Be glad you're still down there and
are missing all the fireworks!

Your father wants to add a few lines and get this to
a friend to deliver to you on his way to work.

Love,

Mom

Don't forget to send your applications to colleges.

Dad

I started to translate this letter to Alejo and Miguelito as
I was reading it, but two or three lines into it, I stopped. It
seemed too real to me in Spanish, and the best I could do
to answer Alejo's questions was simply to say the truth about
Harry, that he had gone crazy and was in a hospital now,
alive and out of the war but nobody knew how long he'd
have to be confined. I skipped the part about the old lady
losing her job. Then I had to tell Martín Segundo, and then
Mamá and Papá, that my brother Harry was now certifiably
insane, the reality sinking in deeper each time.

It was Friday. Father Naboa had taken over monitoring
the Friday school mass in the chapel at San Andrés. We had
all been warned by El Negrito that Father Naboa was going
to take attendance at school masses into consideration when
giving out his final grades in Philosophy and Religion. Father Naboa always sat in the last pew, holding a clipboard
with a senior class list and checking our names off as we
filed in. But we soon discovered that once mass had begun,
Father Naboa generally got up and left the chapel. Once we
caught on to that, it became a kind of senior class game to
see how many of us could get away. We staked out the pews
nearest the side door of the chapel that led to the street,
forcing students from the lower grades to sit in front of us
and around us, covering us. School masses were also open to
the public, so there were a lot of devout maids, old folks
and strangers who walked in off the streets, and we left the
pews closest to the altar to them. After Father Naboa had
risen, crossed and left the chapel, before we had even re-

cited the creed, we seniors peeled off singly or in discreet pairs, ducking out the side door into the street.

Martín and I entered the chapel, knelt, crossed. The first time I had seen the chapel at Colegio San Andrés I thought it looked ugly but I liked it now. It was dim and dark and the pillars went high up. There were already people praying, and the air smelled of incense. There were high, narrow windows that cast a fractured reddish light over the worshippers. The cupola of the chapel ceiling was an ornate painting bordered in gold leaf of San Andrés suffering on an X-shaped cross with an image of Christ in the background showing His tortured hands and looking on in sorrow, cherubs and angels blowing trumpets all around them in heavenly clouds.

I knelt, crossed again, thought of the letter from my mother and started to pray. I prayed for Harry that he would get well and out of the hospital. Then the thought of Harry created flashes of what my brother must have gone through, strapped down to an Army stretcher and raving, then tied down for weeks in an Army hospital in Japan, his arms probably as full of track marks as a junkie's. Through my prayer, I could imagine Harry's voice shouting for me to get him out of there, to please get him out, and then a name, Harry was calling out my own Christian name and the only way to stop his voice in my mind was to try to think of something else. I thought of what Harry's plan used to be, that we would one day live in the city together, just him and me in his own apartment, and how I would go to school and he would pay the rent by playing his guitar and singing. I thought of how often he used to say *my own apartment* in a tone of voice as if dreaming of impossible riches. I managed to quit thinking about Harry and prayed for the safety of all my brothers in the States, and for the old man to make enough money so he could retire to his own photo store like he wanted to, and for my mother to find another job she liked. I prayed for my Argentine Papá, that he would be able to slow down on his financial bicycle and relax more and be able to listen to music and read to his sons like he used to, and for Mamá to succeed with her art gallery, and for Miguelito to pass the sixth grade, and for Alejo to watch out when he crossed busy streets lost in reveries and never to get hurt with his politics, and I prayed that Martín Segundo would learn not to think so much about himself and watch out more for his brothers. El Negrito came to mind, for some reason, and I prayed that he would one day be able to quit running like the wind, as he put it, and then I thought of an expression he used often with the students when they told him he was crazy: *Each one of us is crazy, each one to someone else.* Then I was suddenly thinking about all the good players on the River Plate *fútbol* team I was going to see again on Sunday, and hoping Daniel Onega would score three goals again like he did last week, then I wondered how much I should bet against El Gordo Rojo on the game. I began to feel sleepy with my eyes closed like that, my forehead resting on my folded hands, the ancient prayer cushion like a rock slab under my knees. I knelt there for a while thinking I was praying. Then I felt ashamed of myself for being there at all, a hypocrite of the first water, pretending I really believed I was still a good Catholic. Why would God want to waste His time listening to me? The presence of sincere souls in the pews in front of the altar, of the regular people in off the streets, the fervent widows praying in their black shawls, the devout maids with scarves covering their heads, and lost souls I'd never seen before lost in prayer, the sight of all of them made it even harder to get through the motions of Father Artaud's friendly mass, *May the Lord be with you . . .*

I opened my eyes and turned my head, waiting until Father Naboa stiffly rose from his knees, crossed himself while squinting at the altar as if making his quick excuse to the painting of Christ, and then tucked his clipboard under his arm and shuffled slowly out the main chapel door into the courtyard. I was in the lead this time as three-quarters of the senior class bolted in a group for the side doors, then I was standing in the hot sun on the steps that led up from the street, my palms still sweating, an uncomfortable feeling at the back of my throat.

I decided not to join in the courtyard soccer game that afternoon. Instead, I walked alone down to the broad avenue Comodoro Rivadavia at the bottom of the little hill,

then across the avenue, and hiked up a steeper street to a
small plaza called Primero de Mayo that was like a tiny
park. Sitting in the shade, I remembered praying, and hearing Harry's voice in my head. Something I had read about
the King's Point institution for the insane made me think it
was the kind of hospital where they lobotomized people, a
place where they sent patients too far gone ever to come
back to reality. Thinking this, I was afraid the old man and
the old lady might end up signing papers that would keep
Harry locked away in hospitals forever. But what could I
do? Send a telegram? An international call? None of these
things would work with the old man. To try and tell him
what to do with Harry would be like questioning his judgment, which always resulted in a hardening of his position.
Donny, Tom, Kevin, Willy, all my brothers were likely to
go along with what the old man decided. I couldn't count
on them to step in. Ruling them out, it was up to me to do
something, and fast, because waiting more than a month
might be too late for Harry, that was the situation.

# 9

## Minor Offense

For the next few days, I lived with the pressure that time was running out on me, and not only because of Harry. The International Student Exchange organization had scheduled a series of tours for its students in the provinces. Participation in the tours was voluntary, but apparently nobody had ever turned one down. The first of these trips was going to be a long one, a three-week tour that was to begin in the river-port city of Rosario.

My status was still a little shaky at Colegio San Andrés, and I had to work hard to pull my grades up enough to be absent that long. El Mono was particularly uncooperative. He refused to change his alphabetical ordering of student oral presentations and let me schedule a make-up day to recite to the class a passage memorized from our history text. When my number was up, it was up, and if I wasn't there, tough luck. So I was going to have to swallow a zero on the oral part of my grade in History, meaning I would have to pull off at least an eight, a high B on the final written exam, or I might not graduate.

I should have been excited at the prospect of seeing new landscapes and new cities, but I wasn't. I felt a sense of dread. Here I was just getting myself back together at school, and things were again running smoothly with my family. I had written a strong letter to I.S.E. in New York about the injustice of rejecting Martín Segundo because they couldn't place him, especially when an I.S.E. student was living in his home. I was still miffed at I.S.E. for putting us both in this awkward position, so why should I want to be a part of a trip to promote the organization? And except for the news from home, life was great again. Even in *fútbol*, I was just learning how to kick the ball straight and hard, and how to get it away on defense without kicking shins. Now I would have to think and speak in English again, and I would have to spend time with a class of people in Argentina I had so far avoided—other yanquis.

In Buenos Aires, I.S.E. gathered a large group of yanqui students, six boys and eighteen girls, the kind of odds in these numbers that made me think of Marelli. When I first saw them, I was sure I could fall in love with several of the girls in the first few minutes. But we went through a strange reordering of our behavior as we traveled north on our chartered bus, the boys and girls sitting apart, a tension in the atmosphere like the first high school dance.

The boys were sitting in the back of the bus. There was "Teo," who had spent his year living on a big ranch near a small town like Henderson in the pampas. Teo had decided that he was going to go completely gaucho for this tour and had costumed himself in the baggy gaucho pantaloons called *bombachas*, the big colorful scarf, the wide leather belt studded with coins, the black flat-pan hat and raw horsehide boots—the whole getup. Teo also carried a gaucho guitar which he had only recently learned to play. He had a repertoire of about three Argentine songs, along with the golden oldies "Blowing in the Wind," "Cumbiah," "Hey Jude," "Help" and "The House of the Rising Sun," which was very popular in Argentina. Teo's Spanish was terrible, and he spent most of his time on the tour rattling away manically in English as if he had been starved for conversation all this time. After the first hour of this incessant good-natured chattering, strumming his guitar and singing the same songs over and over again, I couldn't stand him.

Teo quickly fell in with "Carlos," a heavyset fellow from
Ohio who had spent his time in the city of Córdoba, where
all the trouble had been. Carlos seemed mostly unaware of
what had happened in his city. He had been living with a
rich family in an expensive suburb, and had been bothered
only by a few wakeful nights of distant gunfire. Carlos could
hardly speak Spanish at all. He tried everything to make
himself understood, stumbling along, gesturing wildly, but
he had a tin ear for the accent, and the way he twisted his
words around made everyone laugh. This reinforced Carlos'
new role as the group clown. He began to wear his I.S.E.
baseball cap backwards on his head. At our first stop in
Rosario, he did a handstand at a party with a flaming sausage on a stick held in his teeth.

Sitting alone a lot was "Marcello," who was so lean that
his bones stuck out and his brooding green eyes had a pred-
atory look as if he were always hungry. He didn't seem to
eat, and when I asked him about this, he said he was diet-
ing. In his first six months in Argentina, he had eaten so
many tender steaks that he had gained one hundred and
twenty pounds. Marcello showed me a picture, and it was
incredible, the same guy but a real blimp. Marcello said
that for the past four months, he had taken to fasting, starving himself back down to size. I liked him. He had spent
his time in the North, in Tucumán, and there was something
of a jungle version of Hernández-Marelli in the way Marcello had become an Argentine, speaking Spanish with the
slow lilting accent of his province. He was the first to break
the sexual ice, about the third hour of our bus ride, moving
up and down the aisles and visiting with the girls, sharing
his cigarettes. By the time he rejoined us in the back, it was
clear that he had laid the groundwork for three possible
romances with yanqui girls and a sure thing with one of our
chaperones, a very nice university student named Marta,
who had spent a year in Texas with I.S.E. years before and
who spoke English to us with a thick Dallas twang. Marta
was very southern in her way with us, always the genteel
lady but full of the veiled suggestions of a southern belle,
especially with Marcello.

The most capable of all the boys was "Pedro" Goldstein,

who had been living his whole year in Buenos Aires. I had
heard there was another yanqui student in the city, named
Pedro, but I hadn't managed to meet him in all our months,
even though we shared the same coordinator. I was amazed
to discover that Pedro was from Roslyn, a posh town a few
miles further along the North Shore from mine. And what
surprised me more was that Pedro had learned to speak
Spanish better than a native. It was remarkable. I was immediately ashamed of my own street-slang brand of Buenos
Aires Spanish by the way Pedro could sing out the language
with classical intonations if he wanted, like listening to the
King's English spoken by a Shakespearean actor. Then Pedro could switch gears and just as easily rap with me in the
port slang called *lunfardo*, then change over into the gaucho
dialect, and he had even managed to learn a few words of
the northern *indio* language of *guaraní*. I sat beside him for
hours on the bus, listening to him speak Spanish like an
acrobat with words.

He described his year in Buenos Aires, living with a family of journalists who were involved in a Jewish movement
to combat the anti-Semitism of the military regime. His
family's house had been broken into and everything smashed
by a military goon squad one night. Then he had been arrested at a synagogue during an organizing meeting and had
spent two days in jail along with his Argentine brothers and
his Papá. When the Israeli Exposition at the national fair in
one of the parks of Palermo had been burned to the ground,
a group calling itself the Catholic Lions claiming respon-
sibility, Pedro had been one of the volunteers who had re-
constructed the exposition out of aluminum, glass, steel and
concrete, all nonflammable materials, and the Israeli Exposition was back in business in a few days. Pedro was
great, his voice singing with his good language, quoting the
classic Latin American poets as he spoke, like Sor Juana
de la Cruz on love, *"Beautiful illusion for which I happily
die, sweet fiction for which in penitence I live."* And Andrés
Bello on peace, *"The sight of it fills the soul of the world
with serenity and rejoicing."* Then César Vallejo on the
blows that happen in life, *"Those bloody shocks are the
cracklings of some loaf of bread that burns us in the oven*

*door.''* Clearly, Pedro had spent a lot of his time in Argentina studying literature. He had adopted the scholarly Argentine gentleman's mode of behavior, usually well-dressed in jackets and ties or more informally in designer polo shirts and preppie slacks, always with his arm out to escort the girls and addressing them with the grammar of respect.

The other man on the bus was our head chaperone, Rodrigo, a short, balding guy in his late twenties who had recently graduated from medical school. Rodrigo had gone to the United States ten years before with I.S.E. and he had missed it ever since. He regarded chaperoning us on the tour not only as a kind of repayment to I.S.E. for the most important experience of his life, but also as his one big vacation before settling down to a doctor's life. Rodrigo was friendly, but he acted affectedly, way too cool, as if he were reliving a little of his youth by trying to behave like us. He was also interested in some of the girls, and trapped in his role as chaperone. He had to worry about our itinerary, hustle us on and off the bus, and take care of the arrangements to settle us with temporary sponsor families or in hotels. It was soon clear the tour was hardly any vacation for poor Rodrigo. He was run half to death by all the details, and the hassle of keeping track of all the dozens of purses, hair curler sets, hatboxes, hanging bags, and trunk-sized suitcases the girls had brought with them.

I didn't get to know all the girls. There was "Billy," a strange tall girl who played guitar even worse than Teo and who always wore straw hats. She had rebelled against the whole I.S.E. program, it seemed, relying from the start on translators and getting through her year by asking not to be graded at school and teaching her family and anyone she could find to speak English, a sad, distant look about her as if she had never left Indiana.

The most obnoxious was "Nina" from San Diego. Nina kept running to the front of the bus and clapping her hands, then jumping up and down and leading the others as if they were her pom-pom girls in a song to the tune of *When the Saints Go Marching In*, "When I-S-E! When I-S-E! When I-S-E goes marching on . . . Oh, you'll want to be in that number . . .'' and so on, repeating the song over and over

again every time she was seized by her cheerleader's instinct. Teo joined her with his guitar in a group sing-along
of the only Argentine song both she and Teo knew, *Que
Lindo Es Estar En Mar del Plata*, a kind of bouncy pop
tune about how great it was to be at the beach resort of Mar
del Plata. When they finished this song, Nina led her girls
in a vigorous cheer, "Give me an I! Give me an S! Give
me an E! What does it spell? . . ." and so forth, the girls
squealing excitedly and clapping their hands. When Pedro
and I didn't join in, already feeling a kind of reverse culture
shock, Nina glared at us at the back of the bus as if we
were traitors.

There were other, quieter girls, "María" and "María,"
both very nice but painfully shy and unfortunately, like
Marcello, they had gained many too many kilos living their
sheltered provincial lives cooped up and learning how to
cook. The two Marías always looked spooked to be on the
bus somehow, and they sat together, restrained in a very
Spanish way taught by the convent schools they had been
attending. The Marías stayed away from the rest of us, chatting together and working at embroidery in their laps, always dressed in plain dark clothes and acting so properly
that I guessed their time in Argentina had been spent in
strict houses like in Lorca's great play, *The House of Ber-
narda Alba*, in which the mother shouts proudly to the world
that her daughter died a virgin.

There was also "Antonia," a very pretty tall girl who
had spent her time in the beautiful city of Rio Cuarto, stuck
away in wooded mountains that rival the Smokies of Ten-
nessee. Antonia had fallen in love with a young student in
Rio Cuarto, and he was waiting for us when we arrived in
Rosario, a thin, dark Argentine named Gustavo, who had
hitchhiked ahead of us and was romantically blowing kisses
at Antonia with his arms full of flowers as the bus pulled
in. It was Rodrigo's first crisis on the tour to decide if it
was all right for Antonia to share a hotel room with Gustavo, who was clearly broke, and if he could ride with the
group on the I.S.E. bus from Rosario on, which was against
all the rules. Rodrigo finally gave in to Antonia's pleas after

lobbying with each of us in private, saying it was his neck if we ever said a word.

There were other interesting girls, "Cristina" from Illinois, "Mercedes" from Colorado, and "Catarina" from Michigan, and others all very nice, most of them pretty, a cheerful group soon full of energy and enthusiasm for the I.S.E. team. When even Pedro moved up front and started to join in their songs, I hid away alone in back, wrapped my jacket around my ears and tried to sleep. After the first three hours of the songs and cheers and squealing laughter of these yanquis, I made up my mind that I couldn't stand any of them.

Rosario is one of the most beautiful cities in Argentina, overlooking a deep port that, according to the Rosarians, would have made it the ideal city to serve as the capital of the country. Its foundations were as ancient as the Spanish conquest and its culture was refined, with big museums and theaters, and cathedrals whose altars were like national monuments. The *gente bien* of Rosario had decided to welcome the group of yanqui students with a large banquet at a first-class hotel. We were compelled by Marta and Rodrigo to wear jackets and ties for this celebration, where we met the sponsor families we were going to move in with the next day. The mayor of Rosario spoke to us; also the military *comandante* of the district. We were served big plates of barbecued beef and bottles of first-class vintage wine. Afterwards, Rodrigo was a little tipsy, and he suggested that since we had a free night and hotel rooms, some of us might want to go out dancing at a club he knew in Rosario. About half the girls, both chaperones and all the boys ended up riding in a formation of taxis to a discotheque in an old quarter of the city.

I fell in love with Catarina after the first dance. We agreed to speak to each other in Spanish, which she had mastered pretty well, and I discovered she was remarkably mature as she told me about her unusual experience in Argentina, living with a family whose daughter was a famous international tennis player. She had spent almost as much time out of the country as in it, accompanying her Argentine sister to England, France, Spain, South Africa, and even twice

back to the United States on a pro tennis tour. Catarina had
been living a fast-lane life on the tennis circuit as her sister's
companion and roommate in luxury hotels. She was a tall,
dark girl, as angular as a fashion model, very sophisticated
but very nice, and by our second butt-clutching slow dance
the two of us were already breathing as if we had just entered the tropics. Then it was tango time at the disco, a very
nostalgic recording from the twenties coming through the
speakers, *That little blue room of the first passion of my
youth* sung out in a melodious tenor. Catarina knew the
steps and we slunk across the dance floor in a clever, hu-
morous show of tango romance and she was nimble on her
feet as I dipped her, whipped her around, her tall warm
body fitting perfectly in my arms, then cheek to cheek we
started back across the floor. There was applause for us when
the dance was over, and we hugged and kissed in front of
everyone. Then the disco switched back to modern music
and a psychedelic light show was happily flashing across
the dance floor in all its colors. By our third slow dance,
Catarina's pretty cheek resting against my shoulder and my
head dizzy with her good perfume, I was thinking I was
going to like this tour, these yanquis I was with weren't all
that bad, and I felt lucky again, holding her closely like she
belonged in my arms, as sure as I've ever been that all was
right with the world.

   A cry went up at the doorway of the disco. Lights were
switched on as bright as search beams. Men in khaki uniforms, some with their pistols drawn and some holding their
nightsticks as if waiting for the signal to start using them,
were suddenly all over the place. Back and front doors were
quickly covered. Police surrounded the big room. Two officers who were in charge began going through the crowd,
methodically checking national identity cards. Rodrigo and
Marta were at the back of the disco, frantically searching
for students from our group who were scattered all over the
dance floor, waving at us to gather everyone together. Catarina and I were all the way across the packed club, and
we started in Rodrigo's direction half-blindly, knocking into
people, still trying to adjust to the glare of the lights. Shoving our way through the crowd, I saw a police officer give

me a familiar suspicious look and I stopped in my tracks. This police officer didn't like me, that was clear, he thought I was an Argentine and that my hair was too long and my beard not trimmed to his standards. I tried to push Catarina ahead of me to get her out of the way. I reached into my jacket and got my new yanqui passport out before the *capitán* had to ask for it. The police officer looked from the picture to my face, then back to the picture as if he didn't like something he was reading in my passport. Catarina was beside me, hand on my shoulder, and the officer turned to her and asked, "How old are you?"

"Seventeen, señor," Catarina answered nervously. "Eighteen next month. If you want to see my passport, I can get it for you. It's in my purse."

The police officer wasn't listening. He was looking at me with this little smile on his thin lips under his macho moustache and all the signs were suddenly very bad. "There is a law in Rosario now that prohibits a man to dance after midnight with a girl who is a minor," the police officer said. Then he turned from me and called out, *"Teniente!"*

A khaki-uniformed lieutenant broke through the throng, surrounded by a small gang of his subordinates with their nightsticks ready and wearing riot helmets. Without a word to me, this lieutenant began to inspect my passport. By that time, Rodrigo had noticed all the commotion and was trying to get to us with Catarina's purse. He was about to intercede, all humble smiles and little bows, diplomatically trying to push past two or three police officers between him and me to get close to our little problem. Without even looking at me or at Rodrigo, who had started to talk to him, the lieutenant snapped my passport closed and said, "Place this one under arrest."

"What are you doing, señor?" Catarina asked indignantly, one of the riot police already pulling my wrists out and slapping handcuffs on them. "It's not his fault! I'm the one who doesn't have sufficient age!" She raised her voice and was about to put her hands actually on the police officer and try to push him back and I shook my head no, winked at her, smiled, put myself in the way and hissed, *Get the fuck out of this* in English, which stopped her.

Rodrigo also saw what was about to happen and stepped in between Catarina and the police to try to explain the situation but he was too upset, making wild hand gestures and saying, "This can't be! *Teniente!* This can't be! We're an approved international organization! Nobody here has committed any crime!"

The lieutenant looked at Rodrigo with disbelief, at first, then as if he were deciding whether it was best to order his riot police to nightstick Rodrigo or simply to muscle him down.

"*Teniente!* Listen! These students are guests of the mayor! I'm trying to spare the police an embarrassing international incident, I assure you! *Teniente!* Think of your career! If you don't release him right now, this moment, you'll find your name all over in the press!"

Rodrigo's voice rose out of control. He had actually threatened this police lieutenant in front of his officers, and there was no choice after that. With a small motion of his hand, the lieutenant ordered two of his riot police to jump on Rodrigo and wrestle him into handcuffs.

"What are you doing! Please! This is an injustice! This can't be!" Rodrigo was really yelling by now, and he fought back against the officers, trying to yank his arms away from them until one of them shoved a nightstick into his ribs. Rodrigo quit fighting. He looked over at me as if I had just appeared to him in a nightmare. He raised his handcuffs and focused on them as if all he needed to do was blink a few times and he might wake up screaming.

Everything happened fast, too fast. We were pushed quickly out, each of us between two officers. Our assistant chaperone, Marta, appeared at the fringes of a crowd near the disco entrance and called out, "Don't worry, Rodrigo! I'll see everyone back to the hotel and I'll come get you out!"

"Telephone the mayor! The mayor!" Rodrigo shouted, digging his heels in, resisting. Marta raised an *O.K.* sign at him just before a riot policeman shut Rodrigo up and made him go limp by punching a nightstick into his belly. We were shoved down the steps of the disco, then each of us was roughly pushed into the cagelike backseat of a black-and-blue Ford Falcon police car.

Being arrested and locked up inside a small cage in the police station drove Rodrigo out of his mind. He bit his lips bloody, chewed on his knuckles, ground his teeth with a horrible sound. "How could this happen? Me! The chaperone! Here! It's a shame! A terrible, terrible shame!" He was crying, in a rage, beating on his forehead with his fists. Then he lost control and suddenly threw himself against the wire-mesh door, jumping up on it like a monkey and rattling it. This really shot my nerves. I grabbed Rodrigo and pulled him back down to the little bench in our cell and told him to calm down. I offered him a cigarette. The police had taken our belts and Rodrigo's shoelaces but had left us with everything else. "*Che*, it's a good sign they left us with our money and our cigarettes," I said.

It was good to smoke. It helped us to calm down and get a fix on the situation. Three cigarettes later, Marta turned up in the big station room with two men dressed in business suits whom I remembered from the mayor's banquet. We could barely see them as they crossed in front of a partly opened door that led into our little cellblock. Voices were raised in the big room. Rodrigo sensed something was wrong and pressed his face against the cage. "What are they saying? They're not going to let us out? *They're not letting us out!*" He started biting his knuckles again.

Marta was led into our small room with two cages, the other sitting empty across from us. A police officer escorted her, and he didn't have his keys out, a very bad sign.

"It's all right, Rodrigo," Marta said. "It's just a minor offense. I couldn't get through to the mayor, but two nice lawyers came with me and there's no problem. We've paid the maximum fine and they're going to let you out in the morning."

"In the morning?" Rodrigo asked. "Why not now?"

"It's stupid, and they're idiots, that's clear. We're going to give them a hassle about this that they won't forget, but what else can we do? They insist on keeping you until morning."

"But why? Why until morning!"

"Are you awright, honey?" Marta asked me in her Texas English.

"*Macanudo*," I answered her in Buenos Aires street slang, meaning like *really groovy*. "Except that I'm running out of cigarettes."

"Ah'm sorry but I don't smoke, darlin'," Marta said. "You try and get some sleep in here. We'll get y'all sprung in the mornin', don't you worry now."

"But why in the morning? In the morning!"

Rodrigo sat down on the bench in a slow collapse. He looked dazed as the officer led Marta back into the station house, calling over her shoulder to us in Spanish, "Don't worry. Everything's fine. Get some sleep. See you in the morning!"

"Listen, Rodrigo. It's getting late. Why don't you lie down there on the bench and try to sleep," I said. "I'll take the floor. We'll stretch out a few hours, then we'll go out for a nice breakfast in the morning, what do you think?"

"But why aren't they letting us go?" he asked. He stood up from the bench, pacing back and forth about three steps each way. "I don't understand it. Why?"

"How do I know?" I said.

"Those sons of whores," Rodrigo said. "Those sons-of-whore *boludo* fascists! What shit!" he raised his voice. Then he was in a sudden rage all over again and pressed up against the cage, shouting, "Why aren't you letting us go! Why! You sons of whores! Why not! Why! *Why!*" I had to pull him back off the wire again, and roughly this time, before he drew too much attention to us. But it was too late. A big guard with a nightstick in his hands came through the door into our little cell area.

"*Che, Capitán*," I said politely, all smiles at the cage door but half out of my head myself. I was either going to get this officer to do something about the situation or I was going to turn around and murder Rodrigo to shut him up. "My friend here isn't well. He's sick. He needs to get out. He's very fucked up because of this, isn't that clear?" I said. "All our fines are paid, *Capitán*, and my friend here wants to know why you can't let us out. Just tell him why, and he'll be quiet, I promise you."

The officer hesitated a moment near the door. Then the sergeant from the big desk in the station room pushed around him and came in to see what was causing the commotion. The sergeant looked like a reasonable man, gray and experienced, not in any hurry, and not angry, it seemed, as he ambled at a slow, heavy pace toward our cage.

"Thank you. A thousand thanks for giving us a little moment, sir," I said. "I know this isn't your mistake. You've been very tolerant, that's clear, but the situation is that my friend here is sick. He's making himself crazy in here," I said.

"The reason we're keeping you until morning is that we're short on the night shift," the sergeant said bluntly at Rodrigo, who was now seated in a kind of catatonic position on the bench, sulking. "You there," the sergeant said gruffly enough to make Rodrigo look up. "There's no one to type your arrest papers until the new shift comes on in the morning, do you understand? We're very short-handed lately. There's nothing we can do, is that clear? Now will you please calm down and not make problems for yourself?"

"I know how to type," I said. "Pardon me, sir, but I type very fast and accurately."

The sergeant paused at the cage door awhile, taking his time to think this over. He was a careful man, that was clear, and I gently followed up on my suggestion by saying, "Look, it's just you and a few officers here, sir, so who would know? You could tell them in the morning that you did the papers yourself."

"No," the sergeant said after a moment. "How could I say I had done them when I don't know how to type? Listen, I really feel for you, but that's our clerk's job, and we don't have a clerk tonight."

"Look, sir, I have some pesos," I said. "And my friend here has some pesos, too. You can have all the pesos in our pockets. It's not much, but it's a little something to have with your tea," I said. I looked over my shoulder quickly at Rodrigo to check out his reaction. He was already sitting up, pulling crumpled bills out of his pockets and counting them, not a huge sum, maybe fifty or sixty dollars in new pesos, and I had about thirty dollars in new pesos, all together a considerable amount, maybe a week's wages for a police sergeant. But the sergeant didn't make a move to accept my offer, and his expression went suddenly blank. I experienced a moment of panic in which I thought I had landed us in more trouble, they were really going to fuck us over now. But the sergeant was just taking his time, considering the situation, waiting to see how many new peso bills with their portraits of San Martín would spring out of our pockets. When our pockets were turned out, all our change filling our fists, the nice sergeant used his keys.

There are probably moments in every man's life when he says to himself, *This has never happened to anyone else.* That's the way I felt sitting at the antique Olivetti with its loose roller and the keys all out of line, perhaps the first person ever arrested in Argentina who had typed his own police report. After our fingertips were rolled over an inkpad, pressed onto rectangular spaces on separate white cards, soaped, wiped off with a dirty rag, I started with Rodrigo's case first, typing his name and case number on the card. Then there were other, pink forms, and I punched the keys for *Martínez Perrera, Rodrigo* again, then I filled in all the blanks on the pink pages, blue carbons spilling out at the corners in disorder and making sluggish work of typing so many copies with facts like Rodrigo's size, weight, eye color, all of that, his address in Buenos Aires, his occupation, doctor, then his charges, which the sergeant stood over my shoulder and dictated as *conducto radical*. Radical conduct? Disorderly conduct? Did it matter? I typed on, the address of the discotheque, the date and time of the crime committed, and the names and ranks of two arresting officers, neither one of them the lieutenant responsible. The sergeant slowly checked over all the blanks on the forms before he let me roll them out of the machine. Then I started on my own arrest forms, watching the name on my passport jumping out onto the paper, then my address, which I listed as the one in the United States, my occupation of student, and all the rest until my crime, which the sergeant told me was *public lewdness, dancing with a minor after midnight,* the female gender attached to the Spanish word for *minor, una menor*, making obvious that this weird blue law was a crime only charged to men.

As I was typing my own arrest forms, my thoughts began to clear. There was a life decision I was about to make, and I suddenly knew what it was. I was going to get off this tour. Never mind the great beach resort we were supposed to hit at the end of it, never mind another dozen banquets with city officials, another hundred sing-alongs on the bus. Never mind even Catarina, a great dancer but was she really worth it? Maybe so, but I was still throwing in the towel. My decision was to leave this station house with Rodrigo and find a taxi back to the hotel. Then I was going to tell the taxi to wait for me while I went up to the room I was sharing with Pedro and found the rest of the pesos I had with me and the twenty good yanqui dollars I kept hidden away in a ball of socks for this kind of an emergency. Packing would take two minutes, then I was going to get back in the taxi and head straight to the Rosario train station and buy a ticket for the first express back to Buenos Aires. After that, I was going to spend a week to settle business, a week at the most. I was going to talk to my professors and take early exams, or to El Negrito so that he could do whatever it took to get my degree. I was going to spend any money I had left on a few little gifts, toss them and the few rags of my own clothing into a cheap plastic suitcase like the one I had brought with me from the States. I was going to kiss my family goodbye, catch a ride out to the airport and be on the overnight flight back home. My year was over before it was over, and I had responsibilities at home, that was the situation. I.S.E. would think I was a washout, a failure, a chicken, and everyone in both countries would be disappointed in me but I didn't care anymore, I wanted and needed out. If I didn't get out, and soon, I felt like a giant was waiting to catch me and swallow me, Argentina was finally going to drive me crazy.

"I've made a decision that I have to go home," I said to my family just after I arrived the next afternoon. We were all seated at the table for a late lunch. "It's my brother Harry. He's in very, very bad shape in the hospital. I'm not

sure my parents know what to do, and I'm the closest brother
to him, and maybe I can help them. I've got to go home.
I'm really worried about my brother, and I don't want to
take the chance I won't see him again.''

"I'm sorry, my son, it pains me to hear this," Papá said.
"What a shame! What torment your parents must be going
through! But to leave now? Just leave? What about finishing
school?''

"I don't want to throw away my *bachillerato* degree. I'm
going to try to take early exams in the next few days and
pray I get home in time,'' I said, my mouth dry, my tongue
covered with some kind of stickum. "I'm sorry, too, Papá,
Mamá, and please don't think I want to leave. This is hard
for me. It's the hardest decision I've ever made in my life.''
I felt rotten because of the way they were all listening to
me with so much real concern, and here I was leaving so
many things out that I wasn't even sure I was telling them
the truth. We all sat together quietly a moment, my news
sinking in, and I hated myself.

"Listen, my son, I've got an idea," Papá said. "Let me
telephone your parents and tell them we're putting you on
a flight, and don't you worry about the expense. You'll be
able to visit your brother a few days, see what you can do
for your family, then come back to Buenos Aires, take your
final exams like all the others and use your I.S.E. plane
ticket to go home when you were scheduled. Besides, in a
crisis like this, how could you expect yourself to study?
Don't be foolish, my son, we'll go get the ticket right now,''
Papá said.

"But Papá, I think I'll want to stay with him until I know
he's passed the crisis. Who knows how long that's going to
be?'' I said. I looked at my hands. I was twisting a good
linen napkin in them and was about tear the lace border off.
"Listen, Papá, I wouldn't want to burden you by coming
back for just a couple of weeks. That's all the time we'd
have left on my scholarship, do you understand?''

"What burden? To the shit with the scholarship. You don't
need any scholarship to live here,'' Papá said in a scolding
tone.

"Martín, please,'' Mamá said. "You're making things

difficult for the boy." There was a clipped sound in her voice, a hard, distant edge. I realized she understood that I was leaving for good. And still, she helped me. "It would break his heart to have to say goodbye to everyone two times," she said.

"Nobody is saying goodbye in this family," Papá said. "If he goes, then he goes. The important thing is that he knows he is expected back. He can come and go any time he wants, with all our help and assistance, is that clear? Plane tickets, money, anything, with just one phone call. He'll always have a bed in this house. Is that clear to you, Diego? The only way I could be comfortable with letting you go like this is if you know we expect you to return. If you wish, you can even live here and go to the university. The Catholic University is still an excellent education. It might not be a bad idea. The tuition's no problem, you just leave that up to me. And you could find afternoon work that pays well, translating correspondence and that kind of thing, starting in my own office. Do you understand what I'm saying?"

"I don't think I could imagine not coming back," I said.

"You could visit in the summers," Miguelito said.

"That's winter for him, you idiot," Alejo said.

"Soon," I said. "I promise I'll come back soon."

"That's fine with me then, my son," Papá said. "Everything's settled. To the return of our Diego soon, very soon," he said. Papá raised his glass of scotch, all his sons picking up their Cokes, Mamá her seltzer, and everyone touched glasses across the table as Papá said, *"Hasta pronto, Diego!"* We all toasted with him, calling out *"Hasta pronto!"*—their Diego in the most resolute voice.

Colegio San Andrés was thrown into a small furor of activity over the news that I was leaving. There were phone calls for Papá to make to El Rector and to my professors, then papers to take to be signed and then officially stamped by Choto, the administrative secretary of the school, after my early exams had been arranged and completed. Most of my professors were more than cooperative about the exams. Profesor Martinette, who was professor for Trigonometry and Civic Instruction, had me go through an easy exercise with an isosceles triangle. Then he let me write an essay on the spot covering our last quarter's studies on the economy of Argentina. He sat me in the back of his classroom packed full of young students from the fourth year and had me write on the benevolent democracy of the first term of the old Radical party president, Hipólito Yrigoyen, who ruled Argentina during its first golden age when it seemed the nation was a great, developing power and might even grow to match Rio as a playground for the rich. "The regime of Yrigoyen was unsurpassed for its increase in prosperity and its completion of public works. An expanding nation in need of labor brought new waves of immigration, and the southern cone had become one of the breadbaskets for a hungry Europe," I wrote. After about thirty minutes of this, when the bell rang, Martinette looked over my essay for about three seconds then gave me straight eights, high B's, on everything. And Profesora Montiel, the demanding chemistry teacher whom we called La Rata, The Rat, because of her unfortunate sharp nose and buck teeth, grew maternal toward me after my story about my brother Harry's condition, which I stretched a bit for her so that it seemed his life was at stake. In an unprecedented gesture of leniency, La Rata waived my final exam in chemistry. She said I had done well enough on the last *quatrimestre* that she could give me a six for the year's grade, which was the lowest mark that still allowed me to pass.

Later, after school, Music Professor Pérez-Pérez had me sit down with him for about fifteen minutes and simply listen to and identify the prelude to *Tristan und Isolde*. He scrubbed his sharp-nailed hand through my long hair, squeezed my shoulder, rested his hand on my knee, then gave me a perfect score of ten. In a mood of celebration, I found old Father Naboa, weeding through his suncrisp geraniums around the courtyard flagpole under the shade of a big straw hat. "You've been one of the listeners in my class, haven't you?" Father Naboa asked, still at work with his little gardening fork.

"Yes, Father, I think so," I said, on my hands and knees with him by then, pulling up a few weeds.

"Eh?"

"I said I think so!" I raised my voice to a shout.

"If you've been one who's listened, I won't need you to write an exam. Just tell me now what, according to Aristotle, are the functions of the human soul?"

"I, ah, can't be exactly sure, Father," I said, not confident I was breaking through his deafness. "Maybe I could go home, brush up on that, and with your permission, I could write on that point for you tomorrow!"

"There's no need. Give me your own words. What do you remember of what I discussed in class?"

"Very well then," I said. A stalk of geranium as dry as straw came up in my fist. "These flowers don't look very good, Father, they're all dry," I said, stalling.

"What did you say?"

"All dry! The flowers!"

"They always die off in the summer. The truth is, it's too hot for them out here, and all year, they're trampled on," Father Naboa said. "But then, on the other hand, I have the nice work of replanting them."

"It is nice work, Father! You do very nice work out here!" I shouted. Father Naboa sat back on his haunches and examined me through his thick glasses, sweat running into his eyes and making him squint.

"Well? Don't you remember our discussion of *De Anima*? Haven't you read our text?"

"Of course, Father, of course I have," I said. "I'm just not sure what you want me to say."

"Eh?"

"I'm not sure what you want me to say!"

"What did you most get out of it, that's all. And you don't have to shout at me," Father Naboa said with an indignant little wave of his fork. "You. Your own words. You're the only North American student I've ever had in my class, or probably ever will have, and I want to know what you think."

"Very well then. On the functions of the soul, as you discussed," I said.

"Speak up," he said.

"Of course, Father, pardon me," I said. I leaned my head very close to his, shoving my face in under the broad brim of his straw hat. I cupped my hand to my mouth, my lips so close to his ear that I was almost kissing the bristly gray hairs plugging its little black hole. "What I most got out of it, Father, if I'm not mistaken, was the part about lies. In forming opinions, in thinking, we can't get out of the choice of what's true and what's false." Father Naboa began to nod, slowly, knocking the top of my head with his hat. "Our perceptions, our sensations, are generally true, but our thinking sometimes isn't," I said. "We're too emotional. It's the difference between the souls of man and animals, too, that animals can only perceive and aren't able to lie."

Something I had said must have made him happy, because he licked his lips and started into the singsong voice he used in class, "And it follows that thinking . . . is in part imagination, in part judgment . . . imagination is usually false. . . . Sensation and imagination are not the same. . . . Only one is a faculty . . . of the human soul," he sang out into the courtyard. He stopped then and turned to face me, looking into my eyes with a strange intensity. It seemed to be a signal, and I moved my head out from under the shade of his hat into the sunlight. "Very well then," Father Naboa said, no longer singing. "I can only conclude that what you've told me is a misinterpretation of our class discussion, and hardly complete. But maybe I should consider that enough, no? You have been one of the regulars at Friday mass?"

"Of course, Father. Check your lists."

"Eh?"

"Every Friday I was in Buenos Aires!" I shouted.

"Very well then, no need to shout, we're not barbarians. Where are your papers?"

Father Naboa signed my forms on his lap, entering a grade of seven for Philosophy and Religion, the usual C mark with which he blanketed his class. "Wait," he said as I was getting to my feet. I sank back down to my knees in his flowerbed. Father Naboa put his hand on my head, closed his eyes and whispered a blessing, the words so faint I couldn't hear them. I watched his dry lips moving, a strange little whistling sound coming through them, then he finished and said I could go.

I would have had my degree in my pocket that day if it weren't for El Mono, The Monkey, the only one who resisted the idea of letting me off easy. He wouldn't hear of setting up an early exam. "You have already missed your oral presentation two days ago," he said. "If you miss your final exam, I can hardly see how you will have fulfilled the national requirements for graduation."

I caught El Negrito off the schoolgrounds, on his way to run an errand. "That son of a whore El Mono isn't going to let me graduate," I said. "I'm thinking maybe you can do something about the situation."

"El Mono is a very hard man," El Negrito said. "It would take a lot of talking on my part."

"You can tell me how much you want, anything at all, and I'll see what I can do," I said.

"*Che*, what are you talking about? For you, it's nothing. I'll fix everything," El Negrito said. "Or maybe, if you think of it, you might send me some of those nice North American shirts you always wear, medium size, for my nephew. But if not, don't worry. I'll have a little talk with El Mono. Now I have to fly off, I have some last-minute things. Ciao," he said and speedily crossed the street in his lopsided walk before I could thank him, and before I could tell him for the last time that all my nice shirts were Argentine. The next day, when I tried El Mono again, El Negrito had made a deal with him. El Mono would allow me to make up the oral presentation I had missed. With that grade, I could afford to swallow a zero on the final and still pass the course, my last requirement for graduation.

My last two days in Buenos Aires were spent with Martín Segundo, who helped me to memorize and run my lines, eight full pages of textbook which read like an excerpt from an encyclopedia, all of them concerning the life of General José de San Martín. My brother Martín was tireless in helping me, and without him, I would never have graduated. We ducked around the corner for Cokes and pizza on breaks, and it was clear that now I was going to leave he regretted that we hadn't become better friends. So much had gotten in our way; and I realized also how hard I had been on him all along, and how much he had done for me, introducing me at the school, explaining so much for me during my first few confusing weeks. We studied long into the nights, Isabelita bringing in Cokes and trays of her good *empanadas*. The whole family joked about me at meals, saying that I was going out of the school the same way I had entered, remembering the way El Mono had me memorize and recite lessons in Spanish almost every day until he was confident I had learned the language. As a dress rehearsal, I recited the history lesson for Mamá and Papá, but I kept faltering or losing my place and had to start over again, which El Mono never allowed.

My last day at Colegio San Andrés, my *bachillerato nacional* diploma sitting on El Rector's desk, I had to stand in front of El Mono's class in an erect, military posture, legs slightly apart, hands behind my back. My friends were posted in the front row and ready to help—Martín Segundo, El Gordo Rojo, El Judío, Llamas-Pérez and José, each of whom had been passed tiny cribbed copies of my script by Martín Segundo. Martín and El Gordo were closest. I could see how they had their cryptic little pages under the edges of their desks so they could lean back just a shade in their chairs and peek at them. Martín and I had experimented for hours to see what I could read from his lips and how low a whisper I could hear. El Mono sat a little behind me and to one side, monitoring the class. Martín leaned back, peeked quickly at his crib sheet, then winked at me, the signal that he was ready. I cleared my throat, shifted my feet and went blank. The first lines were just plain gone, and without them, where was the rest?

"Very well. You may begin," El Mono said.

I cleared my throat again, opening and closing my fists behind my back. Nothing was in my mind except the outrage that I had gotten myself into this situation in the first place. El Gordo was squirming in his seat, bringing his huge hand up to his mouth as if to cover a cough and about to spit out the words when Martín hissed first, "San Martín . . . José de . . . One of the grandest figures . . ."

"Silence! Silence or I'll throw you out of this class!" El

Mono sang out in his deep baritone voice, rapping on his desk with his bony knuckles. "Now you may begin, señor," he said.

Martín had saved me. The first few words were there, then magically all the rest. I began to recite as fast as I could, the Spanish chattering out of my mouth at superspeed because I was terrified I might blank out again if I didn't jump at the words while they were still in my head. "San Martín, José de . . . One of the grandest figures in the history of the Republic. He was born in Corrientes on the 25th of February, 1778, and baptized into the Catholic Church with the names José Francisco. His parents were Capitán Juan de San Martín, a governor since 1775 in the city of Yapeyú in Missiones province, and Doña Gregoria Matorras. They were married on the 1st of October, 1770. Until the age of four, José de San Martín lived with his parents in Yapeyú. After this, he was entered into primary school in Buenos Aires where, even as a child, he began to organize his compatriots into mock battles . . ."

I went on and on, feeling like a kind of tickertape of memorization. After a while, it was even possible to disengage my mind a little from the machine and I began to wonder what El Mono must be thinking, having me recite all these names, dates, places, regiments in Spain, in Gibraltar, all the military training San Martín went through as he fought with the ranks of junior officers in campaign after campaign for the Spanish against Napoleon. And all the medals and honors he won in Spain while wearing a uniform of white and sky blue, the eventual colors of the flag he would raise after he returned to Argentina and took up arms against the Spanish in rebellion. Why did El Mono insist that this be the lesson?

I went through it all, how San Martín and a group of idealistic and recently unemployed young officers from the Napoleonic Wars set off for Buenos Aires, where they organized and trained the famous *granaderos a caballo*, the aristocratic cavalry with its Prussian code of honor. Then they formed and trained several corps of foot soldiers, a task that took them two years. "San Martín saw the way to liberation to the South. With the help of General Güemes and his force of gauchos, San Martín held fast in the province of Córdoba in order to formulate his continental scheme. In order to achieve this, he had himself named governor of Cuyo, where he began to expand his army into an instrument of liberty. On the 18th of January, 1817, the crossing of the Andes by the great Army of the Andes began. . . .''

The story was long and bloody, full of victories assured mainly by the general's precise calculations, relying on the best advance intelligence and outmaneuvering the Spaniards, cutting them off in surprise attacks, crossing hazardous mountain passes to swarm down the slopes onto their flanks. Suffering from gastric and other ailments, San Martín was pulled across the Andes in a wooden cart. He liberated Chile, then went on to Peru, where he formulated the first Peruvian constitution, one that called for three branches of elected government similar to the new government of the United States, saying on the day of its proclamation, ''The greatest liberals achieve nothing when he who makes the law is he who executes it.''

Peru was San Martín's most exemplary victory, and his idealistic hope was one day to unite the entire continent in at least a loose confederation of similar free democracies. I raced on, recounting the victorious general's best hopes to join forces with Simón Bolívar, who had won battles in the North, and to use their combined force to deal with the growing discord among political factions in the new nations. The whole continent held its breath, waiting for the results of a meeting between the two *Libertadores* on the Pacific coast.

It was a sad story, nobody could deny it, and I wondered if every youth in Argentine schools had to learn it by heart, a story so basic to everything around me that El Mono had decided that I couldn't leave the country without knowing it. ''San Martín met with Bolívar in the Ecuadorian city of Guayaquil. There, San Martín expressed the gravity of the military situation of the two armies of patriotism. He solicited Bolívar for the means necessary to put a final end to the costly war for independence. Bolívar offered three battalions as aid. This was insufficient for the final defeat of the Spanish, and San Martín then offered, in a definitive gesture of his greatness, to serve under the command of Bolívar. But the Venezuelan did not accept the offer, and San Martín came to the irrevocable conclusion that he must abandon the territories of Peru, convinced, as he wrote to Bolívar, that 'my presence was the only obstacle that impeded your entrance into Peru with your command.' . . .''

Bolívar had the bigger army and the strongest ambitions, it was that simple, and he marched on to claim his fullest share of the glory and riches. After that, San Martín elected to retire, renouncing all his military and political titles, and the whole southern half of the continent became embroiled in factional violence. San Martín looked on bitterly from his new retirement as political feuds broke out for control of Chile and Peru, and as Bolívar imposed his autocratic rule in the North. Buenos Aires was filled with dangerous bickering. San Martín's dreams of South American unity became the sure knowledge that he had failed. He turned over his army to the new, chaotic Argentine government in a gesture of unity and peace, tired of war, but even this pacifist act made the violence worse.

"His wife ailing in Buenos Aires, and with threats of assassination because of suspicions he was power-hungry cast upon him by the new Argentine government, he was afraid to visit her. After his wife died in his absence, San Martín returned to Buenos Aires and was given an icy reception. Embittered by this and in grief, he decided to leave the country and put himself into exile in Europe. He returned only once, in 1828, when Argentina called on San Martín to help out in its brief war with Brazil. The aging general arrived in Buenos Aires after a peace treaty had put an end to the war, but never left his ship, possibly because he anticipated calamity. The city was dangerous at the time, split up into factions feuding for control of the postwar government. San Martín stated then, 'My sword will never be unsheathed in civil wars.' He returned to Europe, where he lived out his life in France with his daughter, Mereditas, and his brother, Juan Rufino. He died at three in the afternoon on the 17th of August, 1850, near Boulogne-sur-Mer, and was buried in the cathedral there. It wasn't until the

28th of May, 1880, that San Martín's remains were finally removed from France and his wish carried out, that 'my heart should be deposited in the cathedral of Buenos Aires,' where his remains now rest in a black marble coffer. The coffer is marked by three statues to signify the three nations that San Martín liberated. *Presidente* Domingo Faustino Sarmiento pronounced these words at the ceremony: 'After a long ostracism, these glorious remains return today to rest in our soil, and they will be placed at the altar of the nation, sanctified by the presence of the most illustrious of its martyrs.' . . .''

Hardly before the word *mártires* had left my mouth, Martín Segundo leapt out of his seat and shouted. ''You passed! You passed! You passed!'' The other students left their seats, too, not paying any attention to El Mono, who was rapping his knuckles on the table and calling for silence. During this chaos, El Judeo and El Gordo Rojo got the idea of ending class on their own by picking me up onto their shoulders, and they carried me out that way, Martín and Llamas-Pérez in the lead and chanting, ''Yan-qui! Yan-qui! Yan-qui! Yan-qui! Yan-qui!'' on the way out the classroom door and into the courtyard. Some of the younger students broke out of their classrooms before the bell and crowded into the windows and doorways all over the school, and everyone joined in, ''Yan-qui! Yan-qui! Yan-qui! Yan-qui! Yan-qui! Yan-qui!'' shouting like a stadium crowd, treating me like the hero of a championship *fútbol* game, riding me around on their shoulders as rocky and jolting, giddy and clownish as a blanket-tossing, the whole blue-jacketed gang of them carrying me into the courtyard and making one full circuit around the whole school, still singing my name all the way out and through the archway into the street.

The next day, I left Buenos Aires loaded down with gifts Mamá had bought for everyone in the States. There was a pretty blue poncho for my mother, a polished leather briefcase for the old man, and Mamá had things from Tío Freddi's for my brothers, a leather lariat Casimiro had braided by hand for Donny, a pair of boots for Tom, a gaucho knife with a bone handle for Kevin, a set of *bolas* for little Will,

and a cool black leather jacket to take as a gift for Harry.
Mamá insisted that I pack most of the clothes the family
had bought for me, three brand-new leather suitcases full
of them. She added a gift of a new dark-green suit of light
wool with a striped silk tie, "Good for cold or warm
weather, since you're going to be changing climates, my
son," she said.

She wouldn't take no for an answer. But what was I going
to do back home with a suit like this? Mamá made me
model it for her in the living room, and with my long hair
and goat beard, my appearance in the mirrors was strangely
incongruous, like a backwoods wild man somebody had
dressed for a bankers' convention.

Isabelita was in a rush, ironing, pulling last items off her
clotheslines. Despite my protests, Mamá and Isabelita kept
adding things to my baggage, a whole kilo of *mate* tea and
the gourd and nickel silver straw to drink it with, posters
of the city, two cartons of Particulares black tobacco cigarettes, the fine red poncho of *alpaca* wool that I had used
all year as my bedspread. How was I ever going to carry it
all? Finally, Papá stepped in, asking me around the corner
with him for a little drink. He led the way through the hot
morning in late spring to a little bar and restaurant on the
avenue Santa Fe that had tables set out on the sidewalks.
We sat down, and Papá ordered a bottle of Cinzano, a soda
siphon and *platitos*, tiny dishes of hors d'oeuvres.

"It's pretty to sit like this," Papá said, breathing in the
airs of the classy street. "It's something I wanted to do
before you left us, to sit in a bar like two men, having our
little drink." I said thank you, and we were quiet for a
moment, reaching out for all the good things on the little
plates and nursing our drinks. "I want you always to remember that you have a home here with us," Papá said.
"Our house is your house, and that means forever. You get
things straightened out, see that your brother Harry gets the
best care, you stay for a time, then you come back. Whenever you want, and I mean that sincerely. One phone call
to me and ciao, it can all be arranged. Until then, you are
probably going to need some money. Now don't say anything, because I want you to take this." He reached into

the inside pocket of his jacket and pulled out his large black wallet. "Take this and use it for anything you need," he said, counting out ten small green yanqui one-hundred-dollar bills. He shuffled them into a thin stack and held them out across the table.

"Listen, Papá, I'm going to get a job," I said. "My plan is to work and save money."

"Remember your education, Diego. If someone offers you a gift, a sincere gift, you don't throw it back into his face," Papá said. "It's nothing anyway. Money means nothing to me. It's your security that's important. Now take it or you'll make me angry."

"Thank you, Papá," I said. I slipped the money into my new suit pocket. "I'll put it in the bank and use it for a plane ticket back next year. That's not long. I'll be back home before you have a chance to miss me."

"That's what we hope, *che*," Papá said. "But don't fool yourself, we miss you already. It would break our hearts if you just dropped out of our lives and didn't come back."

"I promise, Papá," I said. "I promise I'll be back."

"Everything's settled then," he said. We sat quietly for a moment, Papá looking off up the sunny street with a sad expression. "It's pretty to sit out here, having a drink like two men," he said, his voice starting to break, then going on. "We should have done this more often, my son, isn't that true?"

For many years, I kept a slide collection of the last half-hour with my family. They were taken in a rush, because we had arrived late at the airport, held up by all the military roadblocks, at each of which we all had to show our papers and Papá had to pay a little "toll." The one slide I took myself showed all five Beneventos standing on the grassy median in front of Ezeiza International Airport after I had checked enough bags for a safari. They were dressed in summer leisure clothes, standing with their arms around each other, in the background the blue sign for *Aerolíneas Argentinas* mounted on the roof of the old terminal.

Mamá had brought her friend Beatrice to the airport, and Beatrice took most of the slides. There was one slide of me dressed in my new suit and tie, holding hands with my little

Mamá, who looked about half my height. There was one
of Martín Segundo and me posing together like friends,
Miguelito and Alejo on either side of us. Another shot
showed all the men in the family, all four boys bunched
around Papá and laughing, hanging off of him in a kind of
wrestling that made him look weighed down. The last shot
was a close-up, taken just inside the terminal with a different lens. The sun had grown fierce outside and everyone
was too hot, and Alejo was saddened by the quick passage
of time. Only Papá was really smiling in that slide, one of
his L&M's lit and held frozen in his fingers, his eyes not
visible behind the smoky green lenses of his prescription
sunglasses. There was a stiffness about me in that shot, an
unnatural hunching of my back and shoulders and a distant
look because my attention at that moment was focused out
past Beatrice on a large clock mounted above the main doors
of the old terminal, on either side of which stood Air Force
guards in their gray uniforms, in full combat gear with sub-
machine guns. The clock over their heads was telling me
that my flight was already boarding. Beatrice was working
her complicated camera and telling us all to get closer. One
of the guards directed his attention to our group, then to my
brothers, then fastened it on me. Beatrice told us to smile
and snapped the shutter. She took the film out of the camera
and dropped it into my pocket with a little kiss. Two of the
guards took a few steps in our direction, then stopped; loudspeakers were announcing the final boarding call and we
were running for the gate.

On the plane, after all the hugs and kisses and tears, I
felt I could breathe again. I took off my jacket and tie and
slipped off my shoes after takeoff, ordered a drink and settled back. I watched the gray and green shimmering sprawl
of Buenos Aires below us until it looked as if it had spilled
into the mud-colored River Plate that was curving under us
like a sea. For a moment, I felt fine, happy enough to be
on my way home, not thinking about what I'd find when I
got there. I tasted my good scotch and waited for the food
and looked the nice stewardesses up and down. I had made
it through the last weeks of craziness and had actually grad-

uated from school, and I felt lucky again, and rich, and proud of myself.

Somebody at the back of the plane, an Argentine, started strumming a guitar and singing. The song was a traditional Argentine goodbye song, "Adiós muchachos," and the voice singing it was sad. It was a tango Papá had played for me in his study, and I thought of that time and wondered when I would hear that song again, and if I would ever come back to visit my family as I had promised. There were a lot of Argentines on the plane, and they were listening to the song, some of them singing along, some of them crying, and I didn't feel proud of myself anymore. *Goodbye boys, companions of my life.* Cold air was blowing on my neck and I reached up to the tiny jet and shut it of. *For all the good times in those good old days.* I finished my drink, leaned my head back and closed my eyes, praying for sleep. *For being with me and starting me off on all the good steaks and all the great pranks and great girls.* Nothing would be that easy again. Nothing would ever be the same. What I was on my way to would be a battle, and those I had left behind were no longer safe. Nobody was safe anymore. Nobody was that lucky.

# 10

## Nortbport

Still, it felt good to land in my own country again. A lot of
my family was waiting at JFK to meet me—my mother,
Tom, Kevin, Carol and Will, the rest still at work during
my noon arrival. I saw them as soon as I was inside the
International Arrivals wing of the terminal. They waved at
me from above, leaning out over the high railing, watching
me pushing a piled baggage cart toward customs. My mother
shouted down at me, "I can hardly recognize you! I can't
believe it's you! You look so thin!" My brothers were all
fooling around up there, little Willy about to get dangled
over the railing by his heels.

I was the last passenger from my plane out of customs.
One look at me, and all my bags were opened and inspected
down to unballing my socks. I was brought into a back
room and frisked by a customs agent. He even made me
take off my new Argentine shoes so they could inspect the
heels. Then when the kilo of green *mate* tea was found in
a suitcase, I had to wait while a sample was taken and
carried off to be tested. It wasn't easy to go through all this
in English. My answers were hesitant, my thinking slow.
Finally, my declaration was stamped, I was allowed to push

my disheveled suitcases through the barrier, and only then did I feel like I was in my own country again.

Maybe it was because the dining room was the only place everyone in my family gathered that I have always thought of it as a battlefield. Everything had gone well up until the homecoming dinner, and everyone seemed glad to see me. I asked my mother about Harry several times, and it seemed she was avoiding giving me a direct answer. "He's still in the hospital, and not doing very well," she said. "Ask your father."

The old man came in from work. He hugged and kissed me, said he was happy I was back in one piece. Then he gave my hair and my beard two firm tugs and said, "This fits in with what's going on now at the high school. We're going to have a talk later about that hair."

Before dinner, the gifts I brought for them were given out in the living room as if it were Christmas. Willy's was the only present that caused trouble, because he smashed one of the lamps in the basement trying to learn how to use his *bolas*. My mother was pleased with her blue poncho. She had found a new job, working for the town's weekly newspaper, and she said how much she needed something warm to wear to the office and how good it looked and that kind of thing. Everyone was pleased with the gifts, and the day was like a celebration until we sat down at the table. My mother said it was my turn to say grace, and I said a quick one in Spanish for them, which made my brothers laugh at the way it sounded. Then steaming dishes of Shake 'N' Bake chicken, packaged green beans and a huge boat of instant mashed potatoes were passed around. I watched my brothers lighting into their plates with both hands in a way I had forgotten. Only Carol seemed like someone I knew, helping my mother serve, gracefully pouring our glasses full of milk. I had forgotten people drank milk with meals. I had forgotten a lot of things. One mistake at this table was all that was needed to disturb its balance, and I was the one who made it. I asked the old man to tell me about Harry. He didn't answer at first, looking into his plate and taking a long time to finish chewing.

"A lot's happened since you've been gone," my mother

said. "There's going to be a change of rooms around here, too. Not only because of Harry, but because Donald is moving out."

I couldn't follow her logic, and my brother Kevin was grimacing at me from across the table to get me to shut up.

"Don? Yeah?" I asked Donny, who was sitting beside me. His hair was long, falling in a dark wavy mass over his shoulders. He looked almost as much of a freak as Harry had before the Army. Don only nodded at me once, carefully not speaking, sensing the dangers.

"Between Donny and Harry, your Mom and I have just about had it," the old man said. "As far as I'm concerned, the sooner the rest of you bums get the hell out, the better. Maybe your mother and I can have some kind of a life for a change."

"Now please!" the old lady snapped. "I worked hard on this dinner!"

"Well I'm telling him. I'm telling all of them," the old man said, starting to raise his voice.

"Calm down, Dad," I said. "All I'm asking about is Harry. How is he doing?"

"Don't you tell me to calm down."

"Excuse me," Donny said and rose from the table, carrying his plate with him to finish eating in the kitchen. Tom looked at me with a tense expression. He rolled his eyes quickly toward the ceiling once, his signal that I had opened my mouth about the wrong thing. Kevin and Willy settled back in their chairs and watched the old man, waiting to see what might happen.

"Harry's in bad shape," the old man said. "There's not much hope. The V.A. wants to dump him. We've got the papers to sign that will send him up to the state hospital for long-term care."

"What do you mean, long-term care?" I asked.

"Are you questioning me, young man?"

My mother put her silverware down loudly on her plate, her gesture to us all that she was ready to declare her dinner ruined. "We had Harry here two weekends ago," she said. "He wasn't ready to get out of the hospital."

"I'll say he wasn't," said Willy.

"You keep your mouth shut," the old man said. He turned to me, pointing his fork at me like a finger. "Harry was here and didn't even know where he was. He talked gibberish. Nobody could hold a conversation with him. Then in the middle of the night, he wanted us to let him go wander off to the city. We got into one hell of a fight. It took Tom and me and our mother, all of us wrestling him, before we could stop him from walking out in that condition. Then Harry found a kitchen knife and threatened me with it. We had to call the police to take him back to the hospital. Before the police got here, Harry went upstairs and smashed his guitar all over the stairwell. Go up and look. I still haven't painted the replastering."

"But what's wrong with Harry, Dad?" I asked. "What do the doctors say?"

"How the hell should I know, I'm not a psychiatrist. If you ask me, all psychiatrists are full of bullshit."

"Your father doesn't understand," my mother said. "Harry's not really crazy, he's mixed up. He can come back to reality if he wants. That's why he's in the hospital. When he wants out of the hospital badly enough, he'll come back to reality."

"But why the state institution, Dad? I've heard it's a real snakepit up there. I thought the Veterans Hospital was supposed to take care of veterans."

"Look, Mister Know-it-all, we know what we're doing," the old man said.

"They won't keep Harry in the V.A.," my mother said. "It's a new policy. They only keep mental patients on a volunteer basis now. We've been over it and over it with them. Even if a patient thinks he's a man from Mars, they can't keep him at the V.A. against his will."

"You mean Harry wants out?" I asked.

"Harry doesn't know what he's doing!" my mother shouted. "Don't you understand? He's not competent!"

"Look what you've done now! Look! You've upset your mother!" the old man shouted. "Get it through your thick skull that we know what we're doing!"

"But Dad . . ."

"Don't *but Dad* me! Harry's all screwed up! Your mother

and I can't handle him!'' The old man slapped his silverware on the table and gritted his teeth to calm himself down. "Enough about Harry," he said. "You'll see for yourself. And I'll tell you another thing, young man. A lot of people in this community are waiting to talk to you. The high school phoned about you maybe talking to classes about South America. The town paper wants to run a photo, and your mother works at the paper. Do you get what I'm saying? How's your mother going to feel when the paper runs a picture of her son looking like a bum?''

"Oh, he doesn't look like a bum," my mother said. "It's the fashion now! All it needs is a trim, and he should gain some weight. Eat. You're not eating," she said.

"I'm sorry, dear, but we've had this out with Donny and we'll have it out with him," the old man said. "Nobody in my house is going to go around looking like a bum. Not anymore. Not after what's happened to Harry."

The old man stood up from the table with a disgusted look at the old lady. He crumpled his napkin and threw it on his plate, then left the dining room in a huff. There was the sound of the doors to the liquor cabinet being unlocked and slid open, then a tense moment when the old man passed the open door to the dining room with a glass in hand, on his way to the upstairs bathroom, where he had the sink and counter all torn up from his latest remodeling project. Nobody relaxed even a little at the table until we heard the sound of his electric drill.

"Somebody at the office asked me today if having so many kids, I loved some of them more than the others. I told her no, I hate all my kids equally," my mother said. "Hate to have you home," she said then, smiling at me across the table.

"Maybe I can borrow the car in the morning and drive out to visit Harry," I said.

"I need the car," she said. "But you can take the train into the city and catch another train out to Northport. Just don't get your hopes up. You'll see what your father means." Suddenly, she was about to cry. She reached a hand across the table and I held it for a moment, a gentle squeeze, then she pulled it away and said, "The rest of you, clear the table! William does the pots tonight! And Thomas, you bring in the dessert!''

Later, Tom and I hung out in the basement and smoked some good weed he had saved for my homecoming. We caught up with each other, he telling me about his junior year in school and what was going on in town. He said almost all the kids were doing drugs up on campus now, growing their hair long, and every day after school, hundreds of them were joining in a two-hour peace vigil in front of the post office at the head of Main Street. He said he didn't usually get to these himself because he was too busy working six-hour shifts after school at the rivet plant, which at one time or another would employ all my brothers. I asked him if I might get on there, and he said maybe there would be an opening after Christmas.

It was good to sit there with Tom, settling back on the old couch in the basement. We listened to a new rock-blues album by a group called *The Electric Flag*, Elvin Bishop and Mike Bloomfield playing together, stretching and bending sounds I had forgotten I loved. Tom said he agreed with the folks about Harry. He said Harry really had grabbed a knife and had thrust it at the old man. As the old lady was dialing the police, Harry dropped the knife and ran upstairs. He opened his guitar case on the stairs and smashed his good Gibson Hummingbird against the banister, the walls, all over the place, the same expensive guitar he had saved up to buy, had polished, babied, and carried with him for years in the city, the guitar he had kept in one piece all through Vietnam. It was hard for me to imagine this. It was the most unthinkable thing Harry could have done. "The old man's right," Tom said. "Harry's gone over the fucking edge."

Donny joined us in the basement for a smoke. He was next oldest to Harry, had graduated high school the year before. Don told me the old man had asked him to move out because of his long hair but for me not to worry, he had fought that big battle and if I got myself a little trim, the old man would cool down. Moving out was fine with Donny. He was making good money waiting tables at the country club, enough to support himself, and besides, he had already found a cool apartment that he had painted with Day-Glo colors, then he had blacked out all the windows with aluminum foil and had hung up ultraviolet lights. When I asked him about Harry, Donny said, "The old man says he knows what he's doing, but I don't know. I think the hospital is just making Harry worse."

The hospital in Northport was a collection of long, low brick buildings on some rolling acres outside of a small, quaint, sugar-maple-covered town on the bay side of Long Island. The place looked from the outside like it would make a big college campus, the buildings scattered over a rolling landscape of damp, browning grass that was awash in the bright colors of fallen leaves. Patients were wandering around the grounds, sitting on benches under the maples. Most of them were older men in heavy gray jackets and gray hospital pants, some of them engaged in raking leaves into piles along the long paved lane that ran through the hospital grounds to the main administration building. Inside the main building, I waited a long time after requesting to visit my brother. Finally, a pretty hospital volunteer in a candy-striped dress led me across the grounds to the numbered building where Harry was kept in a locked ward. A nurse inside inspected me through the window, then unlocked the door. She made me leave my knapsack behind the big desk at the nurse's station.

I found Harry right away. He was sitting on a chair near the entrance door to the second-story lockdown ward. He was whittling on a corncob, and was having a hard time trying to use a nailfile like a penknife. Hair stuck out every which way on his head in a wild growth. He was skinny, his cheeks sucked into his mouth, his eyes deeply set and looking stoned. I stood in front of Harry's chair a long time before he raised his head. He took me in, only smiling a little, as if there were nothing unusual about seeing me. "How you doing?" he asked. "Hey, man, look at this." He held out the stub of corncob. "I was just starting to make this cool pipe for you, which means that somebody was telling me you would drop around. What do you think of that?"

"That's fine, Harry," I said. I tried to move over and give him a big hug but he shifted position suddenly. His tension at my approach let me know he wasn't ready for me to get closer. "Hey, man, I'm really glad to see you," I said. "You made it, man. You made it back."

"Yeah. Right." He turned his attention back to his corncob, digging at one end of it with the point of the nailfile. "They won't let me have my pocket knife in here, but they haven't taken this nailfile away from me yet. Pretty funny, man, wouldn't you say so?"

"Sure is," I said, trying to make my voice sound cheerful. "This place looks pretty funny to me all around."

"This place is not funny," Harry said. "There's one guy in here who tried to punch me out yesterday. I broke the glass on the outside door downstairs trying to get away from this freak. It's not safe for any of us here. The psychiatrists here are gooks, man. We've got this Korean gook doctor who knocks us all to our knees, man, every morning with these shitty drugs they give out in here. But Japan was worse. In Japan, they didn't take the straps off me once."

"Jesus, Harry," I said. I watched my brother turn back to his work, frustrated, missing the corncob and jabbing the point of the nailfile angrily into the palm of his hand. I noticed there were several little stab wounds on his palm, and both hands were covered with bloody scratches. "Listen, man, you don't have to stay in here," I said. "We can get you out any time you want."

"Well who do you think we've been waiting for!" Harry raised his voice. "Shit, man! We've been in these lousy hospitals since August! And we're really pissed off at you, man, you should have gotten me out of here when we told you. So now you turn up all these months too late and of course, these people in here are going to be pissed off! And there he goes again, that stupid little Bobbie Dylan, that little shit telling me what a cop-out you are, man, that's just like him. Can you believe it? I mean, just listen to all these people!"

"To what people?" I asked. "Who are you talking about, man?"

"Oh, man, don't tell me you're going to be just like ev-

erybody else! Don't you hear it? If you can't hear it, man,
that's not our problem. The gooks in this place keep telling
us *It's all in your mind, it's all in your mind*, but we know
we're not crazy. This shit isn't in our mind, man! Now stop
standing there like an idiot and get these people off my
back!''

"What people?"

"Ah, shit, man, just get me out of here."

"Don't worry, Harry, we'll get you out," I said. "Right
away. Right this minute. Come on with me, right now, man.
I've got some money, and we'll take the train into the city.
We'll get you a new guitar, then, well, I don't know, maybe
find someplace to stay." Harry started to laugh weirdly,
moving his eyes around to either side of me as if there were
a whole crowd of other people sitting around us who were
laughing, too. My brother was exchanging looks and facial
signals with these people, then he turned his head to face a
blank wall and started talking.

"This is too much, too much, man," Harry said to the
wall. "They turn up here three months too late and say *to
go with him*? Now? Oh, yeah, now Joanie is going to get in
on the act. But she's the treacherous one. She's the great
white bitch who's going to get us where we live, man." He
laughed again, then stopped suddenly. He turned and focused his glassy eyes on me and said, "No. Not a chance.
You just get us out of it, that's final. Bye, bye. Chieu hoi.
Soc mao," he said and then his voice dropped so I could
hardly hear him. He was talking to something above my
head, as if at invisible people hovering in the air all around
me. "We're going to kill the gook doctor," he said. "He's
a Korean pimp, man, sent in from the White Horse division
to set us up for a case of incurable Asian syph, which none
of these jokers can dig on. So it's all on us, man. We're the
ones who can do it without making a sound," he said. He
stopped talking like a switch had been turned off. He jerked
his head twice, like shaking it loose of his ghosts, then went
furiously back to work on the corncob.

I didn't say anything for a few minutes. I produced a pack
of cigarettes. It was strange to pull a package of Particulares
out of my pocket, and suddenly I wished they weren't black

tobacco, somehow they didn't taste the same. I offered Harry a cigarette and he took it. I bent over close to him and struck a match. As I was holding the match up to his mouth in my cupped hands, Harry whispered, "Hey, man, don't let them know. You're in enough trouble as it is. We don't want them fucking you over the way they did me," he said, looking around us suspiciously as if checking for spies who might overhear our conversation. Deep into the long hospital ward, a few younger men in loose gray clothes were shuffling around in their plastic disposable slippers. Harry waved me away from him, a gesture that I obeyed, stepping back a little. Harry opened his mouth in a yawn, forgetting he was smoking, and I watched the cigarette fall to the floor from his lower lip, then he moved his plastic-slippered foot over to crush it out. I started to jump at his foot, thinking he might burn himself, but he didn't. He pulled his foot away.

"I've been thinking I'll start smoking a pipe," Harry said. "Something like this one. For a change." He bent over the corncob again, poking and digging at it jerkily, moving it around in the palm of his hand. "The problem is to figure out how to gouge an even bowl in the corncob without the sides caving in. You know, if you can't get the sides pretty even, it won't burn right."

"Looks pretty hard with just a nailfile," I said. I watched him work at it a moment. "Come on, man. Let's get out of here and you can finish later. You're going to have to sign some papers, too, at the main building, and we don't want to get hung up too long."

"Nobody gets out of here," Harry said. "You're fooling yourself. Not out of here, man."

"What are you saying?"

"I say hey, man," Harry said.

"Do you want out of here or not?" I asked. I waited for an answer as Harry looked at me with contempt, then he angrily went back to his whittling again.

"Look, man, please tell me," I said. "Tell me how you feel."

"You mean how do I feeeeeel?"

Harry mocked the sound of my voice.

"Yes, that's what I mean," I said. "I want to know if you feel O.K. enough to get out. I mean, if you want out, that's fine with me, I'll get you out, man. I just want to know. There's no way I'm going to see you in here if you want out."

"Sure, man, we feeeeeeeel O.K.," Harry said, grinning. "How do you feeeeeeeel?"

"I feel all right. I'm glad to be back. I'm glad to see you," I said. "Now tell me about you, man. I want to know about you."

"I don't feel anything," Harry said. "I don't have any feelings left. The old man took care of those, and I don't want to see the old man or the old lady ever again in my life." He was moving the dried corncob from one hand to the other, then he grinned at me with a strange lucidity and held the nailfile between his fingers, puffing on it as if it were a cigarette. "You should never listen to the old man," he said, exhaling imaginary smoke, and I crushed out my cigarette. "The old man gives the wrong advice every time."

"Maybe so," I said after a moment.

"You, too, man. Nobody should listen to you. You had your chance and you blew it. You should have been here three months ago."

"Jesus, Harry, I was in South America! You know that! You wrote me letters, and I wrote to you!"

"That's what we mean, man, these people won't leave us alone. We told you what was going down, just after Operation South. That's when we really freaked out, on Operation South. But don't worry, man, as far as the Nam and the rest of us are concerned, nobody has anything to be ashamed of. We made Specialist E-6. Gook-killers all the way. That's pretty far out, man, when you think about it."

"I'm sorry I didn't write back sooner," I said. "But your letters took so long. The postal system down there was all fouled up."

But I had lost Harry suddenly. He was staring off into space as if he could see through me, his eyes looking very stoned now. Then he took in my face, his eyes wide, looking as if he had just remembered something important.

"Hey, man, I haven't told you I got everyone in here calling me Fevertree. Even the little Korean psychiatrist. He considers it a part of my problem, man, and every time I try to explain it to him, it's like I'm goofing on him, you know, he increases my Thorazine dose and says I speak like the ocean. Literally, man, he says, 'You speak rike ochun.' I mean, the best he can do is terrible gook English and he says that it's me who's talking funny. So I quit saying anything at all to him. It's a waste of time."

"All that's over now," I said. "Come on Harry, let's go. I've got some money, and maybe we can check into the Alton House, you remember staying in that place? It wasn't bad, and maybe the rooms are still only ten bucks a night. We'll get you a new guitar, man, and we'll start up again where you left off. I mean it. Come on, man," I said. Then I made as if to turn and leave without him if he wasn't coming.

"I don't play guitar anymore," Harry said. "That's kid's stuff."

"Just come on now, Harry. Let's get out of here, man, please?"

"Yeah. Sure," Harry said. He stood up slowly from his chair, then he laughed with that strange sound again. "But we've got something to take care of first. We're going to kill the gook doctor who did this to us. Shove this right here through his kidney," he said, holding up the nailfile.

I reached out my hand and took the nailfile, Harry giving it up easily. I found the head nurse, who was way off down a hallway. I asked her for my knapsack, then I told her my brother was going to sign himself out of the hospital. "Against medical advice?" she asked.

"If it has to be that way," I said.

She nodded casually, it was nothing to her, and she found the proper forms on her table. She appraised Harry, standing beside me, watching her with a silly grin on his face, then she pressed her lips and led us out of the lockup ward and into the adminstration building. We waited for a few minutes. With the first nurse watching, another nurse filled in Harry's papers, and even as she was doing this, she gave us a speech that on behalf of Dr. Lee, who couldn't be

reached, and the hospital adminstration, it was her respon-
sibility to inform us that Harry still needed psychiatric care
but that it was now against V.A. policy to keep patients
against their will. She gave Harry a bottle of Thorazine
capsules and a piece of paper with a list of addresses where
he could get a prescription filled for more of the same. The
first nurse stood in front of my brother and asked, "Are
you going to take your medication, Harry?"

"Soc mao," my brother said.

"He should take four of these a day," the nurse said to
me. "Good luck."

That was all. Their wards were overcrowded, and neither
nurse looked unhappy to see Harry go even under these
circumstances. As Harry was signing papers letting himself
out against medical advice, the nurse from Harry's ward
gave me a paper bag with Harry's shirt, blue jeans and
underwear in it. Harry went off to get dressed in the rest
room. I talked the other nurse into finding me some extra
hospital packs of soap, toothpaste, shampoo and that kind
of thing. I phoned a cab to take us to the train station and
grabbed up my knapsack, rifling through it and taking out
the leather jacket I had brought for Harry from Argentina.

By the time the cab arrived, I was wondering if I had
done the right thing. Harry was outside, getting happily into
the tough-looking mood inspired by his new leather jacket,
wandering down the paved lane under the trees and striking
matches, setting piles of leaves on fire. It was hard to pull
him away from doing this and get him into the taxi. Harry
watched out the windows of the cab as we drove off the
grounds. He was talking to himself again, answering the
voices in his head.

As I tried to steer Harry through the small Northport
train station that morning, the decision I had made last night
came back firmly in my mind. I was going to telephone my
mother later and give her the news, telling her I loved her
and the old man, and that if they would still have me I
would visit them frequently and tell them what was happening in my life, our lives. I had almost all of Papá's thousand
dollars in my pockets and what I thought was a clear field

ahead. And if things went wrong, well, I felt I knew where
I could find help.

I could have used some help just prying Harry away from
the newsstand, where he wanted to pick up a copy of every
magazine and paper in the display case. I bought *The New
York Times* for him and replaced the things he had taken
with apologies to the news vendor. Then I bought Harry's
ticket and dragged him onto the Long Island Railroad just
in time, the doors closing on us as the train was pulling out
of the station. We took seats facing backwards in the
crowded smoking car, and Harry opened the paper for a
few seconds then started chattering on about a big antiwar
demonstration scheduled for the next day, pointing out the
small heading about it on the front page. I said sure we
could go, not to worry, we could do anything he wanted,
but I didn't take him seriously, and I wasn't sure by the
sound of his voice what he would do if we actually went. I
wasn't that sure we could even make it through the day.
Harry turned to face the window and started talking at the
air again, a continual chatter to imaginary beings that
seemed to be flying everywhere, outside, in front and back
of him, around his head. I saw that I had rightly guessed
he would forget all about tomorrow's plans in a few minutes. He dropped the newspaper at his feet and kicked it
away, pressing his face against the glass.

We sat back together and watched the nice colonial and
modern houses roll by with their neatly groomed lawns,
their well-appointed streets lined with elms and maples.
Then the scene gradually changed to the apartment houses,
warehouses and factories of outer Queens, then the elevated
subway tracks appeared, Shea Stadium, grayer skies.

I reflected calmly on the decision I had made that morning, more confident now that I was carrying it out. My
plans were simple enough. I would stick with Harry and he
would get better soon, once he had a guitar in his hands
and his old life back again. Then I was going to continue
on my own, with plans to work hard, to study hard, and
never to lose track of my two families. Whatever demonstrations there were, on either continent, they would be
massive and spirited, and I would take part in them, if only

from a distance. Perón would come back to Argentina with the help of my brothers, democracy would be restored, the old Turk would give in or die one day and leave a new social order, saving Argentina from its generals. And someday, soon, even the Vietnam War would end. My brother Harry would get steadily better and stay out of hospitals. I believed this with my heart that day, together in our seats in the crowded smoking car, Harry looking happy now, giggling to himself like the gentle madman he had become, his face pressed against the window, one finger drawing the shapes of numbers in the fog his breath made on the glass, then he watched them disappear. We were both happy enough at that moment, even if it would only last this one day. Harry was free now. And I was starting off on my own life, in my own country. We were together again as brothers, finally— a couple of freaks braced against forward motion, expecting to recapture our lives and live them differently, and we went on that way, riding backwards into the city.

# Epilogue

September 4, 1983

My beloved Diego:

Years have passed in which we have searched for you, written everywhere we might find news of you, to your mother and father, and to the last address we had for you. Our letters must never have arrived, because never have we had a response.

We have had great need of you. The * * * * * * * * * * * * after Perón has killed Alejo and Miguel. Miguelito was shot in bed. Alejo disappeared without a trace and we've given up hope. Martín Segundo is living in exile in Paris. * * * * * * * * * * * * * * * * * * * * * * * * * * * * * * * * * * * * * * * * * * * * * * * * * * * * * * * * * *

[These lines were censored.]

We two Beneventos who remain are still looking for our Diego of Arenales Street, the boy who came to live with us once and who once called us Mamá and

Papá. When Miguel and Alejo could no longer call us Mamá and Papá, we had great need of you.

What must have happened all these years? The last we knew, you had graduated from university and were leaving on a trip. You had promised to visit us, as soon as you got your brother off the streets of New York and under a doctor's care again. I answered every letter you wrote in those days, until Papá and I were also arrested. All the time of my detention I thought of you even as I thought about the others, afraid something might also have happened to you. It's strange now to keep writing to you, so many times, but equally a joy for me, because Papá and I remember so much of you and feel sure you remember us. I'm not going to tell you now the horrors that happened in this country, the massacres, the concentration camps, the tortures, because I don't know * * * * *
* * * * * * * * * * * * * * * * * * * * * * * * * * * *

[The next page was missing.]

and this has been a particular ordeal for us. We're still being watched. We still don't get some of our mail.

Please write to us as soon as you can. Now that we will soon have a democracy again, I can pray with some hope that one of our letters will reach you, and yours might reach us. Papá has need of you. He's saddened with Martín so far away, and he has fallen into a depression even as he tries to lead a normal life again, going every day to a new office he's started. One of the things that makes him suffer most is never knowing about you. He's tried to telephone your family but we lost the number long ago and it's unlisted. Nothing gets through. We hope and pray * * * * * * will leave us alone and we won't have to go on in silence.

All we wish is a long letter from you telling us what has happened with you, so we can send you news of us. We don't have much money anymore, the * * * *
* * * * * * * * * * * * * * * * * * * * * * * * * * * *

which is also a grief to Papá. But even in this terrible economy, we might be able to bring you to Buenos Aires to see you again. That would be a miracle and a blessing for us, but most of all please write. You will always be our son.

Go with God, wherever you are.

Mamá

## About the Author

**Douglas Unger** was born in 1952 in Moscow, Idaho. His previous novel, LEAVING THE LAND, was a winner of the Society of Midland Authors award for fiction, an ALA Notable Book of 1984, and a finalist for the Pulitzer and Robert F. Kennedy awards. Unger teaches in the Creative Writing Program at Syracuse University.